[handwritten: Lisa]

THE LORDE'S WAY

The Drama Never Ends…

A Novel

Kenneth D. Perry

[handwritten: Thanks for the Support]

*CRITICALLY ACCLAIMED AUTHOR OF **LORDE BAPTIST:***
GET READY TO MEET THE FIRST FAMILY OF DRAMA

[handwritten signature: Best Blessings, Kenneth 7/24/08]

PublishAmerica
Baltimore

First printing

All characters in this book are fictitious, and any resemblance to real persons,
living or dead, is coincidental.

PublishAmerica has allowed this work to remain exactly as the author intended,
verbatim, without editorial input.

ISBN: 1-60610-385-7
PUBLISHED BY PUBLISHAMERICA, LLLP
www.publishamerica.com
Baltimore

Printed in the United States of America

Also by Kenneth Perry

Lorde Baptist: Get Ready to Meet the First Family of Drama

This novel is dedicated in memory of
My Best Friend
Reginald Morrell Cook
5/22/1971–4/21/2007

~Acknowledgments~

You're in the presence of royalty—it's a sovereign God and King.
We're before your throne, and bow at your feet—worship you Holy King.
—Byron Cage, *The Proclamation*

This book is a work of fiction about two fictional families who struggle to overcome personal demons, relationships, and unforeseen circumstances. The characters are not drawn from life and do not resemble anyone I know personally or have heard about.

I would like to thank God for my gift to put into words what the mind imagines. I realize so many people desire and dream about the ability to write and publish their work and ultimately those same dreams sometimes die with them. On that note, I extend many thanks to PublishAmerica, LLLP for seeing what so many big publishers refused to see...that I do have a talent—*I now have the numbers to prove it*!

Thank you to my many readers—if it weren't for you, where would I be? Thank you to all the book clubs and bookstores locally and nationwide as well as the online stores, thank you, thank you, thank you.

Special thanks to my baby brother, Andre Perry—simply because I love you so much. To my nephews, Dondre' and Dante Perry; and my young cousins...R. Marquelle Perry, B. Aaron Perry, Tamia J. Valentine, Justin R. Walker, Shyniece Wright, Jayla M. Valentine, Taylor S. Perry, Ty'marilyn Wright, Tierra Valentine and Jordan Franchon Wright (2007–2007). They are the reason I want my light to shine positively in front of them. Each of their love for me is unconditional and unwavering...it makes my pursuit of happiness so much easier.

Thank you to my new friend and editor, Regina "Gina" D'Alessio. There is a reason that God places certain people in our lives. If you and Tim had never fallen in love, you would have never moved to South Carolina—thanks Tim! I wish you guys a much blessed future.

Thanks again to Martha Butts and Johanna Gibbs. These two women will

always be a part of my humble beginnings—long before the word *author* was in front of my name. I will never forget either of you.

I must recognize my spiritual father, a man who has such an anointed spiritual covering over my life—the honorable Dr. Reginald E. Grimes (Yes Pastor…some see *Reverend* in the natural, but I see *Reverend Dr.* in the spirit), his lovely wife Henrietta (Lady Grimes, I truly admire your beautiful spirit) and their sons, Jon and Jeremy, along with the entire Four Mile Church Family, thank you all so much.

At this time, I must honor the memory of my best friend; the late *Reginald Morrell Cook*…life hasn't been the same since he passed away. Reginald, this one is for you—rest in peace.

Lastly, but certainly not least, if I have forgotten anyone, please don't hold it against me. I am completing my third novel, I hope you understand. But more importantly, I hope you enjoy reading, *The Lorde's Way: The drama never ends…*

Forever gifted and highly favored,
Kenneth

Characters

Eloise London Lorde—Matriarch of the Lorde family. Mother of Ernest, Jr, Alma, Eleanor and Richard. Stepmother to Miranda, Zondra, Byron and Barron.

Deacon Ernest Lorde, Jr.—Married to the former Overa Hawkins. Brother of Miranda, Alma, Eleanor, Zondra, Richard, Byron and Barron. Superintendent of the Ramblewood county public school district and chairman of the Board of Deacons at the Tabernacle of Praise Baptist Church.

Alma Lorde Hawkins—Married to Deacon Daniel Hawkins, Sr. and mother of Daniel "DJ" Hawkins, Jr. Sister of Miranda, Ernest, Jr., Eleanor, Zondra, Richard, Byron and Barron. Vice-president of Lorde Life and Accident Insurance Company and president of the Tabernacle of Praise Gospel Choir.

Deacon Daniel Hawkins, Sr.—Married to the former Alma Lorde and father of Daniel "DJ" Hawkins, Jr. Brother of Overa Hawkins Lorde. Principal of the Ramblewood High School and assistant chairman of the Board of Deacons at the Tabernacle of Praise Baptist Church.

Eleanor Lorde Christiansen—Married to Thomas *"Snappy"* Christiansen, Jr. and Mother of Emanuel and Christina. Sister of Miranda, Ernest, Jr., Alma, Zondra, Richard, Byron and Barron. Store manager for an upscale women's apparel boutique.

Trustee Richard Lorde—Brother of Miranda, Ernest, Jr., Alma, Zondra, Byron and Barron. Owner and President of the Lorde Life and Accident Insurance Company. Chairman of the Board of Trustees at the Tabernacle of Praise Baptist Church. Best friends with Christopher Christiansen.

Reverend Mychael Dovely—Pastor of the Tabernacle of Praise Baptist Church. Husband of the former Monica Anderson. Physical Education instructor and girl's high school basketball coach for the Ramblewood High School.

First lady Monica Anderson Dovely—wife of Reverend Mychael Dovely and first lady of the Tabernacle of Praise Baptist Church. Daughter of Grace Christiansen Anderson and the late Fernando Anderson. Registered Pharmacist for the Ramblewood Pharmacy.

Joy Lynn Anderson—Cousin of Monica Dovely. Registered nurse for Ramblewood Obstetrics and Gynecology.

Mary Agnes Christiansen Shaw—Married to Deacon Joseph Shaw and mother of Beatrice Shaw. Sister of Grace, *Snappy* and Carolina.

Deacon Joseph Shaw—Married to the former Mary Agnes Christiansen and father of Beatrice Shaw. Deacon at the Tabernacle of Praise Baptist Church.

Beatrice Shaw—Daughter of Deacon Joseph and Mary Agnes Shaw. Finance Clerk for the Tabernacle of Praise Baptist Church.

Grace Christiansen Anderson—Mother of first lady Monica Dovely and sister of Mary Agnes, *Snappy* and Carolina.

Carolina Christiansen—Mother of Christopher Christiansen. Sister of Mary Agnes, *Snappy* and Grace. Also a bank teller for the Ramblewood Savings and Loans Bank.

Thomas *"Snappy"* Christiansen, Jr.—Married to the former Eleanor Lorde and father of Emanuel and Christina. Brother of Mary Agnes, Grace and Carolina. Production worker for a local manufacturing plant.

Christopher Christiansen—Son of Carolina Christiansen. Best friends with Richard Lorde.

Clara Bell London—Mother of estranged daughter Virginia Spudwinkle. Grandmother of Halora, Pandora and Enrique. First cousin of Eloise Lorde.

Halora London—Sister of Pandora and Enrique. Operations Manager for the Lorde Life and Accident Insurance Company.

Pandora London—Sister of Halora and Enrique.

Enrique London—Brother of Halora and Pandora. Investigator for the Ramblewood County Sheriff Office.

THE LORDE'S WAY

The Drama Never Ends…

CHAPTER ONE

It has been a year since her beloved husband passed away. Today, Eloise sat anxiously in a lavender dress—her favorite color. She was covered from head to toe with a matching hat and similar shoes as the installation service was getting underway. She was excited about her late husband's wishes being carried out. During his final hours, the Reverend Ernest Lorde, Sr. was adamant about naming the Reverend Mychael Dovely as his successor.

Eloise conceded that her late husband knew the assistant pastor a lot better than her, and his death bed request only meant he had a tremendous amount of faith in his young protégé. In her heart, she believed her husband had made a good decision, and of course she trusted his judgment. If it were for any other reason, as you already know, she wouldn't be a part of today's ceremony.

She will say, over the years, her late husband had poured so much into his favorite protégé. She believed he wanted more for the young minister and wanted to ensure he received all God had to offer. More times than she cared to remember, her husband had referred to the pastor elect as his spiritual *son*. After hearing it so often, she would remind her husband that he already had two sons, in fact, he had four sons. Lovingly, Reverend Lorde would tell her that his heart was big enough to love the whole world, while also suggesting, that she make a sincere effort to show more of her loving side.

In her mind, Eloise could only assume that Ernest, Sr. was correct, because she knew if her late husband was wrong, and she could count on one hand the times that he had been, as leader of the Tabernacle of Praise congregation, the path Mychael took would be to either follow in his late mentor's footsteps or try to create a path of his own—only time would tell.

The guest minister happened to be another one of Reverend Lorde's former protégés, Dr. Jamison Hamilton-Bryant, whom Eloise personally called to deliver the installation message. Actually, she had dialed his cell phone as she watched one of his pre-recorded sermons on the Word channel. At that moment, she knew he was the perfect individual to preach for this occasion. He was the first person she had called. He was the only person she had called. Before him, she hadn't thought about anyone else, primarily because she didn't want to hear anyone else.

In a sense, Dr. Bryant felt obligated to accept Eloise's invite since he was unable to be the eulogist for his mentor's four-hour funeral. At the time of her husband's death, the minister sympathetically informed her that he was attending a men's conference in the Bahamas. She could tell in his voice that he was devastated by the tragic news and immediately she took on his emotions as he continued to speak to her by phone. Rather than show her disappointment, Eloise accepted the minister's sentiments and his reasoning for not being able to preside over his mentor's funeral service.

Little did Eloise know, Dr. Bryant had so much respect for her late husband that he had arranged for a few of the ministers from Empowerment Tabernacle to attend the service. Their primary role was to be a support to her and her family. It meant a lot to her, and it meant a lot to her children when the ministers arrived and revealed their purpose for being there. They offered their condolences and made themselves available for whatever the family needed. She knew they were only being nice and realized they intended to give their pastor a full report—something she didn't mind at all.

At the time of their conversation, Eloise had everything together—she couldn't recall having any loose ends to tie up. In fact, *time* was the only thing that separated their conversation and the day of the funeral.

Today, she was thinking about her late husband more than she had thought about him throughout the past year. His death hit her hard—like a stone to the head. People didn't realize how much courage she had to gather to walk into his funeral service. That day, she held onto the arm of the city mayor like he was sure to run away from her. A time later, the politician, joked with her about how tight she held onto his arm. As he recalled the memory, he laughed and she laughed to—only out of formality. The city official didn't have a clue as to how scared she was and how much it took

to walk into the crowded sanctuary, with all eyes on you, especially when you're marching down the center aisle of a church as large as the Tabernacle of Praise.

Eloise remembered the comments people had made that she radiated with grace and elegance. Quickly, she begged the differ—she felt there was nothing graceful about her on the inside, and as far as elegance was concerned, she looked the part, but she would have traded in a quick second—the three hundred dollar dress, the two hundred dollar shoes and the hundred dollar hat she wore in exchange for her late husband.

Many people didn't understand her emotions. She felt empty. She felt alone. She felt numb. As first lady, through the years, she had attended many funerals, braving them all. But this wasn't an ordinary funeral. This was going to be the last time she would ever see or touch her husband's now clay body.

No, she didn't shed a tear during the entire service and people found that strange. Some found it to be uncomfortable while others found it interesting. Even though she felt empty, alone, and numb, she knew her husband was in a better place. She knew that he had given her the best years of his life. She knew the person that lay stretched in front of her was an honorable man of God. And quite frankly, screaming and yelling like a fool would have only taken away from all the great things people were saying about the accomplishments he had made in the Ramblewood community.

Throughout the service, Eloise continued to listen to all the honorary remarks about her deceased husband and each one made her proud. Proud to be married to a man who not only gave his heart, mind, and soul to God, but someone who had brought tremendous change to a dilapidated area.

Her family thought she had lost her mind, but they would *never* tell her that. Even still, she was sure they knew how much she loved their father, and her silence had nothing to do with the depth of their relationship. In her mind's eye, she could rationalize how her family found it hard to see her stand when the choir sang, lift her hands when the eulogist preached and hold her head high as she paraded out of the sanctuary behind the bronze casket carrying the only man she had ever loved. She knew why. She knew exactly why. It was nothing more than God's amazing grace.

* * *

"Sista, I gotta go to the bathroom," the female voice said.

"Flossie, can you wait until service is over?" Eloise said, looking at the frail looking woman as she looked at her in return like a small child. At times, Flossie reminded her of a child. She would wait until the most awkward moments to ask to go to the restroom and most times she really didn't have to go.

Flossie Mayweather Lorde was the mother to Eloise's stepchildren and had now been living with her for over six months. She knows what you're thinking. You remember how upset she became when Flossie arrived at her home during the passing of her late daughter Olivia, and how she ran from her house screaming for her to leave the premises.

Undoubtedly, soon after the passing of Eloise's late husband—Flossie's former husband, Flossie suffered a stroke and to keep her children from putting her into a nursing home, Eloise offered to take care of her.

Eloise will admit that it did sound strange, but her late husband's death brought about a change in her—a significant one she would probably say. She had pledged to herself that she was turning over a new leaf, and the bad blood between her and Flossie had to be put aside. The commitment she made to herself was the factor that prompted her offer to her ailing nemesis' caregiver.

At first, Flossie's children were a little skeptical and they had every reason to be. In the past, the two women could really go a round or two about the husband they both shared. Flossie would curse Eloise for a week and Eloise would give it back to her the next. Back then, now that Eloise thought about it, before encountering Flossie, she never used profanity much in her conversations with people. As her grandmother had said many times, it was simply unladylike to use profanity.

As Eloise remembered, she had to admit that her husband's ex-wife really knew how to fit all of her curse words in their rightful place. As for her, she had to learn. She had to study. She even had to practice. But after being the victim of Flossie's tongue lashing for ten or so years, she was forced to do one of two things: stand her ground or succumbed to Flossie's verbal abuse. As you already probably know—Flossie obviously taught her well.

Once the family saw that Eloise was being genuine in her offer to take care

of their mother, they finally agreed to the living arrangement. In all honesty, she had nothing to gain by mistreating their mother, especially a woman who could no longer take care of herself.

Medically, the stroke had caused significant damage to Flossie's short and long term memory. On good days, she would remember her children and other days, she would forget her own name. But for the most part and the majority of the time, she referred to Eloise as her sister.

Some people would laugh when she said it, but Eloise didn't mind that she didn't call her by her first name, and she didn't mind that she referred to her as something that she wasn't. In Flossie's mind, she saw Eloise as her sister, and if that was the case, then so be it, that was the person that Eloise would have to be.

Flossie continued to tug on Eloise's clothes like a defiant child, prompting her to look around the sanctuary for an usher or maybe one of Flossie's children. She was sure one of her children was present since they all had recently joined the family church. Eloise scanned her eyes across the crowded building, making a few people think she was trying to get their attention. Then she spotted Zondra sitting next to her tall husband. She looked very small sitting next to him. Once she got Zondra's attention, she beckoned with her hand for the woman that resembled her deceased daughter to come to her. Zondra looked puzzled. Eloise didn't know why? Zondra should have known she wouldn't be beckoning for her unless it was for something important. She watched as her stepdaughter slowly left her seat and angled her way toward her and her mother. After finding out her reasoning, a smile came upon her face, giving Eloise the indication that she was more than glad to take her mother to the bathroom.

"Mama, come on let's go to the ladies room," Zondra said, extending her hand.

Her mother didn't move, instead she looked at Eloise.

"Flossie, it's okay. She's going to take you to the bathroom," Eloise said to her. The thin looking woman rose slowly from her seat, staring at her daughter then looking at Eloise again. Confused, she plopped herself back on the padded pew. She sat motionless for a few minutes before standing a second time. Once she realized that Eloise was still sitting. She hurried and sat down again.

"It's okay, go ahead. You know who that is, don't you?" Eloise encouraged the Cecily Tyson clone as the woman began shaking her head like she didn't. "That's your daughter, Zondra," Eloise added.

Still confused, Flossie looked at the young woman again, but not showing any signs that she recognized her before saying, "Nice to meetcha."

Sadness filled Zondra's eyes as Flossie no longer recognized her. It wasn't that her mother didn't see her on a regular basis because every Sunday they all ate dinner as a family. Observing Zondra's reaction, Eloise was sure she knew that she was taking good care of her mother and she believed her stepdaughter understood her mother's condition was getting worse. Without wasting more time, Zondra soon disappeared with her mother to the restroom, this time, without any reluctance.

As Eloise sat alone, she turned her head quickly to the touch of her own daughter's hand. "Hey Mother, I guess Miss Flossie has to go the bathroom again, huh?" Alma said, laughing while holding her choir robe in her hand. She was familiar with Flossie's routine because it happened so often.

"Yeah and she didn't even recognize her own child," Eloise said, exchanging kisses with her daughter, before she headed toward the choir loft. Next, her daughter Eleanor entered the sanctuary from a side entrance carrying her robe as well. She didn't stop to kiss her mother as her sister did. Instead she blew her mother a kiss and waved at her with the same hand.

Then Richard arrived dressed in his choir robe. He was in a hurry, briskly passing his mother, also angling toward the choir loft. "Hey there, Eloise," he said jokingly. Eloise jumped at the mentioning of her name, but wasn't surprised that the voice belonged to her son. He found it necessary to tease her in public by calling her by her first name. She shook her head first before waving her hand at her son. She couldn't help laughing at how comical her son thought he was.

Zondra returned with her mother then waited as she sat next to Eloise, who glanced at Flossie as she dried her hands with the paper towels she had brought with her from the bathroom. Eloise had no idea why Zondra didn't insist that her mother throw the brown towels in the trash, and from the way Flossie was moving her hands between the wet papers, she was almost afraid to ask her what she planned to do with them once she was done.

As her stepdaughter turned to walk away, Eloise grabbed her hand and

gave her an encouraging wink. Zondra acknowledged her gesture with a slight smile as she walked away to return to the empty space next to her husband.

Earlier, Eloise had heard someone mention that the program was about to begin. Knowing this, she turned her head to see if the statement was true. In doing so, she noticed her stepdaughter looking at Flossie again. Eloise agreed with Zondra's thoughts that Flossie looked like the woman that she has known all her life, but she no longer acted like the woman she had known all her life. Zondra continued to stare at her mother for a few moments longer, before giving her undivided attention to the worship leader that stood at the podium.

"May we all stand to receive the honorees," he said.

As the musicians played the keyboards softly, parishioners throughout the sanctuary began springing up like flowers. Deacon Chairman, Ernest, Jr. and his wife Overa escorted Mychael and Monica down the center aisle to their seats. Mychael looked very distinguished and well dressed in a navy colored suit as his wife followed in his path wearing a matching a-line navy dress with silver buttons down the front. Eloise thought she could have accessorized the outfit with a hat, but she didn't expect the new first lady to follow in her footsteps so soon.

Before long, the worship leader was introducing the speaker of the hour and Dr. Bryant was now standing at the podium. As he stood there, he scanned the crowded sanctuary, before acknowledging Mychael and Monica, his own wife, former first lady Eloise, the officers of the church, and finally, the members.

Eloise sat back and admired how well the young pastor articulated his words. She couldn't help admiring how handsome he was—his neatly cut hair and evenly white teeth. She even admired the black suit he was wearing—she thought the suit fit him well. She recognized that it was a *Versace* design and the shoes were also by *Versace*. The pants weren't too long, the jacket wasn't too tight, and the shirt and tie blended perfectly. She wondered whether the suit had been tailored to fit his body. She answered her own question. It had to be. Nothing was out of place, *He was definitely wearing this suit,* she thought. She became so mesmerized at how good the young pastor looked she didn't realize someone was standing in front of her.

The usher said she had been standing there a few seconds trying to get her to accept the fan she held in her hand.

"Before I give today's message, I want to recognize someone who could write a book detailing how to be a first lady. This person knew her place in the church and she knew her place in the home. She didn't have a problem honoring her husband as a man of God. And if I didn't have my own little first lady, now that she's single, I would certainly ask for her hand in marriage," Dr. Bryant said.

He paused as the congregation was aroused between laughter and commotion. By the small description that he gave, everyone knew who he was referring to. Following his statement, Dr. Bryant grabbed a white box and opened it, revealing a large plaque. He began to read:

"This plaque is dedicated to First Lady Eloise London Lorde for her service and dedication as first lady. 1980–2006."

"First lady Eloise, even though you are no longer first lady of this ministry, you have left your mark in history as to what a first lady should be. Lady Eloise is such an amazing woman, not only did she tragically lose her daughter, but also the love of her life within months of one another. Only a mighty woman of God could sustain their sanity in times like those. So congregation, I take the time today to introduce to some and present to others, the Mother of the Tabernacle of Praise Baptist Church, Mrs. Eloise London-Lorde."

Applause resonated throughout the sanctuary. Eloise smiled as Dr. Bryant moved his hand for her to stand up. She didn't act bashful or embarrassed, but complied with his suggestion as she waved her hand like she was in a parade. Then thoughts of her late husband and late daughter came to mind. She continued to wave as warm tears streamed down her face.

Dr. Bryant came out of the pulpit holding the cordless microphone in his hand. He grabbed Eloise in his arms and they hugged in the manner of a mother and son. He paused again, but this time trying to regain *his* composure.

He said, speaking to the congregation, "Before we go on with the program, I want you to know that whenever I stayed at the Lorde family home, I was treated like royalty. First, I should say, I have never seen a house so organized and so clean. Babe, even with our housekeeper, no one *can* touch Mother Lorde—she's an immaculate housekeeper. This woman here

knows how to treat a man of God. During my stay, I didn't have to want for nothing, look for nothing or ask for nothing; because she made sure I had everything I needed." He paused again. His voice now cracking, "So Mother Lorde, today I say, thank you."

Dr. Bryant moved the microphone away from his mouth when he asked Eloise was she okay. She nodded that she was as she took the plaque in her hand. She looked at the inscription, and she became proud immediately. He asked her if she wanted to make a comment, and she shook her head that she didn't. She waved her hand at the congregation again then she took her seat as Dr. Bryant returned to the pulpit to continue with the service.

CHAPTER TWO

Mychael was really enjoying Dr. Bryant and he leaned over to whisper his thoughts to his wife, "Boy, this man is awesome." Monica leaned her head towards her husband to hear what he had said, before nodding her head up and down in agreement to his statement. It appeared to him that his wife was also having a good time, he assumed. His assessment was based on the waving of her hands and how she yelled back at the gifted evangelist.

Mychael was glad that the former first lady was persistent about handling the planning of the program. Everything was going perfect. Eloise had done a great job, he thought. He twisted his neck a few times to get a more detailed look at how packed the sanctuary was. He couldn't believe it, he was the uprising pastor of the Tabernacle of Praise Baptist Church. Kudos to Reverend Lorde, Mychael thought to himself. Apparently his late pastor saw something in him that he didn't see in himself. If he had a choice in the matter, he would probably have said he wasn't ready, but Reverend Lorde didn't give him a choice. He remembered his words like it were yesterday. Thinking about what he had told him, in his mind, he knew he had to make a conscious effort to live sanctified and holy. He knew it was going to be rough, but he had to do it. Being the pastor of a congregation this size was serious business, and to destroy it would bring no honor to his late pastor's legacy.

The congregation continued to shout as Dr. Bryant reached the closing of his sermon. His message was unique and it was obvious that he had his own style. Mychael observed his every move and how he kept the crowd on its feet. He took a moment to scan the congregation again and could tell that the people were enjoying what they were hearing.

Moments later, Dr. Bryant was standing on the floor as he paced back and forth, now caught up in the spirit. He had already made the crowd go crazy with his familiar saying, 'Has anybody ever seen a black man preach like this?'

His sermon titled, *after all is said and done, don't forget to repent* was the work of a creative genius. The crowd had followed him through every word. His sermon instructed the congregation to repent for all their wrong doings.

"For every bad thought you had, repent."

"For every thought of jealousy, repent."

"For every act of hatred, repent."

"For times someone needed help and you had the resources, but you refused to help them, repent."

"The angels are rejoicing right now," he exclaimed.

"I say, the angels are rejoicing right now."

"Souls are getting saved tonight. Hearts are getting right tonight. Lives are being changed tonight," he said as he walked around the pulpit clearly in a trance. He fumbled with his suit pocket. Then he brushed his hands down the front of his suit jacket. The spirit wouldn't allow him to keep still. The choir sang, holy…holy…holy one, we adore you. The fifty voice choir had been singing the song for over thirty minutes. It sounded as though they were getting ready to end the verse.

"Keep singing, don't stop. Keep singing. God's not finished. The spirit says we got more to repent for," he instructed as he joined in with the choir with his voice blending in perfect harmony. "Holy…Holy…Holy one, we adore you," he crooned and the sound of his voice was in comparison to Gerald Levert. He left the pulpit and stood on the floor again now surrounded by people engulfed in true worship.

Eloise was now at the mercy of the Holy-Spirit as two female ushers stood at her side while she bucked back and forth on the pew. The women tried to hold her in place, but were unsuccessful. They held her hands and her feet began jerking. Then they held her legs and her head began jerking. The only measure left was for them to keep her comfortable by fanning.

On the other hand, Mychael stood with his eyes closed and his arms stretched outward. He was also caught up in genuine praise for God. It was

obvious to onlookers that his worship to God was true and his submission to Him was forever.

Thirty minutes later, he was walking into the pulpit as the newly installed pastor of the Tabernacle of Praise Baptist Church. It felt different. In a way, he felt overwhelmed. For so many years, he had sat in the same pulpit, but never as the pastor. Today, he had a new responsibility. Today, his life was never going to be the same. Today, it was official—he was indeed the new pastor.

"First I want to give all honor and glory to God. I am so thankful today. Thankful to the late Ernest Lorde, Sr. for naming someone like me, someone who would at least try to fill the big shoes he's left behind. I'm thankful to you all for accepting me as your new leader. I'm going to be honest and tell you, I don't proclaim to be perfect, I don't proclaim to know it all, and I don't proclaim to be the best that you've ever heard. But hopefully you will allow me a little room for error. As Pastor Lorde often said, 'God is looking for a church without a spot or a wrinkle.' And as a human being, I still have a few wrinkles to iron out. However, I promise I will do my best to be the pastor that you will be proud of," Mychael said to the congregation. He waited as the congregation clapped behind his statement.

"I give honor to my lovely wife, Monica. Baby stand up. This is my rock, a beautiful one I might add." Monica stood and waved, turning to face the applauding congregation. He continued, "Mother Eloise….I'm so used to calling you first lady Eloise, I must become familiar with referring to you as Mother Eloise now. Thanks for all your support. Thanks also to the Christiansen, Anderson, and Lorde families as a whole, for all of your support."

After Mychael finished his remarks, he twisted his body to return the program into the hands of Dr. Bryant, who gestured for him to render the benediction while he stood at the podium. Mychael prayed for the church and his own personal growth. Soon after, he was standing at the back entrance along side his wife and the former first lady greeting the worshipers who were exiting the sanctuary. Some of the members came by to either shake his hand or to hug him, but there were others that didn't bother to welcome him as their new pastor or congratulate him on a successful program.

As the last of the parishioners were coming to an end, Mychael felt his cell

phone vibrate. He grabbed the device from his waist and he saw the call was coming from the house of his Cousin Myra. He figured she was calling to congratulate him on his appointment as pastor. He didn't want to miss her call, so he held up his finger to the last member in line as he answered it.

"Hey, Myra, you kind of caught me at a bad time. I'm just finishing up the installation service. I'll have to c—"

"Myke. It's me, Myles. I'm sorry to be calling during a time like this, but I need to let you know that Myra just passed away a few hours ago," Mychael heard his cousin say. He was frozen by his words. A few moments passed, before he spoke again, "What?! Passed away? What are you talking about? I just spoke with her earlier this week. She was supposed to come to the installation service, but she said she was coming down with a cold," he said, pausing, before asking, "Where's Hannah?"

Then he removed himself from the crowd and walked down an empty side aisle. He kept his back to the mingling congregation and didn't know his wife was behind him until he felt her hand rubbing his back. He turned around to face her as she stood in silence. She waited patiently as he continued to speak into his cell phone. As his cousin rambled on, Mychael noticed Eloise greeting the remainder of members that had walked up after he had received his phone call. The former first lady knew how to step in wherever she was needed. He continued to half listen to his cousin as he observed Eloise in action—she was such a pro, he thought.

At this point, Mychael wasn't contributing anything to the two-way conversation—his cousin was doing all the talking. He was going nonstop—like a person with ADHD. He knew it was his nerves and allowed him to babble on and on without interrupting him. Myles finally answered Mychael's question about Hannah, "She's here. We've found Myra's will and it says that you and Monica are to get custody of Hannah if anything were to happen to her."

"I know. She told us about that. Man, I didn't know she was sick. What happened?" Mychael asked.

"Man, Myra had been battling ovarian cancer for over a year. She didn't tell you?"

"Noooooooooo," Mychael said with his eyes filled with tears as he released air from his mouth. His wife moved closer, but continued to stand

in silence. He noticed how she was looking at him—she was searching his face for answers. He took a moment to remove the phone from his mouth to let her know what was going on, "This is my Cousin Myles. He said my Cousin Myra just passed away from ovarian cancer."

"I didn't know she was battling cancer," Monica admitted, also shocked.

"I didn't either. I wonder why she never said anything," Mychael said, returning to the conversation with Myles. "Man, I can't get up there tonight. Is there anyway you and Camille can keep Hannah with you until the funeral? Monica and I will pick her up after the service."

"Okay man, don't worry; she'll be fine."

"I know she will." He paused, before he spoke again. "And Myles….man I appreciate you calling me."

"I know you do, and again, I'm sorry for having to call you with such bad news on a day like today." Myles paused. "Oh and man…congratulations from us all," he said before hanging up.

Mychael disconnected the call from his end and returned the cell phone to his waist. He was still stricken with grief. He thought about the words of his cousin, *Congratulations from us all*. Congratulations, for what? He wondered.

At that moment, he thought about how close he, Myles and Myra were. He loved his female cousin like a sister. She had taken care of him when he was a disruptive teenager and he would be the first to admit, she really straightened him out. A smile came to his face when he thought about how she had bailed him out of so many situations. She was truly one of a kind and was someone who always put the needs of others in front of her own. And today, he realized that more, especially with her not telling him that she had been battling cancer. Mychael held his wife tightly then he grabbed her hand and walked with his head down toward the exit leading to the fellowship hall.

CHAPTER THREE

Six months later…

"Come on girls, hustle!" Mychael yelled from the sidelines. In his mind, he kept wondering, what were these girls thinking? Surely—winning this game wasn't it. It was quite obvious that their minds were elsewhere. Even still, he had to admit aside from tonight's distractions, this was his best team yet. And based on that fact, he was determined to take them to the championship. "Christina, stay focused," he screamed.

He couldn't believe the simple mistakes his team were making. At this point, he had yelled until he was nearly hoarse and it still hadn't turned the game around. All he could do was shake his head when he looked at the score board. The team was only down by four points and three minutes remained in the game. He felt frustrated.

Although this was a single elimination playoff, he had made up in his mind that if his girls didn't win this game, the next day, the entire team would still run for one hour straight. He knew his starting five were tired and he had pushed them to their limit, which prompted him to get the attention of one of the referees as he made a t-sign with his hand. He knew it was beyond time for a time out. Prior to, he could hear the fans in the stands, specifically *Snappy* saying, "All right coach, it's time to give your girls a break."

At the sound of the referee's whistle, the five team members ran to the sideline exhausted, each one grabbing for water.

Christina was among the starting five and one of his best players. She was able to transition successfully into every position on the court. Between her father and Mychael, the two men had taught the young star everything she

27

knew. She was impressive to the college recruiters that watched from the stands. Scouts from near and far came to witness the teenager in action and found it amazing how she was able to move the ball around the court with such rhythm, not to mention her excellent jump shot. And whenever the opportunity presented itself—the six foot one athlete could dunk a basket better than Lebron James. Most of the time, Mychael had to catch himself because he had the tendency to ignore the other players and coached Christina only. It wasn't intentional, but he knew if he could get her to keep her head in the game, she would keep the other teammates in line.

By this time, the team was down by one point and he wanted them to execute the next play with conviction. During the timeout, he grabbed his clipboard with the basketball court diagram and he drew the next play. The fans were growing nervous with fear, but still remaining hopeful.

Monica sat in the stands holding a sleeping Hannah. The toddler had now been living with her new parents for six months and proved to be more than a handful for the both of them. Neither one had had any training raising children. They were basically learning from each other. Thank God they had the assistance of Monica's family.

The Lorde family and a few of the Christiansen family members were also present. Above Monica sat Eloise, her Aunt Eleanor, and her Uncle *Snappy*. Almost near the end of the game, her cousin Joy Lynn and Richard entered the gymnasium. It was normal for Richard to arrive late and he didn't mind people knowing it. The two walked up the bleachers, facing the crowd of family members, and strangers staring at them until they sat down. They were dressed in denim jeans, gray shirts and matching black leather jackets with gray scarves. Joy Lynn took the seat next to her cousin Monica and Richard sat next to her. The two women pressed their cheeks together and grinned like two teenagers. Joy Lynn rubbed Hannah's beautiful curly hair as she slept. The toddler hadn't budged even with all the noise that was being made around her.

Eloise cleared her throat when her son entered to get his attention. The crowd was so thick he hadn't heard his mother nor did he notice that his mother, his sister, and his brother-in-law were sitting a few bleachers above them.

"Son, you do realize that the game is almost over?" Eloise yelled over the people sitting in front of her. "And Joy Lynn, a word to the wise, don't let my son corrupt you into being late for everything," Eloise warned.

Joy Lynn forced a smile to her face, followed by a wave to Eloise. She was surprised the stone-faced woman was in such a good mood. Even still, she wasn't really interested in Eloise's idle chatter as she returned to the conversation with her cousin.

Eloise mouthed to her daughter and son-in-law, "It's something about that girl. She can never seem to look me in the eye," she said. She thought her son had heard what she had said when he turned his body around to face her. "And good evening to you too mother. Besides who said I was late for the game, maybe I'm on time for the victory celebration," he said, attempting to be sarcastic as he waved his hand at his sister and brother-in-law.

The family had become use to seeing more of Joy Lynn and for all intents and purposes, Eloise made gentle conversation with her, but by no means did she like her. Each time the two encountered one another, she would always say it was something about the young woman that didn't sit well with her. Little did she know, her son and Joy Lynn weren't officially dating, but were spending a lot of *serious* time together? She didn't know that Richard was actually excited about the possibility of Joy Lynn becoming his girlfriend as she was about him being her boyfriend. He felt there was something special about her and he enjoyed the times they were around each other, and this was something he wasn't about to let end.

Mychael continued to scribble marks on his clipboard. "Christina, I want you here. Shana, I want you to take the ball and pass it to Christel and Christel as soon as you get the ball in your hands, pass it to Christina to get the basket," he explained in detail. All three of the girls shook their heads with understanding. The five players and their coach put their hands in the circle and yelled in unison, "Panthers!" As the team returned to the floor, the home crowd came alive again and started cheering along with sideline row of young girls, all dressed in the same color. The game clock was now at thirty seconds. The referee blew his whistle and Misty threw the ball inbound to Shana, who then dribbled between two of her opponents.

"Pass the ball to Christel!" Mychael yelled.

The referee had to keep reminding him to stay off the floor. He moved back slightly. In his mind, he said the referee could stop him from coming on the floor, but he was much taller than the referee which enabled him to look over him to see his play unfold. "Shana, give the ball to Christel!" The game

clock was now at nineteen seconds. Shana couldn't find Christel, but she saw that Christina was open at the basket. She passed the ball as hard as she could, but the pass was blocked by the visiting team. The ball bounced loose on the floor as Christina hustled to get to it. She grabbed it in her hands as the game clock ticked at four seconds. Christina dribbled it as far as she could. She needed to get closer, but there wasn't enough time. She eyed the basket and squared her feet on the floor as she released the ball as level as she could. The buzzer went off just as the ball connected with the goal net— she had just completed a three-point play. The crowd went crazy and the entire team ran to the floor as did many of the fans, grabbing Christina in the air and spinning her around.

"We did it, we did it. We made it to the finals," the team yelled. The frustration was now gone from Mychael's body as he was now filled with excitement. He remained calm as he made his way to shake hands with the visiting coach. Winning this game meant a lot to him, primarily since he had once coached the visiting team before transferring to Ramblewood High. Tonight, he and the young coach shook hands and congratulated each other on a good game. He was glad his team had won because the visiting coach happened to be the person that had replaced him after he resigned and accepted his current position.

He looked through the crowd in search of his wife. Before he could walk up to her, she and Joy Lynn walked up to him.

"Babe that was a close call, huh? Christina really came through for the team tonight," Monica said.

"Yeah, she really brought it home for us," he responded, kissing his wife on the forehead then kissing a sleeping Hannah, who had been asleep throughout the majority of the game and wasn't aware of her adopted father's victory.

Mychael moved away from the conversation with his wife and walked into the midst of the cheering teammates and fans, before pulling Christina by the ponytail saying, "Good game sport."

She smiled at him, wrapping one arm around her coach's waist as she leaned her body into his, "Thanks Coach."

CHAPTER FOUR

It was Saturday morning and Mychael was still feeling rather good about his team's victory. The night before, he didn't get much sleep, concerned about the strategy he would use to obtain the championship. He wanted this victory. He could even envision the trophy sitting on the mantle in the front office of Ramblewood High.

Even though Mychael wanted to win, he knew the team he was scheduled to play was tough and undefeated. According to the newspapers, his opponent hadn't lost a game in the last three seasons. With that thought in mind, he had to force himself to remain positive that *his* team was capable of obtaining a victory. They had to. It had been years since the community had won a championship. In fact, Ramblewood High hadn't experienced a championship win since Christina's father, *Snappy* was on the boy's high school basketball team and without counting the exact number of years, and he knew right away it had been a long time.

He walked the halls leading to his church office, and glowed in his excitement as members who had attended the game were congratulating him and *his* team on the chance at winning the finals. He was proud. This was his first time coaching a team with a 12-1 record. In his mind, he had to agree with himself that he had a *good* group of girls. All of them were honor students and didn't have any disciplinary problems.

As he reached the closed door, he turned the doorknob and entered the reception area leading to his office, "Good morning, Sister Beatrice. I missed you last night at the game. Something must have come up?" he said, shuffling through his mail. He waited for her to respond, but she never answered him. He took that as a sign to leave her alone—not even she could ruin his good mood, he thought.

Beatrice had been his secretary since the passing of Pastor Lorde. In her administrative capacity, she also floated between her responsibilities to him and the trustee ministry. Aside from her occasional mood swings, unlike Richard, he thought she did a fairly decent job. The day he decided to hire her, Richard gave him one hundred reasons why he shouldn't put her on the church's payroll. Initially, he thought about taking his advice then he decided to give the young woman a chance. Since his decision, the only problem she gave him was the issue adjusting to her mood changes and he was getting used to those. Not giving her actions a second thought, he moved past Beatrice and entered his office to take a seat behind his desk. He adjusted the level of his chair then he opened his file drawer to look over the information he wanted to discuss during his officer meeting.

This morning, he planned to meet with the deacons and trustees of the church as a group, and following that meeting he was going to address with Beatrice some information that Richard had brought to his attention. She knew they were going to meet, but she had no clue that Richard was going to be present. She had no clue that he was the reason for them having the *special* called meeting. Maybe she did. Quite naturally that would explain the reason for her bad mood, he rationalized.

He closed the folder he was reading and left his office to trail down the hall to the conference room. He entered the open door and found that Beatrice had made copies of all the materials he planned to discuss during his meeting. A stack was placed evenly in front of every empty chair and in the middle of the table stood a container full of water and a second container full of orange juice, along with eight empty glasses. Immediately, he realized why he had hired her—regardless of the fact that she felt a need to call in every Friday. Yes, her absences concerned him somewhat, since Beatrice knew she had been hired to handle all of the daily operations of the church, Tuesday through Saturday. In the beginning, she agreed with this arrangement and worked the schedule without a problem. However, according to Richard's calendar, this month alone, she had failed to show up three Friday's in a row.

Although Richard's information was concrete, he had to admit that his trustee chairman didn't cut their secretary any slack. For some reason, he noticed every error she made and seized every opportunity to address those same concerns with him. He hadn't noticed a problem with Beatrice's

attendance and probably wouldn't have since he was not at the church during the day. However, based on Trustee Lorde's records, the day before Beatrice was scheduled to open the fellowship hall for the plumbers to unclog the toilets in the women's and men's bathrooms and she never reported for work nor did she call to inform someone she wasn't coming. By his estimation, her negligence had cost the church a whopping five hundred dollar service fee and it was a must that they speak to her about her actions.

An hour later, the officer's meeting was going well as the Deacon Chairman gave his report regarding the status of absent and sick members. The remaining deacons gave their input and promised him that they would contact any absent members in their respective wards.

As Trustee Chairman, Richard began his report regarding the financial state of the church. He was pleased to announce the amount of tithes the members were paying and suggested that the church move forward with the education center vision.

"Trustee Lorde, you took the words right out of my mouth," Mychael said. He had been contemplating how he would bring the long time vision of his late pastor up without getting the board in an uproar. Apparently, he was wrong or maybe it was because Trustee Lorde had mentioned it instead. Both the deacon and trustee boards agreed that this was a project that the Ramblewood community needed.

"Okay, since we are in agreement about this vision, Trustee Lorde I am going to need for you to find out the total cost to complete this project and get the information to me as soon as possible," Mychael said.

"I thought you'd never ask," Richard said, pulling out his portfolio of information regarding the construction costs for an educational facility. He began distributing copies to everyone present in the room.

"Bro. Ric— I mean Trustee Lorde, I think I need to look this over before you pass this information out to everyone," Mychael spoke out with caution.

Richard stopped in middle of his pastor's statement. He held the last of the copies in his hand. "What do you mean you need to look at this? My father never had a problem about anything I shared with the board. What is there to be concerned about? This packet only has the figures for

different styles of educational buildings. I think it would be a good idea for everyone to take the packet home and decide what would be economical for the church, don't ya'll agree?" Richard said to everyone.

The deacons and trustees alike shook their heads in agreement with Richard's suggestion. Those that didn't have copies of the packet grabbed for the remaining copies the trustee chairman held in his hand.

Mychael sat at the head of the table feeling outnumbered—dumbfounded. In the back of his mind, he believed Trustee Lorde had already conversed with the board, convincing them all to agree to move forward on the educational center project. It didn't surprise him that everyone would be in agreement since the board was majority family. He felt bamboozled. In fact, he smelled a *rat* and the tail hung from the pants of his trustee chairman. His flesh wasn't quite sure whether the board knew about this information before the meeting, but his spirit was telling him that they did.

* * *

"Pastor Dovely, my dog got hit by a car and died. I was too upset to come in here," Beatrice lied. Truthfully, her dog did die, but that was two weeks ago. She knew the true reason she didn't come in—she was tired. Her boyfriend came knocking at her window around 2*am* and she let him in and they had sex for three hours. Hours later, when the alarm clock went off, she couldn't make herself get out of bed. Now, that was the truth, but she was not about to tell her pastor and boss this private piece of information.

"Sister Beatrice, I understand that you were upset about the passing of your pet, but what I want you to understand is that we had a plumbing contractor scheduled to come here yesterday, and you were not only responsible for being here, but responsible to at least call someone once you knew you weren't coming in," Mychael said.

"I knew you wouldn't believe that my dog got hit by a car. You can ask my mama and daddy, they will tell you what happened. Let's call them right now."

Richard sat back in his chair with his legs crossed. He and Beatrice were like oil and water—he knew not to say anything. He only agreed to sit in on the meeting because Beatrice partially worked for him and he was the one who made his pastor aware of this situation.

"Trustee Lorde, help yo' pastor out here."

Richard paused before he spoke. *First of all, you're not my pastor,* he thought. He knew he had to respect his father's wishes to have Mychael succeed him, but he certainly didn't have to agree with his father.

"Beatrice, Reverend Dovely is correct. It was your responsibility to let someone know if you were not going to report to work. This is your full-time job. The church pays you a salary to be here, Tuesday thru Saturday. Therefore, you have to treat this as though it's a real job."

Beatrice didn't respond. Instead, she cried. Both Richard and his pastor looked at each other before rolling their eyes toward the ceiling.

"Sister Beatrice, it's not our intention to make you upset, but we want you to understand the seriousness of what has happened. On yesterday, by you not reporting to work, the church was penalized to pay a service fee of five hundred dollars and we still don't have the two restrooms fixed. You understand our position, right?" Mychael explained in detail, seeing that his secretary was really getting upset. His explanation didn't help because she continued to give them both the silent treatment. They waited a few moments to give Beatrice time to answer. She didn't.

"Do you have any further questions for either of us?"

Beatrice continued to sniffle as Mychael left the room to get tissue from her desk. As soon as his back was turned, she glared at Richard, who was looking at the paperwork he held in his lap. She stared at him until she got his attention. When she did, she made a sound with her mouth as she moved her index finger across her throat. Richard looked around for Mychael, but he didn't see or hear him. At that moment, he became *scared!* He sprung from his chair, colliding into his pastor as he reentered the room.

"Going somewhere?" Mychael asked as he gave Beatrice the tissue he held in his hand.

"Ah, yeah…Um Pastor, I forgot I was supposed to pick up my dry cleaning before noon," Richard tried to say.

Mychael listened to his trustee's excuse as he walked behind his desk to take his seat. Before he did so, he glanced at his watch, "Well my brotha, you are two hours late, it's almost three o'clock. I hope you weren't planning to wear one of those suits tomorrow."

Still a little startled, Richard stuttered, "Ah…no, Ah…yeah. I mean they

were going to wait until I got there. I mean…I gotta go. I'll see you tomorrow."

Mychael looked at his trustee chairman a little puzzled. All of a sudden, Richard was acting strange and he didn't understand why. He thought maybe it was because he had been gone so long. He would have returned sooner, but Beatrice didn't have any tissue at her desk and he had to walk down the hall to the restroom.

Beatrice was still sitting quietly as her body jerked between her tears. She wiped her eyes with the tissue in her hand. She finally spoke after Richard had left the room, "I know you think I'm lying, but it did happen."

"Sister Beatrice, we've already gone through this, now I want you to take the rest of the day off to get yourself together. We can start anew on Tuesday. I have a few things I need to finish around here; I will answer the phones for the next hour and a half. I hope to see you tomorrow in Sunday school."

Beatrice lifted herself from the chair and returned to her office.

Mychael heard her as she opened and closed a couple of her desk drawers, before he heard her leaving her work area. He sighed aloud, not because he was agitated, but mostly because he was glad the conversation with his secretary was over.

A time later, he realized he wasn't accomplishing any of the tasks he intended to complete, instead, he found himself sitting in silence, marinating in his thoughts. Exactly, thirty minutes had passed, before the office phone rang.

"Thank you for calling Tabernacle of Praise, this is Pastor Dovely."

Richard didn't announce who was. He began talking, "Yo' Reverend Dovely, now you see what I've been telling you. When you left the room that *crazy* girl made a gesture to me like she was going to slit my throat."

He couldn't help but laugh. "Well she's gone for the day; I told her that we would start anew on Tuesday," he informed his trustee.

"Anew what? Yeah, she's going to be new all right, anew style of craziness," Richard said. They laughed aloud when he noticed a sheet of paper lying underneath his desk. At first, he shuffled his feet to reach it then he bent over to pick it up while listening to Richard rant about their assistant.

Once he grabbed the piece of paper with his hand, he screamed, "Oh my God! What is that?" He dropped the receiver and tilted his chair over when he jumped from his seat.

Beatrice had returned and was standing in front of him with her dead dog wrapped in plastic. The dog was dead stiff as live maggots fell from the animal corpse onto the floor. The stench was unbearable.

"Reverend Dovely, I knew you didn't believe me, so I brought Roscoe so you could see that he did get hit by a car and that he was truly dead," she said.

"Get out of here! Get that nasty thing out of here!" Mychael screamed, grabbing his nose, afraid to even breathe. He could still hear Richard on the line saying, "Rev., what's going on? Rev., are you there?"

Once Beatrice had left the room, he grabbed the fallen receiver, explaining to Richard what had happened. Based on Richard's response, it seemed that he couldn't believe what he was hearing. Between laughter he kept saying, "You kidding…man you've got to be kidding me."

He ended his conversation with his trustee chairman before slamming the receiver into the base of the phone. Then he left his office in a hurry to get a can of disinfectant. When he walked through the reception area, he noticed Beatrice sitting at her desk. She was pecking at the keys on her keyboard while holding her dead pet on her lap—the foul order more potent than before.

"Girl, have you lost your mind?!?! I told you to get out of her with that," he said firmly.

"*Shhhhh*…Don't you have any respect for the dead?" she said.

At the same time, he held his nose and covered his mouth while saying, "I'm going down the hall to get a can of spray and when I get back I want you and that dog gone," he threatened, rushing toward the door quickly.

He felt like he was going to lose the contents in his stomach. He put his hand on the door handle to leave the reception area then he looked over his shoulder, catching his secretary glaring at him. Before he could open the door, still holding the dead corpse in her lap, Beatrice took her arm and swiped every item visible from her desk at him. Papers flew in the air—the phone, her desk lamp and computer monitor all went tumbling to the floor. His eyes stretched, he braced himself against the wall as Beatrice's actions paralyzed him with shock. "I want you out of here in the next five minutes or I am calling the cops," he warned her.

"You don't have to call the cops 'cause I'm leaving. I hated working for your *black* ass anyway," she said, walking past her pastor still carrying her dead maggot infested animal.

CHAPTER FIVE

As soon as Richard saw Christopher walking toward their table, he couldn't help laughing again. On the way to the restaurant, he had already laughed to himself several times. First hand, he knew how unpredictable Beatrice could be, but he just couldn't make himself believe what she had done to Mychael.

"What's so funny?" Christopher asked him as he took his seat.

"I told you your cousin was *Crazy*."

"What has Beatrice done now? And stop calling my cousin names."

"She has officially broken the good Reverend in," he said, shaking his head as he placed his napkin on his lap.

"How so?"

After ordering a diet soft drink, he began to tell his friend about the meeting that he and Mychael had with Beatrice concerning her attendance. He could barely wait to tell him about the part involving the dead animal. He knew he wouldn't believe it. He was right. Christopher couldn't believe it himself.

"You gotto be kidding. She actually brought a dead dog for you guys to see."

"No, you're missing the whole point. She thought we didn't believe her, so after I left; Mychael sent her home for the rest of the day. Then I called him to joke around about how she acted during the meeting and as we were talking, she walked in and scared the living daylights out of him. The man literally dropped the phone."

Christopher immediately grabbed his cell phone and called his mother, "Mama, you are not going to believe this. Richard said Bea took her dead

dog to the church because she thought Pastor Dovely didn't believe that her ole retarded mutt Roscoe didn't get hit by a car." He held his phone away from his face as Richard mouthed to him, "What is she saying?"

Christopher mouthed in return, "She's fussing about Bea, Aunt Agnes and Uncle Joe." He returned the cell phone to his ear and listened to his mother go on a little more about her family. He cut her off, "Mama, I'll be home in a little bit and don't you call over there messing with Aunt Agnes and those." He listened to more of his mother's conversation. "Yeah, Mama….Mama….We can talk about it more when I get home. Okay. Okay. Um, humph. I will, okay, bye."

By this time, the food had arrived, but Richard wasn't saying anything. Christopher sighed as he disconnected the call, "My poor mother."

"What, she wants to call your aunt and uncle?" Richard finally asked.

"Yes, when it's none of her business. I told her she cannot control the things her family does," Christopher said, changing the subject. "So what's the deal inviting me to dinner on a Saturday evening?"

"I want to talk to you about something."

Christopher studied the look on Richard's face and could tell that he was now being serious. Also noticing he hadn't said much prior to their food arriving. Earlier, Christopher had ordered his usual grilled salmon salad and Richard had ordered a medium rare rib eye steak with a baked potato.

Richard wondered could Christopher tell that something was different about the evening, maybe he didn't. He had made the decision to take his time to have this conversation with his best friend. He was hoping the longer he waited, the less nervous he would become, but he knew he couldn't stall the inevitable forever.

"I think I'm in love with Joy Lynn," he blurted out.

Christopher stopped in mid-air. His food never reached his mouth. "You think you what?"

"I think I'm in love with Joy Lynn and I'm going to ask her to marry me," Richard repeated, but adding that he wanted to marry Joy Lynn.

The moment Christopher heard those words, his appetite left him and he became cold with anger. He really didn't know Joy Lynn personally, but he still hated her. Over the last year, she had come between his and Richard's time together. She was the reason they had grown apart. She was the reason

every time he called his best friend to invite him to the movies or to dinner, he would say he had plans with her. If he never suspected that something was going on between the two, he got his confirmation tonight.

After his confession, Richard stared at his partially empty plate and didn't look at Christopher for a while.

On the other hand, Christopher looked directly at him, only, because he was pissed. Pissed that after all these years, he now had the notion to fall in love with a woman. Pissed that he wouldn't be moving into the new house and lastly, pissed because he had the nerve to tell him this in public—over dinner. Christopher wanted to cry, but he refused to be embarrassed. He wanted to slap Richard, but he refused to go to jail. He wanted to grab his things and walk out, but aside from being lovers, the two had been friends far too long.

"So, when did this happen?" Christopher said, forcing the words from his mouth.

"I guess since my father passed away. And lately we've been spending a lot of time with each other and it has since turned into something serious," Richard made himself explain. Then he paused. "Man, I want kids and a family. And you know I've always been attracted to women."

"But Richard," Christopher said then he paused, moments passed before he spoke, "We agreed that we were in love and that we were going to be life partners. How has that changed within the last year?"

"Man, so much has changed. I dunno…I'm still in love with you, but Joy Lynn and I share something different. The love between me and her is so special. When I'm with her I feel the two of us are evenly yoked and there's no guilt about the two of us being together."

"So, you're saying that when we were together, you feel guilty afterwards?"

"No, that's not what I'm saying."

"Then, what are you saying?"

"What I'm saying is…Man don't try and twist my words. I'm trying to break it to you easy."

"Oh…Okay, I understand. This dinner was supposed to be your opportunity to break it to me easy," Christopher said, repeating Richard's words. "No, Mr. Lorde, I'll tell you how it's going to be. You go ahead and

marry this Joy Lynn person. Just remember when you get the urge to start dipping and dabbing again, oh, and I know you *will* get that urge again, don't you even think about looking my way."

"Christopher let's not end our friendship like this."

Christopher raised his voice. Others were now looking. "Friendship?! Oh, that's what we had, a friendship? I thought at least I was worthy of being in a relationship with you, but I guess not. Mr. Lorde, the dinner was nice and I wish you well," Christopher said, throwing his napkin into his half empty plate.

"Keep your voice down," Richard said through clinched teeth. He grabbed Christopher by the hand to stop him from leaving the table, but he pulled free. Christopher was now standing, looking down at him sitting. Again, he pleaded further for him to not cause a scene.

"Christopher I told Joy Lynn that we've been friends for years and she wants to get to know you," he said, looking up at a standing Christopher.

After making his last statement, he knew immediately he had said the wrong thing. He knew a friendship with Joy Lynn would be last thing that Christopher wanted.

"You can't be serious. But, in the event that you're not, for your information, I think you should tell your little girlfriend that we were more than friends and furthermore, I don't want to get to know her."

Christopher was boiling with anger and left the restaurant as fast as his feet could carry him. Even the cold breeze that slammed against his face couldn't cool his temper. All the while, his cell phone rang constantly. He knew who it was and he wasn't going to answer it. In route home, he drove recklessly through town and was now walking up the steps to his house; before he entered his front door, he turned the ringing phone off.

Once inside, Christopher put on his best face for his mother. He knew she would recognize that something was wrong. He walked into the living room and joined her as she watched television. Immediately, she wanted to know the entire story about the dead dog again. He gave her the story as Richard had given it to him. His mother admitted that she had called her sister, who didn't see anything wrong with Beatrice digging up her buried pet and transporting him down to the church as evidence to the pastor.

She also told him that she had called her pastor and expressed her

apologizes on behalf of her family. Regardless of the fact that he accepted her apology, she told her son that their pastor admitted that Beatrice really put the fear of God in him. She and Christopher laughed as she recalled how Mychael described the way Beatrice barged into his office with the dead corpse in hand. Not to mention, the way she flung all the items off of her desk.

Christopher listened to his mother speak negatively about her own family, but he only heard part of what she had said. He couldn't concentrate, and it wasn't because he wasn't interested in what she had to say. At that moment, he just had a lot on his mind.

Later, the two went to their separate rooms. In her room, Carolina prayed for her family and her pastor and his family before climbing into bed. In his room, Christopher didn't pray nor did he bother to turn on the lights; he laid across his bed in darkness, crying about the blow that Richard had given to him. A blow he didn't see coming. A blow he was finding hard to process and a blow that was making it difficult to digest a revelation of this magnitude.

CHAPTER SIX

Beatrice decided that it was best to bury Roscoe again since she was becoming annoyed with the foul order. One would guess that she would since she had been riding around all evening with the dead animal in her car. Being that it was winter and too cold to let down the car window, she was forced to endure the terrible stench.

Earlier that night, she and her father had gone outside and placed her pet into its original grave. Initially, she was so upset about Roscoe being killed that she was unable to accompany her father to bury him. Tonight, before leaving the grave, she released more tears for her beloved pet as she ran her finger downward and across her chest. As they returned to the house, her father walked ahead of her as she walked in slow strides behind him. It was the first time in a long time since the both of them had been in the backyard together. At first, she was felling a little depressed, but she snapped out of her state of depression when she noticed the level of bricks stacked at her window. Nervous, she began to hope that her father wouldn't notice the same stack of bricks that she saw when he propped the shovel in his hand against the house.

"Gal, what are you planning to do about that job?" Agnes asked as she walked in the house.

"Agnes, don't start with me," she said rudely.

"You ought to think about apologizing. Carolina said if you are serious about your apology, she thinks that Reverend Dovely will probably give you your job back."

"If he didn't believe me about my dog being killed, I know he won't

believe me when I say I'm sorry," Beatrice said, grabbing a bag of chips from the cabinet then pouring a glass of soda.

In spite of her annoyance, Agnes couldn't do anything but stare at her overweight daughter. *Where had she gone wrong?* She thought—the girl was fat, insecure and stubborn. "If you lose that job, how is your father supposed to know what's coming in and going out of the church account?" Agnes said.

"I guess he'll have to ask the person that replaces me to keep him informed."

Agnes ignored her daughter's suggestion. It was like she never said anything. She went on to tell Beatrice, "You can speak with Reverend Dovely after church service tomorrow."

Sitting comfortably in a chair, Beatrice looked up at her mother standing in the doorway and disrespectfully said, "Agnes, I told you I'm not apologizing. There isn't a need 'cause Reverend Dovely didn't believe me today and he probably won't believe me tomorrow."

She failed to tell her mother all the details that had happened between her and Mychael. Her mother had no idea that she had cursed out their pastor and because of her rampage, left the reception area in a total mess. In her mind, she was thinking that maybe she should mention it to her. Then she wondered what sense it would make? She didn't think it would, so she decided to keep the entire altercation to herself.

Agnes looked down at her daughter eating a bag of potato chips and sipping on a glass of Coke. She had become angry with her so quickly. First, with her defying her authority to apologize to the pastor and secondly, totally ignoring her as she stuffed her mouth with food. She glanced around the room for the closest object she could put her hands on. By reflex and without thinking, she grabbed the family bible and smashed it against her daughter's head. "Gal, wit yo' fat *ass*, I ain't asking you any mo' to apologize to get that job back, I'm telling you that's what you gonna do. So you got all night to think about what you gon' say," Agnes said.

Agnes had had enough of Beatrice and her foolishness. She turned and walked into the kitchen, leaving her daughter behind to clean up the spilled Coke and the bag of potato chips that fell from her lap onto the floor.

Many moments had lapsed when Beatrice thought she still heard birds

chirping around her head. Once she shook herself back to reality, she leaned over to pick up the dismantled bible that was now separated into two sections. As she tried to stand up straight, she became dizzy. She had to get control of her balance before returning the bible pieces on the bookshelf as neatly as she could. She cleaned up the dark liquid and swept the potato chips onto an old envelope and brushed the crumbled pieces into the trash. When she entered the kitchen, she didn't say another word to her mother as she stood at the counter cutting up a five pound bag of white potatoes. She still disagreed with her and desperately wanted to plead her case again, but she chose not to ignite another argument. Without speaking a word, she left the kitchen and walked down the hall to her bedroom. She turned off her television and crawled into her bed. Her head was aching something terrible. In actuality, the room was now spinning more that she was lying down. She had heard the saying that it was possible to actually knock some sense into a person—after having that done, she was seeing things a lot clearer. First, she no longer had a job. Secondly, she no longer had a paycheck coming to her at the end of two weeks and lastly, she didn't have anything to occupy her time between Tuesday and Saturday. Working for the church had been her dream job and she let it consume her. She loved typing the pastor's memos and sending out letters to the members, not to mention, creating the church newsletter.

She wondered if she decided to apologize whether her pastor would give her a second chance. He was the one who always preached about God being a God of a second chance. In one instance, she convinced herself to press her luck and ask for that second opportunity. She thought about writing something down to make her statement seem apologetic throughout. Once she did that her pastor would have no choice but to see that she was sincere, she thought. Then the voices in her head wouldn't allow her to stay focused as they kept reminding her—fool you took a dead dog to church and scared your pastor senseless.

"What I am I going to do?" she kept repeating aloud, entangling her fingers in her long tresses. She caught herself just as her fingers became caught up in her hair. Immediately, she started the breathing exercises Dr. Marson had advised her to complete whenever she would start the nervous behavior with her fingers. It was working. With each breath, she was becoming less anxious.

She began thinking again about how her entire life revolved around her duties at the church. She didn't have any friends. She didn't have a steady boyfriend. At this point, she didn't even have a resolution.

She jumped from her bed and walked over to her bedroom door to lock it. She stepped to her closet and pulled out a black shoe box. This was where she kept all her sex toys. She removed the top of the box and grabbed a penis shaped gadget. She sat on the side of her bed and opened her nightstand drawer. She grabbed a new pack of batteries, opened the package and replaced the old ones. She threw the old batteries in the small trash can that sat next to her nightstand.

In an instance, she pulled her skirt down and slipped out of her panties. She raised over her head the shirt she was wearing and unsnapped the brassier that held her large breasts. She hurried past the mirror because she couldn't stand to look at herself—she looked a *fat* mess. She maneuvered herself around on her bed; she had to position herself just right. She grabbed a pillow to help prop her legs. She spread herself open then she flipped the switch upward and right away she began feeling a steady sensation as she held the gadget in her special place.

Then her private moment was interrupted by light tapping on her bedroom window. She wondered who could it be and she wondered had the stranger seen her pleasuring herself through the window. She rolled out of bed and went to open the curtains. It was Eddie. She was surprised to see him because he's never tapped on her window this early. It wasn't even midnight. Not to mention, it was the weekend and not a weekday. His day to visit was Thursday night, early Friday morning. She could remember this because those visits always kept her from going to work the next day.

She giggled as the skinny Caucasian male climbed through the tight space and landed on her bedroom floor. His hair was greasy and his clothes were both dirty and wrinkled. She enjoyed whenever he stopped by, but sometimes wished that he would take a bath first. She had dropped so many hints until she was tired of mentioning it. Whenever they were about to have sex, she would ask him did he need a towel—he always refused and she never insisted. Instead she would allow him to get on top of her and do his business—most times without a condom.

She knew he wasn't stopping by tonight unannounced for nothing. She

knew he wanted money and he would give her sex in return. In fact, for a year now, she had been letting him through her bedroom window and paying him for sex to finance his drug habit. And as many times as the two of them had had sex, they had yet to get caught.

"What are you doing here? I didn't know you were stopping by," she whispered, standing in front of Eddie naked.

Eddie looked at the bed and heard the sound of her sex gadget vibrating. She had forgotten to turn it off. He grabbed it in his hands and looked at her. "*Miss Bea*, you trying to get your freak on without me," he said, whispering also. She hated when he called her *Miss Bea*. It made her sound old and she was no older than he was and to let him know indirectly that she didn't like his term of endearment, in return, she decided to call him *Mr. Eddie*. It has been a year and he still hadn't caught onto her style of sarcasm as they still continue to call one another *Miss Bea* and *Mr. Eddie*.

"I told you I didn't know you were coming tonight," she said as she climbed back onto her bed. "You wanna watch me?" she asked him.

"Hell yeah," Eddie said with enthusiasm.

Eddie looked at his sex partner strangely when she pulled a rolled up pair of white socks from her nightstand drawer and placed it in her mouth.

She knew her actions seemed strange, but Eddie had no idea how good the vibrating penis made her feel. Sometimes it made her want to scream out loud and rather than screaming, she would bite down on the rolled up cotton. He stood next to her, pulling on his small manhood. It was erect, but it was still small. As she played with herself, he watched and he pulled. He watched some more and he pulled, occasionally, rubbing her breast.

She closed her eyes then she adjusted the stimulation level from low to high. By this time, she wasn't paying attention to her part-time boyfriend. Instead, she was preparing for a rocket explosion. Within moments, she found herself moving around on the bed and wiggling her hips. She pinched the nipples of her breasts with each hand. The sensation was making her feel very good. She started shaking all over. She was feeling like she had stuck her finger in a socket. She couldn't take any more; she snatched the white cotton from her mouth and threw it on the floor. She had to say something. At the same time, she wanted to climax and whisper the name of the person that was in her head.

"Oh, I'm about to cum," Eddie said.

"Me too," she said also. Her mind was fixated on the person she wanted. She was ready. Although, she enjoyed having sneaky sex with Eddie, he wasn't who she really wanted. And in order for her thoughts to come to pass, she knew she had to speak the name into the universe and the only way to do that would be to say it aloud. She panted for breath as Eddie pinched her breast like he was milking a cow—it hurt, but it made her mouth, "*Universe send Mychael Dovely to me.*"

Losing his concentration and his close orgasm, Eddie jumped when he heard what she had said. "Mychael?" he asked, confused. He had heard her talk about Reverend Dovely before and he knew exactly who he was. "Isn't that your preacher? You masturbating and thinking about your preacher...*Miss Bea* that's not right," he said in his southern accent.

She ignored Eddie's comment and proceeded to wipe the moisture between her legs. She really didn't care about his opinion and he certainly didn't understand the crush she had for her pastor. Eddie didn't have to be around Mychael as much as she did, she thought to herself. If he were a woman with her type of needs he would understand. He would know that it requires a lot of restraint to be in the company of a man as good looking as Mychael.

Not wasting time, she popped a piece of gum in her mouth and let Eddie climb on top of her. She couldn't feel any thing, but she liked watching the way he moved his hips. She believed she could get more pleasure standing at the foot of the bed just watching him from behind.

She didn't say a word as she lay with her legs open. Primarily because she didn't want to open her mouth, she didn't like the smell of Eddie's hair. It reminded her of how Roscoe smelt whenever he got caught in the rain. "You like this white dick don't you?" he asked, huffing and puffing.

The thought ran across her mind, what white dick? She had seen bigger in the sex toy shop. While Eddie moved in and out of her, Beatrice didn't know what to say. She didn't know what a person did or how they acted while having sex. Technically, she was still a virgin. She had no experience in having sex before meeting Eddie. He was the first man to show an interest in her. Instead of sounding stupid, she looked at the turning ceiling fan while she continued to chew on her juicy fruit gum.

"I know it feels good," he added.

Beatrice still didn't say anything, hoping that her parents didn't hear the squeaking of her bed. To her it was sounding louder than usual.

Finally, Eddie slid off her and pulled up his pants. As she always did, she went to her purse and grabbed forty dollars and handed it to him. He hurried and gave her a smack on the lips, not really kissing her. Then he crawled through the small space and jumped from her bedroom window. She watched as he barely missed the stack of bricks while making a mad dash around the house, crossing the street into the darkness to purchase his drugs.

CHAPTER SEVEN

It was Sunday morning and Hannah was not being cooperative. She had been running around the room in her pull-up for over thirty minutes and whenever Monica came within an inch of her, she would scream to the top of her lungs. Her antics began weighing on Monica's patience being that she still needed to get dressed for worship service. She was always the last person to put on clothes as Mychael always pranced in front of the mirror straightening his tie. He could hear his wife in the background, pleading for their daughter to behave, but that was all he did was hear because he never turned around to make his defiant daughter listen to the person that took care of her.

"Hannah, honey, come here and let me put your clothes on," Monica said. "If you don't put your clothes on Mommy is going to leave you here alone," she continued to plead, but only teasing.

It was then that Mychael turned to face his wife. It had been eight months now that Hannah had been living with them and this was the first time he had heard Monica refer to herself as the child's mother. He didn't like it. He wanted Hannah to remember his Cousin Myra as her mother.

He paused before he spoke. He didn't want his words to sound insensitive. "Baby, I don't want her to think that you are her mother. I want her to remember Myra as her mother—since she's the one who raised her," Mychael said to his wife.

Monica smiled slightly. She couldn't hide her expression and she knew that Mychael could tell that he had hurt her feelings. It was that apparent— she couldn't hide it. Hannah was almost two years old and she doubted very

seriously that she would remember Myra. Surely, she didn't want to take her adoptive mother's place. But the child hardly paid any attention to the glamour shot photo of the woman that raised her. On occasions, she would say, *'who dat? Or what her name?'*

She looked at her husband and shook her head. She thought he had some nerve telling her not to refer to herself as Hannah's mother. Who did he think was taking care of her? She bathed her. She fed her. She even dropped her off at daycare every morning. For that matter, she was the one that registered her in daycare. *The absolute nerve of him, she thought.*

Mychael recognized that he had made a mistake with his choice of words and what he had said was wrong. He could see in his wife's eyes that her feelings were hurt. He didn't mean to hurt her feelings he only wanted to make her see his point of view. Immediately, he moved over to the bed and sat down next to her. "I didn't mean to sound so harsh, but we got to consider Hannah and the fact that she's lost a lot in the past months. I just don't want her to forget her real mother."

"I understand, but Mychael you don't seem to mind when she refers to you as daddy," Monica brought to his attention.

He was stunned, he didn't see that comment coming, but he knew his wife was correct. On more than one occasion, he allowed Hannah to refer to him as daddy. While he and Monica conversed back and forth, Hannah wasn't paying her new parents any attention. She sat on the floor with her number blocks counting, "1-2-19-5-21...Yeah!"

Monica took a break from their conversation to praise her, "That's right, yeah!"

Mychael continued to speak, "That's different. She never knew her father. Therefore, she didn't have a father figure in her life."

"What about your Cousin Myles? He spent as much time with her as you did. According to you, you hadn't seen her in over a year," Monica recalled.

In actuality, Mychael had been lying to his wife, little did she know, it had been plenty of times when he was heading to or returning from a business trip for the church and he would stop by to spend time with Myra and Hannah. So desperately, Mychael wanted children and when he learned that his cousin had adopted a child, it made him happy. Being that she wasn't married, he figured that the young child would need as many male role models

in her life as possible. So, he tried to spend as much time with the two as he could. Often times, he made his cousin jealous because Myles began to think that Myra was now his favorite cousin. He would never tell Myles this, but actually Myra was.

When they arrived in North Carolina to attend Myra's funeral and to pick up Hannah, Mychael had thought Monica wasn't paying attention. But she noticed when Hannah nearly leaped from her uncle's arms into his. Undoubtedly, Hannah would not go back to Myles, forcing him to hold her during the entire service. He remembered Monica saying to him, 'She's taken a liking to you.' He pretended to not hear her and hoped that she hadn't held onto those moments when Hannah kept referring to him as *daddy*.

"Hannah, come to me and let's get dressed," he instructed.

She looked at Monica as she slowly walked toward her *daddy*. The closer she got to him; she playfully changed her mind and ran into Monica's arms.

"Girl, we don't have time to play games with you," he said, making her laugh by tickling her stomach.

"Dada top, top Dada, top," Hannah said, continuing to laugh.

Mychael looked at his wife, but couldn't bring himself to tell the child not to say *daddy* anymore. He felt bad for his wife. He knew she meant well and she had taken extraordinary care of Hannah. She deserved to be called mom, mother, or mama. At that moment, he decided, if Hannah chose to call Monica one of the above, he was not going to have a problem with it.

Finally they all got dressed and headed for the church. Soon, they were waiting for the line of cars in front of them to turn into the parking lot. To pass the time, he teased with a strapped Hannah in the back seat. He enjoyed making her laugh and the toddler thought he was the funniest person on earth. She laughed at everything he said and every ugly face he made at her.

Today was second Sunday and it appeared that everybody decided to leave home at the same time. Behind him, cars were turning off the main highway one by one. The large capacity parking lot was being filled quickly by every type of vehicle imaginable.

Mychael parked his black BMW in his new parking space. For years, the spot had been occupied by Pastor Lorde, but the officers had changed the sign to now reflect his name. He got out of the car and opened the back door

to retrieve the jacket to his suit. Hannah was grinning and reaching for him to get her. She was ignoring Monica, who was trying to loosen the straps to the car seat and remove her from the car.

He didn't mean to, but when he closed the door tightly, he made his daughter cry. She kicked and screamed like she would never see him again. He walked around the car to help calm her down. "Sweetheart, you have to go with Mommy until later." He was still feeling terrible for what he had said earlier that morning, so purposely, he referred to his wife as Hannah's mother.

Monica didn't say anything regarding his comment. He wasn't fooling her. She knew he was only referring to her as Mommy to smooth over what he had said to her earlier. In fact, she was nobody's fool, she thought to herself as she removed Hannah from the car.

Mychael needed to go by his office, so he kissed his wife, kissed his two fingers before pressing them against Hannah's forehead then they all branched off in separate directions.

During the last eight months, Monica learned that Hannah could be very stubborn and this morning wasn't any different as she made it known that she preferred to walk rather than be carried. She grabbed her small hand as they all walked slowly toward the front of the church. She opened the heavy front door and held it with her hand as Hannah moved along slowly. They entered the vestibule to be swarmed by the hospitality committee. Hannah was dressed in a pink and white dress with the same color hair barrettes on each pony tail also wearing white shoes. She loved the attention she was getting— she laughed and giggled with each kiss and each tickle she received. By the time they made it inside the sanctuary, she had been kissed by at least ten different people.

Monica walked up the middle aisle toward the front. She was dressed in a black two piece suit with similar three-inch heels. Her hair was long and fell below her shoulders. It was flawless, not one strand was out of place. Once at the front, she spotted Eloise and stopped at the second row. She took her seat and leaned over to exchange kisses with the former first lady. Next, she watched as the choir began assembling themselves for the morning processional. Silently, she missed being a part of the choir. Since becoming pastor, Mychael no longer wanted her singing on the choir anymore. A

ministry she had been singing with since she was a teenager. According to her husband, he wanted her to concentrate on being the best first lady she could be. She thought she could handle both, but as Eloise would tell her, she had to be submissive to the man of God and in return, he would be submissive to her. Truthfully, her statements often went in one ear and out the other. This time, she could only assume that Eloise was correct about what she was telling her.

Eloise looked at Hannah and couldn't resist playing with her chubby fingers. It was her first time seeing the small child up close. In fact, she had to glance at the child twice. "You are so precious; I bet people pinch those fat cheeks all the time," she teased.

Hannah had such a friendly personality that she took a few moments to smile at the elder female. Then she went back to her diaper bag search for cookies. She found what she was looking for and bit off piece of the round treat as she turned her attention back to Eloise. Spilling crumbs on the floor, she climbed onto the seat and sat closer to Eloise than she did to Monica. The former first lady looked at Monica, giving her a look of surprise. Truthfully, she was annoyed by the mess that Hannah was making.

As the choir began their morning procession into the sanctuary, Eloise stood to the beat of the music. Hannah kept hitting her on the leg until she reached down to help her stand on the padded pew. Hannah was very excited by the bright colors of the robes. She clapped along with the choir as they marched into the choir loft. "*Nana* look," she said, pointing at the full choir as they rocked from side to side. In the mind of a child, she watched the choir swing from side to side in rhythm with the music. Hannah tried to do the same; except she was shaking her head full of barrettes vigorously, almost hitting Eloise in the face, who was now sitting down.

"*Nana* look at me," she continued to shake.

Eloise was shocked that the child was referring to her as *Nana*. She knew she hadn't been around her enough to know that her grandchildren referred to her as *Nana*. She didn't think about it long as she danced with Hannah until the choir had finished their musical rendition.

Soon thereafter, Mychael was standing before the waiting congregation. "Good morning, blessed people of God."

"Good morning," the congregation yelled at their pastor.

"First giving honor to God, who has always been the head of my life, my gorgeous wife, Mother Lorde and last, but not least my beautiful daughter Hannah."

The congregation clapped as Hannah stood in her seat, clapping also, exclaiming, "Yeah," erupting laughter throughout the sanctuary.

"Well as you can see, Miss Hannah doesn't need any introduction. As many of you know, my cousin passed away almost a year ago and she has entrusted that my wife and I raise her daughter in a Christian home environment. I wish I could, but I can't take the credit for making sure Hannah gets everything she needs. Because of my busy schedule, Hannah is with first lady Monica more than anyone and I must say that I have a wife who's unselfish in everything that she does for our daughter and me. I just want to take a moment to say thank you baby for all you do."

Monica nodded her head and smiled partially.

Eloise leaned over and whispered to her, "Honey, you got a good one. Men don't praise women too much these days."

Monica smiled with the former first lady like she agreed with her comment.

Before Mychael gave the congregation the morning scripture, he looked out among the crowd, becoming uneasy as he made eye contact with Beatrice. She was seated near the back of the church next to her father. Usually, Deacon Shaw sat on the front row among the deacon board, but today, he sat expressionless glaring at his pastor.

"First, we will have a selection by the senior choir, followed by the Tabernacle of Praise youth choir and lastly, the Gospel Choir."

The senior choir rose to sing as Sister Mayweather grabbed the microphone from its stand. She stood nervously as she began singing *Lilly in the Valley*. Her voice was light and weak. The congregation could barely hear her, even with the volume of the microphone at high level. The choir struggled to follow her lead and looked at her as she appeared to lip sync the verses to the song they had previously rehearsed.

Without a warning, Deaconess Mary Agnes grabbed the microphone from Sister Mayweather's hand and took over the song. "There's peace in the valley. There's love in the valley. There's hope in the valley," she sang until the song came to a close. The congregation looked in shock. The choir

looked in shock. Sister Mayweather looked in shock, but transitioned without hesitance from lead to background vocal.

Afterwards, the youth choir stood to begin their selection. As always, they sang upbeat songs and choreographed moves that the youth could relate to. By the song's end, Grace was the only person standing and moving to the beat of the music.

In a circular motion, she swayed her hips. It made you wonder whether she was in a dance contest. As usual, she left her seat and danced in the aisle. She was now repeating the moves of the choir processional. She didn't have any music, but swung her body from side to side, turning her neck far enough to see the back of the church. The entire congregation was laughing and she hadn't noticed.

Mychael kept sneaking glances at his wife. She remained calm and didn't appear embarrassed—she was used to it. Before he knew it, she was exiting the sanctuary, obviously to take Hannah to the restroom for a pull up change. She returned to the sanctuary as the Gospel choir was completing their beautiful rendition of *I need you to survive* by Hezekiah Walker.

He was now standing at the podium, preparing to give the morning scripture and begin his message.

"Pastor, I have a few words, I'd like to share with the people," his mother-in-law Grace expressed. He watched her as she left her seat and maneuvered toward the front of the packed sanctuary. He thought she was going to use the podium and microphone on the floor. But she by-passed them both and headed for the pulpit.

"Mom, you can't come in th—," he tried to say. He had been referring to his mother-in-law as *Mom* since the day he married her daughter. Ignoring him, Grace stepped into the pulpit and began speaking into the microphone, "First giving honor to our highly esteemed Pastor, my son-in-law and to all of you across the sanctuary. I want to share something that the Lord has laid on my heart. God is coming back to get every one of us. It's time out for us to stop playing church. You better get your house in order and the spirit says do it right now."

"Amen...Amen...Give my mother-in-law a hand," Mychael said cheerfully.

Grace smiled at her son-in-law as he helped her from the pulpit. She felt

good that he had mentioned her name. She nodded to several members as she returned to her seat. She didn't sit down until she had waved her hands, nodded her head again and took a bow to the rising applause.

"Thank you Jesus, God is the creator of all things," Mychael said, trying to find his place in the bible. He kept talking—trying to locate the scripture that he was going to use earlier.

"Okay, turn to the book of Hebrews, chapter eleven, and verse one. Faith is substance of things hoped for, the evidence of things not seen. Today's message is titled, "How strong is your faith?"

CHAPTER EIGHT

The morning service was over and as they always did, Mychael, Monica, and Eloise stood at the back entrance to thank members for attending service. Each Sunday, the line was getting longer and longer. Most of the members were beginning to warm up to their new pastor.

Today, Mychael was receiving many comments about his sermon, "Rev. I enjoyed that message," Clara Bell said.

"Thank you Sister Clara Bell, I enjoyed delivering it."

"Pastor, your messages go through me like a fireball. I just can't explain it."

"Okay…. Thank you very much Sister Halley. Where have you been? I haven't seen you in a few Sundays," he said to his estranged church member.

"I'm glad you noticed Pastor, I guess I'm going to have to make sure you see more of me," she replied seductively.

Eloise was greeting members, but could hear her fresh mouth cousin. "Girl, get on outta here," she said, extending a lick to Halora's rear-end. When she turned to face Mychael, she found him mesmerized with the way her attractive cousin sashayed her way out of the sanctuary.

Moments later, after coming back to his senses, Mychael grew nervous when he noticed Deacon Shaw, Deaconess Shaw and Beatrice approaching in the line. He really didn't have enough tolerance left for their foolishness, especially after having to deal with his mother-in-law for over thirty minutes. At this point, he was feeling overwhelmed and he felt could only handle one member of the Christiansen family at a time. He contemplated skipping out and hibernating in his office, but quickly changed his mind since he had his armor barrier standing next to him and that person happened to be *Mother Lorde.*

Deaconess Shaw shook her pastor's hand as she said, "Reverend Dovely, my daughter has something she needs to tell you, but she wants to do it in private, can we speak to you in your office?" she continued.

"Sure Deaconess Shaw, if you don't mind, I'm going to ask Deacon Lorde to sit in with us."

Deacon Shaw laughed aloud and looked at his wife. "Sit in on what? I'm a deacon, don't that account for something?" he said.

"Yes, Deacon Shaw it does, but having you sit in as a mutual party would be a conflict of interest. And since this conversation involves your daughter, you can't have an objective perspective. So, if you don't mind, I believe it's necessary to have Deacon Lorde accompany us during this meeting," Mychael explained to the deacon that caused him the most trouble.

Under his breath, Deacon Shaw said, "I guess so; you're the one with all the answers."

Mychael removed himself from the crowd to locate Deacon Lorde. When he found him, he explained to him as much as he could in the little time they had. Without hesitance, the Deacon Chairman agreed immediately to be a mutual party during the meeting.

Next, he went to his office to have a few moments of prayer prior to the meeting. While in prayer, he heard a knock at the door. He raised himself from his knees then he brushed the wrinkles out of his pants. Standing behind his desk, he invited the person to come in. The door opened slowly as Sister Halley poked her head through the partial opening. He smiled, but was actually surprised to see her.

"Hi Pastor, do you have couple of seconds?" Halley said.

He knew that he didn't have a couple of seconds, but he still glanced at his watch before saying, "That's about all I have Sister Halley. I have a meeting in the conference room."

He became uneasy as he watched her close and lock the door behind her. His nervousness became more obvious when she started walking towards him, cornering him behind his large desk.

"Sister Halley, I really do have a meeting in a few minutes," he managed to say.

Halley ignored him.

"Pastor, I know this is what you want… I know this is what you need."

"Sister Halora, what do you mean what I want and what I need?" he said, placing his hand in front of him to block Halora's advances. Then he continued, "Sister Halora, this is not the time or the place for this. As your Pastor, I'm demanding that you compose yourself as a lady should."

"Pastor Dovely, I am a lady and a woman. As a matter of fact, I am *all* the woman you need," she said to him while rubbing his crotch area until she located the position of his semi hard penis. She massaged it as he backed away, pleading with her to stop, "Sis. Halley, please don't do this here. Someone could catch us."

"Pastor, the door is locked. No one will catch us. Let me give you some *good* head right now."

Before he could decline her offer, a second knock came at the door. They both stopped whispering and looked toward the door, waiting for it to open. The two had forgotten that it was locked.

"Yes," he answered.

He thought maybe it was Deacon Lorde coming to get him since he had been in his office longer than he intended. Surprisingly, it was Monica. "Mychael are you in there? Deacon Lorde said they are waiting for you in the conference room. Why is the door locked?" his wife said out loud, attempting to turn the door handle.

He slid past Halora to open the door to the confused look of his wife. She looked at him, then at Halora, also noticing that she was standing behind her husband's desk.

"Hey baby...I was discussing some personal issues with Sis. Halora, but I think we have them all resolved, right my Sista?"

Halora smiled. Then she flung her long ponytail over her thin shoulder. "Yes, Pastor, you have resolved all my issues," she said, slightly laughing.

Monica eyed Halora as she walked from behind her husband's desk and past her into the hallway.

While the two women eyed each other, Mychael appeared to have vanished into thin air. But he actually had unnoticeably maneuvered out of his office and made his way to the conference room. He decided to have the meeting there because his office wasn't large enough to accommodate everyone. He entered the conference room to the four people waiting. "I do apologize for my tardiness. I had to help a member deal with a crisis," he said, taking his seat.

"That's okay Pastor, no apology needed." Deacon Lorde said.

"Okay, Sister Beatrice, what do you need to discuss with me?" he asked confidently, but still partially upset about yesterday's event.

"I sorry," Beatrice said childlike.

"Sorry for what?" he asked her. He wanted her to reveal to everyone what she had done.

"*Everythang.*"

"Sister Beatrice, I want you to tell everyone here today what you are sorry about?"

"Do I have to?" she answered.

"Yes."

"Now Rev. I think you getting a little beside yourself. My daughter done apologized to ya' and I think that's enough for her to get her job back," Deacon Shaw stated.

"Get her job back!" Mychael shot back, speaking louder than he intended. "Is that the reason why we're having this conversation? If so, I can assure you, Sister Beatrice will never work as my secretary again."

"I told you he wouldn't accept my apology," Beatrice cried, now facing Deaconess Shaw.

Deacon Lorde was confused. He didn't have a clue as to what was going on. All he knew that he regretted sitting next to Deaconess Shaw. She had the odor of a man working in construction. The smell had forced him to cover his nose with his hand and discretely, he sat forward in his seat before asking his pastor for a full update.

Beatrice continued to cry as Mychael updated the Deacon Chairman. Before he could give his opinion, everyone in the room jumped when Mary Agnes backhand slapped her daughter. "Don't you start that Godda—! Oh excuse me Reverend Dovely," Mary Agnes yelled and apologized soon thereafter. Beatrice grabbed her face and dried up the tears as quickly as they had formed.

"Excuse me Deacon Lorde, I'm going to sit in the car, 'cause this stupid *ass* gal gon' make me hurt her. See ya'll just don't understand… but this fat heifer brings out the worst in me," Mary Agnes said in a mouthful as she rose from her seat and turned to her husband. "Joe, I'm gonna ride home with Carolina and Grace," she informed him, exiting the room, but leaving behind her musk.

Deacon Shaw tried to maintain his composure. Along with his pastor and board member, he was shocked by the sudden backhand slap his daughter had received. All three of the men never saw the lick coming.

In an effort to further update Deacon Lorde, Mychael went into more detail about all the things Beatrice had said and done and the reasoning behind the meeting. Deacon Lorde was taken aback and seemed pretty upset by Beatrice's actions and the incident didn't involve him.

Deacon Shaw didn't know that his daughter had cursed out their pastor, but he still attempted to come to her defense. However, the chairman wasn't in the mood for any excuses he was planning to give. To stop his board member from saying another word, Deacon Lorde held up his hand to Joe before saying, "As chairman, I believe Pastor Dovely was justified in terminating Sister Beatrice. She can't expect to disrespect the pastor, pull such foolishness like she did yesterday and not think there won't be consequences." Then he turned to speak directly to Mychael, "Pastor, if you don't have anything further to add, in my opinion, this meeting is adjourned."

Mychael felt like Deacon Lorde was his hero. If he had met with the Shaw's alone, he was pretty positive that he would have been threatened into giving Beatrice her job back. He was always a little afraid of Joe, but now he was becoming afraid of the whole family—Beatrice's actions from the day before and today, the incident with her mother.

Angry that he wasn't given the opportunity to be heard, Deacon Shaw erected himself from his seat, but took the liberty to shake Deacon Lorde's hand. Mychael assumed that his hand would be next. Quickly, he learned that he was wrong. In a Christian manner, he extended his hand to his armor barrier, only to have him move past his extended hand to assist his upset daughter to her feet. Then they both left the conference room and headed toward the closest exit.

Mychael smiled to hide his embarrassment. After the two had left the room, he and Deacon Lorde looked at each other in bewilderment then they clasped their hands together.

"Pastor, sometimes you just have to put your foot down," Deacon Lorde mentioned.

Mychael sighed out loud then placed his hands on top of his head. "Yeah, but I would hate to be Sister Beatrice when she gets home and tells her mother that she didn't get her job back."

"I agree….I totally agree, but while we're in here alone, I need to ask you something," Deacon Lorde said. "Did you smell how musky Deaconess Shaw was?"

"Ah man…come on now…leave my wife's family alone," Mychael said as laughter took over the conversation between them.

CHAPTER NINE

The Lorde family was having a laughing good time. Ernest, Jr. had finally arrived for Sunday dinner, along with Mychael and Monica. Richard had also invited Joy Lynn and all of their half siblings were also present.

Barron and Byron were home for the weekend and decided to attend Sunday dinner. They planned to spend the entire day with their mother. Prior to their weekend visit, Miranda and Zondra had mentioned that their mother's condition was declining, also suggesting that they spend as much time with her as possible.

On this day, Eloise and Clara Bell had cooked a feast similar to the meals cooked for a national holiday. They prepared turkey, ham, chicken, roast, macaroni and cheese, chicken dressing, potato salad, collard greens, green beans, carrot soufflé', yams, corn and every dessert imaginable.

The blended family fellowshipped with conversation, laughter and jokes like it was a family reunion. After everyone had eaten as much as their stomachs could hold, they all moved, one by one from the formal dining room to the family room. Richard couldn't resist teasing Mychael again about the incident with Beatrice. His pastor wasn't as vocal as before, mainly since he was in the presence of his wife and Beatrice was her cousin.

"Look who I found wondering around upstairs?" Eloise said, teasing as she entered the family room holding Flossie by the hand. She had been upstairs taking a nap. As she passed her children, they stared at their frail looking mother as she held hands with Eloise until they reached her favorite chair. Eloise helped her to sit down then she headed for the kitchen to fix her dinner plate.

"Hey Mama, did you have a good nap?" Barron asked. Before she could answer, Byron pushed his twin brother aside and knelt down near his mother's face. "Move out the way, she doesn't know you. Mama, how are you doing today?" he asked. His mother smiled widely as she rubbed her right knee with her hand. Then she said, "Oh Mr. Johnson, I've seen better days, but I believe I'm gonna make it."

"Mr. Johnson?!? Mama, who is Mr. Johnson? I'm Byron, your baby," he said.

Playfully, Flossie looked at him still smiling. "Mr. Johnson, you can't fool me, I know who you are." she said.

Everyone in the room started looking at one another, but saying nothing. They each let their eyes and facial expressions do all the talking. It was obvious Flossie Mae didn't remember her twin son either.

Sadly, he tried again. "Mama, look at me closely, it's me Byron."

The others thought the conversation was funny, making Byron feel guilty. He didn't see this episode as a sign of his mother's declining health, only that he wasn't coming home to visit her enough. It never dawned on him that his mother really didn't remember any of her children and his sisters had to endure this on a weekly basis. In his mind, he was determined that he was going to bring his face and name back to his mother's remembrance. He tried several things. He pulled out photos from his wallet. He turned his face from side to side. Over and over, he kept asking Flossie his name. But no matter what he tried, all of her responses were still the same. To her, he was still Mr. Johnson.

After sneaking a third piece of sweet potato pie, Ernie, Jr. entered the family room and listened to as much from his half brother as he could stand without making a comment. "Mr. Johnson, leave your Mama alone and stop badgering her," he said igniting laughter from everyone in the room. Byron laughed, but he was really disappointed. Before long, all of the family was jokingly referring to him as *Mr. Johnson*. After a few more attempts, he finally left his mother alone, since it was clear that she wasn't going to refer to him as anything else.

Next, Richard entered the room, holding in his hands glasses and two bottles of wine. He handed glasses to all those that wanted to participate in his toast. He wanted to celebrate the official expansion of the Lorde Life and

Accident Insurance Company. The following day, the company was moving into its new office building and a ribbon cutting ceremony had been planned to signify the move. He filled his glass from the first bottle of wine. Then he passed the remaining portion of alcohol around the room.

"I have two announcements and I want my family to be a part of them both. First, I want to give honor to my beautiful and sophisticated mother. Mother can't nobody be Eloise London Lorde like you," he said.

"Thanks son, but have you been drinking something other than the wine?" Eloise responded, also erupting laughter throughout the room.

Richard raised his full glass again. "Mother, please let me finish," he sighed, before he continued.

"Second of all, I give honor to my sister Alma for being such a hard worker and being so organized. If you were to look at my office and compared it to hers, you would think I worked for her. Thank you Alma for being the best sister a person could ask for," he said. Then he remembered his sister Eleanor and he turned to face her. "Eleanor I love you to."

Alma and Eleanor raised their glasses in the air in response to their brother's comments.

He continued, "I'm proud to have my big brother, who supports me in everything I do, not to mention, he thinks I'm the smartest person on earth… And I don't see a thing wrong with that," he said, laughing.

"Now, I know he's drunk," his mother added.

"Mother, if ya'll let me finish, we can toast the occasion."

"Oh, we were supposed to wait until you stopped talking before we drank the wine? I done drunk mine," Clara Bell confessed. "I guess I need my glass filled again," she said, holding up an empty glass.

"I'm glad that I'm going to have my family with me tomorrow at the ribbon cutting ceremony, representing the Lorde name. My three brothers, my four sisters and all of my cousins—I love you guys very much. And lastly, I have something very special I want to share with the whole family."

He reached into his coat pocket and walked over to Joy Lynn as she sat on the stoop of the fireplace. He pulled out a black box and immediately Joy Lynn covered her face with both hands. After seeing the five carat ring she started yelling, "No.No.No. I can't believe this," now shaking her hands as if they were on fire.

"What in the *hell* is he getting ready to do?" Eloise said to her cousin Clara Bell under her breath.

"That looks like an engagement ring," Clara said, before she let out a loud burp.

Mychael and Monica looked on as Richard slipped the ring onto Joy Lynn's finger, asking her to marry him. The two hadn't known that he and Joy Lynn had become so serious—obviously they had. Joy Lynn was now standing over her kneeling boyfriend. She continued to shake her hands in excitement as she took an occasional look at the diamond glimmering on her finger. Tears streamed from her eyes. Her hands were shaking nervously as she held her hand up to the onlookers.

Richard looked at her waiting for an answer. "Well…will you?"

"Yes, Yes, Yes I will marry you." she answered, bending down to kiss him. Love and excitement filled the room. He stood to his feet and spun his new fiancé around in the air. As he settled her on the floor, the two kissed again, but this time more passionately than before. Their lips were pursed together as if tomorrow would never come.

Most of the family hugged and congratulated the couple. Everyone waited for them to commit to a wedding date. On the contrary, Eloise walked out of the room with her son Ernest, Jr. following her to the kitchen.

"Mother, what is your problem?" he said.

"Richard should have discussed this with me first. Something is not right about this girl. I *can't* put my finger on it… And when in the hell did he start dating her? The last thing I knew *he* liked men," Eloise blurted out without thinking.

"Mother hush—you're drunk!" Ernest, Jr. said to her.

"The hell you preach. I'm not drunk. If I were drunk you'd damn well know it. Now leave me alone and find out from your brother when this wedding is supposed to take place. I hope it's not soon because I need time to upstage that *heifer*," Eloise said in a slurred tongue.

Ernest, Jr. returned to the family room as the newly engaged couple announced in unison, "We are getting married six months from Saturday."

CHAPTER TEN

As Beatrice entered the house ahead of her father, she felt disappointed about the outcome of the meeting. She tried to maneuver her steps toward her bedroom while her mother was occupied in the kitchen warming dinner. Agnes hadn't heard her enter the house, probably because she had done it so quietly. Unlike her father, who slammed the door, scaring his wife, yet alerting her that they both were home.

She wondered about how simple her father had the potential to be. She wondered further why he couldn't just follow her lead. All he had to do was ease into the house and purposely close the door without making any noise, she thought.

By the time Agnes heard the door being slammed, she was about to place her feet on the third step headed upstairs. At the same time, she heard her mother say to her husband, "So how did it go?"

She turned around to look at her father. He looked at her and they both looked at Agnes, neither one were bold enough to speak.

"I guess since you and your daddy can't talk, your silence means you didn't get the job back," Agnes figured.

"No Ma'am," Beatrice said, hoping to keep the peace.

"What did he say after I left?"

"He said he should've called the police on you. Agnes, you didn't have any business slapping that gal the way you did," Joe said, attempting to shift the blame.

"That's my child and I'll do whatever I want to her, in front of Reverend Dovely and whomever else," Agnes said like her daughter wasn't standing in the room.

"She's not a child anymore—she's almost forty years old."

Beatrice stayed quiet. If her father felt brave enough to fight her battles, he was more than welcome to do so.

"He said, he wasn't going to hire her back because she told him that she didn't want to work for his *black* ass anyway," Joe said to his wife, repeating what he had been told.

Mary Agnes looked at her overweight daughter. She saw red at the echo of every word her husband was saying. Her anger subconsciously forced her eyes to stretch wide.

"So, you think you can just curse the pastor out whenever you feel like it, huh? If that's the case, I see why he wouldn't rehire your *stupid* ass," Agnes said to her daughter. Then she raised her hand at her, but before the lick could reach Beatrice's face, she grabbed her mother by the wrist.

"Agnes, I'm tired of you hitting on me. You've already embarrassed me in front Reverend Dovely and Deacon Lorde. I'm gonna warn you nicely, don't try that again."

"And if I do? What do you plan on doing about it?" Agnes said, walking towards Beatrice.

They were now standing toe to toe, face to face and eye to eye. Beatrice backed away from her mother. Agnes inched closer. She backed away again then her mother moved in closer again. Soon there was no space between them.

Mary Agnes had each hand balled into a fist. She propped each fist onto her medium size hips then she said, "Let me tell you one thing, you fat—ugly heifer. This is my house and don't you ever tell me where I can and cannot lay my hands."

"I don't care where you lay your hands as long as you don't put them on me," Beatrice said sternly.

Joe looked in horror from the doorway separating the kitchen from the living room. He knew it was about to get out of control. Proceeding with caution, he suggested from a distance, "Agnes, why don't you leave the gal alone? We've talked and she knows that she has to look for another job next week."

"Shut up Joe!"

Listening to the sound of his wife's voice, Joe grabbed the telephone to

dial next door. He was hoping his sister-in-law Carolina would be able to come over before a fight could break out between his wife and daughter.

Right as her husband dialed the number next door, Agnes slapped Beatrice. In return, her daughter grabbed her around the throat. The two women lost their balance and knocked over the coffee table. Beatrice hit her thigh on the edge of the sharp furniture and the impact hurt, but it didn't stop her from rushing her mother onto the coach, while she choked her.

Agnes gagged for air as Beatrice's grip clogged her air passage. Unable to breathe she still kept fighting—fighting for her life. She grabbed a hand full of her daughter's long tresses and used the grip to slam her into the bookcase. As Beatrice hit the wall unit, the impact caused a hundred or more books to tumble to the floor. That didn't stop the women as they continued to tussle, making Agnes' wig fall from her head. The synthetic hair piece fell on the floor, leaving her receding hairline exposed to both her daughter and husband.

Carolina and Christopher rushed into the house as Beatrice continued to get the best of her mother. Carolina screamed at her sister and niece, "Stop it or you're going to hurt each other!" She along with Christopher pulled Beatrice off of Agnes and wrestled more to get her out of the house. Beatrice was mad and full of rage. At this point, she was so angry she was capable of killing somebody—anybody.

Carolina and Christopher were finally able to move Beatrice beyond the door, but couldn't budge her any further. All the while, Beatrice continued to grab for her mother, even though she was down on the floor, squabbling like a fish out of water.

"Bring her to me…Bring her to me," Agnes yelled from the floor, "When I get up from this floor, I'm going to kick her fat ass," Agnes said.

"Be quiet Agnes with your filthy mouth," Carolina said to her sister. A little exhausted, Carolina was soon able to get her niece outside and convinced her to walk next door. In the interim, she told Christopher to return inside to check on his aunt. He walked inside the house and saw Agnes still moving around on the floor. She was trying to get up, but it looked more like she was break dancing. The sour expression on her face made her efforts seem painful. Christopher wondered had Beatrice broken one of her mother's bones?

"Aunt Agnes, are you okay? Do you need any help getting up?" he said.

"Baby, I'll be fine, just help Auntie to her feet."

Christopher grabbed one side as his Uncle Joe rushed to the other.

"Don't you come near me *you* son-of-a-bitch!" Agnes yelled, swinging at her husband. "Damnit, you took her side, so go help her," she added.

A little startled, Joe jumped back at the profanity his wife was using, but more so at her violent mood.

"Agnes, I didn't take anybody's side. I wanted you to talk this whole thing out, rather than fighting each other. But I knew one day you were going to push that gal over the edge and she was going to cut your *ass* like she did today," Joe explained.

"I let her win!" Agnes snapped, trying to pull herself up. The more she tried, the less progress she was making. Christopher wasn't much help since he only weighed slightly over a hundred pounds. He pulled at his aunt's housedress because Beatrice had managed to pull the floral dress over her mother's head. In doing this, not only had she exposed Agnes' receding hairline, but she also exposed the large sized underwear she was wearing and the stockings she had rolled down just above the knee.

"Aunt Agnes, please let Uncle Joe help me get you up. I can't do it by myself."

"Alright."

Joe walked slowly toward his wife. "You're not going to hit him, are you?" Christopher asked.

"No."

Reluctantly, Joe grabbed his wife under one arm as her nephew did the other, helping her to her feet. Agnes eased herself over to the sofa to sit down. She was still breathing heavy. Christopher felt sorry for her as he stared at his aunt as she labored to breathe. Even though she could be hateful and mean, he hated to see her knocked around on the floor. Then again, he knew she probably had provoked her daughter to get to this point.

Carolina reentered the house. She looked at her sister panting for air and rubbing her knees and her arm. "Are you going to be okay?" she asked, concerned. "Beatrice is spending the night with us until the both of you can calm down." She paused, still looking at her sister. Then she said, "And she told me what you did to her in front of Reverend Dovely. I can't believe you

slapped her in front of the pastor and Deacon Lorde. You talk about she's crazy, it sounds to me like you're the one that's crazy. Don't you think our pastor has enough to be concerned about rather than sit around and watch you have a boxing match with your daughter? You were wrong and you are the one who owes her the apology. But like I said, she's going to stay next door tonight. I'm going to get a few things from her room."

"Be quiet! Don't tell me how to raise my child. I didn't tell you how to raise yours," Mary Agnes said to her sister.

Carolina stopped in her tracks and listened to the sounds that came from her sister's mouth.

"And you are not the least bit worried about Reverend Dovely. The only thing you're concerned about is whether I embarrassed the family in front of Ernie," Mary Agnes continued.

She stared at her hateful and miserable sister. "Agnes, I know you are upset, but you don't have to be mean to me. I haven't done a thing to you," she stated as she turned around, now standing in the living room again. She moved her head in the direction of the front door, hoping her son would move toward the door as well. He didn't know what his mother was doing with her head. He was busy looking from her to his aunt.

"Agnes, I see there isn't a bit of help for you. I should've stayed home and let Beatrice finish whipping your behind," she said, refusing to use the same profanity like her sister had earlier.

"I let her win, that's what a mother's supposed to do. Worry about your own business and tell your son whose his daddy."

Now Christopher wasn't staring between the two women, he kept his stare on his aunt. Was she trying to be insulting? His aunt of all people knew that his paternity was a sensitive subject for him, more so, with his mother. She also knew that his mother never told him who his father was.

"Aunt Agnes, what are you talking about? Why are you being so mean after we came over here to help you?" Christopher said.

"Son, I'm not being mean, but I'm sick of your mother trying to run everybody's life and her life is the one that's a mess. It's about time some of her skeletons were brought out of the closet," Agnes said, snatching her head.

"Shut your mouth Agnes. Don't you say another word!" Carolina demanded, pointing her finger at her sister. "Christopher let's go."

"Son, its time you knew…"

"Shut up Agnes!" Carolina continued to say, shoving her son toward the door. As

they moved forward to push the screen door open, Mary Agnes blurted out, pronouncing each word by itself, "Baby—yo'—daddy—is—Deacon—Ernest—Lorde!"

Christopher stopped in his tracks as his mother's hand fell from his shoulders. "W-H-A-T!" He said, his voice now elevated as he looked at his stunned mother. She had gone quickly into a trance. "Mom is she telling the truth?"

Carolina couldn't believe her sister was so evil that she would disclose this type of information—a secret that was intended to stay between the three sisters. Not even Grace in her lowest moment had ever threatened to tell her son about his paternity.

Mary Agnes pulled herself up from the coach and returned to the kitchen to finish her dinner. She maneuvered around singing spiritual hymns, acting like nothing had happened. She was acting like she hadn't changed her sister's life forever. Even more, she was acting like she hadn't changed her nephew's life forever.

Still standing in her sister's foyer, Carolina could hear her son, "Mom, pleeeeeease tell me that she's lying. Mom, I beg you to tell me that she's lying."

By this time, Carolina had come out of her trance, but was now in a daze. Christopher stepped to his mother and shook her several times. The look on her face signified her mind was far—far away. Christopher shook her again, but still couldn't get her to confirm the information his aunt had just shared.

"Mom!" he continued to yell.

"Huh," she finally answered.

"Is Deacon Lorde my father?"

Carolina bowed her head in her chest. She didn't see this day coming. She wasn't prepared for this type of shock value. She had gotten away with this for over thirty years. At that moment, she hated her sister for what she had done. She had no right to hurt her son the way she just did. *She had no right*, Carolina kept thinking.

"Yes, son it's true. He's your father."

Christopher fainted.

Carolina grabbed her son before he hit the floor as Joe rushed to the kitchen to get a wet towel. They applied the soaked cloth to his forehead and face. His mother gently slapped him on each side of his face, but getting no response.

"Do you think we need to call an ambulance?" Joe asked.

"I don't know. I thought he only fainted," Carolina said, holding her son.

Mary Agnes had retired as a registered nurse and knew exactly what to do. She walked into the living room and stood over her kneeling sister and unconscious nephew. She handed her sister something in a white tube. "Here, put this up his nose. He'll be fine."

"Agnes, what is this?" Carolina asked, looking at the tubing, trying to read its label, but the writing was smeared off.

"Don't worry about what it is. It will bring him around."

Agnes was correct. As soon as Carolina put the aroma to her son's nose. He began coughing and pushing the scent away from his face.

"Where am I?" Christopher asked, disoriented.

"Son, you don't know where you are?" his mother said.

"Macy's," he answered.

"No son, you're not at Macy's. You're at your Uncle Joe and Aunt Agnes'," his mother informed him.

"What happened?" Christopher asked. Then he remembered that he had been told that Deacon Ernest Lorde, Jr. was his father. "I know what happened. Aunt Agnes told me that Deacon Lorde is my father," he said, repeating the earlier conversation. After that, he got up with the help of his uncle and mother and stood to his feet. He was a little unsteady, but managed to push the screen door open and walk down the stairs, maneuvering slowly across the yard still with the help of his mother.

CHAPTER ELEVEN

A few hours had passed and Agnes continued to stir around in the kitchen before her dinner was finished warming. She fixed her husband his dinner plate, but chose not to eat with him. Joe took his seat at their worn brown dining table and he looked at his wife like he felt sorry for her. Even though he felt sorry for her, he knew not mention the situation that had happened earlier.

Agnes decided to take a short nap after the incident with her daughter and fixing her husband his dinner plate. One hour later, she was walking out of her junky bedroom, headed toward her filthy kitchen. This time, she entered the area to the sound of her oven timer. She turned the ringing gadget off and opened the oven door to pull out the good smelling peach cobbler she was baking. She moved the warm dessert across her nose as the aroma filled the entire room. She truly had to pat herself on the back because she believed she had put her foot in this one.

Her husband Joe sat in the next room scanning the pictures in the Sunday newspaper because he couldn't read. He did the same thing every weekend, like clock work, he would eat his dinner and scan the pictures in the newspaper. He was still sitting quietly because he hadn't conjured up the nerve to start up a conversation with his wife.

In her mind, Agnes hoped that her husband was thinking it was his birthday and somehow the dessert was for him. Not! She even hoped that he was thinking that it was Beatrice's birthday and the dessert was for her—not times two!

Leaving his recliner chair, Joe angled toward the kitchen. He had finally

gathered the nerve to say something to Agnes. At this point, she would probably say she was approachable—the *cat* nap she had taken had done her body good. But even though Agnes deemed herself as approachable, she never said the *cat* nap had put her in a good mood.

"Something sure does smell good. Did you cook that dessert for me?" Joe asked, putting his empty plate on top of the dishes that were from the current and previous week.

As she ripped a moderate piece of foil from its roll to cover her golden crusted pie, Agnes didn't answer or look at her husband. She waited a few moments. As hard as she wanted to ignore Joe, she made herself answer him, she finally said, "*No*, I'm taking this next door to Carolina's."

"Agnes, do you think that is a good idea? Maybe you should give Beatrice a little time to cool off. It's only been a few hours," Joe said, even though he really wasn't concerned about his daughter's reaction to her mother, but more so about his sister-in-law's reaction to her sister. The image of Carolina's face was fresh in his mind when Agnes revealed to her nephew his paternity. To Joe, it was award winning. It was Oscar worthy. It was for real.

Not paying her husband any attention, Agnes snatched her head, stretching her eyes wide at Joe's suggestion, "I will not. That's my damn sister's house and if anybody has to leave, it'll be her, not me," she responded, walking toward the front door. "I'll be back in a little bit."

Joe watched from the living room window as his wife stepped down the front stairs and took strides across the yard to her sister's. He didn't stay at the front room window long before moving to the bedroom to see if his sister-in-law would actually let his wife, her sister, inside. He continued to watch as Agnes tapped on the front door, only a few seconds passed before she was stepping inside the house.

* * *

Christopher had been the one to open the door for his aunt. He looked at her and thought about her pattern. She was so predictable. Whenever she was wrong about anything, instead of admitting her mistakes, she would bake a peace offering. Usually it was a delicious pound cake, but today, she held a good smelling pie in her hand and it smelled like his favorite.

"Hey, where's everybody at? I made your favorite," Agnes said, placing the pie into her nephew's hand.

"Aunt Agnes, you didn't have to bake me a pie," Christopher said.

Agnes laughed nervously because she didn't know what else to say. There were moments of awkwardness, before her sister Carolina emerged from her room. Many would have thought that the two sisters would have argued about what had been said earlier. They didn't. Carolina rubbed her eyes and stretched her body, before saying anything to her sister. Apparently, she had taken a nap also and woke up when she heard her sister's voice.

"Hey, whatcha done cooked now?" she asked Agnes, referring to the dessert in her son's hand.

"Christopher's favorite. I know Grace will probably want a piece. You feel like walking down the street with me?" Agnes said. Their sister Grace only lived a couple houses down.

"Yeah, let me get a pair of shoes. If you need something to put the pie in, I think it may be some paper plates on top of the refrigerator."

Agnes followed Christopher into the kitchen and added a slice of pie onto a paper plate. She noticed that her sister had remodeled the kitchen. She didn't know Carolina had made these changes and she lived next door. It didn't even look like the same kitchen their mother used to cook in. The counter tops were now green marvel and the floor tile was ceramic with various shades of green. If Agnes had her choice, she probably wouldn't have chosen green as her main color. But despite what she thought, the changes Carolina had made gave the kitchen a brand new look. In her opinion, it was very becoming.

After wrapping the piece of pie, Agnes stood by the front door holding the plate in her hand. She was beginning to feel out of place as Christopher returned to the living room with his bowl loaded with the same dessert saying, "Aunt Agnes, you make the best peach pie in the world."

He knew how to swell his aunt's head. He even knew that if he kept complimenting her about her baking she would continue to bake him his favorite dessert. His comments made Agnes smile broadly at his statement before she was able to say, "Thank you."

"You ready?" Carolina asked as the telephone started to ring. She

stopped at the small table where the phone was sitting. She grabbed the receiver in her hand and clicked the talk button.

"Hey, how you doing?" she said, not giving her son or sister a sign as to who she was talking to. "Yeah… Yeah…okay I'll tell him. Okay, bye," she said, returning the receiver to its base.

Agnes and Christopher both were waiting for her to tell them who was on the other end of the line. She didn't. Agnes took a wild guess, "Tell Joe, he's not getting one piece of that pie, so he can just stop calling."

"How do you know it was him? It could've been my boyfriend," Carolina joked. Then she turned to face her son. "Your Uncle Joe says to bring him a piece of that pie later," she added while she chuckled.

"You better not take him *any*…after the way he stood there and let Bea cut my *ass* this evening," Agnes said, igniting laughter from both her sister and nephew.

In addition to getting her shoes, Carolina had changed clothes also. She was now dressed in a pair of blue jeans and a comfortable fitting sweatshirt. She turned toward the front door, but allowed Agnes to exit first and she second. Then they began their stroll through the neighborhood toward Grace's. They walked at a slow pace, noticing their surroundings. At the same time, they admired the different colored leaves that covered the ground and hated all the cars that sped up and down their street. Since the church's congregation had grown in leaps and bounds, the traffic had increased heavily. They knew the substantial growth was a good thing, but they still hated the traffic. They hated it only because they lived on the road that led to the rear entrance of the church and it affected their street more than any other street in the town.

Continuing their slow walk, Agnes thought about apologizing to her baby sister, but she didn't know where to start. She stopped wrestling with the idea and blurted out what she wanted to say, "I guess I should say I'm sorry about what happened earlier. I just got so worked up with Beatrice and lost my head. I shouldn't have told Christopher something so sensitive. He's always been like a son to Joe and me. And I should've known better," Agnes said, gently grabbing her sister by the hand and squeezing it.

"That's all right Agnes. He was bound to find out sooner or later. As a matter of fact, lately, he's been asking about it more and more. Yes…I wish

I could have been the one to tell him, but what's done is done," Carolina said, accepting her sister's apology.

Agnes wiped the tear that fell from her left eye. "So, you're not mad at me?" she asked Carolina.

"Mad at you? *Jesus*, no. You've got to do something more serious than that to get me mad. Besides, remember what Mama always told us?"

"No, what?" Agnes asked having forgotten what their mother had actually told them.

"That family is always family, no matter what."

"She did tell us that. Mama...Boy do I miss her," Agnes admitted, as they strolled into Grace's yard. Carolina wiped her eyes as her sister wiped her eyes again. At that point, neither one had noticed their sister Grace sitting on the front porch.

Grace watched as her sisters marched up to her steps. She noticed that her sister, Mary Agnes, the older she got, the more she resembled their mother. Her sister Carolina was the youngest and had a combination of both their features and she was the only one with the strong features of their father.

"What are the two of you laughing and crying about?" Grace asked.

"Nothing— but old times. We were thinking about Mama," the two sisters said at the same time.

"If it's nothing, then why are the two of you crying?"

"Didn't we say it was nothing, nosey?" Agnes said, teasing with her middle sister. "Here I brought you some peach cobbler."

Grace grabbed the bowl and inhaled the aroma flowing from the warm plate. She invited her two sisters to have a seat next to her. It was getting dark, but they decided to sit on the porch anyway. Mary Agnes sat first and Carolina followed.

"Did my son-in-law give Bea her job back?" Grace asked.

"Chile, don't bring that subject up," Agnes said as Carolina laughed. Grace looked from one to the other and they knew it wouldn't be long before she asked more questions.

"Why don't bring up the subject?" Grace asked.

"Grace Anderson, you are determined to raise my blood pressure again, aren't you?"

Now Grace was laughing. "What has Bea done now? It has to be

something terrible whenever you talk like that," Grace said, continuing to laugh.

Carolina interjected, "Agnes you may as well tell her cause *Monnie* or Pastor is going to tell her anyway."

"Going to tell me what?"

Carolina went on to say, "Bea got mad with Pastor on yesterday and cursed him out. Then they all met with him today, in which Agnes got so worked up and slapped Bea in front of Reverend Dovely, Ern— I mean Deacon Lorde and Joe." Carolina continued, slightly laughing in between her story. "Then when they got home, she and Bea got into a fist fight over the matter."

Up until this point, Agnes sat quietly. She rocked steadily back and forth as Carolina finished her story.

"What?! Agnes you didn't?" Grace said to her older sister.

"I didn't what?" Agnes said, answering Grace's question with a question.

"You jumped on your daughter in front of the pastor and the chairman."

"I don't know what happened. I just lost my head," Agnes admitted, still rocking.

A few moments of silence rested between the three sisters.

"Is *Three C* going to the expansion tomorrow?" Grace asked, changing the subject. Although Christopher was in his thirties, his aunt continued to call him by the childhood nickname she had given him.

"Probably not. He and Richard are not speaking again." Carolina disclosed.

"Lawd have mercy, them two are like husband and wife. Are they ever on speaking terms?" Grace added.

Carolina said, "I think the same thing sometimes….I think the very same thing sometimes." She didn't say anything further as she got up from her rocking chair. "Well girls, ya'll company is good, but I must get prepared for work tomorrow."

"Tell *Three C* to come by and see Auntie tomorrow. He'll talk to me about it."

"I will and don't forget that Christina's championship game is tomorrow night. I'm planning to go, do ya'll two want to tag along with me?" Carolina said.

"Hummm…they did announce that in church today, didn't they?" Agnes said.

"Agnes, I'll go if you go." Grace said to her sister.

Agnes waited before she answered, "I reckon as long as we don't have to be fooled up with that ole high class Eloise Lorde."

"We are not going to see Mother Eloise, we are going to watch Christina play basketball, remember?" Carolina said.

"I wish you would stop calling her Mother because she is not your mama," Agnes said annoyed. In fact, her face remained twisted long after she had made her statement.

"How long does those games last? It won't interfere with my sleep will it? I need to be in the bed by ten o'clock," Grace interjected, changing the subject again.

"Don't worry we will be home long before ten o'clock," Carolina assured her.

Together, Grace and Mary Agnes rose from their chairs to follow Carolina down the stairs. Before they would separate their conversations always lasted another hour. Usually, Grace and Mary Agnes would walk Carolina home and stand in front of her house talking, then Grace and Mary Agnes would turn and walk in the direction they had come from, ultimately walking past Mary Agnes' house. Before they knew it, the two would be standing in front of Grace's house again. The night usually ended with the sisters fusing back and forth.

"You go inside first and I'll watch for you."

"No, you go inside first and I'll watch for you."

"Okay lets walk inside at the same time and we can call each other to let the other know we made it inside," Mary Agnes suggested.

CHAPTER TWELVE

The news media were taking their places to cover the expansion of the Lorde Life and Accident Insurance Company. Richard and Alma could be seen running over each other. More than anything, they wanted the publicity of the expansion to go over without any glitches. They wanted everything to be perfect.

Richard was excited that the city mayor had agreed to cut the ribbon for the new office building. Plus, a separate local news station had agreed to do an interview about the humble beginnings to the uprising of the Lorde Insurance Company. The new space was a three story building that had been renovated to accommodate the many new departments of the insurance company. The sales division and large call center were the most visible attractions to the renovated space, despite the fact that the third floor was not completed. Initially, the design firm was excited about getting the contract and had so many bright ideas for the renovations. Everything was going as planned and a week before the expansion ceremony, Richard received a phone call regarding back ordered materials. To put it mildly, he was livid. He yelled at the owner of the design firm for his inadequateness and the owner yelled at him for his disrespect. After the conversation was over, Richard didn't have to tell the owner that the delay would tremendously affect the negotiated amount associated with the contract they both had signed. His anger had already said it all.

Doing something she loved, Halora finally appeared on the scene after recording the company's first commercial. She enjoyed being the center of

attention. It took her twenty outtakes, only because she was her biggest critic. Throughout the shoot, she either didn't like the lighting or thought the outfit she wore made her look fat. The camera crew was very patient until they were approaching the hour before the ceremony. At that point, she was forced to get the commercial completed since it was scheduled to debut nationwide the same day as the expansion.

After the commercial was complete, Halora pranced through the crowd frenzy, headed toward her new office. As she walked down the hall, she waved at a few family members and office staff. Once there, she entered her half empty space and sat on the edge of her desk, before pressing the intercom to her assistant.

"Jorge, could you get Mr. Lorde on the line please?" she asked. Jorge was her very efficient assistant. He had been employed with the insurance company for five years—long before Halora was hired. He knew a lot about policies and insurance laws. His knowledge, organization and professionalism were the reason Halora had fallen in love with him the moment she met him.

In the short time of being employed, Halora and Jorge had become instant friends. Jorge was happy to have her as a friend and Halora was happy to have him as a friend and assistant. He was good at his job and he made sure she knew that on a daily basis.

Even though Halora valued Jorge's friendship, she found it hard to believe that he still lived at home and found it more complicated trying to convince her assistant to branch out on his own—based on their conversations, Jorge had no intention of moving out of his parent's house.

"Yes, one moment."

Halora waited a few moments before she heard his voice again.

"Miss London, I'm sorry for the delay, but I've located Mr. Lorde on his cell phone. When I hang up he'll be there."

"Thanks Jorge…. Richard, where are you?"

"I'm on my way back to the center. Alma and I had that interview with the news station, remember? How did the commercial go?" Richard said to his Operations manager through his cell phone.

"I finished about ten minutes ago and from my observation I believe everything will be fine," Halora said not telling her boss that it was completed

only after all her changes and adjustments. "Have you spoken with the caterers about the reception?" she asked. Richard didn't know the answer but she heard him pose the same question to his sister. "Alma says she confirmed with them yesterday," she heard him say.

Halora checked off caterers from the list in front of her. "What about the tour? Did we explain to Melanie the format of how we wanted the tour conducted?" she asked Richard.

"Oh shoot! No, I didn't get a chance to get with her. Could you have Jorge type something real quick? Ask him to explain to her to only take the group to the first and second floors," Richard informed Halora. He didn't want anyone to see the third floor. It wasn't finished.

"Well, I guess that's everything," Halora said, looking at her watch. "We have thirty minutes until show time." Jorge entered her office while she was talking into the speakerphone that sat on her desk. "The mayor is here and the chamber of commerce wants to get everyone lined up outside," he announced.

"Richard, how far are you from the center?"

"We are pulling into the parking lot now. Has my mother made it there?"

Jorge answered, "Yes, your entire family has arrived."

Richard was expecting his mother, his cousin Clara, his siblings and Joy Lynn. Hearing that they were all there made him feel good. He parked his new car near the front of the building. He had recently purchased the new Mercedes 500 series. He wanted everybody to see it.

As he walked toward the crowd of family members and spectators, he was met by his mother, all of his siblings, his cousin Clara and his fiancée Joy Lynn. He was surprised to see his pastor and the first lady. Even though it was championship night for Mychael, he and Monica took the time to support Richard by attending the ribbon cutting ceremony. Richard knew it wasn't all about him. He knew it was safe to assume that they were there primarily at the urging of Joy Lynn.

Richard and his sister Alma kissed their mother first, followed by their sisters then Richard kissed Joy Lynn. The two love birds pursed their lips together for a long time, entangling their tongues together before they let each other go. Richard stared at his future bride for a few moments. Because she was so beautiful, he wanted to kiss her again. Until now, he hadn't realized

how deeply he was in love. Next, he kissed his Cousin Clara Bell on the cheek before moving toward his siblings.

"I'm so proud of you man," Byron said to his brother

"Me too," Miranda said, echoing what her younger brother had said. Richard became misty eyed as Eleanor walked up to him and grabbed him around the waist and pressed her face against his. Then she reached up and wiped his tears with a piece of tissue she had in her hand. She didn't have to say how proud she was, she knew her brother was full aware how proud she was of him.

Alma hugged and kissed her husband as Richard hugged his brother, Ernie, Jr., whose strong hug reminded him so much of their father. The embrace almost reduced him to tears again. Then he hugged his twin brothers a second time because they had stayed over night to be a part of the ceremony also.

Richard returned to Joy Lynn and grabbed her by the hand as they walked to their places behind the blue ribbon. The mayor stood in the middle holding a large pair of scissors. He stood along side Joy Lynn as Alma and Halora stood to the mayor's right. On the count of three, everyone smiled towards the photographers and television cameras as the mayor snipped the blue ribbon, making the expansion an official reality. Then they all stood for more pictures and made brief comments to the news media.

Richard maneuvered his way to the conference hall where the reception was being held. Eloise approached him as she placed her hand on his back. "Son, where's Christopher? I thought for sure he would be here."

"Mother, I haven't spoken to him today. Maybe he had other plans."

"I doubt it very seriously. I'm sure Christopher wouldn't let anything come between him being here. Honey, maybe you should call him?"

Richard couldn't look at his mother. He knew she was right. Christopher knew better than anyone how important this expansion was to him. But he also knew the reason he wasn't there. "I'll call him later," Richard said, trying to end the conversation with his mother.

* * *

At that same moment, Christopher was at home answering the door to a man dressed in a blue postal uniform.

"Hi, may I help you?" he said to the uniformed gentleman.

The postal worker said, making sure he was asking for the correct person. "I have a package for a Christopher Christiansen."

"That's me."

The white male handed him the brown package and the delivery card for him to sign. Christopher inspected the outside of the package before signing the delivery card. After he had added his signature and the postal worker had walked away, he noticed there wasn't a return address.

"Excuse me sir, there's no return address. Do you know who this is from?" he asked.

The man turned to face the sound of Christopher's voice. He smiled and shrugged his shoulders before saying, "I'm sorry sir—I *only* deliver the mail." Then he leaped into his mail truck and drove off to the next house.

CHAPTER THIRTEEN

The gymnasium was filled with students, faculty, family and friends, all of whom were in support of the Ramblewood High School Lady Panthers championship game. Mychael sat on the side line reviewing his plays with his assistant coach. His team was on one side of the gym practicing their shots from the foul line as the visiting team did the same on the opposite end.

Rather than concentrating on her jump shots, Christina took notice of every family member present. Her father, mother and brother were sitting on the top bleachers. A few bleachers below them sat her Uncle Richard and his fiancée, who was caring for Hannah. Monica wasn't present because she had to leave soon after the ribbon cutting ceremony to attend a mandatory training for her job.

Eloise arrived later with her daughter, Alma and son-in-law, Daniel, along with Clara. The four walked up the bleachers with only Alma and Daniel taking the time to say hello to Joy Lynn and Richard. Eloise had not really said much to her son since he had surprised her with his engagement to Joy Lynn, and especially after he wouldn't call his best friend like she had suggested. Richard knew he had two strikes against him and was smart enough to not get his third strike in the same day. He heard his mother suggest that they sit closer to Eleanor, *Snappy* and Emanuel than to him and Joy Lynn.

It was time for the game to begin and the home and visiting teams were no longer on the floor, but on the side line listening to their coaches.

Before the game officially started, Carolina, Mary Agnes and Grace walked in. *Snappy* wasn't surprised to see his sister Carolina, being that she attended a lot of Christina's games, however to see his two older sisters was

87

certainly a surprise. As they sat closer to the floor, *Snappy* came down from the top bleachers to greet and hug all three of them. Grace and Mary Agnes both laughed because they knew *Snappy* was shocked to see them. His greeting was followed by their nephew, who also greeted his aunts with a hug and kiss. Eleanor stayed in her seat but waved at her sister-in-laws from where she was sitting. Then she winked her eye at her best friend and sister-in-law, Carolina, who winked and smiled at her in return.

Christopher and Beatrice were the last of the family to enter the gymnasium. As soon as they entered, he and Richard made eye contact. He pretended not to see his best friend. In fact, he walked past Richard and Joy Lynn without speaking. He was sorry Joy Lynn had to be put in the middle of this, but he wanted to send his ex-best friend a strong message.

Richard's eyes followed Christopher to see where he was going to sit. Christopher didn't know this as he made his way to speak to Eloise, Alma and Daniel before taking his seat. Richard could hear his mother asking his best friend where he was earlier during the day. He tried to listen as hard as he could, but the noise level wouldn't allow him to hear Christopher's response.

Richard waited and watched for Christopher to move away from the conversation with Eloise. His stare followed his best friend as he took his seat. Unaware that Joy Lynn was watching him, he almost spilled his drink when she discretely tapped him on his leg. "Honey, turn around the game is about to start," she said.

The five starters took their places on the court against their five opponents. The referee tossed the ball into the air and the two tallest girls jumped for its possession. The game got off to a good start. The lady Panthers were playing basketball as if they owned the gymnasium. By half time, the entire team ran from the floor to the locker room excited about their eight point lead. They were feeling confident and cocky because the game was going in their favor.

In the stands, Eloise was now holding Hannah. As soon as the young toddler noticed her, she wanted to sit with her *Nana.* She played for awhile then she drifted off to sleep in Eloise's arms. Richard, on the other hand, took the half time moment to talk with his mother. He moved from his seat, stepping up a few bleachers to sit next to her.

"Mother, what did you do with Miss Flossie tonight?" he asked, making small talk.

"Son, Flossie does have children. She's spending the night with Miranda."

"Oh."

"What's going on with you and Christopher? Don't think I didn't notice that the both of you didn't say a word to each other and when I asked him earlier where he was during the expansion, do you know what he said?"

"No Ma'am, what did he say?"

"He said he was busy."

"For real, that's what he said," Richard responded, shocked by what he had heard.

"Yes son, that's what he told me. Now what's going on with the two of you?" Eloise asked her son with concern in her voice.

"Mother…Not tonight. He's the one with the problem, not me."

"Honey, can the two of you get along for longer than five minutes? Surely, you're going to have him in this wedding?"

Richard never answered his mother. He didn't have the heart to tell her that Christopher wasn't going to be in the wedding. If he did, he would have to explain the type of relationship he and Christopher had. He would have to explain why he and Christopher weren't speaking and he wasn't ready to deal with either explanation at this particular time.

Inside, he really wished his best friend would agree to be a groomsmen. He wanted him to be apart of his special day—even though Christopher didn't see it that way. His best friend still felt betrayed. He felt dumped. He felt he had trespassed against him.

Richard saw Alma looking at him, but opting not to come to his defense. Daniel also looked at him, but only raising his eye brows with a *wish I could help look* on his face. They all knew better. He was rescued from further questioning when the basketball teams returned to the floor. He was glad. He knew there would be no end to his mother's questions and inquiries.

As the lady Panthers gathered in a circle, their fans chanted in unison, "Go Panthers!" Christina, Christel and Shana, three of the main players, maneuvered around on the floor. It finally hit Mychael about how close he was to winning a championship. He continued to stand on the side line. Then

for a few moments he would sit. Seconds later, he was standing again. Beginning to sweat, he took off his black suit jacket and laid it on an empty chair. As the lead dwindled to four points, Mychael unbuttoned his tie and rolled up both sleeves. He was growing nervous because right before his eyes, the game was slipping away from his team.

"Christina, keep your head in the game," Mychael yelled after she was cited for a foul. The opposing team was allotted two free shots. Christina was breathing heavy, but she nodded her head that she heard him. The opposing team nailed the two free throws, now the game lead was within two points.

Mychael took Christina out of the game to give her a chance to get a breather and replaced her with a teammate from the second string. He didn't give Tammy the chance to play much since he relied on his first string to carry all the weight. She knew this was her only time to shine in a championship game. Within minutes, she intercepted two passes, converting them into points. The game lead was now at six.

Christina reentered the game, but Mychael kept Tammy on the floor as Christel came out for her breather. The crowd was ecstatic as the opposing team began making simple mistakes, each one being converted into points for the lady Panthers.

The momentum was high and the excitement could be felt throughout the gymnasium. Fans were standing to their feet as they cheered the girls on. The game was down to less than two minutes. The minutes dwindled to seconds, and seconds dwindled to zero, the lady Panthers celebrated by throwing the game ball into the air.

Mychael ran onto the court in the middle of his winning team. He was excited. He was happy. Truthfully, he was ecstatic about the win. He had finally brought a winning championship to the Ramblewood High School and the Ramblewood community.

Blending with the crowd, Mary Agnes and Grace walked up to their niece. "Christina, Auntie is so proud of you," Mary Agnes said, giving her a hug as Grace looked on.

"Mrs. Shaw, I'm not Christina—I'm Christel," the teenager responded.

Mary Agnes and Grace both looked at each other and had to blink their eyes. The young girl was almost the identical twin to their niece Christina.

"I'm sorry honey. I thought you were Christina. Haven't I seen you at church, who's your family?"

"My mom is Shirley Mayweather and my grandfather is Deacon Mayweather," the teenager answered properly. She smiled at the two older women. "It was nice seeing each of you again. I'm going to go now."

Mary Agnes looked at Grace again. "It can't be."

"Agnes, mind your business. Remember, the *Three C* situation?" Grace said.

"Oh hush. I'm not going to say anything, but as many times as I've seen that child, I didn't realize she resembled Christina so much until I saw her close up."

"Do you think *Snappy* has any idea?" Grace asked.

"Oh please…As long as he's been fooling around with her mama. I wouldn't be surprised if he didn't have more than one over there."

"More than one what?" Carolina asked as she walked up. All three sisters looked at each other, but nobody said anything. Carolina didn't pay attention to the silent treatment she was receiving—she was ready to go home. "Ya'll ready to go?" she asked.

"Um…hum…," Grace and Mary Agnes said in unison walking behind their sister to the nearest exit.

After the crowd left the floor, Mychael was able to get his team in line to shake hands with their opponents. He enjoyed all the congratulations he was receiving. He was made to feel even better after the athletic director presented him with the winning trophy. Then he was greeted by the Superintendent of schools, Ernest Lorde, II and the high school principal, Daniel Hawkins.

"I'm very proud of you, I don't know whether I should call you Pastor or Coach Dovely," Principal Hawkins said as he smiled with pride. It meant a lot to Mychael to hear those words come from his boss and assistant chairman. He felt he had arrived. It had been a year since Principal Hawkins had hired him, even after becoming aware of his unstable pattern.

Mychael remembered him saying, '*Dovely, I know you don't come highly recommended. I'm going to hire you only because my father-in-law and brother-in-law have asked me to give you a chance. But if you so much as lay a hand on one of these students, I will have you personally arrested.*'

Outside, in parking lot, the three sisters walked toward Carolina's car

when they saw Christel again. Mary Agnes attempted to be sarcastic, "Carolina, isn't that Christina over there?" Carolina glared at the teenager talking to a young man. "No…If I'm not mistaken, I believe that's Shirley Mayweather's daughter, Christel."

"Oh, my eyes must be playing tricks on me or she looks identical to Christina."

"Well, she should that's her sister," Carolina said, nonchalantly.

"Her sister?!" Mary Agnes and Grace both surprisingly yelled out.

"Oh stop it you two…Shirley Mayweather has said that child was *Snappy's* since the day she was born. I believe her and Christina were born the same week."

"Does he know?" Grace asked.

"I guess he does. He's been sneaking around with Shirley for years."

Mary Agnes asked slowly, "How about Eleanor?"

"I think she does, but she's never asked me about it," Carolina said.

Inside, the gymnasium slowly became empty of all the crowded fans. After his family had left for the evening, Mychael returned to the gym and flipped on the lights. There was no evidence that a game had been played earlier as the janitorial crew had already cleaned the floors and pushed the bleachers against the wall. Carrying his suit jacket draped across his shoulder and one hand in his pocket, Mychael walked to the middle of the floor. He looked around the empty space. He closed his eyes and once more, took in the winning moment. He jumped when he heard the sound of a man's baritone voice.

"Coach, are you the only one here?"

"Ah yes…Mr. Jones, do you have access to a ladder and a pair of scissors?" Mychael asked him.

"I believe we do. Do you need them?"

"If it's not too much trouble, I would appreciate it."

"Oh no sir, it's no trouble at all. After tonight's win, it's not the least bit of trouble."

Mr. Jones returned with a pair of scissors and the ladder. He unfolded it and placed it under the basketball net. Mychael handed him his jacket as Mr. Jones handed him the pair of scissors. He climbed the ladder and snipped the net from the rim. At first, he held it in his hand. He pressed it against his face. Then slowly he climbed down the ladder, handing the scissors back to Mr. Jones.

"I guess that's something to be proud of, huh?" Mr. Jones said.

"Mr. Jones, more than you know…more than you will ever know," Mychael managed to say, fighting back his happy tears.

* * *

An hour later, Mychael had made his way home and was glad that he didn't have to worry about Hannah. She went home for the night with Eloise. He thought to himself that his child was convinced that Eloise was her *Nana* and nobody could tell her differently.

He quickly stepped in the shower and then into a t-shirt and boxers. While in the shower, Monica had called his cell phone and the house phone, only to get the voicemail for both. Once he returned to his bedroom, he relaxed on the bed and began dialing her cell number. He heard her lovely voice on the second ring.

He listened as his wife congratulated him on his win. He enjoyed hearing her repeat that he had won a high school championship. He informed her that Hannah wanted to spend the night with her *Nana* and they both laughed that Eloise had inherited a granddaughter she hadn't asked for. Then Monica informed him that the certification training was very difficult, in return, Mychael reminded her of her brilliance and encouraged her to do her best. Before hanging up, they exchanged loving sentiments then they said goodnight to each other.

He left his bedroom and entered the kitchen to make himself a sandwich. He hummed to himself as he placed a slice each of ham and cheese on wheat bread. He placed the sandwich on a plate, along with a pickle and opened a bottle of water. He sat on one of the two empty stools then he pressed the power button to the remote control for the small 13" television.

He reached for his sandwich and before he could take his first bite, the door bell rang. His first thought was his daughter had decided she didn't want to stay overnight after all with her *Nana*. He walked down the hall toward the door and peeked through the tiny peep hole. It was Christopher, but he had no idea what he wanted. He opened the door, totally forgetting he was wearing only a t-shirt and boxers.

"Hey Brother Christopher what's going on?" Mychael asked.

Before he spoke, Christopher looked down at Mychael's boxers. "Nothing, can I come in?" he asked as he noticed Mychael's thick pubic hairs through the opening in his boxers.

"Ah Yeah," he responded, stepping aside to let his church member inside then he apologized for his appearance, "Man, excuse how I look, I just got out of the shower. So, what brings you out this late?"

"Oh, I just wanted to see what you were up to since *Monnie* was out of town."

Christopher was looking Mychael in the eyes, but his pastor avoided eye contact, instead he glanced at the floor. A few moments of silence filled the room.

"Hey, man I know what you probably came here for, but I don't do that anymore. As a matter of fact, I haven't done anything like that since we were together last," Mychael explained.

"Are you sure?"

"Yeah man, I'm sure and one more thing, I'd appreciate it if you didn't come at me like this again," Mychael said, letting Christopher know where he stood. He watched as the expression on Christopher's face changed. He was sorry for hurting his feelings, but his comment had to be said.

Christopher was disappointed. He was hurt. He was embarrassed. Finally, he turned toward the door without looking back. "Okay, goodnight."

Mychael didn't say anything. He didn't even tell his church member goodnight. Instead, he closed the door behind him and pressed his back against it. Then he turned and pressed his head against the same door. For a moment he thought about it and talked himself out of it. He thought about it some more, but this time he was unable to fight his urge. He went back to the door and opened it. Christopher turned around, responding to the sound of the opening door.

Mychael continued to hold the door open slightly, only peeping through. Quietly, he said, "pssst," to Christopher as he motioned with his head for him to come back. He watched as Christopher climbed the stairs a second time and entered the house.

Christopher whispered, "Myke, are you sure you want to do this? I don't want to force you to do anything." He looked down at Mychael's boxers again and it was obvious he wasn't forcing his pastor to do anything he didn't want to do. "Where are we going?"

"The bedroom," Mychael answered, locking the door behind them.

Christopher knew the location of the bedroom. He had been in the bedroom before. As he led the way, Mychael flipped out all the lights throughout the house. Very easily he had forgotten about his sandwich. He had forgotten about his marriage. He had even forgotten he was now a new pastor.

"Nobody saw you come over here, did they?" Mychael asked Christopher.

"Nope."

"You sure your aunt wasn't on the porch."

"I'm sure. She called my mom earlier to tell her goodnight," Christopher answered, as he pulled down his pants and underwear at the same time. He stepped out of them, leaving all of his clothes in the middle of the floor.

Mychael stared at Christopher's perfect body while he rubbed the front of his boxers. He rubbed his front area like he was trying to calm his excited snake. But his snake wasn't being cooperative. In a quick second, he pulled his erect penis from his boxers and waited for Christopher to climb onto the bed.

"Did you bring a condom?" Mychael asked his sex partner, looking around as if to see one lying around his bedroom.

"No, I thought you had one."

"Why would I have one, my wife and I don't use condoms. Come on...you don't have AIDS, do you? Because I know I don't have it. I'll just pull out when I am about to let go," Mychael said, sounding very stupid.

Mychael climbed on the bed behind Christopher and he didn't waste time. He kissed him passionately on the lips and sucked on his neck. He was so turned on by Christopher's well chiseled body—it made his manhood stay rock solid with hardness. His penis throbbed just seeing Christopher naked. He kissed him more on his chest, moving slowly down to Christopher's stomach to his navel, stopping between his thighs. His tongue mechanics was making Christopher so aroused he tried several times to push him away. He could tell he was driving his lover wild—he intended to. His goal was to make his lover feel his best.

A second time, Christopher tried to push Mychael away, but his efforts didn't make bed partner stop. Mychael couldn't stop. In the heat of passion,

they bumped and grinned into each other then stopping momentarily to lie between each other's legs while their erect penises rubbed vigorously against one another. Mychael looked down at his stiffness also noticing his juices traveling slowly down the neck of his manhood. The beast in him was ready for action.

Breathless, Mychael said to Christopher, "Get on your knees," before he plunged his solid manhood inside of him. The force Mychael put behind his power tool pushed Christopher straight into the headboard. He could tell the pain had pierced right to his soul, but rather than Christopher begging his lover to remove his hard rod of steel, Mychael heard when Christopher gritted his teeth as he moaned and moved his hips all at the same time.

"Oh man, this feel so good," Mychael said between each stroke.

Although Mychael hated doing this, it really felt good to him. In no way could he deny how good it felt—his facial expression wouldn't let him.

Thirty minutes later, the two men were still engaging, but Christopher was now lying on his back with his legs resting on Mychael's broad shoulders. Mychael had forgotten about how much he hated having sex with a man. He had lost all focus and at that point, the only thing he wanted to do now was please Christopher.

The closer Mychael came to ejaculating, the more thrusts he made. His hard muscle moved in and out of his lover with so much force, the pain felt like pleasure to Christopher. It made him beg for more, "Do it harder."

Doing as he was told, the added rhythm had Mychael winded and left him panting to catch his breath. He closed his eyes as he continued to move his hips inward, outward and in a circular motion. He was stroking his lover perfectly. He tried to envision that he was making love to his wife, but he couldn't keep her face in his head. All of his visions kept leading him back to Christopher.

In all his years of being married, Mychael realized that Monica hadn't come close to making him feel the way he was feeling at this moment. He was enjoying the sexual experience he was having with Christopher. He became so caught up in his sexual attraction to his lover that he forgot the promise he had made earlier. Before he knew it, he was letting go inside of Christopher. Right away, he could tell his lover was feeling his hot semen squirt inside of him. He could tell by the way his body jerked—his reaction was similar to

being stung by a wasp. Technically, he knew Christopher hadn't been stung by a wasp, but it did confirm for him, how raw he had made his lover inside.

As the moments passed, Mychael collapsed on top of Christopher. Indeed he was athletic, but now he couldn't move—he was exhausted. For five minutes, he laid in the same position listening to a rapid heart rate. The beats were so strong and similar he didn't know whether it was his heartbeat or the heartbeat of his partner that he heard. He continued to lie in silence as he moved his attention from their rapid heartbeat to taking in the citrus cologne Christopher was wearing. Noticing the time, he pulled his deflated manhood out of Christopher, before rolling on his back still exhausted.

"I'm sorry man, I forgot to pull out," he said, still out of breath.

"That's okay, it's too late now. I guess this is really the last time, huh?" Christopher asked, uncertain.

Slipping on his boxers and t-shirt, Mychael said in response to his question, "Man no…but what happened tonight has to stay between us. You can't show up here anymore, my mother-in-law is too nosey. You need to call me on my cell phone or I'll call you on yours."

As Mychael continued talking to Christopher, he watched as he put on his clothes. Damn, he loved staring at his partner, he thought to himself. To him, Christopher looked like he could have been a tennis player, glancing at him from a side view; he could easily be mistaken for the celebrity clone to the tennis star, James Blake.

He didn't realize an hour and a half had passed until he looked at the clock on the nightstand earlier—it was almost eleven o'clock. Walking toward the front door, he couldn't resist grabbing Christopher by the hand. Then all of sudden, his spirit was now being convicted about what had happened—he was starting to regret it. Next, his flesh took over again and reminded of the last hour and a half. He couldn't erase the thoughts. He couldn't make himself forget. He had to give in and admit that he enjoyed what Christopher had to offer.

They both reached the door and Christopher turned to face him. Mychael pressed his body against his. He didn't want him to leave. He kissed his lips passionately, then, he slowly pulled away—causing a trail of saliva to connect them. Christopher's lips felt like soft cotton to him. He wanted to make love to him again, but they had been together longer than he had intended for him to stay.

"I really enjoyed what happened here tonight. I don't know what it was, but that was a powerful dose of that boy *thang* you threw on me tonight," Mychael admitted, hitting Christopher on his rear-end, "but seriously though…how do you make your muscles tighten like that?" he asked out of curiosity.

Christopher laughed at the look on Mychael's face. He could tell that he was serious about his question, he laughed again before saying. "It's a secret."

"Come on now…"

"Why?" Christopher quizzed.

This time Mychael was laughing. He really wanted to know.

"What's so funny?" Christopher asked.

"I just want to know…because you could teach your cousin a thing or two," Mychael said, also noticing the red mark on Christopher's neck. "I think you're going to have some explaining to do," he remarked.

"What kind of explaining?" Christopher asked, looking puzzled.

Mychael took his index finger and rubbed the area where he had placed the purple mark on his neck.

"You have a passion mark from our lovemaking," Mychael told him.

"Oh goodness, you didn't?!"

"Hey what can I say, I got carried away. I wouldn't worry myself over it. All you have to do is cover it with a turtle neck or something."

"Thanks a lot…I'd better get home," Christopher said, covering the passion mark with his collar. He didn't think it was cute to sport a passion mark when you didn't have a girlfriend to justify it.

Regardless how Christopher felt about it, Mychael smiled with pride about how he had left his mark on him. He could tell right away that Christopher didn't see the humor in what he had done and they didn't exchange words further as Mychael moved his arms around him to open the front door.

Once the door was fully open, they both were shocked to see Richard standing on the porch. The trustee chairman's hand was in mid-air about to ring the doorbell. Surprised, Christopher looked at Mychael, Mychael looked at Richard and Richard looked at the both of them. A few moments passed before anyone spoke a word.

Richard finally broke the silence, "Oh Pastor, I'm sorry that I came by so late. I intended to give you these papers at the game tonight but I totally forgot about it. I need for you to look them over before our meeting on Saturday."

"Ah….Trustee Lorde…thanks, but I wished you would have called first. I could have saved you the trip."

Christopher remained frozen in his tracks. He didn't move. He couldn't move. Richard knew immediately something wasn't right about his best friend being at the pastor's house at that hour. He also knew the first lady was out of town. Joy Lynn had conveniently mentioned it to him earlier

"No, I'm glad I came. It wasn't a bother at all," Richard said, staring at his best friend.

Christopher managed to maneuver past Richard, avoiding contact with his eyes as he skipped his way down the stairs. Richard allowed his head to follow Christopher's shadow to the end of the yard. Then, he turned to look at Mychael again. His mouth hung open, but he couldn't find the correct words to say. He had to make himself smile. Then he shook his head in disbelief.

Mychael finally said, "Well man, if there's nothing else. I'll see you this weekend at the meeting."

He was nervous and his trustee chairman could tell that he was. He hurried and closed the door. He locked it, before leaning his back against it. For some strange reason, he now felt safe behind the bolted locks. He hit himself aside the head with the brown envelope his trustee had given him. He waited a few seconds then he rushed to the window and watched as Richard walked past his parked vehicle to follow Christopher up the street.

CHAPTER FOURTEEN

Christopher had almost made it home, but the sound of heavy breathing prompted him to look behind him. First, he saw his best friend jogging to catch up with him then he noticed Richard had left his car parked in Mychael's driveway.

Richard was jogging faster and the distance between the two was growing smaller. As he got closer, Richard called out to Christopher, his words were more like a whisper, but it was loud enough to get Christopher's attention. Hesitantly, Christopher stopped walking in his fast pace to see what was so important that his best friend had followed him home.

"What do you want?" Christopher answered with an attitude.

"What do I want? I want to know what in the *hell* were you doing at Reverend Dovely's this late?" Richard asked, breathing heavily from the jog.

"None of your business, I don't owe you an explanation and besides he's not only your pastor, but he's mine also and my reason for being over there this late is no different than you deciding to drop by at this hour."

"Do you think I'm stupid?" Richard yelled, but realizing quickly where he was. He lowered his voice before saying, "I can tell by your defensive tone that the two of you were either finishing up or about to do something."

"First of all, I'm not being defensive and second of all, you don't know what you are talking about."

"Then explain this," Richard said, pulling back the collar covering the bruise he had spotted on Christopher's neck. "How did you get that?" he asked.

"Rip, you don't know what you are talking, a bug bit me," Christopher lied.

"Yeah right, a bug bit you all right…A six foot tall bug with Reverend in

front of his name," Richard stated, putting his hands on his waist as he turned to walk away from the conversation. He was having a hard time believing the explanation Christopher was giving him, but he really didn't have any proof. He could only hope that his best friend wasn't sleeping with their pastor, especially a snake in the grass like Mychael.

He walked a few more steps then he turned around to face Christopher again. "Okay, tell me this and I will leave you alone, were you sleeping with him during the same time that he was sleeping with my sister?" he asked Christopher seeming concerned.

Before Christopher could respond, Richard was pointing his finger in his face then he balled the same hand into a fist.

"Christopher man, don't lie to me. I just want to know."

Christopher was pretty nonchalant about the entire conversation. He kept his arms knotted together because the discussion was boring him. He was now finding it hard to believe that Richard was questioning him about his sex life. Apparently, his best friend had forgotten that only a few days had passed since he had admitted to being in love with someone else. Maybe he hadn't forgotten, maybe he thought he was entitled to know his personal business. Well, if that were the case, he was going to be in for a rude awakening, Christopher thought.

The two men stopped conversing back and forth to take notice of the noise trailing down the street. In the dark, it appeared to be a man and woman walking side by side. They didn't know the stringy haired white woman, but recognized the man right away—it was *DJ*.

Richard mouthed to Christopher, "Where are they going?"

"It's an abandoned house that sits behind all those woods. All the crack addicts hibernate down there to do their drugs," Christopher explained, also whispering.

"Thank heavens my father is not here to know that. He would be coordinating a crusade to save their souls too. Knowing *DJ* was living like this…he's probably turning over in his grave, if there is such a thing," Richard said. He kept looking at the couple. He wanted to say something to his nephew, but he said to Christopher instead, "she looks pregnant. Is she smoking drugs while she's pregnant?"

"Rip, she's a junkie, what does she care about being pregnant,"

Christopher stated, "Your father really loved *DJ*. In his eyesight, the boy couldn't do any wrong; honestly, I think that his addiction became worse after your father died, don't you?"

Richard agreed, "Yeah...I often wonder about that sometimes," then he added, "Had my father been alive, *DJ* would not have this bad of a drug problem and that's for sure."

DJ was so preoccupied with the company he was keeping; he didn't notice his uncle or Christopher. And Richard and Christopher had become so preoccupied watching the two crack addicts fight over their drugs, they had forgot their argument. They continued to observe *DJ* who had the crack pipe in his hand and noticed the unknown pregnant female begging for him to give her a *hit*. The two addicts finally disappeared into the wooded area and entered the abandoned house like Christopher had described.

After the short distraction, the two men stood quietly face to face, "I've never slept with Reverend Dovely," Christopher lied again. Then he changed the subject, "Can we now talk about this engagement between you and Joy Lynn? I guess you really are going to marry her?" He paused before adding, "Rip what about us?"

"Christopher there is always going to be us. No matter where I'm living or who I marry—nothing is going to come between the two of us. But I told you I want children and Joy Lynn can give me that. I love her and I love you too, but in different ways."

Richard took his finger and raised Christopher's head from staring at the ground. It slipped his mind again where they were. It was pitch dark, but they were still in front of the row of houses with one belonging to Richard's sister Eleanor and Christopher's Uncle *Snappy*. In fact, Christopher's entire family lived on the entire block.

At that moment it didn't matter to Richard, he began saying, "Joy Lynn satisfies me in a way only a woman can and you satisfy that need I desire only from a man. Baby, she'll never be able to compete with you."

Christopher slid his face away from Richard's hand, giving his attention to the ground again. The words he heard made him feel good, but he wasn't convinced of his best friend's loyalty. He had every reason not to be. Even having his share of doubts, it didn't erase how he felt inside, he felt like a butterfly was trapped inside his body.

Almost letting down his guard, he leaned against the rear of his car as Richard stood before him with his hands in his pocket. The night was still. The sound of crickets chirping could be heard around them. The moment seemed so surreal to Christopher. However, it didn't take away the reality that his best friend was still planning to marry Joy Lynn. It didn't ease the pain of Joy Lynn living in the house that Richard had promised to him. The only thing appeared the same was the love that he held in his heart for the man that stood before him.

"Instead of standing out here, do you want to go to my place so we can talk?" Richard asked feeling attracted to Christopher. He wanted to get him alone, away from the row of houses belonging to his family and away from the eyes of Mychael. Richard's intuition was telling him that their pastor was staring at them through the window. At this point, Richard had no plans of leaving. He wanted and needed to convince his best friend to go home with him.

"No, it's getting late," Christopher said.

He knew Richard's suggestion was out of the question. Mostly, due to him being extremely sore from the good time he had had with Mychael. He didn't want to put himself in a situation for another round of rough sex, all he wanted to do now was take a warm shower and go to bed.

"Come on, you don't have to drive. We can take my car and I promise to bring you home before your Mom wakes up." Richard tried to negotiate.

"No, I've already told you it's too late. Besides you are getting married in a few months and we may as well get used to the idea."

"I told you after I get married things won't change between us."

"And I'm telling you, if you marry her, I'm not having sex with you anymore."

"Why? Because, I'll be married?"

"Partially."

"What's the difference between you sleeping with me and the good reverend? He's married and to your cousin, no doubt," Richard reminded Christopher.

"Keep your voice down. I'm not sleeping with Mych—I mean Reverend Dovely and I wish you'd stop saying that," Christopher said with his words getting tangling up.

Richard became angry again. "Whatever man, you can tell that bullshit to somebody else!" he ranted, walking off. "I can smell his cologne all over you and I know what a passion mark looks like on you, remember? He's turned you into a liar; just like him…I'm outta here," Richard said as he angled toward the street, walking away from the argument between him and Christopher. Before he could move away from the area where he and Christopher were standing, Richard heard Christopher's cell phone begin to ring.

Christopher looked at the display and saw it was Mychael—he answered it. Apparently, he *was* watching from his living room window. He kept watching as Richard returned to his new car and eased out of the driveway.

Christopher was still talking into his phone when Richard drove up to the curve. He rolled down his passenger side window. He said, "I know you're on the phone with the good reverend. You can tell him his secret is safe with me." Then he pulled off and continued down the street.

Christopher spoke into the cell phone a few more minutes before walking up the steps and through his front door. He thought about everything he had said and everything Richard had said. In one thought, he felt Richard was right. In another thought, he felt he wasn't being fair. In so many words, Richard was saying that he wanted to have his cake and eat it to. He wanted to marry Joy Lynn; someone he said could give him children. Then he wanted him, someone who could satisfy the occasional urges he would get being a gay man.

Christopher wanted to tell Richard that they could no longer be lovers anymore. He wanted to tell him that a relationship between them would be inappropriate—especially now that he knew that he was his nephew.

Even though his thoughts seemed realistic, Christopher knew he couldn't follow through with half of the things that circulated in his head. First of all, his mother wasn't ready to deal with the backlash and second of all, he definitely wasn't ready to deal with the fact that Deacon Lorde was his father and not just his deacon.

Instead of continuing his self interrogation, Christopher grabbed a pair of his pajamas and quietly entered the hall bathroom. He had passed his mother's room and noticed that she was fast asleep. She hadn't realized that he had even left the house or that he had even returned. He turned the nozzle

for the cold water and the nozzle for the hot. Then he held his hand out to feel the warmness of the combined temperatures. He pulled his white t-shirt over his head and stepped out of his boxers and pants, before stepping into the shower under the flowing water. He grabbed a used bar of soap to lather his body. He held his head steady under the warm water to wet his hair so he could begin lathering his soft grade with shampoo. He scrubbed and lathered. Then he rinsed. He scrubbed and lathered some more. Then he rinsed. The warm water felt good against his body, he kept his eyes closed tightly as he rinsed the suds away.

Moments later, Christopher opened his eyes to see a red tint in his shower water. He knew it wasn't his shampoo and conditioner because the two combined had never changed the color of the water before. Anxiously, he turned off the shower and wiped his face dry. He was confused. He looked around the shower like he had lost something. At first, he pulled at his wet hair. Then he grabbed the bottle of shampoo—it was his usual *VO5* green tea. Finally, it hit him as he noticed the red fluid running down his leg. *What was going on?* He thought. He realized he was bleeding and he knew where it was coming from. It wasn't dripping slowly, it was streaming rather consistently. He became nervous and his first instinct was to wipe between his legs. When he did, the hand towel he used became saturated with blood. He wasn't in any pain, but the incident made him remember why people shouldn't have anal sex. Softly, he applied pressure to his rectum causing the bleeding to eventually subside.

He finished his shower and later retired to his bedroom. He couldn't resist calling Mychael to inform him about what had happened. He was hoping he hadn't fallen asleep, but when Mychael answered the phone on the third ring, he sounded half asleep.

"Hey, were you asleep?" Christopher asked.

"Yeah, I just dozed off. Is everything all right?" Mychael answered.

"Everything is fine, except I was bleeding like a hog in the shower."

"Hummm…I'm sorry to hear that." Mychael cleared his throat, "I guess in the future, you have to be careful about what you ask for."

"No, I guess you will have to be more careful next time."

Then Mychael said seductively, "Ah ha! I finally got you to agree that there will be a next time."

"Talking about me agreeing to a next time… You were the one who was unsure about there being a next time." Christopher said. Then he paused, before asking Mychael, "Did you *really* enjoy what happened tonight?"

"Christopher," Mychael said then he paused.

"I like the way you said my first name. Not many people call me Christopher."

"Well from now on I'm going to call you Christopher. I like the way it sounds. And when I say it, you'll know I'm saying it with meaning. I *more* than enjoyed what happened tonight," Mychael said.

"Wow…that's deep."

"But we do understand this stays between the two of us, right? Don't tell your friends, family or nobody. I have too much to lose."

"I won't. But I must tell you that Richard thinks he knows something is going on between us. Every time he asked me whether something going on, I lied. Earlier tonight when you called my cell phone, he said to tell you that your secret was safe with him."

"Oh he did, huh? He may be a problem." Mychael waited a few moments. "Do you think he will mention tonight's episode to my wife or his fiancée?"

"What do you mean?"

"During our last meeting, he and I had a disagreement about the educational center project and I told him that he needed to first go through me before discussing any information with the boards. Now, tonight this happens. As you already know, I'm not one of his favorite people. I probably ticked him off with my directive about the education building." Then Mychael added, "But he has to remember that his father is no longer alive and he named me as his successor."

"Mychael nobody can deny that. My fath— I mean Deacon Lorde can validate that. But you have to cut Richard some slack. He's use to his father giving him total control over things within the finance department. Personally, I don't think he will mention anything to Monica. He has nothing to gain by doing that. However, Joy Lynn is another subject—she has his nose wide open."

"I understand that perfectly and I don't mean to be ugly about this. I just want Trustee Lorde to respect me as the pastor."

"He will. I don't doubt that for a minute. Well I'm going to let you get back to sleep, goodnight."

"Before you go, I caught something you said earlier. Did I hear you almost call Deacon Lorde your father?"

Christopher sat quietly on the phone. He thought that Mychael hadn't paid attention to what he had almost said.

"Christopher, are you there?"

"Yes, I'm here. Mychael you can't tell anyone about this."

"About what?"

"My mom just told me that Deacon Lorde was my father," Christopher said with his voice trailing off.

"Wow! So that means that Trustee Lorde is your uncle?" Mychael said slowly.

"Mychael stop. I can't bear to go through this again. I get sick when I think about Richard as my uncle."

"Didn't Sister Carolina know that something was going on between you two?"

"No...she knew we were friends, but she didn't learn that it was more than that until a year ago."

"And she didn't tell you then?"

"No! And Mychael I really don't want to talk about this."

"I'm sorry...I just didn't know. Does my wife know?"

"I don't think so. The only people that know are my mom and her sisters."

"Huh, so my mother-in-law can keep a secret?"

"Leave my Aunt Grace alone and yes, she can keep a secret. She wouldn't dare do anything to embarrass her little *Three C,*" Christopher said with pride.

"Oh, is that what she calls you? Where did she get that nickname from?" Mychael inquired.

"Yeah, she's called me that since I was a baby. She combined my first, middle and last names."

"I know the first and last name begin with the letter C, but where does the third letter come from?"

"Craeg."

"Oh I see."

"Craeg is spelled with a letter combination of my Aunt Grace's name."

"Hummm...I must say, Sister Carolina was very creative," Mychael said. "What time is it?"

"It's late, so goodnight." Christopher said jokingly.

"Goodnight, talk to you tomorrow."

"It's already tomorrow," Christopher said laughing.

"Well I'll talk to you later today," Mychael said laughing also before disconnecting the call.

CHAPTER FIFTEEN

Halora arrived for work, entered her now organized office space when she noticed sitting on her desk a nice basket holding a variety of Veronica's secret beauty products and a box of imported chocolate clusters. Jorge, her assistant, stood up pretending that he was reading an inscription from a folded piece of paper in his hand, "Halora, thank you for such a hot and steamy night, I hope this will remind you of me every time you apply it to your soft brown skin."

Halora laughed out loud. "I know that paper doesn't say that. I can't remember the last time I gave a man some of my energy," she admitted.

"Well, maybe it's your birthday and you somehow forgot," Jorge guessed.

"It's not my birthday. Seriously, where did all of this come from?" Halora asked, still admiring the arrangement.

"They're for you. There wasn't a card attached. It was at the front lobby when I arrived this morning," Jorge explained to his boss.

"Then, how did you know they were for me?" Halora questioned Jorge further.

"I didn't. The security guard said it was brought for you."

Halora's mind immediately went to her encounter with Mychael. He must have felt guilty about rejecting her advances, she thought. He should have. It wasn't everyday that she threw herself at a man, only to get rejected. She continued to smile as she admired all the fragrances in the basket. She opened the first bottle of body lotion and rubbed it all over her hands. Then she placed both hands to her face and inhaled. She had forgotten how much she loved

the scented fragrance of apple cider. She sprayed the same fragrance of cologne around her neck. She didn't care that she had sprayed another brand of cologne over her body earlier that morning.

Gradually, her eyes and attention moved from the *VS* products to the imported chocolate candy, the sweets made her eyes light up. Her mouth even watered. She kept wondering to herself, how did Mychael know that she liked imported chocolate clusters? At first, she wanted to call him and say thank you, but she changed her mind. She figured her silence would be his punishment for rejecting her. Removing the plastic wrapping from the attractive looking box, Halora grabbed two chocolates from the box, placing the candies on a napkin.

"Are you going to share some of those with me?" Jorge asked and he wasn't teasing.

"Do you know how much these chocolates cost?"

"No."

"I figured you didn't, 'cause if you did, you wouldn't be asking me so candidly to give them away."

"Is that a *no*?"

"Yes, it is. Goodbye Jorge."

"Do you need for me to type a thank you letter and send it out? It's obvious you know who this gift is from," Jorge said.

Halora thought about Jorge's offer then she thought about what she had felt in her hands the previous Sunday. It made her smile. Suddenly, she began to think about the possibilities to come. She found herself smiling again.

"No, I'm going to personally thank the person who sent this gift," Halora said.

She placed the first piece of chocolate cluster through her lips. It tasted delicious, forcing her to admire the gift basket even more as she continued to chew. She flung her long pony tail over her shoulder as she noticed other fragrances in the basket that she hadn't seen before. She opened those bottles one by one, placing each one to her nose to enjoy the smell. Then in one mouthful, she gobbled down the second chocolate cluster—it appeared that she had swallowed the second candy whole.

Consumed in her own world, Halora didn't notice her cousin/boss standing in the door to her office. Jorge usually warned her whenever Richard

was on the floor, but he wasn't at his desk. The gossiper was misinforming the office about the mysterious gift basket and the fact that his boss had no plans of sharing her chocolate clusters with him or anyone else.

Halora finally looked up to see Richard watching her, standing with his arms folded across his chest, he laughed at Halora's obvious excitement.

"Appears to me that somebody has a secret admirer?" he said.

"No, it seems to me that Jorge has a big mouth," Halora said, jokingly.

"Well, surely it's not a secret? It's not everyday that someone gets a gift basket sent to them around here. You must have really put something on that brotha." Richard said, followed by laughter.

"Ha. Ha. Ha. It's not one of those type gifts."

"Yeah right, tell me anything. I don't expect you to tell me the truth; I'm *only* your boss."

"As a matter of fact, I really don't know who sent this basket. But I have a general idea."

"Dear cousin…now that's something you don't tell your boss. You really don't know?"

"Okay boss, I know where you are going with this. So you can leave now and maybe I can get some work done."

"No, my real reason for coming down here was to get you to walk me through the marketing presentation you submitted to me last week. I don't understand a few things."

Halora bolted from her chair. "Sure, why didn't you say that in the beginning?"

Immediately, she began to feel dizzy, she grabbed her head. The room was spinning. She was seeing two images of Richard and neither image was staying in place. The images kept hiding behind one another. She held onto the edge of her desk as the nausea came upon her. The same nausea forced her to grab her stomach. She turned in the nick of time to place her head over the trash can that sat near her desk. She began vomiting and showed no sign of stopping as black liquid emerged from her body.

Richard stood over his cousin and employee trying to soothe her by rubbing her back. By this time, Jorge had returned to his desk and heard his boss gagging. He rushed into the office and watched as whatever she had for breakfast mixed with the chocolate clusters gushed out of her body. He and

Richard both looked in horror and concern as Halora's body continued to jerk and her one last attempt to stand straight failed before she collapsed in Richard's arms. Richard held his unconscious employee in his arms, yelling for Jorge to call for an ambulance.

* * *

The ambulance beeped as an EMT worker backed the large utility vehicle under the emergency room parking deck. The driver rushed to open the rear door and assisted the second technician to lift the gurney carrying Halora from the utility vehicle to the ground. The man and woman team entered through a side entrance that was for medical personnel only. Overhead announcements could be heard, "Dr. Orlando Marshall, Dr. Orlando Marshall, please report to the emergency room stat. Dr. Orlando Marshall, Dr. Orlando Marshall, please report to the emergency room stat."

The gurney changed hands with a few on duty nurses. The staff wheeled Halora into a vacant room. Her clothes were now covered with black vomit. Richard was concerned that it was black, but Jorge informed him that she had eaten chocolate candy which was the reason the vomit was the color it was.

Dr. Marshall kept watching Halora's low blood pressure readings. The Isaiah Washington clone seemed concerned. He ordered test and blood work to be done ASAP.

"Did anyone speak with the next of kin to find out what happened?" he asked.

"Yes, Doctor, I spoke with her cousin. Her Grandmother and sister have not made it here yet," the nurse said. "Her cousin said she began feeling lightheaded at work. Then she began vomiting and collapsed," the nurse continued.

In the short time that Halora was his patient, Dr. Marshall watched as her blood pressure continued to drop. It got lower and lower. Her temperature read 106 degrees. She was burning up. Suddenly, she started convulsing.

"Get those tests back to me ASAP!" Dr. Marshall yelled again. "Call the intensive care unit and see if they have an available bed upstairs."

The charge nurse rushed to the nurse's station and called the Intensive Care Unit and confirmed an available bed. She returned to the closed room

and informed Dr. Marshall about the opening and the ICU floor was expecting his patient. She looked at Halora and noticed how young she looked. At the time, Halora was no longer having the convulsions, but she was still unconscious. In that short period, her body had begun to swell and she was no longer a size four, but an easy size twelve.

"Dr. Marshall, do you have any idea what type of illness we're dealing with?" the charge nurse asked.

"Not really, but it appears that she's had an allergic reaction to something. Maybe it was something she ate. The blood work will tell us more. But what I can tell by looking at her, this woman is very ill," he explained.

The transporters arrived to take Halora upstairs to the intensive care unit. As the two men headed toward the staff elevators, they had to pass Richard and Jorge standing in the hall. They realized that Halora wasn't alert as the tubes ran through her nose and various IV's were attached to both arms. They also noticed that she had swollen considerably in such a short period. Her stomach was as large as a nine month pregnant woman.

Richard placed his hand on the moving gurney. He stared at his cousin, "Dr. Marshall, what do we know so far?" he said.

"And you are?"

"I'm her cousin and she works for me. She became ill at work," Richard explained, "her Grandmother and sister should be arriving soon," he added. He looked at the clock on the wall and noticed that it had been thirty minutes since he had last spoke with his cousin Clara.

"They should have been here by now; I may need to give them another call," he said, before noticing his female cousins running frantically down the hall, stopping in the area where Dr. Marshall, Jorge and he were standing.

"What's going on with my grandbaby? Doctor is she going to be okay? I'm her Grandmother Clara London."

"How are you doing Ms. London? I'm Dr. Marshall, but known around here as *Dr. O.* I've been treating your granddaughter while she was in the emergency room. But since she doesn't have a Primary Care Physician, we have assigned her one. He is one of the best Internal Medicine Physicians we have on staff. I assure you that she's in good hands."

"Doctor *O,* I'm not concerned about that. What is wrong with my granddaughter?" Clara said with rudeness.

"Well Ma'am, we don't have any of the tests back yet. But I believe your granddaughter has had some type of allergic reaction."

Jorge added, "It's probably those chocolate candies she received today."

"Chocolate candy…what chocolate candy?" Clara asked.

"Somebody she knew sent her a gift basket and it had chocolate clusters in it."

"It couldn't have been the chocolate clusters. Obviously, it's someone who knew she loves those. She's been eating them for years," Clara informed those standing around.

Dr. O stood listening to the family members go back and forth about the chocolate candies. He looked from Clara to Jorge before interrupting their discussion, "Well I guess that rules out chocolate." Then he walked over to the nurses' desk and handed one of the nurses Halora's chart. He turned to the family standing near. "Folks, it was nice meeting you all, but Dr. Everett Peace will be the doctor taking over Ms. London's case."

After the physician walked away, Richard said aloud, "Dr. Orlando Marshall, I wonder is he related to the Marshall family that attended our church years ago." The name Orlando Marshall sounded familiar, but the person he was talking to didn't look nothing like the overweight teenager he remembered.

Richard walked over to his elder cousin attempting to console her. She was very upset. He led her to the waiting room. The setting reminded him of the time his father became ill and passed away. Actually, they were sitting in the same waiting area.

Hours later, the remainder of the family had arrived and filled the small waiting room. A Hispanic couple sat in the corner among people that they didn't know. They kept their attention towards the wall mounted television but it was obvious how nervous they were about being in the cramped quarters with so many people. Before long, they quietly gathered their belongings and left the room. Now, two hours had gone by and the same couple hadn't returned. The waiting room was now completely filled with the London and Lorde families.

Eloise sat next to her cousin, holding her hand. Clara was still crying. She went in to visit with her sick granddaughter only to see that she had swollen

more. Halora's hair hung wildly over her pillow. She was no longer sporting the long ponytail she loved. The nurses had to remove the extension to allow her to be more comfortable while she rested.

After reviewing the results of the test he had ordered, *Dr. O* informed the family that the test results all came back negative and admitted that Halora's condition was certainly a mysterious one. Nonetheless, he remained hopeful that he would find the reason for her illness. He furthered admitted that once he found what caused her sickness, they would know the type of treatment she should have.

More hours passed as the family sat waiting, and then they were finally greeted with a new development. The new development was that Halora had regained consciousness. She was weak, but she was able to recognize everyone and speak in a hushed manner.

People were coming in and out of Halora's small and crowded hospital room. The room was no bigger than her walk-in closet. But people continued to crowd in. Her throat was scratchy and it hurt when she coughed. She was a little confused and she had no clue *how* sick she was. She just knew she was sick. When Alma entered the room, Halora shyly asked her cousin to stay in the room with her. Afraid, Alma agreed with her cousin, but she really didn't want to. She thought her cousin was going to die and she didn't want to be in the room when she did. She tried hard to hide her thoughts and fears but her face kept holding nervous and scared expressions. Finally, she made herself sit down in an empty chair next to Halora's bed while trying to comfort her as best she knew how. She held her hand as they both listened to the constant beeping of the heart machine in Halora's room.

Halora didn't realize it, but while sitting next to her, the majority of the time, Alma kept her head down as she silently prayed to God for Him to turn this whole ordeal around.

"Am I going to die?" Halora said to her cousin.

Alma raised her head, but not really hearing what her young cousin had said, "Honey, did you say something?"

In a weak and feeble voice, Halora repeated her question, "Am I going to die?"

Alma stood to her feet and gave her cousin an encouraging smile. "No, honey you're going to be fine." She kissed her cousin's puffy face. She

brushed her hair. She kissed her forehead. She brushed her hair again, but this time causing a clump of hair come out in her hand. The incident shocked Alma with numbness, but concerned her more that Halora didn't flinch as the hair disconnected from her scalp. Discretely, she laid the patch of hair to the side, out of sight. The hair loss had made a visible bald spot.

"What is happening to me?" Halora continued to question Alma. She knew she didn't feel well and she knew her body felt weak. Even if she wanted to she couldn't lift her head from the pillow. In fact, her head pounded from a severe headache and her face was now feeling tight to her from the swelling.

"Honey, the doctor's are trying to figure that out. You will get well soon," Alma encouraged her young cousin.

"Why does my face feel so tight? Is my face swollen? Is there a mirror in here?" Halora questioned Alma more as the room continued to spin.

"Honey, I don't have a mirror. You don't need to be worrying about any of this. Just try to concentrate on getting better."

Halora ignored Alma, weakly she said, "Go ask the nurse to give you a mirror."

Alma looked at Halora and knew right away she didn't need to see an image of herself in a mirror. One, her face and body were swollen beyond belief and two, the big patch of missing hair from her head was far too noticeable. In a quick second, no longer worrying about the mirror, Halora began to slip in and out of consciousness.

"Halley…. Halley…Halley," Alma called out to her. Halora didn't respond. Alma slightly shook her cousin and the movement only caused her to partly open her eyes.

"I'm so tired. Can you close those blinds because that sun is so bright?"

Alma looked around the room and the blinds to the window were already closed. In that instance, she decided to leave the room to speak with one of the nurses. As she got to the door, a smile came to her face. She saw Mychael and first lady Monica about to enter the room. She spoke to them both as she kissed her pastor first and his wife second. She shared with them the latest information that was available to the family.

Mychael and Monica was dressed as if they were going to dinner with Mychael wearing a pair of brown slacks, a casual shirt under a brown

checkered blazer. Monica was dressed in a tan leather skirt and a matching tan cashmere sweater. She sported a pair of tan colored boots that stopped at her calves. She clutched with her fingers an expensive *Coach* handbag. As usual, her hair was gorgeous, flowing below her shoulders.

Alma stepped away from the two and angled toward the nurse's station. Mychael and Monica entered the room together. At first look, he turned to his wife. "It's hard to believe she was fine yesterday," he mentioned sympathetically.

"She was, wasn't she?" his wife said, responding to her husband.

Alma returned, only peeping her head far enough to say, "Pastor Dovely, can I see you for a moment?" Mychael continued to look into Halora's face. By this time, she was non-responsive. Then he turned from her bedside and walked away saying to his wife, "I'll be back in a second," before hurrying toward the door. Monica nodded her head in response to her husband as he and Alma disappeared from the door. She walked slowly over to the bed, placing her handbag on top of the empty serving table. She called out to Halora and she didn't get a response either. She touched her puffy hands and Halora didn't respond to her touch. Water uncontrollably flowed from Halora's eyes and mouth. It looked disgusting, but Monica didn't attempt to wipe any of it dry, instead, she wrinkled her mouth in disgust. She touched Halora's swollen face. She was cold as ice—again no response.

Monica noticed all the equipment she was attached to. She wasn't a doctor, but she was a registered pharmacist, making her familiar to some of the medications she saw hanging from the tall iron pole. She took notice of the branch of tresses lying on the table next to the bed then she looked at the bald area in Halora's head. Another large chunk came out in Monica's hands when she brushed her hand through Halora's hair also. She laid the second patch of hair on the table covering the first. She looked around the room and realized that she was still alone. She knelt down as if she were whispering a prayer to the deathly ill patient, her husband's church member. Then she whispered into Halora's ear, "Bitch, you should've thought twice about trying to seduce my husband!"

CHAPTER SIXTEEN

On this particular night, Christopher wasn't quite ready to go to sleep and he sat in his bedroom about to open the mysterious box he had received the week before. For the life of him, he couldn't imagine what could be in the box. He hadn't ordered anything and he kept asking himself, who would send him a package without a return address? A week had now passed and this was his first opportunity to open the package. He ripped at the moderately sized box that was covered with brown paper. The box had been secured really tight with clear tape. Somebody didn't intend for him to open the box so easily, Christopher thought.

The contents were sealed so tightly that Christopher had to remove himself from his bed to retrieve a box cutter from the kitchen drawer. Before returning to his room, he looked in all of the cabinets and the refrigerator in search of something to snack on. His mother really needed to go grocery shopping, he said to himself.

He returned to his room and sat on the bed again. Then he made a second attempt to open the carefully wrapped package. He kept thinking to himself that someone had taken a lot of time to make sure the contents of the box was going to be safe and secure. Anxiously, he wondered what was inside. Was it someone playing a trick on him or were the contents inside something special—maybe an expensive gift? He couldn't wait.

He slid the box cutter into the cardboard box and found the contents to be a stack of papers and the addresses of several people. He was confused as he shuffled through the papers, looking at the front and back sides of each. At first, he thought this was all a joke until he read the reports and realized

the information he was reading involved the investigation of Richard's late sister, Olivia and accordingly to his mother, his late aunt.

The report summary detailed a lot of information that he didn't recall being discussed with the Lorde family. The toxicology report indicated that there was a very small trace of labor inducing medication found in Libby's blood stream. He knew for a fact, this information was never disclosed to the family. However, the report did indicate that the trace wasn't great enough to be a reason for the cause of death of the deceased.

Christopher walked around his room as he read the pages one by one. He wondered as to why this box of information had been sent to him. He wasn't an investigator. He had no vested interest in the case involving Libby. At this point, he didn't even have a clue as to what he was going to do with the information he held in his hands. Maybe the postman delivered it to him by mistake? He grabbed the box and looked at it again from all sides. True enough, it was addressed to Mr. Christopher Christiansen, 123 Marble Drive, Ramblewood, South Carolina. At first, his mind thought about Investigator Martinez. He thought maybe he was playing tricks. His suspicion made him grab the phone from its base and dial the number for the downtown precinct. A female voice answered, "Ramblewood Police Department, Officer Lowe speaking, may I help you?"

"Ah, yes, may I speak with Investigator Kindness Martinez?" Christopher said, deepening his voice.

"I'm sorry sir, but Mr. Martinez has not worked at this precinct in over a year. He transferred to another precinct last year."

Christopher was really surprised. He wasn't aware that Martinez had moved. He knew he hadn't seen him around town or hadn't heard from the investigator, but moving was the last thing he suspected.

"Do you know where he transferred to?" Christopher asked knowing the woman probably wouldn't tell him, but he tried anyway. He was correct in his assumption.

"I'm sorry sir, but we are not at liberty to disclose the transferring locations of our investigators. For safety reasons, I'm sure you understand."

"Yes, I certainly do," Christopher agreed.

"Is there something else I can help you with? Maybe another investigator can assist you?"

"No thanks," Christopher said, disconnecting the call.

Christopher went to his nightstand and grabbed his address book. He flipped the pages to the *m* section and located Martinez's cell phone number. He never programmed the number in his own cell phone—he had no plans of ever using it. He said the number aloud so he could remember it as he dialed the ten digits.

"You've reached the voicemail of Amy Price. I'm away from my phone at this time. Please leave a message."

Not only had Martinez moved, he had also changed his cell phone number and the number now belonged to someone else. Puzzled, Christopher pressed his back against the headboard of his bed. He compared the numbers written in his address book to the numbers he had entered into the phone. They were the same. By this time, curiosity had gotten the best of him. Especially, trying to figure out the list he held in his hand. He didn't know any of the names and addresses of the people from North Carolina. Strangely, he wondered even more why he was sent a list of names and addresses without telephone numbers. *What was he supposed to do with this information? He thought to himself.* He had no idea, who was Myles Dovely? Who was Myra Dovely? And what did they have to do with the death of Olivia Lorde.

Christopher grabbed the phone again. He was thinking that he should probably share this information with Richard. Then he remembered how sarcastic Richard had become and realized his ex best friend had come too far in his grieving process to spring this type of information on him. And knowing Richard, he would probably think he was trying to be cute to pay him back for breaking things off.

Later, instead of playing a guessing game, Christopher decided he would probably have to pay Myles and Myra Dovely a visit. He stacked all the papers in order and was about to return them in the same box when he noticed two additional pieces of paper folded in half. He removed both pages from the box and began reading them. The top page was the first page of an adoption document and the second piece of paper was a birth certificate both concerning a Baby girl Dovely. It listed the birth mother as Joy Lynn Anderson and the birth father as unknown.

Christopher noticed that the page he held in his hand was actually the first

page of an adoption packet—one of ten pages. The first page read that an adoption transpired between Joy Lynn Anderson and Myra Dovely. The same page also stated that Myra Dovely was single, making Christopher wonder. From the documents, he had gained a general idea of who Myra Dovely was, but who was Myles Dovely? And why did Joy Lynn give her baby up for adoption?

Christopher returned all the pages neatly in the small box with the exception of the list with the addresses. He walked into the den where his mother sat watching television. He turned on the computer and logged onto the internet.

"Sister Clara's granddaughter is sick and they're saying it doesn't look good," Carolina said to her son.

"Who is Sister Clara?" Christopher answered, taking a moment to glance at his mother then turning his head back to face the seventeen inch computer screen.

"Mother Eloise's cousin—the older lady that joined the church last year. She moved here from up north after her granddaughter started working for Richard."

"W-h-a-t! Halley London?! What's wrong with her?" Christopher asked, turning around in his chair to look at his mother again.

"Nobody knows. She got sick at work and had to be rushed to the hospital. Every one of the tests they've run so far isn't revealing anything."

"Do you want to go with me to the hospital tomorrow?" His mother asked.

"No, I have something to do tomorrow."

"Like what?"

"*Mom*......That's personal."

"Okay....Okay, I didn't mean to invade your privacy."

"You're not invading my privacy, but some things are personal," Christopher explained to her. "Just let them know they are in my prayers," he added as he typed in the search engine the name and address from the list.

Immediately, the name, address and telephone number appeared for a Myles and Camille Dovely. Christopher typed in his home address and printed out the results for the directions to the North Carolina destination. He did the same for Myra Dovely, nothing came up. After he received what he needed, he shut down the computer and walked past his mother.

"Goodnight," he said to his mother returning to his bedroom.

CHAPTER SEVENTEEN

Concerned, Clara called the hospital before she arrived to be told that her granddaughter's condition had not changed. That was four hours ago. She and her Cousin Eloise were now walking into the waiting room about fifteen minutes before visiting hours. Eloise sat quietly, but Clara was anxious and nervous watching the other family's converse back and forth about the conditions of their respective loved ones.

Ten minutes later, an elderly volunteer, wearing a pink jacket, came into the waiting room. She called into the intensive care unit then one by one she informed family members that it was okay to go inside for visitation. From a list, in alphabetical order, she checked off each family name, omitting the *London* name, but never saying anything to Clara or Eloise.

Without confirming with the volunteer, Clara and Eloise assumed the woman had overlooked them and they both took the liberty of exiting the waiting room and entering the ICU ward, walking toward room six before a nurse stopped them from entering.

"Ladies, I'm sorry, but Dr. Peace is on his way and he doesn't want Ms. London to have any visitors until he can examine her," she said to Clara and Eloise at the same time.

Clara twisted her neck at Eloise, who was standing nearby. Eloise looked at Clara in return; Clara saw a worried expression appear on her cousin's face. She was also worried, but she tried to hide her fear better than her cousin did.

"But the volunteer called back here and they said it was okay for her to have visitors. I'm her grandmother and this is my sister. Has she taken a turn for the worse?" Clara said.

"I'm sorry... Ms. London, is it? I told the volunteer that all the family members could come back, except the family members for the patient in room six," the nurse explained then she continued, "Dr. Peace will be able to explain everything to you when he arrives. He should be here shortly. He said he was about twenty minutes away. If you don't mind, you can return to the waiting room and I will let him know that you are here," she said politely as she walked from behind the nurse's station.

By this time, Clara had taken all she could take. She was no longer able to hide her emotions. She buried her face in her hands, shaking her head from side to side. "Eloise, she's not going to make it," she said.

The same nurse, a caramel colored woman grabbed Clara by the shoulders. "Ms. London, my telling you that you can't see your granddaughter doesn't mean that she's not going to pull through this. I'm only sharing with you the orders of Dr. Peace. I'm sure he will explain his reasoning for all of this. If you lose your composure, you won't be any good for your granddaughter," the nurse said.

The nurse walked Clara toward the exit of the Intensive Care Unit. She turned to speak to Eloise, "Mrs. Lorde, sh—" Only having turned her back for a second, the nurse found Eloise sitting in a chair as another nurse fanned her. She had told the second nurse standing next to her that she felt like she was going to faint. "Mrs. Lorde, are you okay to return to the waiting room?" the younger nurse asked.

"I think so. Thank you darling, but Halora is like one of my own children."

"I understand Mother Lorde," the nurse said, referring to Eloise by her church title. She was familiar with the Lorde family and was a member of the Tabernacle of Praise. "Does Pastor Dovely know that Sister London is here?" she asked.

"Yes, he knows. In fact, he and the first lady came by the other day to visit her," Eloise said then she took a second look at the young woman. "Honey, I know you are a member of my church, but for some reason I can't remember your name," she added.

"I'm Claudette Mayweather. Deacon Mayweather is my father. I'm sure you know my son Ashton, he sings with the gospel choir."

Claudette was a large woman, slightly overweight with chocolate colored skin. She reminded you of the actress Mon'que. She had chubby cheeks and wore hair weave down to her shoulders. Today her face was covered with

123

make-up. She had on the full package—lipstick, eye shadow, mascara, and blush. The amount she was wearing today, any beauty sales consultant would be glad to see her coming.

Eloise had noticed Claudette earlier as she strutted from one room to the next. At the time she didn't recognize her. She also notice the scrubs she wore were tight and form fitting. Realizing that even though she was a large woman, she had a small waist line and her stomach was near flat. She saw that Claudette was carrying the majority of her weight in her buttocks and hips.

"Oh yes, I remember you now. You moved back to Ramblewood about a year ago. Shirley Mayweather is your sister, right?"

"Yes and that's why I understand your situation, I love my sister's children like they were my own," Claudette said, helping Eloise to sit down once they had reached the family waiting room.

"Mother, I told you and Cousin Clara to wait until someone could bring the two of you over here. You know the both of you together aren't worth two cents," Richard said, attending to his disoriented mother.

"Oh be quiet! I'm stronger than you give me credit for. I only got weak after I saw Clara falling apart," Eloise explained.

"Thank you ma'am," Richard told the nurse.

"No problem. We have other family members that do the same thing," the nurse informed him.

"These two are different," he said then he recognized the nurse. "Claudette? I almost didn't recognize you. I didn't know you worked in the intensive care unit. How long have you worked on this floor?" he said, now sharing a hug with the woman.

"It's been about six months now. I transferred from labor and delivery," she explained to Richard. "And I've been meaning to tell you, congratulations on your engagement," she added.

"Thank you, thank you, thank you," he said, happily. "Again, I am sorry for the inconvenience. These *two* Thelma and Louise characters are hard headed, knowing good and well, when one goes down, the other goes down," he said to Claudette. She laughed at his comment before walking away from the family, throwing her rear end from side to side until she had reached the nurse's station. The family could see her still laughing as she spoke to the other nurses.

* * *

Dr. Everett Peace walked into the Intensive Care Unit and walked directly to Halora's room. He entered the area and stepped back quickly. Halora was now three times her original size. There was tape holding her eyes shut and the way she looked, reminded Dr. Peace of the incredible hulk.

"Bring me the results from those tests. This is one of the most difficult cases I've ever seen. I have no idea what is going on with this woman. Why is she swelling like this?" he said to himself as he read the notes from the overnight shift then focusing his attention on the test results once again.

He removed the tape from Halora's left eye. When he tried to open it, he realized her eyeball had swollen and was on the verge of coming out of the socket. He looked at the night chart report again and scratched his head. Her eyes had been taped shut around midnight. *The notes on the chart said, eyeball coming out of socket and fluid draining heavily from eyes.*

He looked at his patient. He hated to tell the family that there was nothing more he could do. As he glanced through the entire chart, he noticed she was an organ donor. But as young as she was, her organs wouldn't be any good to anyone. He shook his head in defeat.

Then without warning, the brakes on the bed slipped and the bed collapsed almost to the floor. His patient's large body lifted slightly from the bed. The machines and monitors went tumbling to the floor all alarming at the same time. A doctor attending to a patient in the next room came rushing in along with three nurses.

"Stand those monitors up!" Dr. Peace yelled, scrambling to take Halora's pulse. "Call downstairs and tell them to send as many men to ICU as possible."

Within seconds, the unit was flooded with male nurses, men from environmental services and the cafeteria. They all surrounded the four hundred pound patient and on the count of three transferred her from one bed to another. The old bed was soiled with a black substance that had an unbearable odor.

The male helpers all left the room, holding their noses and covering there mouths. Since he wasn't finished examining his patient, Dr. Peace put on a

face mask, but the smell eventually made its way through the mask and into his nostrils. It even made its way into the hallway, making the nurses all scram for cans of disinfectant.

Halora remained unresponsive throughout the entire episode. She now had a shallow pulse and her heart rate was low. Dr. Peace regretted having to face such a loving family with this type of bad news. But they were entitled to know, he kept telling himself. He took a deep breath and walked into the waiting room.

"Good morning, Could I speak with the members of the London family?" he said, after he pulled the mask from his face.

Richard, Eloise and Clara stood to their feet and followed the doctor into the hall. The doctor was wearing a defeated look on his face. Truly, he hated to disclose such disappointing news to such a loving family.

"I'm sorry, but medically we have done all that we can do here at the Ramblewood Medical Center. Ms. London's condition remains a mystery to me and my colleagues. She is continuing to swell and it's a matter of time before her organs will shut down. If she has any children or other immediate family, I would suggest you contact them."

"Are you going to be okay?" Richard asked a speechless Clara. At this point she couldn't utter a word. All she was able to do was nod her head as tears escaped from her eyes.

"I'm sorry Ms. London; we really have tried everything medically here. We are going to keep her on the antibiotics and hope for the best. I do believe in the power of prayer. I will encourage you and your family to pray for a miracle."

Richard held onto his cousin with one hand and extended his free hand to the doctor. "Thank you for everything Dr. Peace. My family and I really appreciate it," Richard said.

Finally able to talk, Clara said, "thank you Dr. Peace. Is it okay for us to go in to see her?"

"Yes and Ms. London, I know this is your granddaughter, but you really need to brace yourself before you go in there. She doesn't look like herself. She has swollen more over night. All of her hair has come out and we are now draining this thick black fluid out of her body."

"Dr. Peace, do you know where this fluid is coming from?" Richard asked.

"No, we've sent it to the lab and the results produced nothing.

"Cousin Clara, are you sure you want to see her like this?"

"Yes, that's my grandbaby and I want to be with her until the end. But let me get myself together first," Clara said aloud.

"Dr. Peace, how long does she have?" Eloise asked.

"Possibly, twenty-four to forty-eight hours," Dr. Peace estimated.

After seeing her granddaughter, Clara returned to the waiting room and sat down quietly. She grabbed her purse with her daughter's telephone number. She wasn't in any condition to talk to anyone, so she gave the number to Richard, and asked him to contact her daughter to explain Halora's condition. Clara instructed Richard to give her daughter Virginia one option and that option was for her to get on the next flight to South Carolina. Richard took the paper Clara had given him as he held onto her directive in his head. He walked out into the hall to use his cell phone in private.

Clara took a few moments to close her eyes and to say a silent prayer to God. She knew God was able to do anything miraculous and she was not about to doubt Him now. She opened her eyes as a woman dressed in old rags came and sat between her and Eloise. They both looked at the woman when the scent from her rear-end traveled into their nostrils. Clara just stared at the woman, but Eloise fanned her hand in front of her face to rid her nose of the smell. The woman seemed friendly and hadn't noticed that her body odor had offended the two women. She smiled like nothing had happened.

"How ya'll doing?" the woman said.

"Fine, thank you." Clara replied, now eyeing the homeless looking woman from head to toe.

"That young gal in there belongs to you, I suppose?"

"Yes, that's my grandbaby, why?" Clara answered.

"My husband is here also. The nurse let me go and pray with your granddaughter," the woman said. She paused and waited until the third family had left the room before she continued. The only people present in the room now were Eloise, her, and Clara.

"There's an evil spirit in that room. Your granddaughter has become the victim of voodoo. Somebody has put a *hex* on her," the woman told them.

"Ma'am, how do you know this for sure?" Clara asked, showing an interest in what the woman was saying.

"That odor... that odor is the smell of voodoo. If you don't mind, I can give you something to help fight the evil she's come in contact with."

Clara and Eloise's eyes followed the woman's hand into a large bag that sat between her legs then watched as she pulled out a mason jar full of a yellow liquid. She handed the jar to Clara, who could smell the odor as soon as the woman removed it from the bag, it made her twist her nose and lips before saying, "And what am I supposed to do with this?"

The woman watched the door. "Hopefully, it's not too late for you granddaughter. Tell the nurses that you want to rub her down in this. And in twenty four hours you should see a turn-around. If she doesn't pull through after twenty four hours, the voodoo has consumed the body."

Eloise wasn't asking any questions. She was scared. It always unnerved her when people spoke about black magic, hexes or voodoo. Even though she knew that these type of things happened, it still made her uneasy.

"Clara, do you believe in this mess? I don't think you should be engaging in stuff like that," Eloise finally said as Richard reentered the waiting room. He only heard the end of the conversation, so he decided to keep quiet. He let the two cousins continue to exchange words between each other.

"You wouldn't. It's not your granddaughter," Clara said, sharply.

"Clara Bell, that's not what I mean. You should let God work this out." The woman interrupted Eloise. "The liquid will not serve its purpose if those around you don't have faith," she said, directing her statement to Eloise.

Clara lifted herself from the place where she was sitting. She waited a few moments for Eloise, who didn't move. Waiting a few more seconds, Clara said to her, "Eloise, are you going to help me or what?"

"No Clara, I can't help you this time. But I'll be here praying for Halora," Eloise said, staying in her seat.

Clara took the yellow liquid and walked out of the waiting room, down the hall and into the Intensive Care Unit. She walked up to the nurse's station and made her request known to the two women sitting in front of her. The woman she addressed didn't give her any argument. In fact, she gave her the few white towels she had requested.

Back in the waiting room, Eloise was still sitting with her legs crossed as her son sat next to her. She looked at him in disgust. She wasn't disgusted with him but she was indeed disgusted. She shook her head from side to side.

She looked at her son again. Her high blood pressure gauged between her anger for the strange looking woman and her cousin.

"Now isn't that some *shit*," Eloise said, obviously upset at her cousin's course of action.

Trying to change the subject, Richard said, "I got in touch with Cousin Virginia and she said she's taking the first flight out." He waited a few moments then he added, "Mother, Cousin Clara feels this is her only hope. You can't control the actions of people... I keep trying to tell you that."

"The *hell* I can't!" Eloise said removing herself from the spot she was sitting in. The strange woman didn't comment, but stole glances at Eloise from the opposite side of the room.

Eloise began walking toward the waiting room exit. Richard called out to his mother. Eloise turned to face her son and caught the homeless looking woman staring at her again. Before she answered her son, she said to the woman, "What the *hell* are you looking at?"

"Nothing ma'am," the woman said, sounding a little frightened. "I don't mean you any harm," she added.

"Ma'am, please excuse my mother's behavior," Richard said, begging the woman's pardon.

Clara entered her granddaughter's room and closed the door behind her. She braved herself as she started her sponge bath. It was heartbreaking; the person she was bathing didn't look anything like the baby she had once cradled. She didn't look like the child that fell asleep on her lap every night. She didn't even look like the child that was afraid of the dark until she was fifteen.

Clara started the bath beginning with her granddaughter's arms. Then she moved to her chest, stomach and legs. She bypassed her feet—they were bandaged because they had split wide open. Clara stared at her granddaughter's legs as she shook her head in sadness. Then she finished her task by dabbing the yellow liquid around Halora's face.

In her mind, Clara Bell kept realizing that her granddaughter didn't resemble the beautiful and vibrant young woman she once was. Her head was now completely bald. Her finger and toe nails had all fallen from their nail bed and her entire body was now black as coal.

At this point, the only thing that remained the same was the radio Pandora

had placed in her sister's room. The radio was playing gospel music over Halora's head. At that moment, *"Incredible God, Incredible Praise,"* by Youthful Praise was echoing lightly through the speakers.

Quietly, Eloise walked into Halora's room as Clara was closing the top to the mason jar of yellow liquid. She stretched her eyes and immediately grabbed her nose. Clara could tell from the way Eloise reacted that she couldn't bare the smell of the liquid she was using. Eloise didn't get a chance to say anything to her cousin before scramming out of the room, still covering both her nose and mouth.

CHAPTER EIGHTEEN

Christopher arrived in North Carolina around noon. It was Saturday and he really hated using his weekend to investigate a matter that really didn't involve him. Driving cautiously, he weaved in and out of the Charlotte traffic before bearing off onto the downtown exit according to his directions. He cruised through downtown and was surprised to see the attractive business building bearing the granite name Lorde & Lorde, Attorneys At Law. He had to admit, he was impressed by what he saw. He thought about stopping and speaking to the two brothers and according to his mother, his uncles, but he didn't want to run the risk of them mentioning his visit to Richard.

He drove along a little more and the further he traveled, the more congested the traffic became. He didn't think he would ever make it to his destination. It seemed to him like he was stopping at every traffic light and turning at every corner. He drove a while longer eventually escaping the downtown traffic as the scenery changed from tall buildings and four traveling lanes to trees and two lane roads. After driving another twenty minutes, he was finally turning into a small and secluded suburban subdivision.

The mysterious box had now made Christopher more curious than he wanted to be and his curiosity made him determined to put this puzzle together. Prior to the trip, he decided he was going to pretend to be an adoption advocate, who was conducting a follow up visit concerning the adoption of baby girl Dovely.

A fraction after one o'clock, Christopher was pulling into the driveway of an average size ranch style home. There were two cars in the driveway. A bucket of water was sitting next to the smaller vehicle and a green water

hose was spread across the yard. He didn't know who was responsible, but somebody was wasting a considerable amount of water. He noticed as the water flowed freely from the hose into the street.

He grabbed the manila folder marked baby girl Dovely and eased out of his rental car. He was ready to make his bogus investigation work and he knew he had to make a believable effort to be professional. His intention prompted him to create a few business cards to make his identity as Jason Brooks seem credible. At least, he thought it was a smart idea, even if it possibly wasn't.

He walked up the concrete driveway when a middle age man appeared from the side of the house angling toward the front yard. Christopher was greeted with a giant smile. He didn't know who the man was and was pretty sure the gentleman he was facing didn't know him. Whoever he was, he seemed friendly.

Myles sat the second bucket he was holding in his hand on the ground then turned off the water supply flowing through the green hose. He shook hands with the person that introduced himself as Adoption advocate Jason Brooks. Immediately he asked to see his business card. He flipped it front and back, examining it thoroughly to see if it was authentic. Apparently, he was satisfied. After the short exchange, he opened up like the *red sea* before inviting his visitor inside his home. Prior to the invite inside, Myles had already given Christopher more information than he had expected.

The house smelled clean. It was neatly organized. Right away, Christopher noticed all the awards that aligned the wall. Obviously, Myles was the president of the Omage-Omage fraternity. He had a separate award for all his years of services as president.

The two men sat at a moderate sized kitchen table as Myles continued to speak without taking a breather. During their conversation, Christopher listened as Myles informed him that less than a year before his sister had died of ovarian cancer. Then, Myles left the room for a few seconds and returned with an eight by ten photo of his attractive late sister. The woman Christopher saw was beautiful, but most glamour shot photos are. The features the Star Jones clone held were similar to those of her brother.

Myles explained to the person he thought was an adoption advocate that his sister had found out years ago that she couldn't have children and she

decided to adopt. The only problems she faced were the fact that she was single and she had been diagnosed with stage three ovarian cancer. Myles explained further that when his late sister decided to give up hope of becoming a parent; a young woman, miraculously came forward, offering a baby girl.

"How old was the baby she adopted?" Christopher asked, as he jotted down a few notes. He had to remain believable.

"The baby was a newborn from my understanding. Shouldn't you have all this information Mr. Brooks?" Myles asked.

"Well, actually I should. But the last adoption advocate kept poor notes and was unorganized. Basically, I have to start from scratch. As a matter of fact, the only information I could find about the adoption was the first page of the entire adoption document," Christopher explained, also realizing at the same time that Mr. Dovely was a sharp individual. He pulled from a manila folder the front page he had received with the mysterious package. Myles took the paper in his hand and read it.

"Actually, I have a copy of the entire adoption packet. My sister had it in her safe deposit box. I only have a copy though…I gave the original to my cousin. He's the one who now has custody of the child. My sister arranged for him and his wife to rear the child in the event she wasn't able to beat the ovarian cancer," Myles mentioned.

"That's strange. Why didn't she arrange for you to care for the child since you lived here in Charlotte?" Christopher quizzed, becoming comfortable in his fictional role.

Myles smiled before he spoke, "Well, Mr. Brooks, that wasn't an option. My daughter and son are grown and both my wife and I travel extensively, me with my job as a district manager and my wife with her employer. We just didn't have the time to raise a young child. I'm sure my sister would have wanted her daughter to stay here in Charlotte, but since she trusted our cousin like a brother, she decided to give custody to him. And quite frankly, I didn't have a problem with her arrangement," Myles said, smiling again slightly. He held his sister's picture in his hand subconsciously and glanced several times at the smiling woman. A couple of times, he even traced the frame with his finger before sitting the picture to the side.

"If you don't mind me asking, what company do you work for?" Christopher asked off the subject.

133

"I'm a district manager for a women's apparel chain." Myles answered. "Now if you don't mind me asking, what does that question have to do with this adoption?" Myles said.

"No particular reason, I was just curious," Christopher explained mildly.

Next, Myles removed himself from his seat and disappeared into another room. He was gone for more than five minutes before returning with a ten page document in his hand. He handed the copied pages to Christopher and allowed him to scan the document, settling on the last page. The page read, contact information of the birth mother was an address in Ramblewood, South Carolina and employment information of the birth mother was the Ramblewood Gynecology & Obstetrics. The document also had the full name of the adopted baby, it was Hannah Marina Dovely and it was signed by Joy Lynn Anderson.

"Do you think this paperwork will help you get up-to-date?" Myles asked.

"I believe they will get me more than up-to-date," Christopher announced. He nodded his hand up and down as he scanned the pages again. "If you don't mind, can I take this with me to make a copy at the office and I promise to send the original back to you?" he asked, waiting for a response from Myles.

Mission accomplished Christopher thought to himself, when Myles agreed for him to take the papers with him. Maybe Myles wasn't as sharp as he had thought. Who would allow a complete stranger to take such an important document and trust that person to return the original? If it were him, Christopher knew that he wouldn't have released the documents so freely. However, Christopher realized it wasn't his place to understand why Myles was so naïve and he didn't intend to waste anymore of his time. In the event, he had a chance to think about what he had done and change his mind.

Christopher rose quickly from his seat and clasped hands with Myles. "I really do appreciate you taking the time to speak with me, Mr. Dovely."

"It was my pleasure. I wish you could have met my wife and our daughter. Actually, my daughter is the evening news anchor for Channel 4 Action News. You may have heard of her, Tamara Dovely? Unfortunately, she and my wife are at the mall shopping today," he said.

Myles walked Christopher outside and to his car. The two men shook

hands again. In many ways, Christopher thought he resembled Mychael, except his hair had more gray than his cousin, plus he had a neatly trimmed gray mustache and goatee. He was light-skinned, a shade lighter than Mychael. He was tall and slender and even had a lazy eye similar to his cousin. The two relatives definitely had similar features and it was quite obvious they were related.

"I'm sorry that I didn't get a chance to meet your wife and daughter. I probably won't need to come back because it appears that baby girl Dovely is doing fine," Christopher said,

Christopher opened the door and got into his rental car then he put the gear in reverse. He eased out of the driveway as he watched Myles brandish a smile similar to his Cousin Mychael. On the drive home, Christopher simmered over all the information that he had received from his investigation. But how was he going to use it to figure out this mystery? He tried to play around with the information in his head, but he was having a hard time trying to keep it all together. It was obvious the daughter that Mychael and Monica were raising was adopted by a woman named Myra and Myra was Myles' sister and Mychael's first cousin. But how did Joy Lynn fit into the picture? Richard never mentioned that when he met his fiancée that she was pregnant. Surely if she was, he would have noticed, Christopher thought.

In the middle of the highway, Christopher slammed on brakes. "Oh my Goodness!" he said aloud, also hitting the steering wheel. "Joy Lynn worked for Ramblewood Gynecology and Obstetrics and she and Monica are cousins. She must have told Monica that Olivia was pregnant," Christopher continued talking to himself. "I'm willing to bet you that Hannah is Libby's daughter and Joy Lynn had something to do with Libby's death. Maybe she's the one who took the baby." Christopher paused, before saying, "Richard is not going to believe this and Mychael probably doesn't even know that he is caring for his *own* daughter and he's sure to be shocked to find this out," Christopher thought.

CHAPTER NINETEEN

Parishioners were all standing around fellowshipping with one another as Sunday school was finishing up and worship services were about to begin. Today was communion Sunday and the missionaries and female choir members were all dressed in off white dresses and the male choir members and church officers were all covered in black suits.

"Honey, I love that outfit. Where did you get it from?" Eloise asked her daughter.

"I ordered it from a catalog a few months ago. I ordered Eleanor one too."

Alma was wearing an off-white ankle length skirt and a matching jacket. She had on a pair of off white shoes with a clear three inch heel. She moved her feet from side to side to show her mother the style of her whole shoe.

"Why didn't you tell me about the outfit? I would have ordered one," Eloise said, still admiring the ensemble.

"Mother please, you don't wear this kind of stuff. I'm sure you ordered the outfit you're wearing months ago. Besides, what I'm wearing didn't cost five hundred dollars."

While the mother and daughter were talking, one of the Deaconesses passed the two women, grabbing Eloise by the hand and pressing her face against hers, "Sister Eloise, you sure are wearing that dress. You don't look a day over thirty," the missionary said.

Honestly, Eloise didn't look a day over thirty. At times, people had to look twice when they saw her and her daughters shopping in the mall—she looked as put together as her two younger offspring.

Today, she was really wearing her two-piece off white outfit. The skirt

stopped just above the knee and flared like a poodle skirt, minus the poodle, and the jacket fitted comfortably over the waistline of the skirt. At first glance, you could easily mistake the two piece outfit for a dress, but it was actually two separate pieces. She wore flesh colored hosiery and off white heels that strapped around the ankles.

She propped her hands on her hips, embarrassed, yet flattered, "Ya'll young people keep me on my toes," she remarked, pointing her finger at the recently installed missionary. She smiled as the woman walked away before returning to the conversation with her daughter. By this time, her daughter Eleanor had walked up.

Eleanor exchanged kisses with her mother also wearing an exact replica of the dress her sister had on.

Seeing her second daughter dressed, Eloise was now truly jealous as she gave her daughter a once over look.

"Baby, you and your sister really look nice today. I'm *so* jealous. How much did you say the dress cost?" Eloise said while inquiring about the price.

"I didn't. But it cost $89," Alma answered.

"Oh yeah, you're right. My body would break out in hives if I wore that type of cheap material," their mother said, laughing.

"See…that's what I'm talking about. Oh, there's Sister Monica," Alma noticed.

Eloise turned to face the first lady as she walked down the center aisle. She was shocked to see her dressed in a soft pink skirt and matching jacket. The jacket and skirt were form fitting and it didn't appear that the first lady had on a slip—her business was no longer her business. Eloise thought to myself, *has she forgotten today is communion?* She didn't give it a second thought as she returned to face her daughters.

"Did you get a chance to go by the hospital yesterday to check on Halora?" Eloise asked, directing her question to Alma.

"Yeah, I sat up there for two visitations. But I didn't get a chance to see her. Claudette said nothing had changed and I called this morning and she said again her condition was still the same," Alma informed her mother.

"Lawd have mercy, my poor cousin is going to have a fit, if that child doesn't pull through. She's hoping some yellow liquid a *bum* gave her is going to cure the girl," Eloise said.

"What yellow liquid?" Alma asked.

"I don't know what it was. It looked like *piss* and smelt like sh—" Eloise said to Alma, covering her mouth after realizing where she was.

"Mother, what are you talking about?"

"Chile I will fill you in later. Church is getting ready to start. Where is your brother?"

"He's probably on his way."

At the same time, Monica walked up with little Hannah in hand. "Hey *Nana*," the toddler said to Eloise.

"Hey Buttercup," Eloise said, lifting Hannah into her arms. "How are you?"

Eloise looked at Monica again from head to toe. She thought she was going to be able to ignore how she was dressed. Before she knew it, a comment almost left her tongue, but she fought with herself not to say anything. With Hannah in her arms, she slid into her seat, leaving enough room at the end of the pew for only the first lady.

With only moments to spare before worship service, Monica left Hannah behind to go over to speak to her own mother and her Aunt Mary Agnes. On her way back to her seat, she bumped into her cousin Joy Lynn. The two spoke briefly with Joy Lynn reminding her about the photo shoot of her in her wedding dress along with the wedding party.

Also during their conversation, Monica invited Joy Lynn to sit next to her. She entered the pew first and realized right away there wasn't enough room for her and Joy Lynn. She stood close to a sitting Eloise. At first, she looked at Joy Lynn then she smiled at the former first lady before saying, "Mother Eloise, do you mind moving over a little?"

Coldly, Eloise responded, "As a matter of fact I do. She's not a deaconess nor is she a missionary. She shouldn't be sitting in this section."

Joy Lynn looked at the serious expression on Eloise's face and the way she rocked back and forth while holding Hannah in her arms. Then she looked at Monica as she said to Eloise, attempting to be friendly, but more sarcastic, "Well good morning to you too Mother Eloise."

"Morning," Eloise said, glancing quickly at her future daughter-in-law. "And I'm not your mother," she added, under her breath, reaching for the toy Hannah had dropped on the floor.

Although Eloise had spoke her comment in a soft tone, Joy Lynn still heard her loud and clear. She backed out of the pew and mouthed to Monica, "I'll see you after service."

In a state of shock, Monica sat down slowly trying hard to ignore the former first lady. She pretended to be playing with Hannah, who was sitting in her *Nana's* lap and enjoying every moment of it. Eloise continued to rock the toddler back and forth unable to hold her peace any longer, she said, "First lady Monica, why did you come to church dressed like that?"

"What do you mean? I purchased this outfit a week ago," Monica said.

"Do you know what today is?" Eloise asked her.

"Of course I do. It's Sunday."

"Its communion Sunday and you are dressed like you're going to a street party. Have you noticed that every female in this church is dressed in off white, even your mother and aunts are dressed in off white, in fact, everyone is dressed appropriately, except for you and what's her face?"

"Mrs. Lorde, with all do respect this is hardly a party dress and my cousin's name is Joy Lynn."

"You need to go home and change before communion. You still have time if you leave now," Eloise advised Monica.

"I'm not going all the way home just to change my dress," Monica said, giving Eloise word for word.

Eloise turned her head toward Monica. "I'm not asking you, I'm telling you that you need to take your role as first lady a little more serious. A day like today is not something you forget. Now get your keys and skedaddle on home," Eloise said, motioning her hand for Monica to get going.

Monica settled on the seat more, pulling at her form fitting attire. "I'm not going home. I'm sorry if you have a problem with my suit. I'm comfortable taking communion in this outfit," she said.

A few moments of silence rested between the two women.

"Oh goodness, I need to run to the ladies room right quick. Could you hold Hannah until I get back?" Eloise announced aloud.

Monica didn't answer. She didn't even look at Eloise. She just held out her hands to receive her adopted daughter. Hannah exchanged from one hand to another and Eloise brushed the wrinkles out of her skirt and disappeared through the door entering the fellowship hall. Ten minutes

passed and she was returning to her slightly warm seat. She extended her hands to receive Hannah, but Monica out right ignored her.

"She's fine. You should concentrate on the communion services to make sure everything goes well," Monica said.

Eloise laughed at the first lady's comment. Then she folded her arms across her stomach and watched as the choir prepared to begin the morning processional.

A few minutes later, Mychael appeared in the doorway. He was trying to get his wife's attention, but she was looking straight ahead. One of the missionaries sitting behind her tapped her on the shoulder and Monica turned her head to face the woman, who then pointed toward her husband. Mychael waved his hand for her to come to him. Instead of giving Hannah to Eloise, she laid her comfortably on the empty padded pew in front of them. She got out of her seat and went to speak with her husband, who could tell she wasn't happy. In fact, she wasn't smiling—compliments of Eloise. Mychael greeted his wife with a smile, but Monica maintained her frown. When she got within arms reach of him, her husband gently grabbed her by the hand and pulled her through the double doors. The two could be seen talking from a distance.

Moments later, Monica returned in a haste grabbing Hannah with one arm and her handbag and diaper bag in the other. She didn't say one word to Eloise, but glared at her, before walking off. Her looks didn't bother Eloise and the fact that she was upset didn't phase her either. She was going to teach her to be the best first lady she could be, one way or the other.

Soon, the choir marched into the choir loft and Mychael entered the pulpit. He was wearing a brand new off-white robe, a garment that Eloise had recently purchased for him to wear on communion Sundays.

"Good morning, blessed people of God!" Mychael stated.

"Good morning," the congregation yelled at him in unison.

CHAPTER TWENTY

"That Eloise Lorde is a *nasty* bitch, isn't she? She's just a busy body," Joy Lynn said about her future mother-in-law.

"A gray haired one if you ask me. I don't understand her logic of complaining to *my* husband about *my* outfit and I can't believe Mychael had the nerve to follow her up," Monica said still angry at both Eloise and Mychael.

"I saw you when you got up and went out of the sanctuary, what did he say to you?" Joy Lynn said.

"He told me that I needed to go home to change my outfit and I told him that if I left I was staying home."

"And what did he say when you told him that?"

"You know my husband...he thinks that he can give you a kiss and everything will be fine."

"How did you get home, I thought you rode with him?" Joy Lynn quizzed.

"I walked. Joy......have you forgotten we only live around the corner from the church?"

"Oh, that's right."

Truly, Monica was still upset with the disturbance Eloise had caused in her marriage. She felt the former first lady had no right to question her about the clothes she chose to wear. While simmering in her anger, she declared she was not going to tolerate it. The former first lady may have bossed around her own family and possibly Mychael, but she was not going to tell her what to do—under no circumstance.

"I know one thing. She should've put the same time and energy into

keeping a leash on that *slut* of a daughter of hers. That's the one she should've been mothering," Monica said to her cousin.

She was still a little heated and showed no signs of calming down. As soon as her husband walked through that door, he was going to get it—literally. She felt like she knew her husband well enough that if he even thought about eating Sunday dinner with the Lorde family, he knew he would certainly be in hot water.

After worship service, Mychael decided to skip going by Eloise's for Sunday dinner. It was tempting, but he declined. She reminded him that she had made all of his favorites, but he still declined her offer a second time. His decision was difficult because her cooking was the only home cooked meal he ever received and even though her offer seemed very tempting, he knew his priorities were at home, making amends with his wife.

Mychael didn't know why, but he felt uneasy about Monica storming out of church after he suggested that she change her clothes. It crossed his mind that his wife looked very attractive in the outfit, even with Eloise not thinking that her outfit was befitting for a first lady. Especially, to wear that color and to wear an outfit that was so form fitting on communion Sunday.

During their conversation, Monica had informed Mychael that she would not return if she left worship services to go home. He heard what she had said to him, but he didn't believe what she had said. He learned later on, she meant every word of her ultimatum because when he looked at the seat next to Eloise, he found the space empty of his wife and their toddler daughter. At this point, he had no idea what he would face once he made it home.

Mychael arrived home and entered a quiet house. He didn't hear the sound of the television or the radio. He saw Joy Lynn's car parked outside—so he knew someone was there. He called out to his wife—she didn't answer. He removed his suit jacket and laid it on the sofa. He grabbed his tie and pulled it away from his neck. Then he entered the bedroom to find Monica sitting Indian style on their bed. She was not dressed in the soft pink outfit she was wearing earlier that morning. She was now covered in powder blue sweat pants and a similar powder blue sweat jacket. Her hair was pulled behind her ears and she gripped a wad of white tissue in her hand.

Joy Lynn was sitting on the same side of the bed. Quickly, she sprung from her position and touched her cousin on the leg. "*Monnie*, I'm going to go. I'll call you later to tell you about the photo shoot."

Monica nodded her head then she wiped her face of tears. Joy Lynn glanced at her cousin's husband as she passed him. "Mychael."

"Joy."

Soon after, the front door slammed. Mychael sat in the same space that Joy Lynn had sat in prior to him. He pulled his shoes from his feet, then…

"You really missed a good service. I hate you decided not to come back," he said.

Monica didn't say a word—she continued to wipe tears from her eyes.

"Are you going to give me the silent treatment or are you going to act like an adult?"

Mychael had angered his wife earlier, but he had really hit a nerve with his current comment. As soon as Monica heard what Mychael had said, she jumped from the bed and stormed out of the room. Mychael followed her to the foyer now wearing only his slacks and a t-shirt. He grabbed her arm. "*Monnie*, what's the matter? Why are you crying?"

Monica wiped her eyes again. "Mychael you embarrassed me," she finally said.

"Embarrassed you, how?"

"When Mother Eloise told you that I should go home. Instead of defending me, you agreed with her idea that I should leave the service and change my clothes," she explained.

"Oh, baby, you're reading this all wrong. Mother Eloise only has the church's image in mind," he said, pulling his wife's face up with his hand. He moved her hair away from her face. He kissed her on the nose. He kissed her cheek then her lips. "What's really going on? I know you're not getting all worked up because Mother Eloise suggested that you change outfits. Tell your husband what's the real problem."

Monica didn't say anything.

"Do you want to talk about it?" Mychael continued to inquire.

Monica shook her head that she didn't. Mychael lifted her head again to face him and kissed his wife on the lips. "I'm sorry if you thought I embarrassed you. Do you forgive me?"

His wife nodded her head. She was no longer upset, but for some reason she couldn't stop crying. She didn't want to argue, nor did she want to slap her husband anymore, but the tears were running out of her like a broken

faucet. Instead of standing in front of her husband looking foolish, she moved from the foyer where they were standing and entered the family room—there she sat in quietness.

Mychael walked in the opposite direction and returned to their bedroom to finish changing his clothes. After changing clothes, he walked into the family room holding a pair of athletic shoes. He was now wearing a matching nylon jogging suit. He sat across from his wife as he slid his feet into his shoes. He watched as his wife continued to sit in silence. "Do you want to go out to get something to eat?"

"No, I'm going to fix something later," she answered.

"Well I'll pick up something on the way back. I promised Sister Clara that I would come to the hospital and have prayer with her granddaughter."

"I wish you wouldn't go to that hospital to see her," Monica suggested, primarily because she still hated Halora for trying to seduce her husband.

"But why? Baby she's one of my members, I have to."

"Mychael, did you forget how she tried to seduce you?" Monica reminded him.

"I know and I hate it happened, but I can't control the actions of people. Besides, if I should say so myself, if I were her—I would try to seduce me too," Mychael said, laughing. Monica didn't laugh with him mostly because she failed to see the humor in his statement.

Mychael moved from his seat to sit next to his wife. He moved closer to her than she would have liked. He kissed her again on the cheek. He kissed her on her neck. Then he rubbed his hand in places that aroused her. He wanted to make love to the woman he found to be very sexy.

At first, Monica moved her head from side to side, enjoying the wet kisses her husband gave. She returned each kiss with as much passion as her husband had given to her. He pulled at the zipper to her jacket. "No Mychael, I'm not in the mood," she said.

"Come on baby, I'll get you in the mood," he said, continuing to pull at her jacket. He pulled her head back and sucked on her neck. It felt good. Monica really didn't want him to stop.

"Come on, let's go to the bedroom," he said seductively, breathing heavily. He lifted his wife into his arms and carried her to their bedroom. He laid her down on the bed and pulled his own jacket off his body, dropping it on the floor.

He massaged with his hands every inch of his wife's body. She moaned. They kissed and bumped and grinned into one another. Then she stopped.

"I can't do this. I'm just not in the mood," she said.

"Are you serious?"

"I'm just *not* in the mood," Monica repeated again.

"Monica, I can't believe you just did this," Mychael said, jumping from the bed, grabbing his jacket from the floor. He stared at his wife for a few moments, but decided not to argue with her. Instead, he picked up his keys and cell phone from the dresser. As he walked toward the front door, he heard his wife declare how sorry she was. He didn't stop. He didn't even look back. At this point, he didn't care how sorry his wife was. He got into his car and sat in disbelief. He looked down and saw that his manhood was still noticeable. He placed his car in reverse and looked over his shoulder as he backed out of the driveway. He drove down the road headed out of the subdivision when he grabbed his cell phone in his hand. He began dialing a memorized set of ten digit numbers. A familiar voice answered.

"Where are you?"

"Why?"

"I need to see you."

"Where are we going to go?"

"The Marriott on Main Street—it's about thirty minutes away. You go ahead and get the room. Call me with the room number and I'll come up behind you."

"Tell me where it is again."

"It's the Marriott on Main Street!"

"Okay, you don't have to yell. I'm getting on the interstate now. Bye."

* * *

Later that evening, Monica answered the phone and on the other end was her Aunt Agnes. She was calling because she didn't know what was going on with Beatrice. She explained to her niece that her daughter was sitting on the toilet in severe pain and wanted to see if she could come over to take a look at her. True enough, Monica was a registered Pharmacist, but her aunt thought that was on the same level as a doctor.

Monica grabbed a cranky Hannah and rushed a few houses up the street. She entered the house to find her Cousin Beatrice now lying on the living room sofa. Before taking notice of her cousin, she looked around her aunt's junky house…well it was beyond junky—it was filthy.

Next, she looked at Beatrice who was wearing a blouse and the other part of her body was covered in a white sheet. At the time, the only person home with her was her mother and she didn't have a clue what to do. In a calm manner, Monica handed Hannah to her aunt and she sat in a chair next to Beatrice. First, she felt Beatrice's head for a temperature and realized that she didn't have one.

"Bea, where does it hurt?" Monica asked her.

"My stomach, I'm having severe pains at the bottom of my stomach. I think it could be possible food poisoning. I ate from a Chinese buffet last night."

After feeling Beatrice's head, Monica took her hand and poked around the bottom of her cousin's stomach. Right away, she knew something didn't feel right about her cousin's large abdomen—it was too firm and had far too many stretch marks. As she went to pull Beatrice's shirt over her belly, Beatrice screamed as she fought to keep Monica from lifting the blouse.

"Bea, are you pregnant?" Monica asked, wrestling with the muscles in her face.

"Pregnant?!" Agnes repeated what she had heard her niece say.

"No, it's food poisoning. I'm not having sex," Beatrice exclaimed.

"Girl, stop lying, you are pregnant. You're in labor. Aunt Agnes dial 9-1-1 to get an ambulance," Monica instructed, still trying to keep from laughing. She knew she couldn't travel along with them to the hospital because she didn't have anyone to keep Hannah and she was determined not to call Eloise, who she knew would have gladly kept Hannah. Instead, she tried several times to reach her husband on his cell phone, but all of his calls went directly to his voicemail.

At the same time, Agnes and Beatrice were now arriving at the Ramblewood Regional Medical Center emergency room. Agnes was fuming. If she had been a firecracker, she would have exploded. She ranted as the nurses rushed her daughter from the emergency room to labor and delivery. If she had the time she needed, she would beat her daughter aside

the head just as the baby was coming out of her. But she realized she didn't have time to beat or curse her daughter, before she was standing in the delivery room with Beatrice, listening to her scream bloody murder.

"Oh my God…it hurt so badly!"

"Gal, you may as well shut up that foolishness, it wasn't hurting when you were getting this baby," Agnes said, arousing laughter from the nurses in the delivery room as well as from Dr. Martin. Twenty minutes passed and Beatrice was having her final contraction. Dr. Martin had already indicated that this would be the last push needed to birth the baby. Being a retired registered nurse herself, other than her own, Agnes had never witnessed the birth of a child. She moved from standing near Beatrice's head to an area where she could see her first grandchild being born. She could see the head—her eyes grew big. Now she could see the hair—her mouth flung open.

"Well, I'll be *damned*! Agnes said slowly, grabbing her mouth after cursing. She shook her head as she looked at her daughter while listening to her give it all she had to bring forth a bald headed, pink looking baby boy. Agnes could not believe what she was seeing.

Later in Beatrice's room, Monica had arrived and she was admiring her newborn cousin. It was apparent that there was still a lot of tension between her aunt and cousin. By this time, her Uncle Joe had arrived as well and he and Agnes both sat in silence. Beatrice tried to break the tension and make small talk with Monica, "I told Agnes that they mixed up the babies. That's not my white baby," she said.

Monica didn't say anything as she continued to rub the hands of the little infant. He was so cute.

"The *hell* you preach. Gal, don't start that damn lying. I saw that baby come out yo' *ass* and anybody with as many gray hairs on their *pus*—as you is too damn old to be having a baby," Agnes mouthed, obviously still upset with her daughter.

"Agnes, do you have to talk so nasty?" Joe asked his wife.

Monica smiled at the cut and dry personality of her aunt. She knew better than to even attempt to come to Beatrice's defense. Instead, she continued to admire how cute the full term baby boy was.

CHAPTER TWENTY-ONE

Alma and Eleanor both arrived at the hospital together. It was an hour before visiting hours would be over. They met Pandora in the hall and they all entered the waiting room to the voices of Eloise, Clara and a few church members talking among themselves. Pandora had just left the intensive care unit visiting her sister. She informed the others that it seemed to her that her sister had given up.

In reality, Halora had given up. She was now swollen beyond recognition. Body fluids were draining from her eyes, nose and mouth heavier than it had been previously. Her eyes were swollen shut. The yellow fluid that the mysterious woman had given to Clara wasn't producing the results promised. It was obvious that Halora had taken a turn for the worse. The nurses didn't mean to be insensitive, but they were now complaining that the order of the liquid had become unbearable.

Noticing her daughters, Eloise stopped talking in mid sentence in response to their stares, "What have I done now?" she asked.

"Mother, why did you hurt Joy Lynn's feeling this morning?" Alma asked, sitting down next to Eloise.

"Hurt her feelings, how?" Eloise said, pretending not to know what Alma was talking about.

"She told us that she was trying to be nice by speaking to you this morning and you were very cold to her when you said you were not her mother when she called you Mother Eloise."

Eloise chuckled because her future daughter was correct in two instances. One that she was rather rude to her and two, she wasn't her future daughter's

mother. "Maybe, I was a little rude to what's her name," she admitted.

"Mother, her name is Joy Lynn," Eleanor reminded Eloise.

"What?"

"Mother, don't pretend like you can't remember her name."

Eloise chuckled again.

"I can't help she has one of those names that a person has a hard time remembering," she said laughing also arousing laughter among her sister circle.

"Sister Eloise, you are a mess," one of the sisters said.

"Call me what you want," Eloise said. She paused. "But my son could have gone through the trash and found better than that," she added with a straight face. "If I have my way she'll never change her name to Lorde."

"Mother…" Alma said, embarrassed.

"Whoa….If that don't say she doesn't like her son's fiancée, I don't know what else will," another sister said.

Alma and Eleanor couldn't do nothing but look at their mother. Of course, they were ashamed by the way she was acting. Instead of chastising her in front of her missionary sisters, the two left to visit their cousin and chose not to tell their mother about the precious moments they had shared with their future sister-in-law.

Earlier, Joy Lynn was scheduled to take her pre-wedding photos. She wanted her two matrons of honor and bridesmaid to take photos with her. She had reserved an upstairs room at the *Rest in Peace* funeral home for three hours and luckily, the funeral home didn't have a death or a funeral scheduled this particular day.

She mentioned to her soon to be sisters-in-law that Monica was not able to make it. She went on to tell them what transpired between her cousin and their mother. It wasn't surprising to them; they knew their mother could be a piece of work.

At the shoot, the two sisters helped Joy Lynn into her wedding dress. Once she was covered in all white, she looked like a different person. Her hair was done in an upsweep style with two long tresses hanging on each side of her face. Alma and Eleanor both were excited about the photo session and actually ecstatic about the upcoming nuptials; this was the first wedding of a sibling.

After that, the photographer suggested that Joy Lynn take a photo gazing into a full length mirror, the sisters watched as her emotions came down. Until now, she hadn't seen herself before that moment. It was obvious that she realized that in less than a month she would be becoming Mrs. Richard Anthony Lorde.

The photo session continued with the future bride taking photos with her matron of honor and bridesmaid. The photographer was very impressed with the entire session and took the liberty of making Eleanor blush when he told her that she was very photogenic.

Following the session, the two sisters helped their future sister-in-law carry her wedding gown and accessories to her car. This was the first time they had seen her black Ford mustang with the license tag, *All Joy.* They admired the leather seats and sporty rims. While Alma and Joy Lynn placed the wedding dress and accessories comfortably in the trunk, Eleanor found herself behind the steering wheel pretending she was driving the parked vehicle.

Once at the hospital, the happiness they felt for their brother and the wedding was short-lived. After visiting Halora, the tears streamed down their faces like a waterfall. Alma braced herself against the wall as Eleanor stood next to her sister as she gathered her composure. Alma felt numb. Her stomach was twisting in knots. All the memories that she was responsible for bringing Halora to South Carolina, she thought maybe if she hadn't hired her, Halora could possibly not be in this condition.

"She's giving up. She's not going to make it," Alma said.

"Don't talk like that. God has the final say. We have to pray," Eleanor encouraged.

"No, Eleanor, Halora is not there. Her spirit has gone on to be with the Lord."

Eleanor didn't respond to the remarks of her sister. *What did she mean her spirit had gone on to be with the Lord?* As far as she knew, Halora was still alive—unless she was misreading the monitors in her room, Eleanor thought to herself. She walked slowly with Alma as they returned to the waiting room. Again, the sisters entered the waiting room to the sound of laughter and chatter. Clara was even laughing and talking with her visitors. *Had she come to terms with Halora's condition?* Eleanor wondered.

"*Lawd* have mercy! My baby finally made it!" Clara said, raising both hands in the air. She leaped from her seat and maneuvered her short legs and wide hips toward the waiting room entrance. Everyone sitting in the waiting room turned toward the door. The middle age woman she greeted looked very sophisticated. Her hair was styled similar to the hairstyle of Nancy Wilson. Her small face was expressionless. She didn't resemble Clara in the least. In more ways than one, she favored Grace Anderson. The eyes, the mouth, her facial expression, her everything, screamed that she could be possibly related to the Christiansen family.

By this time, Eloise was standing near and Clara introduced her and her family to her daughter. Virginia was cordial, but she didn't hug any of her relatives. She hugged only her mother and their embrace lasted a long time. She stood in silence as Clara chattered before taking her to see her dying daughter.

Virginia Spudwinkle hadn't traveled alone. She was accompanied by her Caucasian husband Donald, who was the same man that took her away from both her mother and three children. The Regis Philpin look-a-like didn't exchange pleasantries with his wife's family. He followed Virginia and his mother-in-law into the intensive care unit. It had been a long time since Virginia had laid eyes on her oldest daughter. The person she was looking at didn't resemble the child she handed over to her mother more than twenty years prior. The amazing part of the reunion was that she wasn't afraid of her critically ill child. She walked over to the bed and grabbed her swollen hands. Then she noticed her missing hair, her swollen eyes and her cracked skin. None of that made her afraid to touch her daughter.

Soon thereafter, Pandora returned to the hospital with her brother Enrique. The two made brief eye contact with their mother. They knew she was coming. She looked the same to them, but much older. They still hated her and didn't want to be near the woman that had abandoned them and the two elected to stand on the opposite side of her. They watched as she spoke to an unconscious Halora, referring to herself as her mother. The siblings didn't like what they were hearing, she wasn't their mother—she handed over those rights twenty years ago. Hugging each other around the waist, the two realized now wasn't the time to deal with their estranged mother. Instead, they focused on their dying sister.

Many moments passed before Virginia bent over and kissed her daughter on the cheek. Her husband comforted her with his hand against her back as she turned to walk out the room. Then she heard the sound from behind. A loud gasp was followed by alarms from the monitors. She couldn't bring herself to look back. Even with her back towards her family, she recognized her mother's screams, she recognized the wailing of her beautiful daughter, then came the masculine sobs of her handsome son. If she didn't know any better, he sounded like her husband, who she knew was walking beside her. Her oldest daughter was now gone to a better place and the only memory she could relate to her life was the day she walked off and left her twenty years prior.

CHAPTER TWENTY-TWO

Christopher made it home around 3am. His mother was still awake, she was having problems sleeping. At the moment, she was watching old sitcoms on television. He walked into the family room and noticed the broadcasting of an old episode of the *Jefferson's* on the TV land channel. He laughed along with his own mother as Mother Jefferson pretended to fall on the floor to get the attention of George and Louise.

"Sister Halora passed away this afternoon," Carolina informed him.

Christopher was stunned. He sat down in an empty chair, not realizing he was still holding his jacket in his hand.

"It's amazing how God works. Her mother made it just in time. She died as soon as she arrived at the hospital. Oh, and this evening my *crazy* niece gave birth to a baby boy and didn't tell a soul she was pregnant." Carolina said.

"Oh, she did? I thought Halley and those didn't know where their mother was. Didn't somebody say she didn't have any contact with her children?" Christopher said, not surprised by what his mother had said about Beatrice.

"Well apparently they knew where she was because she showed up to that hospital today. Did you know that Bea was pregnant?" His mother said. He tried to dodge her questions. But his mother didn't get the hint that he wasn't going to answer her.

"And you know the family was calling Mychael all evening and *Monnie* said she didn't know where he was and he wasn't answering his cell phone. Pastor needs to stop going places without letting his members know how to get in touch with him. Deacon Lorde didn't even know where he was."

"How did you know he couldn't get in touch with him?" Christopher said, now questioning his mother.

"He called here looking for you. He thought maybe you knew how to get in touch with him."

"And how was I supposed to know how to get in touch with him? I'm not his keeper," he said defensively.

Christopher knew right away that Richard probably pushed his brother up to call and question him about Mychael's whereabouts. Honestly, he really didn't know where Mychael had been. He had been hanging out with his best buddies, Pierce and Jorge. The three had gone out to dinner then to the movies.

"Did they know what happened to her?" he questioned his mother further.

"Not that I know of, unless the family is keeping it all a secret," Carolina answered. "Earlier tonight, I spoke with your Aunt Eleanor and she was saying the same thing, the cause of death was unknown. She even said the mortician said she was going to need an extra wide casket."

"My goodness....She had swollen that much?"

"That's what Eleanor said. She said it will probably be a closed casket too."

Christopher asked his mother to give him Beatrice's room number. He was going to call her and he wanted to dial directly to her room. Next, he lifted himself from the chair he was sitting in and walked to his bedroom. He slipped out of his shoes and placed his jacket on the back of his closet door. On his bed, he noticed an envelope marked media mail lying on top of his comforter. He grabbed the package in his hand and looked it over. Again he didn't see a return address. *What type of media mail could this be?* He thought.

He opened the envelope immediately because he wasn't going to wait a week like he did with the other package. He was now a self proclaimed investigator and a good investigator used every piece of evidence to their advantage. Inside, he found a DVD.

Immediately, he powered on his player and placed the disc inside. Then he closed the door to his bedroom and locked it. He didn't want to run the risk of his mother entering his room without permission. She had done it so many times before.

Christopher looked at his 27" television and tried to focus his eyes on the

fuzzy picture that was very hard to view. He knew it wasn't his new television, but was a poor copy of a surveillance video. At first, he didn't recognize the area and then he realized it was the neighborhood where Libby once lived. After twenty minutes, he saw someone driving a car with the license plate, *All Joy*. He watched closely as the camera recorded an unknown female getting out of the sports car and making her way up to the front door.

The video showed a petite woman looking around nervously, as she stood on the porch for only a few moments, before a second female was standing in the doorway. The two women laughed and it appeared that the unknown woman went inside. After another few minutes, the tape went black and ejected itself from the DVD player. Strange ending, but it was enough to peak Christopher's curiosity.

Christopher had to watch the recording again to be sure of what he was seeing. Now, he was sure. Joy Lynn was the woman that had visited Libby the day before she was found dead. His mind automatically began putting together a few more pieces to this complicated puzzle.

He sat back on his bed. He was sleepy, but he wanted to play with the new pieces of the puzzle he had in his possession. Thus far, he had the complete document of the adoption of Hannah, who is actually the adopted daughter of Mychael's Cousin Myra; however, Joy Lynn's name was listed on the child's birth certificate. And lastly, Joy Lynn had contact with Libby before she died. In his mind, Christopher felt he had enough information to make his next mission to be a confrontation with Joy Lynn—before she became Mrs. Richard Lorde.

Really sleepy, Christopher laid the papers he held in his hand on the nightstand. He grabbed the telephone and dialed directly to Beatrice's room, she answered, "hello."

"I guess you couldn't wait on me, huh?" Christopher teased with his cousin.

She laughed at his humor, but was glad to hear his voice. He was the only person that wouldn't cast judgment on her the way Agnes and Joe had done before leaving the hospital to go home.

"Where were you? We called next door first. Chile, I thought I was dying."

"I bet you did. I went out with Pierce and Jorge tonight. How does the baby look?"

"He's half white if that's what you're asking. And Agnes is *not* happy. She keeps asking me about the father. I can't tell her that he is a drug addict and I certainly can't tell her that he was conceived in my bedroom."

"No, you sure can't or you will be out on the curb," Christopher remarked. "Is he in the room with you now?" he asked.

"No, they had to come to get him earlier. He wouldn't stop crying. He cried so much until he was all red and shaking," Beatrice disclosed. Then she paused, changing the subject. "Is it true that the girl from our church died? They said the family was so upset they sent for Joe to go upstairs to help calm them down."

"That's what Mama told me tonight."

"Is it true she was related to us?"

"I'm not sure. I think that was only a rumor," Christopher said, also pausing, having nothing more to say.

"That's not what Joe said. When he came back to the room, he said the girl's mother was the spitting image of Aunt Grace."

"I don't know, I guess time will tell. Okay, I'm going to say goodnight and don't worry about the baby, he'll be fine. You just try and get yourself some rest."

By no means was Christopher a doctor nor was he a drug counselor, but he knew that the newborn was experiencing withdrawal and he didn't want to tell his cousin this. So, he disconnected the call with her while assuring her that he would come by to see her the next day. Then he returned the phone to its base, followed by him sliding under his thick comforter and soon falling to sleep.

CHAPTER TWENTY-THREE

Clara and her daughter agreed to have Halora's body cremated. For once, they were thinking on the same level and realized that Halora should not have to lie in state as some would say as *concerned* and *nosey* spectators paraded past her swollen corpse. At the time, Clara couldn't speak for her daughter Virginia, however, in her mind, she believed her granddaughter was worth so much more than that.

Halora was a beautiful and vibrant young woman and her grandmother would be the first to say her grandchild didn't deserve to die the way she did. Clara never mentioned it to anyone, but she happened to see the homeless looking woman again and the woman invited her to her home. Ironic as it was, the same woman was instrumental in revealing to Clara what had happened to her late granddaughter.

For days prior, Clara whelped and kept asking herself, "Why my granddaughter?" She had to admit, when the woman gave her the disturbing news, she literally scared the living daylights out of her. As you can imagine, she second guessed herself and wondered why she even chose to meet with this person. Not to mention, agreeing to meet her at her home or as the stranger mentioned several times—her place of business.

The homeless looking woman was strange in every sense of the word. She had a strange style of decorating. She had a strange style in the way she dressed. Everything about her was strange. Personally, Clara didn't like the various shapes of skull heads and photographs of snakes that covered the woman's beige walls. She entered a slightly pitch black house, at first, she saw a glimmering shadow of the woman. But the more steps she took down

a long narrow hall, the darker the house became. Between being afraid and in the dark, Clara bumped into a table and a few chairs before being guided to her seat. At that very moment, the house and the atmosphere both were now giving her the creeps. In her mind, she knew the woman probably intended for her décor to have that affect. It was working, Clara thought.

She hated being in this predicament, and more so in this environment, but she realized that sometimes you have to give a little, to get a little and the information the woman was sharing with her was shedding a lot of light on some very dark areas in her life.

During her visit, ten minutes had passed when the woman struck a match and lit a medium sized candle. It gave a glowing light to the room—enough light to make Clara crook her neck when she noticed a black python lying motionless in an open cage. At first, she thought the reptile was dead or asleep rather. Then it moved. She started to shake. She was frightened more with fear when the woman revealed to her that the reptile's favorite dish was human foods—Clara could only speculate what the woman meant by that.

She learned by accident that the strange woman's name was Mablean and did so as she drove up to the spooky looking house, noticing the flashing sign outside. She thought maybe the sign was fictional until she saw her business cards sitting on her wisdom table and the same name was listed with psychic reader behind it.

By now, Clara was unable to hide her nerves and she thought Mablean noticed it to. She assumed she was trying to convince her further because she made it a point to tell her she could tell the future. Honestly, Clara didn't care that she could. But the woman promised to read her palms whenever she wanted it done. What had she gotten herself into? Clara thought to herself again. It was obvious that this woman was involved in more than psychic readings, she was the *real* thing.

Meanwhile, Clara thought maybe she should have listened to Eloise when she told her that God was better than a witch doctor any day. Unfortunately, Clara had to learn the hard way, but to her this was a lesson worth learning. Especially after Mablean revealed to her that the person responsible for killing her granddaughter would not live beyond one year of her death. Inside, Clara thought the person Mablean was referring to was somebody from that job her granddaughter enjoyed or that humongous church her family loved

so much. Knowing this, Clara decided she would wait patiently for the next person to die and she didn't care whether she had the right or wrong person. In her frame of mind, the next man or woman that closed their eyes and was a member of the Tabernacle of Praise Baptist Church or an employee of the Lorde Insurance Company would be the person she blamed for bringing death upon her granddaughter.

As the week continued and the days passed, Clara was surprised that her daughter Virginia didn't give her the grief she knew she was capable of doing. She had to concede and say that her daughter was strange—but not strange enough to realize she had technically given up her rights as a mother twenty years ago.

After making the appropriate arrangements, the family gathered for a private memorial service. Mychael delivered a short eulogy and a few of Halora's classmates traveled from New Jersey to give reflections as friends.

One of her friends in attendance was a young woman that Halora had gone to college with and the two were the same age. She was of Korean descent and spoke highly of the fifteen year friendship that she and Halora had shared. Her words were beautiful and appropriate. But no one will forget the compassionate words that Jorge spoke regarding the overbearing boss that he admired. The young man was so devastated that he sobbed throughout his entire remarks. His tears brought out the emotions in everyone. By the closing, his mother had to leave her seat to escort him back to the place where he had been sitting. He had everyone in attendance crying, everyone except Clara's daughter.

Throughout the service, Virginia sat stone-faced along side her husband, entangling her fingers with his. Clara observed her behavior and to her it seemed like her daughter was afraid of her own family. *What is her problem?* She thought. She knew money had the tendency to change a person, but she didn't think it would make you act crazy.

In her mind, Clara wondered whether her daughter had the good sense that God had given her. But before she could pass judgment on the distant acting woman, she had to remember who she was related to. And with that being said—she had to cut her only child a tremendous amount of slack.

If she were to be honest, Clara would say, she seriously wanted Virginia to cut a rug. She wanted her to scream and holler her granddaughter's name.

She even hoped that she would faint and have to be carried out of the service. Instead, her daughter sat quietly and contently. Not a cough—not a sniffle—not even a sigh.

Early in the week, Clara learned that Virginia was now the mother of six rather than three. Her younger children ranged in age from twenty years to seventeen years old; Donald, Jr. was twenty, Mary Elizabeth was eighteen and Clarina was seventeen.

At first, Clara thought they were going to have a problem as they lined up to enter the small chapel. Eloise walked in with her and Enrique and Pandora walked in together, followed by their mother and stepfather then their half siblings. As they all took their seats, somehow, Pandora was left to sit next to her mother and being the hateful person that she was, she kindly got up to exchange places with her brother, leaving him to sit next to their estranged mother.

Forty-five minutes later, the family was walking out of the chapel. The parking lot was full of church members, but the people that stood out the most to Clara were the Christiansen family. *What in the hell did they want?* She knew what they wanted. They wanted to get a closer look at her daughter and Halora's funeral would be the only way that they could.

Personally, Clara didn't have a problem with their curiosity because her daughter knew how was conceived and she knew who her father was. Clara just didn't think a memorial was the time and the place for her daughter's family to peek their curiosity. Frankly, she could only hope that no one would make the mistake and say the wrong thing to her daughter. Even though she was grieving, Clara was still coherent enough to kick *some* ass.

Clara would have to agree with everyone's assessment that Virginia and her daughter's niece, Grace were similar to twins. When she first saw Grace, she had to snatch her head twice, even take a third look because the resemblance was unbelievable.

Like a lioness, Clara eyed *Snappy* as he walked up to her daughter. She waited and listened to the words that came from his mouth. He was smarter than Eloise gave him credit for. He introduced himself, not as Virginia's nephew, but as her cousin's husband. She watched as her daughter smiled slightly at him, before moving through the crowded parking lot, angling toward her.

Virginia didn't mingle with any of her family—not even her mother's relatives. She bypassed them all, stopping her strides when she reached Clara. That was when she realized that her mother was wearing a frumpy looking black dress and a pair of black flat shoes—she wasn't wearing any stockings. Virginia's thoughts went directly to how Eloise was dressed and how her attire made her own mother look like Cinderella's stepsister. To put it mildly, she was embarrassed by the way Clara was dressed; nonetheless she still owed the woman that stood before her a lot and no matter how she was dressed, Clara was still her mother. Virginia gave Clara a kiss on each cheek before speaking a few words, "Mudear, the children, Donald and I will be leaving now to catch our flight. I hope we can keep in touch," she said then she angled toward a waiting limousine.

"Honey, don't you want to talk with Pandora and Enrique before you leave?" Clara asked before Virginia could walk away. She was fully aware how her grandchildren felt about their mother. But she knew her grandchildren needed to make an attempt to mend the relationship with their estranged mother—her estranged daughter. She felt she was up in age now and she knew she would not live forever and whenever God chose to close her eyes, she wanted things to be right between her grandchildren and their mother.

"No Mudear, if they haven't forgiven me in a week then they have their minds made up," Virginia said, seeming distracted.

"You didn't give them a chance to forgive you. You stayed away from us all week. They don't hate you, you're their mother. For me, please try to work things out with your children. At least, introduce them to their brother and sisters? If not, introduce them to me. Honey, I don't even know my own grandchildren," Clara pleaded.

Virginia walked back toward her mother and held her round face in her skinny hands. Her nails were well manicured with burgundy paint. She paused and spoke slowly to her mother like she was a child. "There isn't a need to make them relive the past. Pandora and Enrique are your children now. You raised them. I have my own family to look after. I'll keep in touch."

Virginia was correct in assuming that her son and daughter would not forgive her. They had not exchanged two words with her during her week long stay. Afraid of being isolated, she decided not to stay with her family,

opting to make her reservations at a hotel. She spent all of her time with her husband and her three children. Right then she made the decision not to introduce her children to their half siblings, their grandmother or their entourage of cousins.

Excusing herself from the conversation with her mother, once again, Virginia made her way to a waiting limousine. Her husband stood at the door as she entered. He entered, the children all entered one by one. They didn't look back at the crowd of people they didn't know. The driver closed the door and returned to the driver's seat then he put the limousine into drive. He drove slowly out of the parking lot. As the long vehicle moved past her, Pandora gave those inside an evil stare. She couldn't see them, but she was hoping that they saw her. And they did.

Inside the limousine, Virginia had held it together as long as she could. She laid her head on the shoulder of her husband. She sobbed uncontrollably. Her son, Donald II handed his mother a tissue. Virginia continued to cry. She clutched her husband's hand tightly as the elder Spudwinkle remained quiet—he was reserved. During this entire time, all he wanted was to be was his wife's rock—her support. He was feeling rather guilty because he hadn't seen Halora, Pandora or Enrique since they were small children, since the day he told his wife that he didn't want to be a step-father to her *bastard* children. He remembered vividly what he had told her twenty years ago. 'I'm too young to be a father to your children. Marry me and we can leave the state and have our own children—our own beautiful children,' Donald recalled in his head.

At the time, Donald didn't give Virginia time to think about her decision, before driving her to her mother's apartment. He remembered the day, month, and year when she dropped the three children off to Clara, who was sleeping off the late shift she had worked the night before.

Clara asked her daughter about her plans for coming back for the children. Donald remembered hearing his wife, his girlfriend at the time say, 'Mudear, I'm not coming back. He doesn't want these children in our lives.' That day, Virginia walked away from her mother yelling, 'Honey, what am I going to do with three young children?' Virginia never looked back. She entered Donald's car, the way she entered the limousine today. She got in and never looked back.

Virginia eventually married the man she thought would give her a better life. The couple moved to California and Donald became a successful business man. In time, Virginia gave her husband the beautiful children he wanted and he gave her the lifestyle she never had. Little did he know, one of the children they had left behind, he had actually fathered. Virginia knew it, but was afraid that if she told him, he would refuse to marry her. She thought being Mrs. Donald Spudwinkle would afford her opportunities she never had. She was correct. As his wife, she was able to live in a three story mansion, drive Jaguar and Mercedes cars and to have their own housekeeper and a nanny. She had it all, but at the cost of her three little children.

Throughout the years, her husband never forbid her from contacting her mother and children, in fact, he encouraged her to reach out to them. She was the one who decided not to keep in contact with her relatives. Not only did she not keep in touch, she didn't send her family birthday cards. She didn't send them Christmas gifts. She didn't even send them a gift when they each graduated from high school and college. It was only last year, when she decided since her mother was getting older, she would reach out to her. On an expensive note card, she mailed her mother the family address and telephone number. She was unaware that her mother no longer lived in New Jersey and had moved to South Carolina. She sent the note card to the last address she had known. Luckily, the information was forwarded to her mother's new address.

Thirty minutes had now passed, Virginia was still crying as she arrived at the airport. Her emotions were so heavy it prevented her from having a conversation with her children. They respected their mother's grief and talked among themselves. It was more like whispering. They noticed immediately that Enrique and Donald, Jr. looked too much alike and wondered was he their father's son. Being that their mother was still grieving heavily, they had no intention of mentioning it to her, but would be sure to bring up the subject to their unsuspecting father.

Virginia stepped out of the limousine and walked up the long corridor inside the boarding terminal. It was another hour before their flight would leave. She stood and stared through the open window as other planes landed and took flight. Her arms were folded. She was still dressed in the attire she

had worn to the memorial. The pearl necklace still hung around her neck and her narrow feet were still in her black four inch heels. She was even still holding onto the tissue her son had given her. She couldn't stop crying, so she took a moment to dab both eyes.

"Virginia my love, I understand your grief," Donald said.

"I wish you did," she said back to him.

"I really do. Halley was my step-daughter."

She paused before she spoke. "Donald, you were the one who didn't want me to bring them with us. I never should have turned my back on my children," she explained to her husband.

"I know, but that doesn't say that I didn't love them."

"If you loved them, you would have suggested that I bring them all to California. So don't say you loved them—because you didn't."

"Virginia let's not argue about who loved the children more," he suggested.

"Donald, there's nothing for us to argue about. I just attended the memorial service of a child that I carried for nine months. I just saw two children that I hadn't seen in twenty years and I treated them like they were strangers. I don't expect you to understand how I'm feeling right now. I didn't lose my oldest child this week. Truthfully, I lost all three of my children twenty years ago," she said in a mouthful.

The hour wait seemed like eternity. Finally, the family was able to board their flight, stopping in the first class section. Virginia was not crying now. Her mood had now changed. She was quiet—she was slowly adjusting to being a mother of five instead of six.

CHAPTER TWENTY-FOUR

It was almost lunch time when Christopher arrived at the Ramblewood Office of Gynecology and Obstetrics. Rather than getting out, first he circled the parking lot. He was looking for a black mustang with the license tag, *All Joy*. He wasn't sure whether Joy Lynn was working this week or not, but her parked vehicle confirmed for him that she was. He hurried to park his car then gathered the manila folder that sat on his front seat. He waited a few seconds to gather his nerves before springing from the driver's seat. He rushed through the half empty parking lot and into the luxurious doctor's office.

Once in the lobby, Christopher looked at his watch and realized it was *exactly* ten minutes before the office was scheduled to close for their lunch hour. By observation, he noticed how expensive the building looked from the outside, but the lavish décor inside was an indication that he was entering a very successful establishment.

Immediately, Christopher was greeted by a female receptionist, "Sir, if you're looking for a patient, our last patient left about five minutes ago," she said to him.

"Thanks, but I'm Christopher Christiansen and I'm here to take Nurse Joy Anderson to lunch," he lied.

The unknown female couldn't keep the smile off her face. It was obvious what she was thinking, Joy Lynn was about to get married and another man was there to take her to lunch. As she rose from her seat, she suggested that Christopher take a seat while she informed Joy Lynn that he was there.

Quickly, Joy Lynn appeared at the hall door. She looked at Christopher with her hands on her slim hips. Her expression was such that he knew she

didn't like the idea of him showing up unannounced at her place of employment.

"What do you want?" she mouthed at Christopher.

Christopher got up from his seat and walked over to the pale looking nurse. In his hand, he held copies of all the information he planned to present to Joy Lynn. "I need to speak with you in private and it's very serious. Either you speak with me now or we can speak with Richard tonight—together!" he said boldly.

"Christopher you really have caught me at a bad time, plus I'm not in the mood for your antics," Joy Lynn said, looking around.

"Joy, are you going to be okay?" the receptionist said, causing both Christopher and Joy Lynn to look in her direction.

"Yes, I'll be fine."

"Well, I'm going to go ahead and leave. Remember to set the alarm," she reminded Joy Lynn.

Once the receptionist had closed the door behind her, Christopher got right to the point, "Joy, do you have a room where we can speak?" he demanded.

Reluctantly, she removed her hand from the door she was holding. She led Christopher into a small room with a table and four chairs. The space was very tight. The room had one picture on the wall, a small television and a DVD/VCR player sat on a table in the corner. Joy Lynn sat in the empty chair closer to the door. She didn't say anything as she watched Christopher take his seat.

Christopher wasted very little time with small talk as he opened the packet and slid the paperwork in front of Joy Lynn. She looked at the manila folder and studied the documents—her facial expression revealed what he had hoped, that she was surprised by what she saw. She should have been. At this stage in his investigation, Christopher knew he had all of his ducks in a row. The documents, plus the additional information he had gathered all spoke for itself.

"Do you have anything to tell me Ms. Anderson?" Christopher asked Joy Lynn, sounding like a true investigator. He had to admit, he was getting good at this.

"I don't know where you got this information, but this doesn't mean anything," she said.

"Oh, I beg your pardon. I believe it means everything. It means that you knew that Libby was pregnant by Reverend Dovely. It means that you told Monica about the pregnancy and the two of you devised a plan to get rid of her. The day before Libby was found dead, you picked up a prescription from the Ramblewood pharmacy that would send her into labor—I don't have to explain how you received that. Would you like for me to continue?"

"This is all lies. What is your problem? Are you so resentful about my marrying Richard, that you will do anything to stop this wedding? Richard won't believe a word of this far fetched set of lies," she denied.

"Yes, he will. I plan to present this information to him tonight," Christopher stated.

Joy Lynn stood to her feet and pointed her finger in Christopher's face. "Mr. Christiansen, you are way out of your league. You won't be presenting anything to Richard," she said, ripping the manila folder and its content in half. Then she ripped the two half pieces in half as she leaned on the conference table, pressing her fingers against its surface. "Are you done? Now let me take a trip down memory lane. Remember, when the high school won the state championship? Of course you do, you were there. But as you may recall, my cousin—your cousin was out of town," she said as she paced the small quarters like she was an attorney making an opening statement. "If my mind serves me correctly, you paid a visit to your pastor around nine-thirty and didn't leave until around eleven o'clock. I wonder did Mychael ever tell his wife about your visit. I'll answer that. He didn't. He never mentioned it because he knew she would be upset. He knew she would accuse him *again* of having a homosexual affair with her cousin. Oh…he knew it would be a problem. So, Mr. Christiansen, do you still really and truly want to tell my fiancée about this little eye spy investigation of yours?"

Christopher sat back in his chair. He laughed out loud. He had Joy Lynn figured out so well. "I knew you would do that. The papers you just ripped in half were copies. I have the originals in a safe place. And as for your sorted story… Reverend Dovely is my pastor and I can stop by to speak with him anytime day or night and Monica is just going to have to deal with that," he explained, realizing she must have gotten the scenario from her fiancée. True enough; the scenario scared him as to whether Monica may have had her and Mychael's house bugged. How else would she know what time he arrived

and what time he left? He wasn't sure about that. But what he knew for sure was he couldn't let Joy Lynn know that her statement was getting under his skin.

"These documents don't prove anything. You have nothing that puts me at this woman's house before she died."

"As a matter of fact I do," Christopher admitted. He pulled from the outside pocket of his shirt a copy of the DVD he had received in the mail. He lifted himself from the chair and walked over to the television and DVD/VCR player. He powered the electronics on and placed the DVD inside.

Joy Lynn watched as Christopher pressed the play button using the remote that sat on the table nearest him. She watched the surveillance recording of her arriving at Libby's house, carrying a white bag. The Ramblewood Pharmacy logo could be seen on the bag. The recording also showed her speaking with Libby for a few moments and eventually going inside.

She sat down slowly. In her mind, she saw her perfect wedding day going down the drain. She was now white as a ghost and wasn't as vocal as she was earlier. In a pleading nature, she grabbed Christopher by the hand. She now sounded desperate. "Christopher, you can't tell Richard about this. He will call off everything. I promise I won't mention anything about my suspicion of your affair with Mychael. Richard and I are in love—doesn't that mean anything to you?"

"You *damn* right he's going to call off the wedding. He would never marry a woman like you. You can't imagine how difficult his sister's death was for him. The man you fell in love with was not the same man over a year ago," Christopher said, then pausing. "You took one of the closest people to him. You devastated that entire family. But all you and Monica cared about were your own needs."

"Christopher, I'm sorry. Please don't tell him. His sister was still alive when I left with the baby. I didn't think she was going to die. Can we keep quiet about this until after the wedding? Richard will be devastated if we don't get married."

"No! You'll be devastated if he doesn't marry you. I can't keep all this information in good conscious," he informed her.

Christopher ejected the DVD from the player and gathered the torn

pieces of the folder in his hand. Then he followed Joy Lynn out of the small conference room into the hallway. By this time, the office was empty and no one was there but him and Joy Lynn.

"I guess I'll have to tell Richard tonight. Wait right here while I get my purse," Joy Lynn said.

"I'll go with you."

"Christopher you don't have to follow me around, you can see both exits from here." Joy Lynn informed him.

Christopher was a little leery, but he waited for her in the hall. He pulled a small note pad from his pants pocket. He turned to press down on the countertop as he wrote notes about his and Joy Lynn's conversation. In a sense, he felt like a true investigator, but he knew that he wasn't. At least it felt good pretending and he knew that Richard and the Ramblewood police department were going to be proud of his involvement in solving this case.

"I'm ready," Joy Lynn said.

"Its abo—" Christopher attempted to say as Joy Lynn hit him over the head with an object she had hidden under her jacket. He fell to the floor unconscious as she stood over him. "Christopher I told you that you were in way over your head. Why didn't you believe me?" she said to her silent victim. She knelt beside him like a mental patient. She moved the coat she was holding around about her hand. She kept shaking her head as she cried. "Christopher, why didn't you just leave? Why wouldn't you leave us alone? Richard is mine…didn't you know I would do anything to become Mrs. Richard Lorde?" she said to an empty office. Then she grabbed him under his arms and proceeded to pull him toward the back entrance. She rushed out to her car and backed her vehicle up to the rear entrance then struggled more to put his heavy body in her trunk. Once she got him inside, she slammed the trunk shut and dialed numbers into the keypad of her cell phone.

"Ramblewood Pharmacy, this is Monica speaking."

"*Monnie,* we have a problem," Joy Lynn spoke into her cell phone.

"What kind of problem? Girl, I have to call you back, we are swamped."

"Christopher has figured out everything. He has information linking us to Libby's death and Hannah's adoption," Joy Lynn said, hysterical.

"What? Calm down Joy. How much does he know?"

"*Monnie*…he knows! He has a surveillance recording of me going to the

house the day before they found Libby dead. He has the adoption papers between me and Myra. He's already spoken to Mychael's Cousin Myles and he suspects that Hannah is Mychael and Libby's daughter. Now, he's threatening to tell Richard everything. I don't know what else to do," she continued, still hysterical.

"Joy Lynn you have to calm down. We will figure this all out when I get off this evening. I'm sure Christopher won't mention this to Richard before then," Monica said. Then she asked through clinched teeth, "Where is he now?"

"In *my* trunk!"

CHAPTER TWENTY-FIVE

Richard's male family members succeeded in convincing him to have a bachelor's night out. Initially, he was totally against the idea and regretted that he had agreed for Joy Lynn to have the wedding rehearsal the week before rather than the night prior to the wedding. If he had insisted that she stay within the traditional guidelines, at that moment, he would be standing in the sanctuary of the Tabernacle of Praise Baptist Church, rehearsing what they would be doing the next day. However, he understood his fiancée's logic since the week before was the only time that the entire wedding party could be there and being the perfectionist that his future wife was—she wouldn't have it any other way.

His family thought he was kidding when he said *no* bachelor party. He really wasn't kidding. He didn't tell them this, but he really didn't want a bunch of strippers grinding and shaking their breasts all in his face. Yeah...Yeah...Yeah some would call him different. He was different, he was the chairman of the trustee board and he was now proclaiming to be a true and honest man of God. He realized that most men would have loved to have a party like this on their last night of being single. But Richard didn't. That's not how he wanted to celebrate his last night as a single man. He was thinking on the level of something simple—and it didn't include strippers!

He hadn't heard anything from anyone; therefore he assumed his family had agreed with his suggestion for something simple, like a small prayer service. He learned how wrong he was when his nephew *DJ* called to ask what time they were leaving for North Carolina. His nephew thought his uncle knew about the trip, but learned quickly that nobody had mentioned the details to him. *DJ*

171

explained to Richard further that the male family members were going out of town to North Carolina to avoid any controversy from potential church members. After his nephew had supplied him with all the details that were supposed to be a secret, Richard felt obligated to offer him a ride to his surprise gathering in North Carolina.

That evening, as they drove up to the establishment, Richard recognized his twin brothers standing next to a burgundy Cadillac Escalade. Byron was pacing as he spoke into his cell phone while his twin waited patiently next to the parked Sports Utility Vehicle.

Richard got out of his own SUV along with his brother, Ernest, Jr., his brothers-in-law, Daniel and *Snappy* and his nephews, *DJ* and Emanuel. They all united with handshakes and hugs. He was glad to see his half brothers as it had been a few months since he saw them last. He could tell they were excited about having the responsibility of planning his bachelor's night out. He should have been excited, but he was more nervous about what all his half brothers had in store for him.

"Hey Mr. Johnson," Ernie, Jr. said, joking with his baby brother Byron about the name his mother had given him. They all laughed at Ernie, Jr. and his comedy. Everybody there knew why he was calling his brother *Mr. Johnson.*

"Ha. Ha. Ha," Byron said, still talking on his cell phone.

"Man, you going to have a funky good time," Barron said to his brother.

The club's parking lot was very clean and partially full. The establishment looked like an exclusive hotel. The men made a single line, listening to the loud music as they walked into the building. The twin brothers had reserved a small area for the eight of them. As they took their seats they were introduced to two sleazy dressed waitresses that would be providing them customer service.

"Good evening gentlemen my name is Alfonso and I'm the general manager. I would like to introduce to you your servers for the evening. This is Brandi and this is Aliza," he said.

Brandi was dressed in a pink bunny suit with a small white bunny tail attached to her costume and Aliza was dressed in a black leather halter top and mini dress, along with her fish net stockings and high heals.

The man that introduced himself as the general manager was dressed in

a red three piece suit accessorized with a red hat. He looked at the group of men like he was trying to analyze the caliber of customers he was dealing with. They all joked among themselves that they each saw dollar signs appear in Alfonso's eyes when they walked in.

"So, who's the groom?" Alfonso asked.

Everybody pointed to Richard as he held his cell phone to his ear. He was calling Christopher to ask him again about his plans to attend the wedding. He had been calling him for the last month in an attempt to change his mind about attending the wedding. Again, he didn't get an answer then and he wasn't getting an answer now—this call also went straight to Christopher's voicemail.

"Man, you need to put that cell phone away. This is your last night as a bachelor and you are about to get the show of a lifetime," Alfonso said, speaking directly to Richard.

"Don't do me any favors," Richard said under his breath.

Later in the night, Alfonso took the stage in preparation of introducing the dancers. The club was very upscale. There were three stages and each had a steel pole in the middle of the floor as two smaller stages were on the side of the main stage.

First, he introduced Chocolate Thunder, who was a rather large woman weighing about four-hundred pounds. She took the stage wearing a two-piece bathing suit and she wasn't embarrassed that her huge stomach hung over her yellow bikini. The *Norbit* looking woman had her long weave pulled away from her face as she grabbed the pole and spun herself around it with such limberness.

The fat woman crawled to the edge of the stage like a female panther. *DJ* jumped from his chair and ran to the area where she was dancing. He held in his hands a stack of money, mostly one dollar bills. She opened her mouth and allowed him to feed her dollar bills like she was a change machine. She shook the money from her mouth and spread her lips again for more.

The family group of men laughed as *DJ* enticed the obese stripper. He stood in front of her holding his drink. His father could be heard in the background yelling, "Go get her son," prompting the group of relatives to laugh again.

Then a second woman emerged from behind the red curtain to take the

second stage. She was slightly thin. She also spun around the pole, throwing her head back. She raised herself and stood side by side with the steel pole. She eased herself to the floor in a split, before rolling onto her back, holding her legs open to the crowded club. All the men gasped as some rushed to the stage with the group of curious of men including; Emanuel and Barron. They stuffed dollars into the g-string of the nude dancer. She moved from her back to her knees and shook her breasts in Emanuel's face then in Barron's. They both smiled with excitement. She let the men kiss her. Barron rubbed the inside of her wet womanhood with a twenty dollar bill. He put the same twenty dollar bill to his nose before placing it in the stripper's g-string.

"Damn, it's just the way I like it, wet and funky," he said.

Emanuel laughed at his uncle. Then he said, "Come over here and let me smell it." The stripper moved in front of him and spread her legs wide. From where his father and uncles were sitting, their nephew and son looked like a Gynecologist, as Emanuel placed three fingers inside of the woman. He moved them in and out of her. He laughed and appeared excited about what he was doing. He put the same three fingers to his nose. He too enjoyed the smell as his uncle did earlier then they clasped their hands together in agreement.

Alfonso returned to the stage to introduce the final act, "Well gentleman, what you've been enjoying is what we call the appetizer. But now we are ready for the main course. The next dancer is not a stranger to our regulars. She cute, she's fine, she's freaky and she's all mine. Please welcome to the stage…Brown sugar."

Alfonso thought of Brown Sugar as his secret weapon. He didn't look at her as a stripper, but more like an entertainer. He loved her personality and style. She had class. In his opinion, she was nothing like the other girls that worked for him. She showered before and after every show, she took pride in the costumes that she wore, and she never took up men on their offers to pay her for sex—she wasn't that type of girl.

The lights around the club dimmed and the spotlight was on the attractive young woman that emerged from the curtains. She walked down the runway to the music by the Commodores, *Brick house.* She was certainly a brick house as men began crowding the stage with ten, twenty, fifty and hundred dollar bills in hand. She was wearing a leopard cat suit. Her face was partially covered with a face mask. Her hair was flowing. It wasn't weaved—it was all hers.

Brown Sugar grabbed the pole and spun herself around. She was demanding the attention of the crowd. She was in control. She threw her head backward, forward, and around. The stage was crowded on all three sides as the patrons watched her walk to the left as she pulled on a small string causing her top to fall to the floor. Her perky breasts were now exposed to the lusting crowd—the men went crazy. Their eyes shined like a kid in a candy store. She was a natural. The regular customers enjoyed her performances, only because she never performed the same routine twice.

She moved to the right side of the stage and ripped off her pants. The group of men became aroused as they stared at the nakedness of a woman with not one ounce of body fat. The only hair on her body was the long tresses that hung at her shoulders. Her breasts were perfect. Her *ass* was perfect. Her waistline was perfect.

Brown Sugar returned to the pole and spun herself around, never once touching the floor. She crawled. She rolled. She opened herself. She excited the crowd even more.

"Yo' come over here," one patron yelled. The stage was covered with money. It covered her. A few bills fell to the floor. Her customers were honest men and they grabbed the loose money from the floor and threw it at her.

Brown Sugar continued to dance around the stage. The lights were still dimmed, but she moved around the stage like a cat walking in the night. The dimmed light was the reason she was able to zone herself out—she wasn't able to see the faces of her patrons. She wouldn't have to remember. She wouldn't recognize them at the Convenience store, the Laundromat or at the Mall. Right now, she was giving her audience the performance of a lifetime. They loved it, they cheered her on.

Richard, Ernest, Daniel, and *Snappy* were all now standing around the stage. They all agreed that the woman before them was truly putting on a show.

"Dance baby…Dance for daddy," the crowd begged. She danced. She danced. She danced.

Then she beckoned for a male patron to take the stage with her. A nerdy looking man tried to come up—she pushed him away. Then an elderly looking white guy wearing a tailored suit tried to climb on the stage—she pushed him away. Then an intoxicated *DJ* climbed on stage. The engineers

lowered the stage lights more. It was obvious *DJ* was aroused. She kissed him. He gave her five dollars. She unbuttoned his shirt and kissed his chest also sucking on his nipples. He gave her a twenty. She grabbed the chair that the bouncer was handing her. She led *DJ* to the empty seat. She knelt down in front of him and unzipped his pants, fumbling with the opening of his boxers. The crowd was going wild as *DJ's* long and thick manhood sprung forward. It was shaped like a banana. The crowd was literally going crazy.

"Suck it. Suck it. Suck it," the crowd chanted.

Brown Sugar leaned into *DJ* and whispered in his ear. "Do you want me to suck it?" she asked him, but he was so mesmerized by this private attention, all he could say was, "Yeah."

The group of men couldn't believe the show they were getting. Ernest, Jr. smiled widely as he rubbed his head. Daniel was proud of his son for scoring so big. All throughout the club, men were laughing, joking and being obnoxious.

"Man, stick that *dick* in her mouth," a second patron yelled.

"Make her deep throat it," another hollered.

Brown Sugar massaged the banana looking muscle. *DJ* was drunk, but it felt good to him. Then she began sucking on him. She consumed all of him then she slid her mouth slowly from the base to the head. She pulled on the head of his penis with her mouth. She looked like a baby sucking a bottle. *DJ's* pants and boxers were now around his ankles. At that moment, he began sliding out of the chair. He lifted himself up. He was enjoying the twenty minutes of pleasure as he bumped his manhood inside Brown Sugar's mouth. He grabbed a hand full of her hair. It *was* real. He grinded inside her mouth from left to right. Then his arms went limp and dangled on each side of him. His eyes flickered like someone being electrocuted before he let go inside Brown Sugar's mouth. The crowd went crazy again. It sounded like a pep rally was going on.

DJ pulled his pants and boxers up to his waist, putting away his deflated manhood. He staggered. He shook his head. Then he grabbed the pole he was standing next to. It helped him to keep his balance.

A bouncer came to his aid and helped him step down to the floor then the same bouncer grabbed all of the scattered money, packing it inside a bank bag as Brown Sugar blew kisses and waved to her patrons until she had left the stage.

"We want more…We want more…We want more," the patrons chanted.

DJ returned to his male family members. They joked with him about his twenty minutes of pleasure. He couldn't return their humor, he was exhausted. He was drunk. He was in love.

After getting himself together, *DJ* walked over to the general manager and asked could he speak with the dancer that just gave him the pleasure of a lifetime. The woman made him forget about his drug addiction. He had to meet her in person, away from the excited crowd.

Alfonso propped his hand on *DJ*'s shoulder. "Man, I know she made you feel good and all. But for safety reasons, we don't allow the patrons to interact in private with our dancers, especially with *my* Brown Sugar. Get the hint?"

"Man come on now, I'm not a convict. My uncles are the ones who arranged for us to be here. They operate their own law firm, Lorde and Lorde, Attorneys at law."

"Sure you right…And your name is?"

"My name is Daniel Hawkins, Jr., everybody calls me *DJ*. Go over there and ask them," he said, pointing in the area where his uncles were sitting.

"All right, Mr. Daniel Hawkins, Jr., there isn't a need for any introductions. I'll let you speak with Brown Sugar, but only for a few minutes. 'Cause time is money. She has another show to do in an hour," Alfonso explained. He observed the time on his watch. He looked at a waiting *DJ*. He shook his head and laughed, "Damn, you got whipped after getting a little head. I hate to see what you would've done, if she had given you the *pussy*."

Next Alfonso led *DJ* backstage, stopping at Brown Sugar's dressing room. He tapped on the closed door. They both heard as she yelled, "Just a minute."

They waited. A few seconds passed, before she appeared at the door. She was dressed in a silk bathrobe, but she wasn't wearing her face mask.

"Oh shit!" she and *DJ* both said at the same time.

"Oh shit, what?" Alfonso repeated what he had heard, looking from his dancer to the star struck patron.

Brown Sugar moved from the door. She maneuvered around in her dressing room like a mental patient. Her boss was still unaware as to the

reason for her shyness. She had met customers before and she was never shy.

"Baby, what's going on? My partner here only wanted to meet you in person. What can I say, the dude is star struck," he teased, still unaware.

DJ left Alfonso and Brown Sugar in the small dressing room. He didn't say another word to the woman. He returned to the front of the club, sitting down to the table with his family. All of a sudden, he felt sober.

In the dressing room, Brown Sugar kept her back turned as she spoke to her manager, "Alfonso that was my cousin." She felt like she was going to hyperventilate. She felt nauseous. Despite, how she felt, Alfonso was stunned. He pointed his finger in the direction where *DJ* once stood. "You mean to tell me, you just gave your cousin a blow job on stage. Didn't he know you worked here?"

"No, he doesn't know I'm a stripper," she answered.

"Ah… he does now."

"Alfonso, you're not helping."

Pandora sat in her dressing chair. She usually felt like a celebrity whenever she danced. At that moment, she didn't feel like the popular Brown Sugar— she felt ashamed.

At that same time, *DJ* was informing his family that the masked woman that gave him oral sex was Pandora. The good time the family was having was now replaced with shock and embarrassment.

Barron raised his hand. He said, "Well, technically, she's not related to Byron and me." The others couldn't help but laugh. Then *Snappy* said, "And Daniel and me only married into the family," his statement arousing more laughter. "Oh be quiet *Snappy*, you should be more ashamed than any of us, she's your first cousin," Ernie, Jr. pointed out.

"Shit, that's right," he agreed then saying, "But that rumor hasn't been confirmed and if it were, I would have to say, my cousin has one *nice* ass," he added, turning the half bottle of beer up to his mouth.

Soon thereafter, Alfonso emerged from backstage to see the group of patrons leaving the club in the same single line as they had entered. The group realized they all had a long day ahead of them. It was going to be the day that their brother and uncle would make his bride elect, Mrs. Richard Anthony Lorde.

CHAPTER TWENTY-SIX

Guests began filling the sanctuary early in anticipation of the wedding of the year. Two hours before the ceremony, all three areas of the church were packed, leaving little room for the guests that were now arriving. The church family had waited on this day for years, they were excited that Richard had finally decided to get married, and everybody who was anybody wanted to be in attendance to witness the blessed occasion.

The sanctuary was decorated beautifully with peach colored ribbons, flowers and candles of the same color. The wedding director was marching back and forth holding her clipboard. She had no idea where she was going to seat the guest waiting to get inside. The bride and groom had instructed her not to use the choir loft and that was the only space she had left.

The groomsmen were dressed in black tuxedos, white shirts, covered by a peach colored cummerbund. Barron and Byron escorted the female guest to their seats while Richard, Daniel, Blaine and Ernie, Jr. entered through one side of the fellowship hall as the groom was dressed in a white tuxedo with a peach cummerbund as his brother, brother-in-law, and friend were dressed in black tuxedos and peach colored cummerbunds similar to Barron and Byron.

Alma, Monica, Eleanor and Joy Lynn all entered the church from the opposite entrance of everyone else. The two matrons of honor and bridesmaid were already dressed. Each dressed in peach colored gowns with their tresses styled in an upsweep. They were helping Joy Lynn carry her wedding gown and accessories to the bridal suite.

"Joy, I need to ask you something," the wedding director said. "I know

179

you and Richard mentioned that you didn't want anyone in the choir loft because of the pictures, but we have run out of space. And I spoke with the photographers and they said it won't be a problem for the guests to sit in that area. They assured me that they can remove anything from the background of a photo."

Joy Lynn was excited and vulnerable. She was on cloud nine. She didn't clearly hear what the director had said. At this point, she would have agreed to anything.

As Joy Lynn spoke to her director, Monica's shawl slid from around her arms. She dropped Joy Lynn's overnight bag trying to keep the sheer material that matched her peach colored dress from hitting the floor.

"Lady Monica, I didn't know you had a tattoo on your forearm. What does the *T* stand for?" Alma noticed.

Embarrassed, Monica answered quickly, "It stands for *tough*…it was my line name in college," she explained. She had never allowed anyone to see her tattoo. She hated that her shawl had slipped away exposing the one stupid decision she had made in college.

"As long as all those people don't show up in my pictures, it's fine with me," Joy Lynn said.

"They promised me that they won't."

"Is it really that crowded out there?" she asked, surprised.

"That's an understatement," her wedding director answered, as she exited and Joy Lynn's make-up artist entered. He placed his supplies on the counter next to Joy Lynn's accessories then he began applying cosmetics to her face. Within minutes, her pale skin was transformed into a vision of beauty. She was also sporting an upsweep hairstyle. After her makeup was fully complete, she slid a blue garter onto her right leg. Then she stepped into her wedding gown. Monica helped to close her zipper as her cousin sat before a half mirror allowing Alma to clamp her pearl choker around her neck while she inserted her pearl earrings into each ear. A knock came at the door. She and Alma turned toward the sound as Eleanor opened the door slightly. It was an older gentleman. His hair was silver, along with a neatly thin silver trimmed mustache.

He smiled at Eleanor. Then he said to her, "Is my daughter ready to get married?"

"Daddy!" Joy Lynn screamed from her seat.

The older gentleman walked into the room. He introduced himself to the two women he had never seen before. "I'm Franklin Anderson, Joy's father," he said, shaking Eleanor's hand first then moving to Alma.

"Daddy...I mean Uncle Franklin, it's good to see you," Monica said, kissing her uncle on the cheek.

"*Monnie*, your father would be so proud of the woman you've become. A certified registered Pharmacist and the first lady of this beautiful church."

Both Eleanor and Alma were surprised to hear the gentleman call Monica by her nickname. They had known her nearly all her life and they never heard anyone call her that. Now they knew two things about their first lady, one that she had been tattooed, and two, that she had a nickname.

Embarrassed a second time, Monica gently slapped her uncle on the hand. "Stop it Uncle Franklin, you're going to make me blush."

Franklin moved from his niece to his daughter. He looked at Joy Lynn through her reflection in the mirror. He stood over her and placed his hands on her shoulders. He squeezed them gently. "*Bunny rabbit*, you look absolutely stunning today. I'm really proud to be your father," he said as he placed a kiss on top of her head.

Joy Lynn blushed as she kissed her father's hand, leaving behind her lip print. After her kiss, she smiled at Monica, before moving her eyes back to her reflection in the mirror.

"Daddy, I thought the day would never come for me to get married," she said. Then she paused. "But when I first laid eyes on Richard, there was something about him. He was a gentleman, comical and caring. It felt good...It just felt right," she added.

"Honey, I know. I felt that same connection when I married your mother. I believe she's looking down from Heaven right now. I know Richard is more than capable of giving you the love and lifestyle you deserve," her father said. "Speaking of Richard, I want to meet his mother, is she here yet?"

"Yes, she's here," Alma answered. "My sister and I will take you to meet her and that will give Lady Monica and our future sister-in-law some time alone."

Inside the sanctuary, Eloise was sitting near the rear of the church. She looked amazing. She didn't look like a bride, but she came close. She was

wearing a peach colored evening gown, matching shoes, hat and purse. She wanted desperately to upstage her future daughter-in-law and if she couldn't, she intended to give her a good run for her money.

Alma and Eleanor hadn't seen their mother before now. To them she really looked stunning. They introduced Franklin to her and apparently he thought so as well.

"Franklin Anderson, this is our mother, Mrs. Eloise Lorde."

"The pleasure is mine," he said, kissing Eloise on the hand. She was flattered. It showed in the way she looked at the tall and handsome gentleman.

"Well, Mr. Anderson, you really know how to make a woman feel special. I'm sure your wife has to keep a watchful eye on you," Eloise flirted.

"I'm sure she does from Heaven above. My wife passed away fifteen years ago," he explained, still holding Eloise's hand.

Rising from her seat, Eloise said, "In that case, the pleasure is mine." The two stared at each other. Then he said, "Mrs. Lorde, before I leave, we must arrange to have dinner. I would like to know all of my son-in-law's family."

"Franklin, is it? I was thinking the same thing. If you are not busy tomorrow, I would like to invite you to our family dinner after worship service. Is there anything in particular you like to eat?" Eloise said.

Franklin thought about it. He thought about several things he would like to eat, but he decided on his favorite. "Pig's feet. I haven't had those in years," he finally answered.

"Pig's feet it is. I guess I will see you tomorrow."

Franklin confirmed the address and time before walking away. He stopped at the front of the church to speak with his sister-in-law Grace and a few others.

"What just happened here?" Eleanor asked, attempting to be comical.

"What? I was only trying to be nice to the man and he is handsome. I may be old, but I'm not dead...Now, help me figure out where in the devil am I going to get raw pigs feet this late in the evening?"

"Eleanor, I don't know what just happened, but there was some strong chemistry going on between those two," Alma said, ignoring her mother as they all laughed together.

"Knock it off girls and help me figure out how to get those pigs feet," Eloise said.

"Mother, don't worry about that. Somebody will take you to the 24-hour market and pick up a pack. How much do you plan to cook?" Eleanor said.

In the bridal's suite, Joy Lynn and her cousin were now all alone. Monica went to the door to make sure no one was standing in the hall.

"So far, so good. Do you think Carolina is going to get suspicious about Christopher?" Joy Lynn asked.

"No, I called and told her that he couldn't get in touch with her and he called me to let her know he was going out of town this weekend."

"She didn't ask any questions?"

"No, she knew that Christopher was bothered by this wedding. So, she figured he went out of town to clear his head. Did you go by the warehouse last night?"

"I didn't have time. But he had enough food and water there to last for a few days."

"I really hated doing that to Christopher. What is that beeping?" Monica asked, looking around.

"Oh goodness, it's probably Christopher's cell phone. Richard called it all day yesterday and three or four times last night."

"Where is it?"

"It's in my purse," Joy Lynn admitted.

Monica ran to the beeping handbag and removed the cell phone. She looked at the display screen. It read: Richard On Cell. She removed the battery from the phone and threw it in the trash.

"This could have gotten us caught. Most phones nowadays have a locator inside them and Carolina could have easily found out that we were telling a lie by you having this phone."

"I'm sorry, I didn't know."

"I have to get rid of this phone," Monica said, discretely leaving the room. She looked back at Joy Lynn, "I'll be back."

Joy Lynn turned to face the mirror once again. She placed her tiara comfortably on her head. She maneuvered the chocker she wore around her neck as a knock came at the door.

"Come in."

No one entered.

"*Monnie*, it's open."

The door squeaked as it slowly opened and Christopher stood in the doorway.

"How did you get here?" Joy Lynn said, shocked to see him.

Christopher stood holding his stomach. His beige shirt was ripped in two places and covered with dirt. His shirt tail hung outside of his pants. He was weak. He leaned against the door. He grabbed his head in the area where he had been hit. The blood had dried in his hair.

"I've called the police and they are supposed to meet me here. You won't get away with this," he weakly warned Joy Lynn.

Joy Lynn turned away from him and looked at her image in the mirror. She wanted to see herself one last time, before she became Mrs. Richard Lorde. She brushed her eye brows with her finger. "Christopher, that's where you are all wrong, I don't know how you got here or how you even got loose from the warehouse, but I'm about to marry the man of my dreams."

Christopher moved aside as two police officers entered the room. Joy Lynn saw them through the reflection in the mirror. She looked at them in horror.

"Joy Lynn Anderson you are under arrest for the murder of Olivia Lorde, unlawful use of a prescription drug and the kidnapping of Hannah Dovely and Christopher Christiansen."

A female officer placed Joy Lynn's hands behind her back and continued, "You have the right to remain silent, and if you give up the right to remain silent, anything you say, can and will, be used against you…"

The officer tightened the handcuffs on her wrists. "Ouch! They're too tight."

"Cool it. They will loosen eventually," the officer said, escorting Joy Lynn to the door.

Richard was now standing in the hallway along side his brother, Ernest, Jr. He ran toward his fiancée. "Officer what is going on?" he asked, confused.

"Sir, I need for you to step back."

"Officer, my brother has a right to know what's going. This is his fiancée. As a matter of fact, they are about to get married in less than an hour," Ernest, Jr. said.

"Well mister, there will not be a wedding today," the male officer informed.

Monica appeared from outside. They all turned to face her standing in the doorway. She saw Joy Lynn crying and in handcuffs. At that moment, she knew their cover up had been exposed.

"Let her go," Monica yelled, now pointing a small handgun in the direction of the two officers.

"Ma'am, drop your weapon or we will shoot," the officers requested.

"I said, let her go," Monica demanded again, this time louder than before. She moved the gun from one officer to the other.

Now, Mychael entered the fellowship hall and everyone turned a second time to the sound of the opening door. He was dressed in the black and white robe he was going to wear to perform the ceremony.

"Sir, don't come any further. Put your hands in the air," the male officer requested, moving his gun from Monica to Mychael.

"He's fine. He's the pastor," Ernest, Jr. stated.

"And he's my husband," Monica added, holding her weapon straight and steady.

"Ma'am, drop your weapon or we are going to shoot. On the count of three, we need for you to place the gun on the floor."

Before the officers could begin counting, Monica raised one hand in the air and with the other, lowered the small handgun to the floor. Then she raised it quickly. Everyone in the room ran for cover. Mychael yelled, running to protect his wife, *"Noooooooooo!!!!"* As one officer fired one shot and his partner fired two from their separate weapons.

CHAPTER TWENTY-SEVEN

In the sanctuary, Eloise sat alone as she watched the clock on the wall. One minute later, she was looking at the time again, but this time on her gold wristwatch. Time was slowly moving closer to the event of the hour. So far, she had silently wished one hundred times that her son would change his mind about this marriage. Over the last six months, she had tried everything imaginable to show Joy Lynn that she was *not* welcome in her family. The first instance was when she and her son had arrived at her house and it was pouring rain. Joy Lynn sat in the car because Richard had planned only to stay a few minutes, but took the opportunity to use the bathroom. As time passed, Joy Lynn got out of the car because she thought Richard was taking longer than usual and she grabbed her umbrella to see what was taking him so long.

Through her partially open blinds, Eloise watched as her future daughter-in-law slid out of her son's vehicle. She continued to watch her walk up the stairs, leading to the front door as she closed her blinds completely and moved quickly through the foyer to her front door. She closed the door just as Joy Lynn was about to press the door bell. She laughed to herself as she listened to her future daughter-in-law ring the doorbell repeatedly and even banged on the front door a few times.

Richard remained in the bathroom while his mother peeked through the closed blinds that were covering her bay window, watching Joy Lynn leave the front porch to run towards the Richard's car. As Joy Lynn reached the vehicle, Eloise laughed more before using her son's extra set of keys to activate the alarm system to his car.

This day, it was raining fiercely, which caused the cheap umbrella Joy

Lynn was holding to collapse on her head. Eloise found great pleasure in watching her future daughter-in-law's frustration while Joy Lynn tried to enter the alarm code into the door keypad. Before Eloise moved from the window to kiss and see her son to the door, she as well as Richard listened as Joy Lynn set off the vehicle alarm. But they didn't see her when she stomped the ground in frustration and anger.

After his mother closed the door behind him, Richard was shocked to find his blushing fiancée soak and wet. He didn't need an explanation. He figured fast what had happened as he shook his head while looking at his mother peeking through her closed blinds.

Eloise had to admit, the second instance was the work of a true genius. Immediately after Sunday school, she placed two small thumb tacks on the empty space next to her. Cleverly, she covered the tacks with her bible and purse. When she saw her future daughter-in-law walk into the sanctuary, she waved her hand for her to come in her direction. Joy Lynn looked shocked since her future mother-in-law had run her away from the section so many times before. As her arms lay next to her body, Eloise grabbed her future daughter-in-law and pulled her into her, planting a big kiss to her pale cheek. Yes, she shocked her twice. Then she complimented her on her outfit as she invited her to sit next to her—two things she had never done before. Joy Lynn was shocked a third time, but she accepted the offer as Eloise moved her purse and bible discretely as Joy Lynn sat her bottom perfectly upon the two sharp thumb tacks. Even today, the thought still makes Eloise laugh at the sight of future daughter-in-law almost springing into the air.

"Oooo…what was that?" Joy Lynn had said, looking down at the pew. She didn't see anything. Then she looked at Eloise as she backed slowly out of the pew. Eloise tried to keep a straight face, but found it hard to do as she watched Joy Lynn sashay toward her regular seat with the two tacks lunged in her petite behind. By now, you would think Joy Lynn would have a hint that her future mother-in-law didn't like her and had no plans to hide it.

Today, Eloise was laughing with some members of her sister circle and teased with a few ushers that passed her. She looked around, realizing something she had not thought about before. The place was packed. Every section was full, the choir stand was full and the only space available was the pew that she was sitting on. The wedding director had saved this area for

some reason or another. She moved her head from side to side in search of at least one of her children. She saw her stepchildren, but that's not who she wanted. Where did Alma and Eleanor go? She wondered.

Then she jumped along with the rest of the guests when she heard what sounded like three firecrackers. It sounded close. Eloise sat up and looked around. The other guests were looking around also. Someone ran into the sanctuary and yelled, "There's been a shooting in the fellowship hall." People could be seen running for cover, some were ducking between the pews. Eloise didn't run nor did she duck between the pews. She got up, gathering her gown slightly that it wouldn't drag on the floor—she had paid too much money for it. She made her way through the chaotic crowd and angled herself toward the fellowship hall. As she passed the double doors, Franklin met her. They moved from side to side like they were dancing. But actually, he was trying to stop her from going any further.

"Franklin, what is going on? Someone said there's been a shooting. I want to know what happened," Eloise said.

"Eloise, you don't want to go back there, "he said, pulling her in the opposite direction.

At that moment, Franklin wasn't concerned about his daughter being arrested. He wondered how he was going to pursue his flirtatious attraction for the former first lady, now that his daughter was being arrested for her late daughter's death. He was really in the dark, more than he knew. He had no idea that it was more than Joy Lynn being arrested—but had everything to do with his daughter's love for her cousin, his niece's jealousy of her husband and lastly, Mychael's affair with Eloise's deceased daughter.

"Where are my children?" Eloise asked Franklin.

"Eloise, your children are fine. I will drive you home," he answered.

"Franklin, I just met you. I can't allow you to take me home."

"Eloise, I am not going to murder you," he said, realizing he had probably used the wrong word. "I will get you home safe," he added, holding her by the arm.

Eloise knew that the man standing in front of her was only trying to be nice, but she didn't understand why he was being so persistent. She snatched away from him and once again began stepping toward the fellowship hall. He grabbed her arm again. By reflex, Eloise slapped him, before she thought about what she had done.

"I said I can't go home with you. Now take me to my children," she demanded with a straight face. An expression she used to intimate people. It wasn't working to her advantage now.

Franklin wasn't intimated, he was shocked. As a matter of fact, he was still holding his face. The lick Eloise extended to him was given with such force the hand print was embedded into his left cheek.

"I was only trying to protect you from this entire ordeal. I already told your daughters and sons that I would make sure you got home safely," Franklin said.

Hearing his explanation, Eloise's attitude softened. She was now ashamed as she fumbled with the front of her dress with one hand and clutched her small purse under her arm. She fought with the muscles in her face to keep from laughing at herself. She didn't think laughing was going to erase what she had done.

"Franklin..."

"I understand. Not only are you beautiful, you're head strong and a bit of a spit-fire. But Eloise, at some point, you have to allow someone to take care of you."

"I know...I've gotten so independent since my husband passed away. He did everything for me and sometimes, I feel like I have to now do everything for myself."

As Eloise spoke, Franklin listened attentively, and then he spoke. "Is that your subtle way of saying I'm sorry? If you are, I accept." He said. Then he stood waiting, allowing Eloise to entangle her arm with his.

They walked through the nearest exit and headed toward his car. Franklin opened the door and waited as Eloise gathered her gown and carefully pulled it inside the front seat with her. Franklin was such a gentleman, Eloise thought. She had not told him, but she believed he knew the dress she was wearing was expensive and obviously, she didn't want to damage it. Finally, he closed the door and jumped into the driver's side of his luxury car.

Franklin drove from the opposite side of the church and Eloise never saw all the crime tape that roped off the side entrance to the fellowship hall. She never saw all of the uniformed officers and investigators scattered about the church parking lot. She was clueless to the shooting. She was clueless to the death of their first lady. Furthermore, she was clueless of the arrest of the person that was being accused of killing her daughter.

Feeling more comfortable, Eloise gave Franklin directions to her house. He proved to be a safe driver as he weaved in and out of traffic. He made the left turn into her subdivision perfectly. He pulled all the way into the driveway and placed his top of the line Jaguar into park. He looked at Eloise. She looked at him. She had been patient and by this time, she was waiting for an explanation. But the expression on Franklin's face told her that he was trying to think of something to say.

"Well Franklin, if my children are okay, then don't you have something to tell me? Obviously, my son is not marrying your daughter and if you don't mind, I'd like to know the reason why he's not." Eloise said. Honestly, whatever reason the wedding wasn't taking place was good enough for her, she thought to herself. But out of curiosity, she still wanted to know.

"Eloise, once I tell you this, I hope it doesn't change the strong attraction between us," Franklin said. He paused. Then he took a long sigh. "My daughter was arrested for the death of your dau—," he tried to say. Eloise didn't let him finish. She began frantically grabbing at the locked door handle. Franklin rested his masculine hand on her arm. "Don't touch me! How could you think that this wouldn't be a problem for me?" she said, as she jumped out of the car almost tripping on her gown.

Eloise was now outside the vehicle, moving fast to get to her front door. Franklin was close behind her. At that time, she didn't care how much her dress had cost. She wanted to get as far from Franklin as possible.

"Don't follow me," she said to Franklin.

"Eloise, I had no idea what my daughter had done until today. I am as equally disappointed in her as you," he said.

Eloise walked into her house, but left her front door open. She didn't know whether she left the door open because she wanted Franklin to come in or that she had forgot to close it behind her. She looked around and noticed how he stood at the door. She tried to ignore him as she placed her purse on the counter. Moments later, she looked again and he was still watching her through the closed storm door. She observed the pitiful look on his face. She observed his gray eyes. Then she observed his flushed skin. She still didn't invite him in. They looked at each other as the moments passed. Many more moments passed as they continued their stare at one another, then Franklin pointed at the door handle with his finger. Finally, Eloise nodded her head to

let him know it was okay for him to enter. Was she making a mistake? If his daughter was a murderer, maybe he was to, she thought.

Franklin stepped inside was immediately taken aback. He was impressed, as most people are. Every piece of furniture was in its place, every rug was lying straight on the floor, not one speck of dust could be found. The home was gorgeous and spotless, a showcase no doubt.

"You have a beautiful home," he said, nervously placing his hands in his pockets. He was still wearing the tuxedo that a father of the bride wore when they were about to give their daughter's into marriage. He hadn't changed. He looked very young and handsome in his tuxedo. Eloise really didn't want him to change. She didn't care that he looked younger. Well maybe she did.

"How are old are you?" she asked.

"I'm fifty-five. Why?" Franklin said.

"I was curious. You look so young."

"Thank you, if that's a compliment."

"Shouldn't you be trying to bail your daughter out of jail?" she said.

Franklin didn't say anything. Instead, he looked at his ringing cell phone. He thought about what Eloise had said. He looked at the display on the cell phone again. It was his attorney calling. He knew the call was probably concerning his daughter. Eloise was right; he really needed to leave to find out what was going on with his daughter. "I guess I'd better get down to the precinct to find out what's going on. Are you going to be okay?" he said.

"Yeah, I'll be fine. Someone from my family should be along soon."

"Can I call you later?"

"For what?" she snapped.

Responding to Eloise's attitude, Franklin stood non-verbal in the middle of the floor. Eloise realized she had caught him off guard. He didn't expect her to answer his question with a question. "Just to see how you are doing," he finally said. Then he turned to leave, but not before saying, "Eloise, I'm not the enemy."

CHAPTER TWENTY-EIGHT

Myles sat in his leather recliner while his wife prepared dinner in the kitchen. At the time, he was sipping from a bottle of water, relaxing before the tennis match between Venus Williams and Maria Sharapova was scheduled to broadcast. He loved watching Venus play tennis, she was talented—a much better player than her sister. In his opinion, Serena needed to lose weight. She thought her large behind was one of her assets, but Myles didn't think her large butt was an asset, he thought it was more like a fat *ass*.

The match was about to begin and while the commentator was talking, the program was interrupted.

"Good evening everyone, I'm Tamara Dovely, thanks for joining us. We have breaking news regarding a shooting at the Tabernacle of Praise Church in South Carolina. Investigator reporter Tyler Lewis from our affiliate station WRAM is with us live. Tyler, can you update us about what's going on…"

"Yes, Tamara. We are here at the Tabernacle of Praise Church, in Ramblewood, South Carolina, what some have said was supposed to be the wedding of the year, has turned deadly. As you can see, we are not close to the sanctuary, but sources are telling us that one person is dead and she is described as an African American female. The entrance to the fellowship hall has been roped off with yellow crime tape and Tamara, if you would look closely, in that general area, you can see people dressed in peach colored dresses and black tuxedos. Some of the guests appear to be very calm while others are visibly upset. We are standing here with the chief investigator from the Ramblewood Police Department. Sgt. London, could you tell us what's going on?"

"As Tyler has mentioned, there has been a shooting. About two hours

ago, the department received a 9-1-1 call stating that the deceased and her accomplice had allegedly kidnapped a member of this congregation. When the officers arrived to execute an arrest warrant, her accomplice to the crime, pulled out a weapon. The victim was asked several times to surrender her weapon, when she refused, several shots were fired, thus resulting in her death," Sgt. London explained.

"Sgt. London, at this time, can your department disclose the identity of this woman?"

"Yes, we can. The next of kin has been notified. From our understanding, the victim has been identified as Monica Anderson Dovely."

The cameras moved from Sgt. London back to Tyler. "There you have it. We will continue to follow this story and give you updates as they become available. Tamara back to you."

Reading the prompter, Tamara said, "Tyler…Tyler…is it true that the victim is the wife…is the wife…is the wife …of the Reverend Mychael Dovely and the first lady of this church?" Tamara said slowly, now realizing the names she had just read. The Nia Long look-a-like couldn't hide her emotions. She pursed her trembling lips together, trying to hold back her tears. Her eyes were now glossy as her emotions silenced her.

"Well, Tamara, just as the investigator was leaving; another source confirmed that she is indeed the wife of Reverend Mychael Dovely. We will have more for you tonight on the evening news. I'm Tyler Lewis, reporting live at the Tabernacle of Praise Church. Tamara back to you."

Trembling and her voice shaking, Tamara managed to say, "Thank you Tyler for that breaking news report. As he said, we will bring you more updates tonight on the evening news. Please stay with us as we return to our regular scheduled program."

Before the newscast could go back to its regular programming. The screen showed the shaken anchorwoman rising from behind her news desk saying, "Oh my God, my cousin is the pastor of that church. The woman that was killed is his wife. Oh my God, I've got to call my parents," she said, holding her stomach and covering her mouth with her hand.

Myles bolted from his comfortable chair, at the same time, yelling for his wife. Camille didn't know why her husband was acting hysterical. She stood silently as she watched him press the keypad on his cell phone.

"What's wrong?" she asked.

"Damn, he's not answering, it's going to his voicemail."

"Who's not answering? Myles you are making me nervous, what are you talking about?"

Before he could explain the tragedy to his wife, he rubbed his head. Then he dialed his cousin's cell phone number again. No answer. He grabbed his address book and looked up the number for Tabernacle of Praise church.

"Myles! What's wrong?" Camille asked her husband again.

"The news just said Monica was killed at a wedding. Call the station, Tamara was the anchor person that broadcasted the report. She's upset."

"What? What kind of wedding was she attending?" Camille asked, grabbing the cordless telephone.

"I don't know. Myke is not answering his cell phone. I'm going to call the church. Just call the news station and make sure Tamara is okay," Myles said as he transposed the telephone number from the phone book to a note pad.

Myles began pressing the same numbers into the keypad of his cell phone. A male answered on the second ring. "This is the Tabernacle of Praise Church, Sgt London speaking," the male voice said.

"Ah yes, my name is Myles Dovely and I am a relative of Pastor Mychael Dovely, is it possible for me to speak with him?"

"Mr. Dovely is unavailable at this time. May I take your name and number? I will make sure he gets the message," the man said.

"Sir, is it true that his wife was killed?"

"I'm very sorry sir, but you may want to speak with Mr. Dovely. I will give him your message if you desire to leave one."

"Thank you," Myles said as he slammed his cell phone closed, looking at his wife before saying, "Damn whoever that was. Let's go, I'm driving to South Carolina."

Within two hours, Myles and his wife were pulling up to the big church where his cousin served as pastor. He had no idea the church he was leading was that large—it was impressive. The entire campus was huge. The parking lot was half empty, but was still swarming with uniformed officers. Some of the shirts said *Investigator* and other jackets sported the title *Police*. It was obvious that something had happed. He circled the parking lot and parked his car in a space next the curve. He got out along with his wife. They walked

toward a couple of police officers that were directing people away from the church.

"I'm sorry sir, only family are allowed in here," one of the officers said.

"I am family. I'm the cousin of the pastor here. I just heard that his wife was killed."

"Immediate family sir, cousins are not considered immediate family."

"Young man, Reverend Dovely and I were reared like brothers. I drove here from Charlotte, North Carolina and I would like to see him," Myles informed the officer, now showing how annoyed he was with his ignorance.

"I'm sorry sir; I am only following orders from my superior."

"And who is your superior? You need to get them on the line immediately," Myles demanded.

The insensitive officer spoke into a radio that rested on his shoulder. "Sheriff Roundtree, I'm having a slight problem. There is a gentleman here demanding to see a Mychael Dovely, do you know the person he's talking about?" the office said.

Myles couldn't believe what he was hearing. He was being considered a slight problem. He held his tongue because he wanted to make sure Mychael was okay. He continued to watch as the officer listened to the directive given to him by radio. The voice stated that he was on his way out.

A suit and tie officer emerged from the fellowship hall. As the medium built gentleman walked towards him, the two men began laughing because they recognized each other. The Sheriff happened to be Myles' fraternity brother in the organization where he served as a board president.

"Officer Matthews, it's okay. Mr. Dovely can come with me," he said.

Myles and his fraternity brother shook hands and walked together down the long concrete walkway.

"Man, he didn't say who you were. I apologize for the inconvenience," the Sheriff said to his fraternity brother.

"No problem man, I don't believe you've ever met my wife, Camille?"

"I don't believe I have," he said, extending his hand to Camille. "There's no need to be alarmed about your cousin. He's speaking with our investigating team, but I must warn you that he is very upset about the shooting death of his wife and even more since we have cleared the two officers of any wrong doing. He felt we should have charged them with

murder. I hope you can get him to understand that they were *only* doing their jobs."

"I can only imagine how upset he must be, but that's why we're here."

Sheriff Roundtree led Myles and Camille into a small conference room. Mychael was sitting on the opposite side of the table near the wall. He jumped to his feet when Myles and Camille entered the room. He was still covered with his wife's blood.

"Man, she's dead. They killed her," he sobbed in Myles' arms. Camille rubbed his back as he released his emotions for his deceased wife. Myles hugged him in a compassionate and brotherly fashion before helping him return to an empty seat. After the investigators learned who he was, they updated him as to what had happened.

"They didn't have to kill her. She wasn't going to hurt anyone," Mychael said, continuing to cry.

"Where is Hannah?" Camille asked.

"She's with Monica's family. They've all left the church already."

Myles and Camille sat around waiting for the investigative team to finish questioning Mychael. Myles was shocked to learn that his late sister was apart of an adoption scam initiated by Mychael's now late wife. He was shocked even more to learn that Hannah was the product of an affair that Mychael had had with the former pastor's daughter. In the lobby leading to Mychael's spacious office, many thoughts ran through his mind as he changed the channel to the wall mounted 32" television.

"This concludes tonight's news program and before we close out our broadcast, the channel four news family would like to send our condolences to the Dovely-Anderson families in Ramblewood, South Carolina and a special condolence to my cousin, the Reverend Mychael Dovely and the Tabernacle of Praise Baptist Church. I'm Tamara Dovely; we thank you for joining us. Goodnight."

CHAPTER TWENTY-NINE

Joy Lynn was escorted into the Ramblewood detention center. Her hands were no longer cuffed behind her, but now in front of her. She cried during the drive over to the center and the constant tears had made her mascara create black lines from the inside and outside corners of her eyes. As they pulled into the congested parking lot, reporters and cameras could be seen waiting for her arrival. Thank heavens for the compassion of the two transporting officers—a side she didn't see in them earlier when they shoved her into the police car.

These officers weren't the same officers that had placed her under arrest. The arresting officers had to stay behind to be questioned for killing her Cousin Monica. *She couldn't believe she was dead.* Despite the way the previous officers treated her at the church, the present officers allowed her to enter the center through a back entrance and she didn't have to face the line of reporters congregating in the front parking lot.

Her expensive dress was now tied in a knot and wrinkled from the rough handling by the previous police officers. Her feet were hurting from the high heels she had been wearing for the last three hours. When she purchased the shoes, she did so with the anticipation of only wearing them for a few hours—not three. She limped down a long corridor leading up to the desk where a male booking officer was sitting.

"Major, we are booking Ms. Anderson for the death of Olivia Lorde, unauthorized use of prescription drugs and kidnapping," the female officer said.

"Take her through. Officer Lowe should be back there," the desk officer said.

Before they reached the woman the desk officer was referring to, Joy Lynn started crying again. She saw from a distance as the Forrest Whitaker looking woman sat behind a metal desk waiting for her. Once she and the arresting officer reached the second desk, she was handed off to the manly looking woman, who grabbed her by the arm. The manner in which she handled her was rough—it hurt. Officer Lowe stopped at a short metal cabinet and grabbed an orange uniform in Joy Lynn's size. She unlocked the handcuffs and shoved the uniform at her.

"Put this on," the officer said.

Joy Lynn didn't say anything as she slowly slipped out of her shoes, stockings, dress and slip. She was still wearing the blue garter around her right leg. It made her think about Richard and the fact that he would never get the chance to remove it from her thigh. She cried silently. Not wanting to waste time, she slid the blue ring down her leg and placed it along with her other belongings.

"It appears somebody was about to get married," the officer said as she watched Joy Lynn undress.

Joy Lynn ignored the officer's second comment and began stepping into the orange outfit. The officer stopped her. "Not yet. I need to check you for contrabands," she said.

"You saw that I came in here wearing a wedding dress, how is possible for me to have any contrabands?" Joy Lynn said.

"I'll be the judge of that. You'll be surprised where some women hide things. So spread 'um!" Officer Lowe said.

Joy Lynn didn't hesitate. Instead, she did as she was told and watched as the burly looking woman grabbed two latex gloves and placed one on each hand. At first, Officer Lowe took a long stare at her prisoner, making Joy Lynn cringe as the woman ran her hand against her breast. She was so turned off by the woman's actions that she hadn't noticed when the officer pulled her hairpins out of her hair causing her long tresses to fall wildly in her face.

"Are you a virgin?" Officer Lowe asked her.

Joy Lynn remained quiet because she couldn't believe she was being subjected to this. But she should have thought about this long before. If she would have followed her first mind months ago, she would have told Monica that her suggestions weren't worth her freedom.

"I asked you a question, are you a virgin?" the officer asked. She was now close to Joy Lynn's face. Her breath smelled like she had been eating Doritos. Joy Lynn realized right away she was not going to leave her alone, the officer's action made her cry like a ten year old. She turned her head away in embarrassment from the officer. Then she answered, "Yes."

"I thought so, but you won't be when I finish with you," Officer Lowe threatened.

"No, stop it!" Joy Lynn yelled at the woman, refusing to open her legs. They wrestled until they both fell to the floor. Protocol would have been for her to call for backup, instead the overweight woman continued to wrestle with Joy Lynn until she had overpowered her.

"Open your legs bitch!"

"No!"

"Open your goddamn legs before I break them," she demanded, finally able to pry Joy Lynn's legs a part.

"OOOOUUUUCCCCHHHH! Joy Lynn screamed as loud as her voice could go. But her screams didn't help her at all. No one came to her rescue. She knew the other officers were in the next room. She even heard laughter, but no one appeared at the steel door to rescue her.

Once Office Lowe was done with her inspection, she stood on her feet. She removed the bloody gloves from her hands and threw them in the trash. She walked in front of Joy Lynn doubled over in pain as she lay naked on the floor.

"If you tell anybody about this, I promise you, I will make sure you get rapped with a pool stick every night, understand?" Officer Lowe said.

Joy Lynn couldn't even bring herself to answer her interrogator. She just nodded her head, causing her hair to once again fall. She was no longer wearing the upsweep hairstyle that she had loved so much. Her hair was now hanging and covering the greater portion of her face.

A half hour later, Joy Lynn was fully dressed in an orange uniform and she was being escorted down a long concrete hall as women yelled at her. She didn't have any changing shoes, so she was forced to keep on her four inch heels that were intended to be worn only with her wedding gown. The shoes were painful. They were uncomfortable. It was torture of the worst kind. She kept thinking in her mind that she didn't deserve to be treated like this.

Not only was she walking in the most painful shoes that Nine West has ever made. She was further humiliated, when the same officer wouldn't allow her to wash her face. Looking like a clown, she took her mug shots with the black mascara streaming down her face. Not that she wanted to look like a beauty queen, but she thought she should have been allowed to at least wash her face of her makeup.

Joy Lynn was taken to a holding cell and was allowed to make one phone call. She dialed her father's cell phone number and he answered.

"Daddy, you've got to come to get me out of this place, it's filthy," she said, letting her tears flow freely. She didn't care that the other four women in the cell with her were calling her a wimp and a classic jailhouse diva.

"Bunny rabbit, the judge just denied your bail. The prosecutor said that you could be a flight risk because of your financial resources," she heard her father say.

"Daddy noooooo….I can't stay in here. You have to try harder."

"Honey, I'll do what I can. If the judge doesn't set your bail, you may have to stay until your trial," Franklin said to his daughter. Joy Lynn didn't want to hear what she had been told. She wanted her father to use his influence to get her out of this hell hole. Her father had always given her what she wanted and this time would be no different. She disconnected the call then she returned it in its place again the wall. She sat down in an empty space behind the rusted prison bars. In sadness, she leaned her head against the filthy metal because she wanted out and she kept hoping that her father would do everything within his power to make that happen.

Chapter Thirty

Mychael listened as the funeral director assisted everyone to get into a waiting limousine. They only needed one since the Dovely family was small. He was dressed in a black suit, carrying his inquisitive daughter in his arms. He had her dressed in a white dress with similar colored shoes, as white bows clamped the ends of her long ponytails.

Hannah sat in her father's lap as she watched the remainder of the family get into the limousine—some she knew and others she didn't. Mary Agnes entered the limousine, then Grace, followed by Carolina. They were going to escort their sister into the funeral service of her *only* child. Myles and Camille, Mychael's family, were going to meet him at the church. They didn't want to cause any conflict by riding in the family car because technically they were not Monica's family.

"DaDa… way we going?" Hannah asked, yawning. She was getting sleepy. He heard his toddler daughter, but he ignored her. It wasn't her fault but her talking was making him so agitated at this point. The more chatter he heard from anyone, the faster he was losing his patience. This wasn't occurring only with his daughter, but with everybody. At this point, he was terribly missing his wife and she had only been dead a week.

"We are going to say goodbye to Mommy," Mychael said to his daughter, straightening her dress.

"Way her at?" Hannah inquired more.

"She's waiting for us at the church. Now daddy needs for you to be quiet."

"Yeah, Mommy…Mommy…Mommy. I go see my mommy," Hannah chanted. He felt sorry for the child he had learned was his biological daughter.

This was the second death she had experienced in less than two years. As thoughts circled in his head, he could hear the sniffles of his Mother in-law Grace again, she had been crying off and on throughout the week and especially today. She couldn't stand to hear anyone talk about her daughter, Mychael's wife.

"DaDa, why her crying?" the toddler asked, pointing at an emotional Grace.

"Hannah, be quiet please!"

"But her crying," she continued to say, watching the two women comfort their grief stricken sister.

The family reached the church and emerged from the cars and walked up to the church entrance. As they promised him, Myles and Camille were waiting at the church entrance. Myles stood to Mychael's left and accepted the bible he handed him as Camille stood to his right while he carried an anxious Hannah in his arms. Myles tried not to look inside the sanctuary. From a distance, he could see Monica's casket and the sight of her made his heart race. His legs were becoming weak.

A string of ministers lead the processional, followed by Monica's female classmates, both high school and college and behind them were her male high school and college classmates who were bearers of the casket and the church deacons were honorary pallbearers. Mychael marched into the church as his legs wobbled the long distance to the front. They were shaking badly. Walking down the aisle seemed like forever. He thought he would never make it to the front of the church. In times like these, twenty steps seem like twenty miles to a grieving family.

Finally, Mychael reached the casket then he looked down at his wife, *a vision of loveliness she was.* The Rest in Peace funeral homes had done an outstanding job. Next, Hannah looked down at the second mother she had lost in two years. She surprised everyone when she said, "Bye mommy, I love you."

Mychael became weak; so weak, he almost let his daughter slip out of his arms. Thank God Camille was there to grab her. Hannah really didn't know what was going on as she held a puzzled look on her face while staring at her father. Foggily, Mychael remembered Myles guiding him to his seat next to him on the front row. By this time, he was close to being out of it. He recalled

Hannah sitting in Camille's lap, making no attempt to get to him; she sat contently, staring at him, but overall, he was spaced out.

The remainder of the family was seated and the program continued as Reverend Alton Givens was now standing at the podium, he was a friend of Mychael's from college. His subject for today's service was *do you have an anchor in this storm?"*

The short and slender minister flipped through his bible as he addressed the family. "First giving honor to God, to the bereavement family, my friend Mychael, I extend God's strength to you during this hour of grief. When Mychael called and told me what happened, I immediately went into prayer. Praying for him, and his young daughter, but mostly, praying for this community and this church. The devil can and will come in all forms of disruption. Tabernacle of Praise, Satan is not happy about this church being packed beyond capacity every Sunday. He's not happy that this man of God is walking in God's purpose. And he's definitely not happy about him being a man that can keep his hands to himself, devoting all his love and attention to one woman. I'm sorry to tell you, but this is something that has been in the works for a long time. Satan is slick, he's cunning, and he's a devourer. He had to come up with something that would destroy the head because he feels that if he destroys the head or if he distracts the head, the body will eventually die or go astray."

Reverend Givens continued to preach. He had gone into his sermon without knowing it. He intended to give a scripture, but he didn't.

"If your pastor and his family were to ever need you, it would be now. And I don't mean for you casserole sisters to be at his door every evening or you brothers who *think* and I put an emphasis on *think* that since he's grieving and vulnerable that you can convince him to go to the other side. I'm talking to the members who genuinely have their pastor's best interest at heart."

The congregation laughed, but knew the minister was telling the truth. Mychael was even able to laugh at the comment. He was now holding an alert Hannah. He looked down at his daughter who still didn't have any clue as to their reason for being there. She didn't understand that today was going to be last time she saw her adopted mother. Nervous, Mychael took the time to straighten out the different layers to her white dress and moved the long ponytails out of his daughter's face.

Eloise sat on the front row directly across from her pastor. Once Mychael had regained his composure, he took the time to look at her and she winked at him. He was able to give her a half smile in return. He knew Eloise understood his feelings because *this* ordeal was making her relive her daughter's death. He was glad she decided to set aside her own feelings and forced herself to attend the service.

"In times like these, do you have an anchor?"

"In the midst of the storm, do you have an anchor?"

"Prayer is your anchor."

"The word of God is your anchor," the eulogist said, waving his worn bible in the air.

"Family, God doesn't make a mistake. This tragedy was ordained since the beginning of time. God knew that Monica was going to grow into the beautiful woman she was. God knew that she was going to fall madly in love with the handsome and athletic Mychael Dovely. God knew that she was going to marry him and become the first lady of this church. Storms like these are not new to our almighty God. That's why I ask you today, do you have an anchor in this storm? We know who it is today, but we don't know who it will be tomorrow. So, do you have an anchor?" he said.

As Reverend Givens preached, the musician and choir members played and sang softly the lyrics to Kirk Franklin's, *"The Storm is over now."*

Mychael sat and observed his friend and college room mate bring the eulogy to a close. He nodded his head in agreement, raising his free hand to reverence God. He kept his eyes shut as tears slipped through his closed eyelids.

"Bring the volume up choir, that's right, *the storm is over now*. Those of us that have an anchor can honestly say *the storm is over now*. If you don't, I suggest you get an anchor because that's the only thing that will keep you during the storms. Mychael didn't tell me to do this; however, I feel with as many people here today, I need to open the doors of the church. If you feel that God is calling you to be linked with this church family, I encourage you to come forward right now. Come quickly, I need for you do it very quickly."

People began leaving their seats and walking briskly toward the front of the church. From where Mychael was sitting it appeared to be between forty

to fifty people. Every one of them crowded around his wife's closed casket. Some people were raising their hands and some were jumping around caught up in the spirit. Mychael thought to himself, in death, his wife was still able to bring unsaved souls to Christ.

"At this time, I would like to give my friend the opportunity to give any remarks if he chooses to do so," Reverend Givens said, motioning his hand toward Mychael.

Mychael handed a sleeping Hannah to Camille and left his seat, buttoning his jacket as he walked into the pulpit. He hugged Alton and told him thank you while they embraced each other. He really did appreciate his words of encouragement.

Mychael was now standing behind the wooden podium. He wrinkled his mouth and shook his head from side to side as he hit the edge of the podium gently with his hand. He was nervous. He found himself flipping the handkerchief that belonged to Alton back and forth.

"First, I should say thank you to the many of you who have stood by my family and me this week during this very difficult time," Mychael said, forcing himself to smile. "Mother Eloise, you were right…walking into this sanctuary today was the longest walk I've ever taken and I personally thank you for all of the advice you gave me. I promise you that I won't ever disclose to anyone the things we shared. It really did mean a lot, but life goes on. I am going to miss the presence of my beautiful and gifted wife, but the devil is a liar if for one minute he thinks that I'm going to question the mighty God I serve."

The congregation was yelling and echoing behind their pastor's statement. A few people stood up as others clapped.

"I've got an anchor…I know where my strength lies," Mychael said, feeling like he was about to preach. "The word says weeping endures for a night, but *joy* cometh in the morning. I believe that today. You may see my head hanging down today, but *joy* cometh in the morning. You may see my family grieving today, but *joy* cometh in the morning. You may even see the loneliness in my eyes today, but *joy* cometh in the morning. *Joy…Joy…*I say, *Joy* cometh in the morning," Mychael said, stepping down from the pulpit and returning to his seat.

The congregation stood up all over the sanctuary, extending an ovation

to their pastor for almost five minutes. At that moment, Mychael felt so much love coming from his parishioners, he felt obligated to stand again and wave his hand toward each section to show them that he appreciated their support. Then he sat down again and watched as Alton wiped tears from his own eyes and instructed the morticians to come forward.

CHAPTER THIRTY-ONE

Six months later…

"All rise. This court is now in session. The honorable Judge George Mathis is presiding," the bailiff said to all those in attendance for Joy Lynn's murder trial. The middle age man walked into the courtroom and took his seat behind his elevated desk and grabbed the folder handed to him by the bailiff.

Joy Lynn sat next to her high profile attorney covered in a gray dress without the accessory of any jewelry. She was advised by her legal expert to coordinate an outfit that would make her look as plain as possible. At the time, she didn't know why but she obliged her attorney—at least her father did. She later learned the woman defending her didn't want her expensive taste to be associated with her father's wealth.

The first outfit Franklin showed his daughter's attorney, she rejected. The second outfit he showed her, she rejected that one also. By the weeks end, he had carried twenty different outfits to her office for approval, all rejected. So, to keep from being sent away again, he finally decided to stop by the Goodwill store and there waiting for him was the dress Joy Lynn had on today. It defined everything her attorney had said earlier about being plain and boring.

Her attorney was a young African-American female with an unprecedented reputation of demolishing her opponents. Unlike the other lawyers her father had in mind, this woman was known as the killer shark of the sea— lioness of the jungle—bear of the woods. After meeting with the woman several times, she had no doubt that her attorney would get her acquitted and if she didn't she knew she would definitely go down trying.

The courtroom was full, a lot fuller than Joy Lynn had anticipated. The courtroom was so crowded, making some people have to stand along the walls. The entire Lorde family was present and they all sat together, filling up one row after the other. Joy Lynn could tell by the look on their faces, they all wanted justice. They wanted to make sure she was undoubtedly convicted for Libby's death.

Personally, Joy Lynn didn't have a large family and this was a time she wished she had one. She was glad to see her father but she would have appreciated if her sister could have been there as well. They were so close. Still she was glad to have the support of her father.

She'd heard through the grapevine that her father had become smitten with Richard's mother and *she* was the reason that he and Eloise weren't speaking. She hated that she'd put her father in the middle of her troubles. She knew he deserved to experience love again, the way she and Richard had done. On the contrary, she would have preferred if he were attracted to someone his own age and not to an *old* bat like Eloise. But she understood that things don't always go as planned and as hard as it was for her to admit, she believed Eloise would have made her father very happy.

For the longest, Joy Lynn thought her father was the one who had severed all communication with Eloise. She remembered when he mentioned that it seemed awkward pursuing his attraction for her when she was on trial for murdering her daughter. In truth, it was awkward. He felt awkward whenever he arrived at Eloise's for Sunday dinner and the entire family refused to share the dinner table with him. He felt awkward when he would call to speak with her and her family would lay the receiver down and never call her to the phone. He even felt awkward when the family had gatherings and everybody shared conversation with everyone in the room, except him. This is what she thought. She later learned she had been all wrong when her father admitted that Eloise was the one who had been avoiding all of his calls and not vice versa. He told her that he didn't understand the sudden change and he was afraid to ask for an explanation. All he knew, the closer it came to her trial date, the more distance the woman he was attracted to seem to put between them.

Eloise found it easy not to look in Franklin's direction, and basically treated him like she wanted nothing to do with him. In her stubborn mind, the

closer the trial date came upon her, she began to see Franklin as the parent of a murderer. She fought with her spirit. She fought with her flesh. Then she decided what was best for her and for that reason alone; there was no way she could continue a friendship or even a relationship with him.

The male prosecutor stood and called his first witness to the stand. "Your Honor, the court calls Christopher Christiansen to the stand."

Christopher walked through the open doors located at the back of the court room. He was dressed nicely in a suit, shirt and tie. He took the stand and before he took his seat, he held up his right hand then swore to tell the truth, the whole truth and nothing but the truth, so help him God.

"Mr. Christiansen, do you know the woman on trial today?" the prosecutor asked him.

"Yes," he said.

"How do you know her?"

"She was engaged to marry my best friend."

Richard watched Christopher on the witness stand and was surprised that he still referred to him as his best friend. He appreciated it, but he agreed with his conscious that he had given him a bad deal. *He was a fool, he thought*. In a quick moment, flashbacks began to appear in his head about how he had sprung the news about his ex-fiancée on him. *Yes, he was a fool, he thought again.* He was actually planning to marry and have children with a woman now accused of killing his beloved sister. As he sat there, he saw Christopher sitting in the witness box, but he didn't see a young man dressed nicely in a suit and tie, all he could see was Christopher storming out of the restaurant and the hurt in his eyes when he left. The image was still haunting him.

"Did you know Olivia Lorde?"

"Yes."

"How did you know Ms. Lorde?"

"She was a member of the church I attended and she was the sister of my best friend."

"Can you tell the jury, how you came to be involved in this cold case?"

"I received a mysterious package in the mail and it contained several documents about the adoption of a young child and a toxicology report for Ms. Lorde," Christopher explained, making sure he stated only the facts to the prosecution.

"Mr. Christiansen, would you explain to the jury how you took this document and launched your own investigation to help the local police solve this case?"

"After I received the addresses, I located the family it involved and I went to visit them in North Carolina."

"Objection your Honor, hear say. No one knows that Mr. Christiansen went to North Carolina."

"Your Honor, Mr. Christiansen is only trying to provide a time period explaining his involvement in this case."

"Overruled," Judged Mathis announced.

"I went to visit the Dovely family, who happen to be relatives of my pastor and Mr. Myles Dovely gave me information explaining the adoption of the young child"

"And who is the young child this adoption involves?"

"Hannah Dovely."

Others in the courtroom gasped, but the Lorde family weren't surprised that Hannah was Mychael's biological daughter. They had all come to terms with the fact that she was the product of the affair between him and Olivia. At first, Eloise was a ball of emotions. She was mad. She was angry. Then she felt a sense of peace that she now had a part of her deceased daughter. Hannah was the splitting image of her late mother.

Strangely, Eloise always felt a connection she couldn't explain from the time she first laid eyes on Hannah. The toddler had never seen her before, but immediately began calling her *Nana*. She ignored the eyes. She ignored the impressions that reminded her of her late daughter. She even ignored all the things that stood out to her. Subconsciously, she didn't want to see her daughter's characteristics and personality in the child. It made her focus too much on the child she carried for nine months—the child that was no longer alive.

"Your Honor, I would like to present exhibit *A* for the jury to observe." The prosecutor waited as the bailiff clicked the screen to reveal a copy of Libby's toxicology report. The screen highlighted the drugs found in her blood stream.

"Your Honor, I would like to present exhibit *B*. It's a surveillance video of Ms. Anderson arriving at Ms. Lorde's residence. I would like for the jury

to take notice of the date and time of the video. It was approximately nineteen hours before Ms. Lorde was found dead in her home."

"Objection your honor—the prosecution doesn't have a definitive time of death."

"Your Honor, as a matter of fact I do. If you will notice, the toxicology report states that Ms. Lorde was dead between 15-20 hours. Therefore, I feel I would be correct in stating that it was 19 hours."

"Objection is overruled," Judge Mathis announced again.

"Mr. Christiansen, could you tell the jury how you put Ms. Anderson at the residence of Ms. Lorde?"

"Because of her car tag."

"Objection your Honor, what does this have to do with the case?"

"Your Honor, Ms. Anderson has a personalized tag which is very distinctive."

"Objection is overruled," Judge Mathis said.

"Mr. Christiansen, could you tell the jury how you determined the person at Ms. Lorde's residence to be Ms. Anderson?"

"Her license tag has *All Joy* on it."

"No further questions, your honor."

The judge scribbled on a yellow pad. He turned his attention to the female attorney.

"Counsel—your witness," he said.

The woman left her seat, fumbling with a pen in her hand. She looked at the jury. Then she walked up to the witness stand, standing in front of Christopher.

"Mr. Christiansen, how well do you know the Lorde family?"

"I know them very well. I was practically reared in their household," he said.

Richard was getting anxious. He began fidgeting in his seat. He folded his arms across his chest. His mother noticed right away. She looked in his face, then down at his nervous feet. He shuffled them back and forth. As a child, he only did those things when he was nervous. She didn't say anything, but turned her attention back to the cross examination.

"It's funny you would say that," she said, slightly hitting herself on the lips with the pen.

"According to your testimony, you said you knew the family well and you were practically reared in their household. Would you say that you were happy or disappointed regarding the engagement of Ms. Anderson and your best friend?" she asked.

Christopher paused. He looked around the courtroom. He glanced at Joy Lynn then he glanced at Richard. A few moments passed and he hadn't answered the question.

"Your Honor, please instruct the witness to answer the question."

"Mr. Christiansen, please answer the question," the judge directed.

"No, I wasn't happy that they were getting married."

"But Mr. Christiansen, why, according to you, the defendant's fiancée' was your best friend, right?"

"Yes. Ah…but…It was something about Joy Lynn that didn't feel right to me."

"No, Mr. Christiansen, it had nothing to do with your intuition about Ms. Anderson! You didn't want your best friend to marry her because you and her fiancée were more than friends. More than high school buddies. More than choir members—the two of you were homosexual lovers, weren't you?"

"Objection your Honor! Objection your Honor!" the prosecutor yelled as he stood behind his wooden table.

"No further questions, your honor."

"Order in the courtroom…I said, order in the courtroom," the judge kept stating.

Joy Lynn looked at Christopher and his eyes were wide open. As bad as she disliked him, she felt sorry him. Cameras were flashing all over the courtroom and news reporters were running from their seats out into the foyer. She had a feeling this uproar was going to be a headline for the newspaper. She watched as Christopher rose from his seat and slowly moved from the witness stand—he passed the jurors—he passed the Lorde family, according to his mother, his family, angling toward the exit doors. Then the judge put the trial on a fifteen minute recess.

During the break, Joy Lynn sat quietly as her attorney studied the list outlining the next group of witnesses.

"Boy that was brutal," she said to her attorney smiling.

"I know and I won't be as easy on the next one," she said. "The faggot should learn to mind his own business. Next time, he'll think twice before he tries to play detective again," she added.

"Wow," Joy Lynn said. "I would sure hate to be an attorney opposite you."

"Girl, you haven't seen anything yet. I didn't go to law school all these years to gain a reputation of being the underdog," she said.

Joy Lynn sat back in her seat afraid to look around the courtroom. Instead, she watched her attorney continue to scribble a few notes on a note pad. After that, her father walked up behind them. "Counselor, that was a pretty good show you just put on," he said while resting his hand on her shoulder as well as the shoulder of his daughter.

CHAPTER THIRTY-TWO

Richard stepped into his house still numb about the fiasco that happened earlier in court. He couldn't believe the audacity of the attorney representing Joy Lynn. She had some nerve, especially when she attempted to misinterpret his and Christopher's friendship. He guessed he couldn't hold it against her, she was only doing her job and a portion of that was to prove that her client was innocent at any cost, even if it was at his.

As he moved into the foyer, he took in the scent of brand new wood. The smell immediately reminded him of his family home. A home his mother took great pride in keeping clean and organized. He had to admit that his roommate/friend was doing a good job keeping their new house clean. He was grateful of his efforts, but by no means was his roommate Eloise London Lorde and he didn't expect him to be. He was just glad he didn't have to keep reminding him of his expectations.

Richard was not only Larenz's roommate and friend, but his lover of many years. During college, the two had been roommates for four years and was successful in conducting their relationship in secret. At least it was until he asked his little *secret* to move in with him. He told him that he no longer had an interest in women and he was now totally into men. He didn't come out and say it but Larenz figured changing his sexual preference from bisexual to homosexual was the result of his wedding disaster.

During his transition period, he didn't try to mend fences with his best friend—if you remember, he did a very good job at ruining their friendship. In fact, their relationship had been over for a year now. Until today, the two had hardly spoken to each other, but seeing Christopher in court gave him

the opportunity to speak with him away from the courtroom chaos. The two decided that they had been friends far too long and their friendship was worth salvaging. During the same conversation, the two men decided that it would be best to be friends and not lovers anymore. Richard agreed, but wondered why. Christopher told him that he had his reasoning for cutting off the sexual part of their friendship and truthfully he did.

Standing in the foyer, Richard shuffled through the mail sitting on the table next to the staircase. "How did court go?" Larenz said to Richard as his partner turned to kiss him on the lips, "How was your day?" Richard asked him in return. Then he said, "I guess you could say court was fine. The only major thing that happened was the prosecutor implied that Christopher and I were lovers," he informed him.

"What? Who was there from your family?"

"Ah…the entire family—in-laws and all. So, I hope you understand, I am not in the mood for much conversation," he warned Larenz.

Rather than question Richard further, Larenz backed off and returned to the kitchen to finish dinner. He had anticipated that the day was going to be long, so he prepared Richard's favorite. He was planning to cook a juicy steak, a baked potato and a salad, which was chilling in the refrigerator along with a bottle of wine.

Today was Larenz and Richard's six month anniversary since they had moved in together and he wanted their celebration to be special. As he wrapped two potatoes with foil then placed them both in his heated oven, he remembered how reluctant he was about getting serious with his college roommate. At the time, he knew he could be getting himself into a mess—based on the long history between the former best friends. In his mind, becoming a live-in lover is nothing compared to someone that will be available for a quick round of sex.

Larenz had become comfortable being a piece on the side and couldn't blame anyone but himself. Over the years, he had accepted everything that Richard had done to him simply because he didn't feel he was worthy of better treatment. He was overweight, had poor self-esteem and considered himself unattractive. His negative mind frame always made him think he wasn't good enough to be with someone like Richard—a millionaire. A man that had so much going for him—his good looks, his education and his

charisma. All three combined had always made room for his live-in lover in the outside world.

Now things were different for Richard since he no longer had someone he could call his best friend or lover. Not by choice, but he was now available to see whoever he wanted and that person happened to be Larenz. A person who didn't give the invitation a second thought and willingly came running into Richard's arms—arms that were unsafe and possibly on the rebound.

Walking up the spiral staircase then down the hallway to his bedroom, Richard pulled his jacket from his shoulders. Minutes later, he was stepping into a hot shower and fifteen minutes after that, he was walking into the den, now dressed in comfortable clothes as he found a place on his plush sofa. He opened the folded newspaper and began reading it.

Larenz waited awhile before following his partner into the same area. He sat next to him to let him know that he had finished dinner. Richard had told him that he wasn't up for much chatter, how easily did he forget, he thought.

"What did I do?" Larenz said.

"I told you that I didn't feel like talking," Richard said to him again.

Before Larenz could come back with a response, the phone rang. He removed himself from the sofa to answer it.

"Hello," he said.

"Larenz, why are you answering my son's telephone?" he heard Eloise say.

"And how are you Eloise?" he said, attempting to be sarcastic. Because Eloise was always rude to him, he refused to refer to his elder as Mrs. Lorde, Mrs. Eloise and definitely not, Mother Lorde.

"Put my son on the phone," Eloise continued with rudeness. "I don't know where in the *hell* my son finds his group of friends," she continued to say to someone in the background. It was apparent she didn't care whether Larenz was listening or not. He was, as he kept the phone to his ear, he listened until Eloise had finished ranting then he passed the phone to Richard.

"It's for you—its Mommy dearest," he said, hoping the elder Lorde heard him as he rolled his eyes toward the ceiling.

"Hello."

"Son, why is he answering your phone?" Eloise asked Richard. He knew his mother didn't like Larenz. For some reason, she didn't like anybody in

the Mayweather family. Whenever someone mentioned the Mayweather name, she cringed. Her hatred was personal and it wasn't just for the Mayweather family but for any of Richard's friends. She had a problem with everyone one of them, everyone, except Christopher.

"Mother, not now, I have a headache. Did you need something, I was about to sit down to dinner?" he told her.

"No, I just wanted to check to see how you were doing," she paused. "Alright, I'm going to let you go and eat dinner. I love you son."

"Okay Mother, I love you too…Mother, Larenz doesn't live here," Richard lied. "I'll make sure he doesn't answer the phone again," he said, winking his eye at his partner.

Richard disconnected the call with his mother as he noticed that Larenz had left the room. He sat with a blank stare on his face then he returned to reading his newspaper. He still meant what he had said earlier, he didn't want to be bothered. He had hoped that his partner had got the intended message or in fact, remembered their earlier conversation.

Larenz didn't say anything to Richard throughout dinner. He finished his food first and Richard finished his soon after. He stood at the sink washing the small amount of dishes they had used during dinner. As he moved his hands around in the soapy water, he thought about how his and Richard's living arrangement was a secret. Even though he had told him that he was the head of his household, he still wasn't man enough to tell his mother the truth.

Richard pushed his plate to the side and began scanning the portion of the newspaper he had brought with him to the dining table. He read the section while listening to the sound of plates and glasses being placed in the cabinets. Then he heard the refrigerator open and assumed that Larenz was placing the leftovers from dinner inside it.

All of a sudden, Richard said, "I feel sick. I think I'm going to throw up," as he ran from the table to the downstairs bathroom. The nausea overwhelmed him and he couldn't stop releasing his dinner into the toilet.

Larenz listened from the kitchen as his lover gagged and regurgitated all of his dinner from his body. He listened longer as Richard threw up, gagged, threw up and gagged again. Finally, he couldn't listen any longer from the next room and now he was standing at the doorway of the same bathroom.

"Are you going to be okay?"

"I think so; I don't know what is going on with me," Richard said, looking at the pink mixture in the toilet, before flushing it down.

Truly, he didn't know what was going on with him. For the last six months or so, he had been regurgitating every time he ate. It had gotten to the point where he no longer ate lunch during the day, fearing he would bring his food back to the surface. He moved from the toilet to the sink and splashed water on his face. His face still felt hot. He dashed more of the cold water on his face and grabbed the towel that Larenz held in his hand.

"I brought home those papers for you to sign," he managed to say.

"What papers?" Larenz asked. He had forgotten about the discussion they had previously. Unsure, he followed Richard to his study and sat down on the opposite side of the desk as Richard sat on the other.

Richard showed him the locked cabinet where he kept his last will and testament. He explained all of the papers that he saw in front of him, also handing him a blue ink pen to sign all the documents making him the beneficiary to all his insurance policies. Then he showed him where he had added him to all of his checking and savings accounts. In a separate folder, Richard let him see where he was leaving the insurance business to his mother. He didn't like it. Richard saw the way he wrinkled his nose, but that was something he had to do.

"Richard, why are you doing this now?" Larenz asked, confused. "Do you need to tell me something?"

"It needs to be done sooner or later," Richard responded.

Larenz had changed his own insurance policies to name Richard as his beneficiary and he made his sister aware of his changes. Claudette didn't have a problem with the changes he had made because she knew her brother was gay and she knew the type of relationship he had with Richard. She made it appear easy for him because she respected his partnership with Richard.

But, the situation was quite different with Eloise, who had no idea her son had signed over his hefty insurance policies to his partner. She knew the two were roommates in college, but she didn't know they were secret lovers. She didn't even know they were living together. Once she found out the changes he had made, Richard knew she would vow with every ounce of conviction within her to make Larenz's life a living hell. It wouldn't matter that the insurance policies were an agreement between he and Larenz. It wouldn't

matter that he had known Larenz longer than he had known Christopher. Once she found out, not one thing would matter.

"I hate when you start doing stuff like this," Larenz said, holding in his hands the folder with the copies Richard had handed him.

"Didn't you start this a few months ago?" Richard said, reminding his partner about the papers he had signed for him months before.

"I know, but I didn't know you had all this invested. All I had was a few policies and an old car," he said.

"And we're going to fix that, I custom ordered you a brand new Honda Accord. It should be here next week," Richard said.

"A brand new car?" Larenz quizzed.

"Top of the line...don't you think you deserve it?"

While looking at his papers, Richard suddenly thought about his father. He remembered it was the week before his father had passed away when he stopped by the church unannounced. Like always, his father was glad to see him. They sat around while his father updated him about everything going on with the congregation. Then he asked him about his friendship with Christopher. At the time, Richard was very surprised at his father's questioning. As long as he could remember, that particular day was the first and only time his father had followed up idle gossip.

Richard laughed that day the way he was laughing now. Today, it was easy to recall the story for Larenz, but a year ago, he had been under so much anxiety before he revealed to his father that he and Christopher were lovers. In that moment, he was prepared for a long sermon. Instead, he received comforting words from a man full of compassion for God's people. He remembered his father saying to him, 'Do you love him?'

Keeping Larenz engaged with his conversation, he also recalled for him how uncomfortable he was to have that type of conversation with his father. He admitted that the opportunity to disclose his sexual preference had lifted a load from him. That day, he told his father that he was planning to build a new house and he and Christopher were going to live as partners. He remembered that his father didn't respond to him in a negative manner, but he told him that he had his own cross to uphold. But if he were going to have that type of relationship that he needed to sit down with Christopher to discuss what happens after one or the other passes away. Richard mentioned

to Larenz that his father's only suggestion to him was that he leaves the insurance business bearing the family name to a member of his own family.

And today, that's exactly what he was explaining to Larenz. He believed he understood his position. At least, he hoped he did since he didn't comment either way.

"It's not that much, but for publicity sake, I'm going to keep my mother as the executor of my estate. Therefore, I'm going to leave her the house and the family business. Do you have a problem with that?" Richard lied. He knew his estate was worth millions and even though he trusted Larenz, he wanted his mother to handle his will as he had outlined it.

"Not really, as long as she gives me time to find somewhere else to live."

"I'm sure she will. My mother isn't as hard as she appears. She's really a sweet woman; people just have to get to know her."

"Whatever."

"Whatever what?" Richard asked, defensively. He was looking at Larenz becoming offended about his attacks against his mother.

"She's your Mama, I expect you to say that."

"I'm serious. She's really sweet in her own way. She just doesn't take any stuff."

CHAPTER THIRTY-THREE

It was Saturday morning and Mychael stumbled from his bedroom to the front door. It was nine o'clock, and he and Hannah still weren't stirring around. He looked through the peephole, surprised to see Christopher standing on the other side of the door. He opened it. He was still covered in a t-shirt and his pajama bottoms.

"Sir you order breakfast," Christopher said, mocking the dialogue of a Chinese delivery person.

Mychael laughed at his new secretary's imitation. Recently, he had hired him in the position that Beatrice once held. When he interviewed him, he joked, but was really being serious when he asked him was he *crazy* like his cousin.

"No, I didn't, but I'm sure I can find some place to put this order," Mychael said in return. He grabbed the two carryout plates, lifting them to his nose. Whatever was in the containers smelt similar to his favorite breakfast item? Hungry and anxious, he led the way to the kitchen then he opened one of the tightly closed containers. He was correct. It was his favorite—salmon croquet. One plate had a small portion, obviously for Hannah and the other was piled with grits, croquets, link sausages and scrambled eggs, obviously for him.

"Man, yo' Mama really know how to treat her pastor. Please tell her I said thank you," Mychael said.

Chris looked at him then he handed his pastor his cell phone.

"No, you call her," he said.

Mychael took the phone in his hand and began pressing numbers into the

keypad. He said, when Christopher's mother answered, "Sister Carolina, I was telling your son that you really know how to treat your pastor." He listened for a few moments then he laughed along with her. He said, looking at Christopher, "Yes ma'am. I will be looking forward to this every Saturday and by the way, your son makes a good delivery guy, he has the Chinese dialogue down to a science," Mychael said, laughing again.

As Mychael spoke into the phone, Christopher took the liberty of looking at the papers lying on the counter. Mychael hadn't mentioned it, but he was now a very wealthy man. The copies said he had received over a million dollars as the beneficiary to Monica's life insurance policy. Plus, $700,000 from her job and other small policies the two had together.

Mychael disconnected the call with Carolina and returned his attention to Christopher. He stood at the island counter with one foot propped on top of the other. He continued to stir margarine into his grits, adding his eggs and salmon.

"What kind of promises has my mom made to you?" Christopher asked.

Mychael didn't answer him right away, he continued to stir his food, smiling at Christopher for a few seconds then he looked down at his plate again. He knew if he kept staring at his houseguest mischievously, he would make him feel uncomfortable. He meant to do it.

"She said next Saturday would be your turn to fix me breakfast," Mychael said, changing around the conversation between him and Christopher's mom. Carolina really said she would be the one fixing him breakfast on Saturdays, but he used the opportunity to joke around with Christopher.

"Huh…I know my mom didn't say that. 'Cause she knows that I don't cook for anybody, but myself," he said.

Mychael put a spoon full of food in his mouth and swallowed, waiting a few seconds before he spoke. "So, you're telling me that you wouldn't cook breakfast for your pastor?" He asked his secretary.

"Nope," Christopher countered.

"Even…if I was starving?"

"Even… if you were starving."

"I don't believe you. I think next week, you are going to try to out do your mother." Mychael stated confidently.

"Wait on it."

"I can't wait."

"Mom said that if you had something to do today, she would keep Hannah for you," Christopher said, changing the subject.

"She told me and I certainly appreciate it, but this is Mother Lorde's turn to get her and she doesn't play about her weekends," Mychael let Christopher know. "Ask her can I have a rain check?"

"I'm sure she'll give you one."

"When were you going to tell me that you were moving out?" Mychael asked a shocked Christopher. He didn't have to think twice about where he had received his information. Undoubtedly, his mother shared too much of his business with their pastor.

"I would've told you before I moved. Don't you think it's time for me to be on my own?"

"Yes, it's past time," they both laughed.

"Are you going to give me a key?"

"And why would I do that?"

"I'm your pastor and I may need to come by to lay hands on you," Mychael said. They both laughed again. The sound of their laughter echoed throughout the house.

Moments later, Hannah appeared in the kitchen rubbing her eyes. Although half asleep, she still looked as cute as a button with her chubby cheeks, carrying her brown teddy bear. She angled past Christopher into her daddy's lap. Christopher watched Mychael and the way he interacted with the toddler, he seemed to be a natural.

"How's daddy's little girl this morning?" he said to his daughter. Hannah didn't say anything, but turned her face away from Christopher. She seemed to be embarrassed in front of him. She turned her head away a second time when Mychael tried to feed her some of his food.

Mychael looked up long enough to ask Christopher, "Where are you moving to? Are you buying a house or renting an apartment?" He tickled Hannah as he waited for his answer. He already knew where Christopher was moving to, in spite of his information; he wanted to see whether Christopher would tell him the truth.

"DaDa top...top DaDa...," Hannah said trying to get away from Mychael's wiggling fingers.

"I'm renting Richard's condominium," Christopher answered quickly, then he changed the subject, "Hannah, you have some fat cheeks," he added, attempting to pinch them.

"Tut-up!" Hannah said, with a mean look on her face.

Christopher drew his hand back in fear. Actually, he wasn't afraid of Hannah's actions, but he did raise his eyebrows while looking at Mychael.

"Hannah...that wasn't nice. Tell Mr. Christopher that you're sorry," Mychael said.

"No."

"Yes."

"No."

"Yes or you are going to get a spanking," Mychael threatened her.

"Tut-up DaDa," Hannah said, embarrassing her father. He tapped her on her hand. He had barely smacked her when she jumped from his lap, screaming and hollering on the floor. In the midst of her tantrum, she managed to kick Christopher a couple times on the leg.

"Hannah, stop it," Mychael kept demanding, sounding more like he was pleading. Then he threatened her again, but now sounding more like he was negotiating with her. "Okay, if you keep acting out, you're not going to see *Nana* today."

"Nana....way her at?"

"She's at home."

"My *Nana* way her at...DaDa way her at?" Hannah kept asking. She walked out of the kitchen, calling out for her grandmother. *"Nana*, way you at? *Nana...Nana.*"

Christopher was surprised by how fond the child had become to Mother Eloise.

"She is really crazy about Mother Eloise, huh?" he said.

"Yes, that's an understatement," Mychael answered with a small ounce of jealousy in his voice. Then he spoke directly to Christopher, "Out of all the places to live in Ramblewood, you have to lease a place from *him*."

"Come on, don't act like that, I told you, Richard and I don't get down like that anymore. It was just a deal I couldn't pass up."

"I bet it was," Mychael said still sounding jealous. "Well, we both know what will happen if you can't pay the rent," he added, placing his empty carry out plate in the trash.

Mychael left Christopher in the kitchen alone to find Hannah. He found her in the den, watching a program he didn't recognize. She was smart enough to turn on the television, but had to watch whatever was on since she hadn't figured out how to change the channels. Mychael flipped the channels for her and stopped on the cartoon network, causing his daughter to become instantly entranced by the animated characters on the television screen. He thought she was going to stay behind to watch the cartoon program, but when he turned to leave the room, Hannah followed behind him. He moved his head quickly to face her, "Baby…go back and watch television." Luckily, she stopped at the sound of his voice. She looked at him for a few seconds before returning to sit in front of the television as she was told.

Mychael returned to the kitchen and intentionally walked close enough to brush up against Christopher. It worked. He got him to take his attention away from the papers he had spread across the table. He stopped behind the island counter, opening the fly of his pajamas, releasing his excited manhood.

"Is this what you really came for?" Mychael said low enough to be a whisper. Christopher didn't answer, but fell to his knees and began sucking Mychael's hard manhood with his mouth. He licked the piece of steel like it was dinner and seemed to enjoy it. He pulled so hard his suction was pulling Mychael further into his mouth. All Mychael could do was tilt his head back as his mouth hung open.

"Oh, this feels good. Keep sucking. Ah…man, suck it harder for me," Mychael begged. He held onto the counter top as he moved around in Christopher's wet mouth. One minute he watched the door, the next minute, he couldn't help looking down at Christopher. He was enjoying the sight of his manhood move in and out and around Christopher's mouth. Christopher was a pro, Mychael thought. His suction was similar to his late mistress Olivia—Christopher's late aunt.

Christopher continued to suck Mychael, then he would swallow him whole, he didn't gag. He sucked harder, before he swallowed him whole again. By this time, Christopher's suction had become so strong, Mychael literally felt like he was going to pass out.

"Ooooooooooo I'm about to cum," Mychael said, standing on his toes and moving his hips faster. He stood by one leg as he propped the other on the nearby stool. He moved his hips faster. "Here it comes," he warned his lover.

CHAPTER THIRTY-FOUR

This was the second week of the murder trail. The audience of spectators had not changed. Christopher had completed his testimony and Joy Lynn's attorney decided rather than the jury hearing one side, it would be best for her client to give an account of her actions. She felt this would prevent the jury from basing their verdict on Christopher's testimony alone.

Joy Lynn agreed with her legal expert that she should give an account of her actions. *No one could tell the story the way she could, she thought.* Again, her attorney suggested that she try to be as conservative as possible with her wardrobe. She agreed with that suggestion as well—only because this time, her attorney used the term conservative and not plain. In her mind, she could work with the idea of being conservative, it was the idea of being plain she had a problem with.

This day, Joy Lynn was wearing a navy blue pants suit and a pair of flat—causal shoes. It was obvious that her attorney was satisfied with her dress because she smiled at her when she stepped from behind their table and walked across the courtroom into the witness stand.

"Ma'am, raise you right hand," the bailiff said.

Joy Lynn raised her hand as she was told.

"Do you swear to tell the truth, the whole truth and nothing but the truth?"

She answered, "Yes." Then she took her seat in the hard wooden chair. From where she was sitting, she could look around the whole courtroom. She could see everything...pictures of previous judges lined the back wall. People were walking in and out the rear door. Looking from this angle, she didn't have to miss anything. It was one thing to be sitting with your back to

the spectators, but now she was forced to face all the people she had hurt—Richard, his mother and her father. A tear left her eye without a warning.

"Ms. Anderson, please tell the court how you came to know the deceased," her attorney said beginning her portion of questioning.

"She was a patient at the Ramblewood Gynecology & Obstetrics office where I worked," Joy Lynn said, looking down and rubbing her hands together. Her palms were sweaty, but she had to keep in mind what her attorney had told her. She had told her to make sure she addressed all her responses directly to the jury or make sure she glanced at the jury every now and again. She had to admit, right now, she wasn't doing a good job.

"Had you known the deceased before then?"

"I knew of her, but I didn't know her personally."

"Would you elaborate for the court, what you mean by knowing of Ms. Lorde, but not knowing her personally?"

"I attended worship service a few times with my cousin and Ms. Lorde's father was the pastor. I'd heard the name Olivia Lorde, but I hadn't seen her until I visited the church."

"How did you hear of the name?"

"By my cousin—she suspected her husband was having an affair with Ms. Lorde."

"Objection your Honor. Ms. Lorde is the deceased and she's not the one who's on trial."

"Objection overruled. The witness may continue with her answer."

"As I said before, my cousin suspected that Ms. Lorde was having an affair with her husband. Therefore, when she came to the office for a visit, her regular nurse was on maternity leave and I was assigned to work in her place. It was at that time, I recognized Ms. Lorde from church."

"Did you have any reason to kill Ms. Lorde?"

"No."

"Is it your sworn testimony that when you left Ms. Lorde, she was alive?"

"Yes."

"No further questions, your honor."

The judge looked at the prosecutor before saying, "She's your witness."

"Ms. Anderson, could you explain to the court the reasoning for visiting Ms. Lorde?"

"She called the office for Dr. Martin—"

The prosecutor interrupted Joy Lynn's statement. "Your Honor, please let the court take note that the Dr. Martin she is referring to is the Obstetrician of the deceased."

"So noted, continue with your cross examination prosecutor," the judge said.

"Ms. Anderson, does the Ramblewood Office of Gynecology & Obstetrics make house visits to all their patients?" the prosecutor asked.

"No, but the Ramblewood Pharmacy does. Ms. Lorde requested that a medication be delivered, rather than her picking it up."

"Okay, so you work part-time for the Ramblewood Pharmacy? Is that what you are saying?"

"Objection your Honor, the prosecutor is trying to put words in the witness' mouth."

"Objection is overruled. Counselor you know exactly what he's doing. Ms. Anderson can answer the question."

"No, I don't work part-time for the Ramblewood Pharmacy."

"So, how did you get the prescription?"

Joy Lynn paused for as long as she could. "My cousin Monica gave me the prescription," she said, putting her head down. She couldn't bring herself to stare or glance at the jurors.

"It's your sworn testimony that you delivered medication to Ms. Lorde, given to you by registered pharmacist Monica Dovely."

The Prosecutor was feeling good about himself. At this point, he knew this case was an open and shut one.

"Yes, from my understanding, the day before, Ms. Lorde had been to the emergency room because she was having false labor pains. Her file said she was given medication to stop her labor and allowed to go home. The next day, she called the office because she was having a reaction from the medicine and needed something for nausea. Her doctor called in a prescription for Ms. Lorde for nausea. Later that day, my cousin, who's the Pharmacist for the Ramblewood pharmacy called to let Dr. Martin know that the pharmacy was very busy and there wasn't anyone available to deliver the medication and that Ms. Lorde was unable to pick it up. At that time, being that she was a patient of Dr. Martin, I volunteered to pick the medicine up

and take it to Ms. Lorde. That evening, I arrived at her house with the medicine and she let me in. She said she was experiencing more labor pains, but she didn't want to go back to the emergency room. I got her a glass of water and gave her one of the pills before helping her to get in bed. I asked her did she need me to call someone. She said, no," Joy Lynn explained. "I didn't know the medicine that I gave to her was a labor inducing drug. Plus, when I arrived, according to her, she was already experiencing labor pains."

"Ms. Anderson, did this look like an emergency situation?"

"Sure it did. But she wouldn't let me call 9-1-1. Instead, I called my cousin at the pharmacy and asked her what to do."

"Is it your sworn testimony that you didn't know the medication that you delivered to Ms. Lorde was a labor inducing drug?"

"Objection your honor, for fear that my client may incriminate herself," Joy Lynn's attorney said.

"No…Yes…Not until my cousin told me over the phone. By that time, I had already given Ms. Lorde one of the pills. But she was already in labor when I arrived." Joy Lynn said aloud.

Her attorney rose from her seat, "Objection you honor, if my client continues, I will have to step down as her attorney," she said.

Joy Lynn looked at the woman that had been hired to get her acquitted. She pleaded with the woman to allow her to continue. She felt in her heart that Olivia's family needed to hear what she had to say. She needed to tell them what actually happened in that house. She wanted them to know that Olivia was alive when she left her. Her attorney stood for a few more moments then she slowly sat down.

She continued, "I could see that she was in labor, I checked her and sure enough she was crowning. My cousin told me to make sure I didn't leave until the baby was born. So, I waited and the contractions grew worse. I really felt sorry for her. She said the pains felt like they were ripping her insides apart. After about an hour, she delivered a healthy baby girl. I cut the umbilical cord and tied it with a string. Then, I convinced her to let me take the baby to put it up for adoption. It took her awhile to agree, once she did, I wrapped the baby in a blanket and laid her at the foot of the bed until I got Olivia cleaned. I swear to you, she was fine when I left her. She was talking and very coherent. Mrs. Lorde, I'm sorry, I didn't kill your daughter," she said, breaking down.

Eloise covered her face with her hands and sobbed out loud. Her children moved from their seats surrounding their upset mother.

"Order in the courtroom, order in the courtroom," the judge said, hitting his gavel down on the desk.

"Ms. Anderson that was a well thought out story, but how do we know that you are telling the truth? Also, if that was the case, why didn't you come forward to explain this to the authorities?"

"There wasn't a need. The child had been adopted and the investigation was closed based on Olivia dying from complications in child birth. Besides, my cousin threatened me not to say anything. She didn't want the child in her husband's life. She was the one that gave me the name and address of her husband's cousin. She told me to pretend that I was the birth mother and to let the woman adopt the baby."

"How did you create the false birth certificate?"

"That part was easy. I sent the paperwork from Dr. Martin's office to the county public health department, using Dr. Martin's rubber stamp to validate his signature. In a week, I received an original birth certificate by mail then I forwarded the copy to Mychael's cousin in North Carolina."

"The adoption papers?"

"My cousin found a sample document on the internet."

Joy Lynn looked at her attorney. The woman was finally able to smile. She was now feeling good about herself. Despite her client's admission, she felt as though her client had pulled at the heart string of the jurors.

"Your Honor, the state rests its case."

"Your Honor, the defense rests."

"Court is in recess until we get a verdict from the jury pool. Jurors you are excused to begin deliberating," Judge Mathis instructed.

* * *

After four hours of deliberation, the jury returned with a verdict. The families were called to return to court. All those that were present earlier returned to the court room to hear what they've waited so long for.

Joy Lynn stood nervously next to her attorney as the jury foreman stood with the verdict written on paper. The bailiff handed the folded paper to the judge and returned it to the middle aged woman. She began to read:

"In the case of Joy Lynn Anderson vs. the state of South Carolina, we the jury find in the case of kidnapping—guilty, the case of unauthorized use of a prescription drug—Not guilty and the case of murder in the first degree—NOT GUILTY!"

"Jurors, thank you for your service. You may be excused. Ms. Anderson, you are sentenced to five years probation on the charge of kidnapping," the judge said.

Screams echoed throughout the courtroom. Eleanor screamed and cried, "Murderer…Murderer…You murdered *my* sister."

"Order in the courtroom, Order in the courtroom," the judge yelled at the hostile crowd.

Ernest Jr. and *Snappy* grabbed Eleanor as she continued her screaming rampage from the courtroom into the hall. Richard grabbed for his mother. She couldn't move. She sat frozen stiff. A few moments had passed and she remained expressionless and numb—unable to believe what she had heard.

Eloise was confident that if the jury hadn't found Joy Lynn guilty on first degree murder, they would at least get her on involuntary manslaughter. She wasn't found guilty on either.

The remainder of the family rushed out into the foyer of the courtroom. On one side of the foyer, Eleanor had screamed so much until she fell unconscious and now lay passed out on the floor. She was surrounded by the onsite medical team that rushed to her aide. On the other side of the foyer, Richard became so angry with the whole judicial system that he smashed his feet through a wooden bench. He leaned his arm and head against the wall. "She got away with murder. I can't believe she got away with murder. She left my sister there to die. I know she did it on purpose, she meant to leave her there to die," he said, shaking and crying.

Back to her senses, Eloise grabbed her son and pulled him away from the wall. They walked hand and hand toward the nearest exit as the paramedics rushed Eleanor to Ramblewood Medical Center's emergency room. Meanwhile, Ernest, Jr. spoke with the court bailiff to make arrangements to have a check sent over for the damage done to the vandalized bench.

Throughout the commotion, Franklin had walked past the upset family and was standing outside when they emerged from the courthouse. As they individually walked past him, he kept his back turned while speaking into his

phone. Eloise walked up to him and she didn't care in the least that he was talking to someone. "Mr. Anderson, you tell that daughter of yours, she may have gotten away with murder today, but if *only* my son had listened to me…he would've left her ass in the gutter where he found her," she said as she walked away along side the remainder of her family.

"Mrs. Lorde, do you have a comment regarding the light sentence that Ms. Anderson just received?" One reporter asked.

"Mrs. Lorde, can you give us a statement as to your state of mind right now?" Another said, pushing a microphone in Eloise's face, awaiting a response.

Declining to comment, the family walked in sequence toward their parked cars. Cameras continued to flash as several news stations continued their efforts to get a statement from them. Guarded by her family, Eloise was whisked away to a waiting SUV. As she approached the open door of the vehicle, she collapsed in the arms of both of her sons.

CHAPTER THIRTY-FIVE

One week later…

Clara Bell lay in pain on her cousin's expensive couch. Eloise didn't like it, but she had to deal with the situation since her favorite cousin had injured herself while helping her move a few boxes from her backyard storage. The large woman had been in the same place for the past two days, constantly complaining about the severe pain she was in. Eloise thought otherwise. She suspected Clara Bell was being deceitful and somehow she was going to prove it.

Clara Bell remained adamant that it was difficult for her to move, but found it easy to ring a bell to get refills of her water glass. Lovingly, Eloise obliged her, at the time she thought she was truly in pain. Then one day, she stood at the top of the stairs, watching her obese houseguest maneuver independently around the family room like God had miraculous healed her of her back injury.

After her discovery, Eloise kept quiet, allowing Clara to pretend that her back pain was unbearable. She never gave her cousin any indication that she knew different. This day, she walked into the family room, holding Flossie by the hand as she led her to sit down in her usual rocking chair. Flossie's condition has gotten worse, making her act more like a small child. She was now holding conversations with herself and sometimes she answered her own questions. It didn't bother Eloise though. She had become used to it.

"I'm bringing you some company," Eloise teased, walking past Clara as Flossie mumbled to herself a language only she understood.

"Gee thanks. Now, I know I really won't get any rest," Clara said.

"Now…now…don't be mean. Miss Flossie here won't cause you a bit of trouble," Eloise said to her cousin.

Once in her rocking chair, Flossie rocked back and forth as she moved her fingers around like she was doing sign language. Lately, for some strange reason, she was now titling her head to the side. Eloise had asked her doctor was her change in behavior a new medical issue and he assured her that it wasn't. He told Eloise like he had mentioned to her before, Flossie was suffering from old age. Specifically, becoming more senile that old. Eloise didn't need a doctor to tell her that, because she could look at her patient and tell that she was. But despite Flossie's rapid decline in her health, she still managed to remember two things, her son Byron was still *Mr. Johnson* and Eloise was still *Sista.*

"Clara do you want something from the kitchen? I'm about to start dinner," Eloise said, hoping her cousin would tell her if she needed something, rather than wait until she had left the room to start ringing that *stupid* bell.

"No, I'm fine, but I don't know what is going on with me," Clara said. "I may need to go to the doctor to get a prescription to help relax these muscles in my back," she added.

"Hummm…," Eloise mouthed. "Chile please, if I were you, I wouldn't waste my money." She added.

"*Sista*…she too fat isn't she?" Flossie said, laughing out loud. Eloise stopped and looked at Flossie because she had caught her off guard. She had never heard her talk like that before.

"Eloise, when you get back, you may be short one patient," Clara said, sarcastically.

Flossie rocked in her brown rocking chair her children had purchased for her the previous Christmas. She began mumbling to herself again. "I know what's wrong with her. She too fat," she repeated, this time raising her voice, "*Sista,* isn't she big like fat Albert?" Flossie said, laughing as she rubbed her hands together.

"Eloise! You better take that heifer out of here," Clara yelled at the top of her lungs.

"Ooooooo goodness, my ears—you talking too loud," Flossie said. "*Sista*, make her be quiet."

Eloise didn't know who was more comical, her cousin or Flossie? "You

girls please behave while I get dinner started," she said. Before she could walk towards the kitchen, she heard keys jingling as the front door opened. She wasn't startled. It had to be one of her children since they were the only people that had keys to her house. She stood in the foyer and waited until the door was fully opened. A smile came on her face once she saw that it was her daughters stopping by after a day of shopping. They had purchased her a pair of shoes.

"Hey, Cousin Clara, hey Miss Flossie," they both said, following their mother to the kitchen. Alma handed her mother the plastic bag holding a box of shoes. Eloise pulled out the shoe box and opened it. She immediately fell in love with the shoes. They were hunter green, the same color as the pantsuit she had purchased when they were shopping the week before. She and Alma exchanged small talk about the shoes as she glanced a few times at her daughter Eleanor, who kept glancing at her watch. It was obvious she wasn't paying her mother or sister any attention.

"Mrs. Christiansen, do you have somewhere to be?" Eloise asked.

"No. Why?"

"Well, you keep looking at your watch."

"I was just seeing what time it was."

Eloise placed the shoes back in the box and the box back in the bag then she handed the items to her daughter to take upstairs to her room. After Alma left the kitchen, she walked over to the sink to rinse her dinner vegetables.

"Well, I can't hold it any longer," Eleanor said, sounding anxious.

"Can't hold what?" her mother said.

"I finally convinced Carolina to go on a date with my district manager."

"Oh my goodness, Chile aren't you a little old to be playing match maker and besides, if your sister-in-law hasn't caught a man by now, she should probably call it quits," Eloise said.

"Mother, don't say that. She's been trying, but Mr. Right hasn't come along yet."

"Chile please…and at her age, he probably never will. I hate to say it, but time has run out for the girl. She need to face it, she's just too long in the tooth."

"Who's too long in the tooth? And what does that mean, anyway?" Alma asked, returning to the kitchen.

"Please don't get her started," Eleanor suggested.

"It's an old saying about animals when they are too old to mate. They can tell whether they are able to mate by the length of their teeth."

"Oh."

"Alma, don't you think there's still a chance for Carolina to find someone?"

"Goodness yeah, the poor thing has wasted her whole life hoping Ernest, Jr. would realize his mistake and marry h—"

They all jumped. "What was that?!?!?!" Eloise asked. Then they all ran to the family room, Eloise was first, with Alma and Eleanor behind her. Once there, Eloise found Flossie on the floor holding her head and her face covered in blood.

"Clara what happened?" Eloise said.

"I'm sorry. She got up and started hitting me with that magazine and I gently pushed her away and she fell and hit her head on the end of the coffee table."

Flossie was still holding her head and was now talking in a slurred tongue—like she was drunk. The cut seemed to be deep. Hurriedly, Alma ran to grab a wet towel as Eleanor dialed 9-1-1.

The paramedics arrived within minutes and rushed the elderly woman to the emergency room at the Ramblewood Regional Medical Center. Eloise had to ride in the ambulance with Flossie, or she wouldn't go otherwise. Alma and Eleanor arrived the same time as Kenneth and Miranda. Zondra arrived moments later.

It was a busy evening in the emergency department. The nurses and doctors were in and out of the different curtains as Eloise stood by Flossie's bed side.

"*Sista* what is this?" Flossie asked, referring to the needle in her arm.

"That is there to give you fluids. They said you were dehydrated." Eloise explained.

"Deactivated…I ain't deactivated. I want to go home. These people don't know what they doing." Flossie said, trying to pull the line out of her arm.

"Flossie you can't take that out," Eloise kept trying to explain; She was about to look out the curtain when Miranda walked in. She didn't ask about her mother's condition, she spoke directly to Eloise.

"I would like to see you outside," Miranda said with a straight face.

"Okay honey, let me get a nurse first," Eloise said, unaware.

Eloise returned with a nurse and they all agreed since Flossie kept trying to pull the line for her fluids out of her arm, it would be best to tie her hands. She stayed around until the young female nurse put the soft restraints around Flossie's wrists.

"Sista, what is this on my arm?" Flossie asked Eloise.

"A bracelet, aren't they pretty?" Eloise lied.

Flossie looked at her like she was the one who was becoming senile. She stared at the restraints again and repeated what Eloise had said to her, "A bracelet?" She didn't look like she was convinced.

"Flossie, where did you get those pretty bracelets from? Those are nice," Eloise said trying to distract her.

"I dunno," Flossie said, moving her wrists from side to side. "These things don't look like a pair of bracelets to me. They look like a set of handcuffs," she added.

Then Dr. Peace walked in. He held an encouraging and handsome look on his face. He recognized Miranda standing in the corner. She had a scowl expression on her face. He was almost afraid to speak to her, but he did, "Hi Miranda, how are you? Is Mrs. Lorde related to you?"

"Yes." She said very short.

"See my pretty bracelets," Flossie said, moving her hands as far as the restraints would allow.

"I do, those are nice. Where did get those from?" the young physician said, winking his eye in a teasing manner at Eloise and Miranda.

"Over there." Flossie said, not really pointing in any particular direction.

"I was coming to let you know that the x-ray came back fine and the cut is not as deep as we had first thought. Mrs. Lorde will only need a few stitches. First, I am going to numb the area and come back in thirty minutes to close up the wound."

After Dr. Peace numbed a fighting Flossie, he left the room. Seconds later, Miranda reminded Eloise that she still needed to speak with her. Holding Flossie by the hand to keep her calm, Eloise attempted to leave the room.

"Sista, are you are coming back?"

"Sure darling, I need to speak with Miranda for a second."

"Who is that?"

"Honey, Miranda is your daughter."

"Oh she is."

Eloise and Miranda returned to the waiting room to a group of sad faces. Everyone seemed to be concerned about Flossie's prognosis.

"What are all the sad faces about? Dr. Peace said the cut will only need a few stitches, after that she should be fine," Eloise informed everyone.

The small area of the emergency room where they were standing was quiet. Eloise studied everyone's faces again. She couldn't get anything from none of them. Zondra—nothing, Alma—notta thing, Kenneth—zilch and Eleanor—nothing.

"Let's go outside," Miranda insisted. Eloise didn't have a clue as to why her stepdaughter was being so curt. Once outside, she learned quickly as they stood face to face.

"How did my Mama fall and hit her head on a coffee table?" Miranda asked. "You can't be watching her, if you allowed that to happen."

"No honey, its nothing like that, my cousin tried to make her stop hitting her with a magazine and made her lose her balance and she fell. Kind of like horse playing," Eloise explained.

"Horseplay, huh? Who was the horse and who was doing the playing?" Miranda said. Then she added, "I'm sorry, but my family and I are filing charges against you for abuse and neglect."

By this time, the remainder of the family was now standing outside witnessing the altercation between Miranda and Eloise.

"You plan to *do* what?" Eloise asked because she wanted to be sure of what her stepdaughter had said.

"You heard me—my brothers will be here soon to begin proceedings."

To keep from slapping her step-daughter, Eloise backed away from the conversation they were having. Then she got back in her face. "You mean to tell me I've been taking care of your mother for over a year and now you and your siblings are going to accuse me of abuse and neglect." Eloise said, raising her voice. At this point, she was heated. In fact, she was ready to *kick* some ass.

"Eloise, we can't take things like this lightly," Miranda rambled on.

239

Eloise turned her head to look at Zondra, who didn't mumble a word—she was letting her older sister do all the talking. Eloise nodded her head up and down because she couldn't believe the nerve of the two sisters. She was more heated now than she was before.

"I tell you what…Alma, I need for you to take me home, so go in there and get my purse out of that room." Then Eloise said, pointing her finger at Miranda, "But you….you little ungrateful bitch! I was good to ya'll Mama and to accuse me of neglect is a direct slap in the face. Effective today, you and your siblings need to make arrangements to take your mother some place else." Eloise walked away along side Eleanor. Alma had handed them her set of keys and she returned to gather her mother's belongings from the room where Flossie was being treated.

Eloise and Eleanor had almost reached Alma's car as Barron and Byron parked their car. The twin brothers jumped from their vehicle, running toward their stepmother.

"What happened? How's mom?" the twins asked her.

"I don't know, go ask your sisters," Eloise said with as much rudeness and attitude as she could find. She kept walking as she spoke—not even stopping long enough to get a mental picture of what the two men were wearing.

"What's wrong with her?" Byron mouthed at Eleanor.

"Miranda just told her that you all were going to file charges against her for abuse and neglect of Miss Flossie," Eleanor explained. Byron and Barron both looked at each other, surprised by what they were hearing. They walked with their arms open toward their stepmother. "Mrs. Lorde, if that's what Miranda told you, that is the farthest from the truth. Byron and I would never think that you would neglect our mother. Don't worry about this, we will handle our sister," Barron said.

Eloise didn't exchange conversation with her stepsons. In fact, she continued to ignore them as she stood on the passenger side of her daughter's car, waiting for Eleanor to unlock the door. She and Eleanor sat in the car waiting for Alma to return.

"That ungrateful big lip bitch!" Eloise mouthed.

"Mother, do you have call her all that?" Eleanor said cautiously.

"Well that's what she is…Going to try to charge me with abuse and neglect, after I done took care of her *black* ass Mama. I be damned…if she

will. She better use her contacts to get her mother in a nursing home tonight because I'm packing her clothes first thing in the morning," Eloise ranted.

Alma jumped in her car and through her rearview mirror, she could see her four half siblings arguing. Her mother and sister turned their heads also to witness the argument that had no audio. They could see hands and heads moving back and forth, but didn't know what they were saying to each other.

"Chile ya'll missed it, them boys don't take any stuff from Miranda. They got her butt straight and told her that she had better apologize to you tomorrow. Her husband even tried to come to her defense and they told him that they weren't one of his patients and to mind his business," Alma recalled for her mother and sister.

"Apologize to me for what. I've washed my hands of all of them," Eloise announced.

Eleanor corrected her mother. "Mother, it's not all of them, Miranda was the one doing all the show boating."

"I don't give a damn who was show boating. That cockeyed Zondra didn't say a word in my defense. And since she couldn't speak up for me— let her and that *black* ass husband of hers, take care of their Mama."

"Mother, do you have to use the word *black* to describe everybody? My husband is dark skinned and you make me feel like you are prejudice against dark skinned people," Eleanor said.

"No, I am not prejudice, but if yo' husband were to piss me off tonight, I would call his *ass* black too," Eloise ranted to her daughter, ending one statement then beginning another, "Call your brothers and tell them to meet me at the house."

"Why? Are we having a family meeting?"

"Yeah, tell them that."

For a few seconds, she thought about Flossie. "She's not going to go to sleep unless somebody sits in the room with her until she dozes off," Eloise spoke aloud, propping her hand against her head.

"Mother, that's not your problem anymore, let Miranda and those worry about that now," Alma said.

By the time they pulled into the driveway, Eloise could see that her sons had already made it to the house. Richard could be seen standing in the doorway. She entered first, followed by Eleanor then Alma. She walked past

her youngest son, entering the family room, as her two daughters behind her, pressed their faces against their brother's lips. She interrupted the conversation between her oldest son and Clara Bell—she didn't speak to him either.

"Hello to you too mother," Ernest, Jr. said.

"Clara, I hope you are satisfied. Flossie had to get stitches this evening. Get your *ass* up—Ernie Junior and Richard are here to take you home," Eloise informed her.

"We are?" The brothers responded together, surprised.

"You done caused enough trouble around here."

"Eloise, you know I can't get up, my back is out," Clara reminded her cousin.

"I knew you would say that. That's why they are going to carry you to the car. I don't like what you did and you know damn well you pushed Flossie too hard. The woman doesn't weigh a hundred pounds compared to your three hundred."

"Eloise blood is thicker than water. I can't believe you sending me home sick like this," Clara said.

"*Shut up!* Don't think I haven't seen your fat ass wobbling around here. Ain't a damn thing wrong with you—Ernie Junior….Richard, take her outta here. Alma, go upstairs and get her things."

CHAPTER THIRTY-SIX

Recently, Christopher had moved into the condominium he was leasing from Richard. Out of guilt, Richard tried to get him to live in the condo free of charge. He knew that wouldn't work because as soon as Mychael learned that was the arrangement, he would become suspicious. For weeks, the two played tug of war in an attempt to finalize the lease agreement. Richard wanted him to live there for free and Christopher wanted to pay as if he was a regular tenant. Finally, they agreed that he would pay $900 a month for rent.

Christopher didn't mind because he loved the condo. He loved it when Richard lived there and he loved it know that Richard was gone. The bonus to the arrangement was he was allowed to keep all of Richard's old furniture, but from what he could see there was nothing old about the furniture Richard had left behind.

Today, he was officially moving and he had his best friends, Jorge and Pierce helping him. They were doing more laughing and joking than they were unpacking. Christopher knew he was lucky to have Pierce and Jorge in one place long enough to help him—so he savored the moment.

In the middle of unpacking, Christopher stopped to answer his ringing cell phone. It was Richard—he wanted to know how his move was coming along. He was still talking on his cell phone when his friends followed him into the living room. One sat on the sofa and the other sat down on the loveseat. They watched Christopher as he walked around the room brushing his hand across the television that sat inside his entertainment unit. He wrinkled his face and lips at the amount of dust he had on his hands. No longer facing the television, he turned to look through the open view window as people moved

about the streets. He wasn't talking but listening to Richard talk on the other end of the line.

"Everything is fine. Yes, he changed the locks and gave me both keys," Christopher said into the phone.

"Who is that?" Jorge mouthed.

"Richard," Christopher mouthed to his friend while he covered the phone with his hand. He saw Jorge when he rolled his eyes toward the ceiling.

"Okay, bye." Christopher said. Then he plopped down on his new sofa next to Pierce. "Whew, Mama *is* tired," he joked.

"Alright, *Miss thang*…give us the dirt. I know you are living here rent free," Pierce said.

"I wish I was," Christopher responded. "You guys just don't understand. Rip and I are history."

"So you say. A lie don't care who tell it," Jorge added.

"Whatever. Enough about my business, I promised that I would buy us pizza for dinner, what kind do ya'll want?"

Pierce said, "I want sausage."

"Me to," Jorge agreed.

"Sausage it is." Christopher said, missing the joke between his two friends. Then he got it, "Can you two ever think of anything else besides that?"

"Nope," they said at the same time.

Christopher should have known the answer to his question before they answered. The three of them had been friends for a combined twenty years. In fact, they had gone through so many things together—good times, bad times, deaths, financial hardships, you name it—the three of them had experienced it together.

Jorge was a thin brown skin looking brother with full lips. He stood a little over 5'8" in height. He worked as an administrative assistant for the Lorde Life and Accident Insurance Company. A job he hated, but loved because of the pay. Over the last six months, he had threatened to quit several times and could probably have done so since he still lived at home with his parents. But for some strange reason, after payday, he always seemed to change his mind.

According to him, he has been gay since the day he was born also claiming that he's a virgin. One would probably say Jorge was highly attracted to men,

despite his fear to go all the way. On a daily basis, he had to fight off the bi-curious brothers that were attracted to his petite figure and boyish good looks.

These days, especially following the passing of his boss, Jorge looked thinner. The pair had grown to become good friends before the woman died mysteriously last year. He blamed himself for delivering to her the anonymous gift basket filled with beauty items and the *deadly* chocolate clusters. It took him the longest to recover after her untimely death and sometimes during conversation he always manages to bring Halora's name up.

"Ya'll know what I dream about sometimes?" he said.

"What?" Christopher asked, going through the address book in his cell phone.

"Do ya'll think Monica had something to do with sending those chocolate clusters to Halora?"

Christopher sighed, before saying, "I dunno… I didn't know she was so crazy about ole' Rev., but I can certainly understand why," he added, laughing as he bobbed his head from side to side. At that exact moment, he was remembering the previous Saturday and how the good reverend gave it to him fast, quick and in a hurry.

"Okay, we're listening," Pierce said. He was a caramel colored brother with a medium build. He was of average height and slightly muscular. It was hard for people to tell that he was gay, at least until you spoke with him. His voice told it every time. He dressed very manly and tried tirelessly to convince his buddies that he was a top and not a bottom. They knew better. Jorge especially, since he had actually seen his friend many times in action and from what he had observed *Miss Pierce* was never on top.

Pierce was certainly a horse of a different color. He lived alone and had recently purchased a house in an expensive neighborhood. He didn't purchase the house because he could afford it, but he wanted to live among the wealthy and rich. Needless to say, his expensive taste keep him in debt whereas he had to spend all of his time working full-time for the Ramblewood Park & Recreational department and part-time at the city mall to make ends meet.

Personally, Christopher enjoyed the time they all spent together. They had so much fun laughing, especially when they made jokes about life and

each other. Sometimes they would laugh so hard until their sides would ache. They told each other their most intimate secrets and they all knew that each one had the other's back. They were as close as friends could get.

"Is that the doorbell I hear ringing?" Christopher pretended, jumping from the sofa and running to his bedroom to keep from responding to Pierce's statement. He left his friends behind with serious looks on their faces. They didn't hear a door bell and moments passed before they caught Christopher's sarcasm. Of course, once they caught his style of comedy, the two friends left the room in pursuit of him, "Oh no…you must tell us. Are you sleeping with the good Reverend?" the two friends asked, when they found their friend in his master bedroom, removing a king size mauve colored comforter from a plastic bag. They each grabbed a portion of the comforter to help him spread the material evenly across the bed.

"I don't care whether you are or not. Just tell me, is it big like people say?" Pierce asked.

Christopher couldn't help revealing the information to his friends. They told each other everything. He waited a few moments. Then he gave them a boyish look, before he shook his head up and down, confirming what they had asked him.

"Oh my God—now heifer you should be ashamed. Were you sleeping with him when your cousin was alive? My spirit says you were," Pierce joked. Once again, Christopher couldn't keep the answer to himself. This time he laughed as he shook his head vigorously up and down again. All three of the friends laughed until they fell at different angles onto the bed.

"You should count your lucky stars that Monica never found out because I would hate to think what she would have done to you and Pastor Dovely both," Pierce stated.

"I wasn't scared of Monica and her hexes. She's not the only one with a few hocus pocus tricks up her sleeve," Christopher said, now serious.

Pierce stood to his feet as he grabbed his vibrating cell phone before saying, "Now…talking like *that* reminds me why I don't eat your cooking." Then he looked at the display while saying, "What does he want?"

"Who's *he*—one of your men?" Jorge said.

Pierce rolled his eyes upward. He mouthed at his friends, "This little punk will not leave me alone." Then he pressed the green key on his phone. "Hello,

hey man what's up?" he said, walking out the bedroom, leaving his friends behind to wonder. They could hear him talking, but couldn't gather anything from his conversation. He returned to the bedroom to find Jorge lying across the foot and Christopher lying across the top of Christopher's king size bed.

"Who was that?" Jorge asked immediately, not giving Pierce a chance to tell them.

"This punk from the choir," Pierce answered.

"Could you be more specific, there are plenty of young and old punks on the choir?" Jorge commented.

"Ashton Mayweather."

Propping himself up by his elbow, Christopher said to his friend, "Wait a minute...you trying to get with a teenager?"

"He's eighteen...thank you very much."

"I don't care that he's eighteen...Michael Jackson—you're not eighteen. In fact, you are eighteen times two."

"Excuse me *Miss Thang*; don't try to get all righteous with me. You've had some young cocks in your mouth before," Pierce informed, moving his hand across the air as he snapped his fingers.

"Never!"

"Liar! And besides, I didn't give him my cell number and I'm not pursuing him. But damn it, if he keeps calling, I promise you I'm gon' bend that little *virgin* ass over the closest couch and bust him wide open...Okay!" Pierce vowed.

Once Christopher saw how serious Pierce was about his statement, he said, unable to keep from laughing, "Boy...there is no help for you."

Pierce didn't know how ridiculous he sounded talking about what he was going to do to Ashton. His friends knew he was serious and was probably looking for love in any manner or fashion that he could get it—even if it meant getting it from someone young enough to be his son.

Christopher will be the first to admit that his friend has had his share of bad relationships. One relationship that stood out more than any others was the long term courtship between Pierce and his live-in lover *Fuzzy*. In his opinion, he thought the man was a straight nutcase—the worst kind of nutcase. And yes, his mother named him Fuzzy Walter Benjamin, II. After getting high from his weeklong binges of crack cocaine, he would return home, he and Pierce

would fight for days on end—both in public and sometimes in private. On one occasion, it was a summer evening, Christopher recalled they were all were sitting around at house. Enjoying each other's company, *Fuzzy* became angry when Pierce wouldn't give him more money to buy drugs. He would have if he had it, but *Fuzzy 's* habit had drained his lover's bank account completely dry. Pissed off, he began punching Pierce in the stomach and chest. Pierce tried to defend himself, but he didn't stand a chance against his muscular six foot tall lover.

Christopher remembered the altercation getting so out of control that *Fuzzy* ended the squabble by stuffing his friend's head into a half full garbage container. He and Jorge were so embarrassed for him. But Pierce was embarrassed the most as he pulled his head out of the filthy trash can with lettuce leaves and shredded carrots covering his head and face.

The doorbell rang. "Now that really is the door bell ringing, our pizza is here." Christopher said, leaving his bedroom, walking to the door. He grabbed his checkbook from the counter and prepared to pay the delivery person. He swung the door open without asking who was there.

"Hey, I hope I'm the first houseguest?" Mychael said.

"Mychael I didn't know you were going to stop by." Christopher said surprised.

"Should I have called first?"

"No, but I have company. I thought you were the pizza guy."

"*Pizza!* My favorite, especially since I haven't eaten today, I hope you ordered enough," Mychael said. Christopher looked over his shoulder to see his two friends. They were sticking their heads out of his bedroom door. "Come in," Christopher eventually said with little enthusiasm.

Mychael walked into the spacious condo. He was dressed in a pair of jeans, a tan sweater and a pair of cowboy boots. He was wearing the *Polo* cologne Christopher loved to smell on him. Whenever he wore it, long after he was gone, the scent lingered in every room. The way it was doing this evening.

The two friends emerged from the bedroom, filing into the living room. By this time, Mychael was sitting on the sofa, flipping through some old magazines that were lying on the crowded coffee table. Christopher had to make his visit seem innocent, so he didn't call Mychael by his first name.

"Reverend Dovely, I think you know my friends, Jorge and Pierce, they joined the church a few years back." He introduced.

Mychael stood to his feet, pulling at his form fitting jeans, before extending his hand to his members. "You guys sing in the choir right?"

"Yes sir."

"Well it's a pleasure to meet you both. Friends of Brother Christopher are definitely friends of mine," Mychael said with a smile.

Jorge noticed right away that he said Christopher, and not Chris. Nobody called their friend Christopher. He also noticed that his pastor didn't appear the least bit nervous, but his best friend sure was.

"The pizza should be here soon." Christopher said, leaving the room. He heard his friends having a civilized conversation with their pastor, something he didn't think they were capable of doing. At the time, he was in the kitchen, unpacking the boxes that his dishes were in. He pulled from the second box, four plates and four glasses. He rinsed and dried them off. Before he could place them on the table, Mychael walked into the kitchen where he was.

"Brother Christopher, I guess I have to take my own tour of the place. From what I've seen so far, this condo is really nice. Do you need some help setting the table?" Mychael said.

"No, I got it." Christopher answered with even less enthusiasm.

Mychael turned away from their conversation and walked through the two bedroom—two bathroom condominium. After giving himself his own tour, he returned to the dining room table, this time taking the plates and utensils from Christopher's hands. He placed a plate in front of each chair. Jorge and Pierce observed from the living room as Mychael and their friend interacted.

"The fork always goes on the right." Christopher said to Mychael.

"Excuse me. I guess I need to go to the school of etiquette," Mychael said followed by laughter.

"Maybe you do."

Mychael lowered his voice to a whisper, "Maybe you can give me private lessons," he said as they both laughed, leaving the onlookers in the dark. The doorbell rang again. This time, Jorge went to answered it.

"The check is on the counter." Christopher yelled from the dining area.

Jorge handed the delivery guy the check and the delivery guy handed him

the pizzas, breadsticks and a two liter soda. Then all four men sat at the table and demolished the two large pizzas in less than thirty minutes. They were full.

All throughout dinner, Pierce discretely watched as Mychael and Christopher stole glances at each other. He also watched how his pastor touched his best friend's hand when passing the pizza box, and lastly, he watched how he filled his and Christopher's glass with soda, but passed the same two-liter for him and Jorge to pour their own.

Surprisingly, the two friends didn't know that their pastor was so down to earth. They saw a side of him they had never seen before. He had a great sense of humor and from what they could see, he seemed happy to be in their company. They even found it strange to see him in this mood because usually from the pulpit, he was expressionless, especially when he was about to deliver the word.

"Well Christopher…Jorge and I have to go and get ready for service tomorrow." Pierce said, winking at Jorge. He thought he was being cute by referring to his friend as Christopher and not Chris. Christopher shocked him by his response. "I thought ya'll were here to help me to finish unpacking. Can't ya'll stay a little while longer?" he said, prompting Mychael to turn his head quickly in his direction. He apparently had other plans.

Frankly, Mychael was glad his church members were leaving early because three was too many and four was *definitely* a crowd.

"No, we better go. I haven't laid out anything to wear for tomorrow," Jorge added.

"What are you talking about? We are wearing robes tomorrow." Christopher said before following his friends to the door and talking with them for an additional twenty minutes. He stalled for as long as he could then he returned inside.

"What's going on with you? You act like I make you nervous or maybe having me and your buddies in the same room makes you uncomfortable?" Mychael said.

"I'm fine. You caught me by surprise. I didn't know you were coming over this soon." Christopher said.

Mychael didn't like what he was hearing, he paused before he spoke. "Are you saying that I should've called first?" he asked again, entangling his fingers with Christopher's. Christopher didn't answer his question. He had

already told him that he didn't have to call. But he couldn't help remembering what he had said to him. *Never show up to my house unannounced.*

"Well, yes and no. Remember, you told me to never show up to your house unannounced." He recalled for Mychael.

Pierce and Jorge were gone now and Mychael didn't have to say Brother Christopher anymore. He could simply call his lover by his first name. "Christopher, I was married then and you knew the reason for me saying that. Even still today, you can't tell your friends about us. I'm the pastor of a church with a membership of 2,000. Do you think it would be good for business if the congregation knew I was a homo…? I mean… that I'm ga—?" Mychael tried to say, unable to label himself.

"No, I don't really *think* people would take that too well." Christopher agreed.

"Then it's settled, I don't want you hanging around Jorge and Pierce anymore. If they figure out something is going on between us, my position as pastor could be threatened."

"You don't have to worry about that. My friends will never use something I tell them against me or you."

"Christopher, you don't have a choice in this matter. There is too much at stake, now promise me that you will end your friendship with Jorge and Pierce."

In no way did Christopher want to break ties with Pierce and Jorge, but to appease Mychael, he slowly agreed. Truthfully, he didn't have any intention of ending his friendships. But he would just have to figure out a way to keep his friends and Mychael separated. No matter what Mychael thought about Pierce and Jorge, he and his friends have never kept secrets from one another and they weren't going to start now.

Moments later, Mychael interrupted Christopher's thoughts when he took his hand and lifted Christopher's head to face him, "You do understand, right?"

"Yeah," Christopher said mildly.

"And it's not yeah, it's yes sir. If you don't make this happen, this thing we have is over," Mychael said mixed with a hint of an ultimatum.

Their conversation was interrupted when Christopher's cell phone started to ring. He could see from a distance that it was Pierce. Mychael

didn't give him a chance to pick up the talking device before he grabbed it in his hands to answer it.

"Hello," he said.

"Ah…may I speak with Christopher?" Mychael heard Pierce say.

"No you may not. I'm sorry man, but please don't call this number again, Christopher is in a leadership position and I don't want you guys distracting him from his leadership role."

"Excuse me! Look here bishop…I got your num—" Pierce attempted to say, before Mychael cut him off. "It was nice talking to you, but you heard me," he said then he flipped the cell phone closed. He scrolled through Christopher's cell phone address book and deleted Pierce's number, moving to Jorge's, deleting that one also.

Christopher was still in shock—he couldn't believe what had just happened. If he had known accepting the position as Mychael's secretary and financial clerk would change him like this, he would have never accepted the offer. He thought about his earlier meeting with him, he remembered him saying, "Brother Christopher this is the best decision you've ever made. You and I are going to make a great team." It was something about the way he said, they were going to make a great team. It sounded strange when he said it then and it still seems strange now that he was remembering the words today.

Lost in his thoughts, Christopher didn't realize Mychael had left his seat, walking toward the bedroom. Mychael snapped him back to reality when he looked over his shoulder and noticed him still at the dining table, "Are you coming or what?"

CHAPTER THIRTY-SEVEN

After the big altercation between her and Eloise, Miranda was forced to take a leave of absence to take care of her ailing mother. She was determined to prove to that *prune* Eloise that she was capable of taking care of her own mother, as good as, or even better than she ever could. Indeed, she was a nurse administrator and she had a strong background in patient care. *It couldn't be that difficult,* she thought. But if she were to be honest with herself, she would have to admit that she wasn't doing a good job.

Since her arrival, Flossie wasn't being cooperative nor was she sleeping during the night. After four failed attempts to run away, she forced her daughter and son-in-law to install dead bolt locks on all the doors. She was determined to find her way back to Eloise, her *Sista.*

"I want to go home. Where's *Sista*?" she would say to Miranda. She out right refused to do anything her daughter asked of her and that included eating her cooking. "I don't want to eat this, it taste like slop," she added, moving the spoon from her mouth, knocking the plate to the floor. "Call *Sista*, she'll cook me something."

Over time, after refusing to eat so many times, she lost a tremendous amount of weight. She was so tiny and frail that you could see the weakness in her eyes and the bone structure of her face. No matter how hard Miranda tried, her mother was making it difficult to take care of her, but as any offspring would, Miranda kept trying to give her mother the best care she deserved.

Today was Tuesday, it was mid-morning and Miranda was dreading to get out of bed. She was tired. She was exhausted even. Earlier, she had been

sitting in the room with her mother until around four o'clock in the morning. While sitting in her mother's rocking chair—the same chair Eloise had sent over by express delivery. As soon as she would doze off, her mother would say out loud, "*Sista*, you sleep? I got to go to the bathroom." Miranda didn't know whether this was her punishment or a curse, especially since her mother was actually wearing a diaper. She tried to explain the concept to her mother, who only looked at her confused and still half asleep. A few moments would pass before she began humming to herself and after an hour she eventually dozed off to sleep again.

The digital clock now said nine o'clock. Miranda should have been up two hours ago to allow ample time to get her mother her medications and breakfast. Her husband kept telling her to get up and informed her that he was leaving to make his rounds at the hospital then to his office to see patients.

She really didn't have a legitimate excuse for not being out of bed. She was awake, but resting in bed gave her quiet time to figure out how she would apologize for the twentieth time to Eloise. She had called her stepmother twice, only to have her hang up on her each time. She had sent her three apology letters only to have them all returned—addressee unknown. She even approached her several times at church, only to have two male ushers escort her back to her regular seat. The final straw was when she showed up at Eloise's house, not only did she not open the door, but the next day, she was served with a limited perimeter restraining order.

Now, the phone was ringing and the sound was interrupting her thoughts. She grabbed it on the second ring, "hello."

"How's Mama?" Miranda heard Byron say. She didn't answer her brother's question, rather she immediately began sobbing into the phone, "Zondra and I can't take care of Mama alone, you and Barron need to come home more often to help out."

Byron lit into her without pausing, "I don't care what you can't do, make it work. Because it was your doing to offend Mrs. Lorde by accusing her of abuse, now you figure it out." Then he took his turn to hang up on her.

After hearing her brother's words, she cried harder, but eventually forced herself to get out of bed. She moved from the bedroom to the bathroom and stepped into the shower. After she finished drying herself, she put on a fresh pair of silk pajamas and a matching bathrobe. She walked into her mother's

bedroom and as she walked up to the bed, she didn't hear her mother talking, in fact, she was positioned towards the wall. Since she had been living with her, she had never slept that way. She always slept facing her bedroom door.

"Mama it's time to get up." Miranda said, not getting a response. She shook her and still no response. She felt her pulse, it was shallow.

Frantically, she grabbed the telephone to call for an ambulance. Then she phoned her sister. She didn't reach her at first, Zondra was in the middle of an English class, but her secretary said she would give her the message. She stayed at her mother's side until the paramedics arrived. When she heard the doorbell ring, she ran to the front door to let them in. Not wasting a moment, they rushed by her, but waited until she could show them the location of her sick mother.

Zondra arrived at the house as the paramedics took her unconscious mother out on a stretcher. By this time, Miranda had thrown on some clothes, grabbed her purse and locked the door, before getting in the car with her sister. Zondra drove similar to a maniac behind the blinking ambulance, refusing to stop for red lights or stop signs.

"I think we need to call Mrs. Lorde and let her know Mama is going back to the hospital." Zondra suggested.

"She's not going to come up there." Miranda said.

"We don't know whether she's going to come or not, but it's our responsibility to let her know. And if she decides not to visit her, at least we've told her."

"Okay, if you say so… Good luck."

Miranda pulled her sister's cell phone from her purse and handed it to her. Zondra had Eloise's number on speed dial, next she listened as the rings sounded in her ear.

"Hello," she said to whoever answered the phone. Miranda could only assume it was Eloise. Zondra continued, "Mrs. Lorde, this is Zondra, I was calling to let you know that Miranda and I are on our way to the hospital, Mama got sick again and I wanted to call to let you know."

Today, Eloise was in a good mood. At least, she didn't hang up on her stepdaughter and that was a sign that she was. Zondra kept talking, updating Eloise about her mother's current condition. From what Miranda could tell, Zondra didn't receive an indication whether their stepmother was planning to drop what she was doing, to get to the hospital to see their mother.

"Thanks honey, I appreciate you calling," Eloise said.

"I knew you would. I'll keep you posted."

Later that evening, at the hospital, Flossie could be found drifting in and out of sleep. She was now attached to a fluid drip and her arms were tied to the railings of her bed. She would sleep awhile, then, she would wake up to yank at the restraints.

Miranda was now at the hospital alone. Earlier, Zondra had to leave to get her son from daycare. She promised her sister that she would come back once her husband made it home from work. Miranda sat quietly in the chair next to her mother's bed. While her mother slept, she had made several attempts to take a nap, but her mother only slept in five minute increments.

"What am I doing here?" Flossie asked, confused.

"Mama, you are sick. Please try to calm down," Miranda tried to explain. She could tell from her reaction that her mother didn't understand what she was saying.

Flossie waited before she said anything else. Miranda saw the expression on her mother's face and she could tell from her stare that she didn't know who she was. Flossie waited a while longer then she said as she pulled her restraints, "Who are you? Where's my Sista."

At the same time, a knock came at the door and the distraction forced Flossie to stop pulling at her restraints. Together, she and Miranda stared at the opening door. It was Eloise, Alma and Eleanor. Upon seeing Eloise, Miranda became sad immediately when she saw her mother's response to Eloise.

"Sista—Sista, take me home. These people don't know what they're doing," she yelled, reaching out to Eloise as far the restraints would allow.

"Mama, please calm down and be still," Miranda said.

Earlier at home, Eloise had received a call from Byron, asking her to find out the status of his mother's condition. This was her only reason for being there. Based on the conversation she had with Byron, he and his brother both were tied up with court cases and weren't able to take the trip to Ramblewood. She agreed—she had nothing better to do. So, having the opportunity to walk into Flossie's hospital room made her feel vindicated, but she resisted the urge to rub her vindication in the face of her stepdaughter.

Before arriving at the hospital, Alma and Eleanor had convinced their

mother not to be rude to Miranda. She agreed with her daughters that her stepdaughter had been taught a valuable lesson. In addition, her stepdaughter didn't know that her brothers had been keeping her up to date about her becoming overwhelmed caring for their sick mother.

"Hello," the three ladies said, one behind the other.

"How's everyone doing?" Miranda responded, smiling slightly. There were only three chairs in her mother's private room. She left her chair to hug her two half sisters then she stretched her arms open to hug her stepmother. She immediately became a victim of her raft.

"Don't press your luck," Eloise said through clinched teeth, "How's she doing?" she asked, not really looking at her stepdaughter, more so speaking into the air.

"The doctors said she's going to be fine. Her blood sugar was low."

"See *Sista*, that's what I'm talking about. They are accusing me of stealing a bag of sugar. I didn't steal any bag a sugar."

Eloise fought to keep from laughing. "No honey, they said your blood sugar is low, not that you stole a bag of sugar." Her presence was helping Flossie to calm down. The elderly woman kept insisting that she wanted to go home. And she didn't mean home with her daughter—she meant home, as in home with Eloise.

"*Sista*, are you going to take me home? Please don't let me go back with them people," Flossie pleaded, referring to her daughter like she was stranger. She even turned her back to her daughter to engage in a conversation with only Eloise. She began to whisper as if her daughter wasn't in the room. "Her food is awful, she doesn't cook like you. She won't let me feed myself and she's always trying to shove that dog food down my throat," she continued to say.

"Mama that was meatloaf I was feeding you, not dog food." Miranda corrected her.

"I want to go home...I want to go home," Flossie kept saying, trying to slide out of bed. She had already managed to get loose from one of the restraints.

"Calm down honey, we'll see about you going home." Eloise assured her.

* * *

At the same time, Daniel was at home. He was entertaining someone his wife didn't know anything about. He knew her visit to the hospital would keep her away for awhile. Although, Daniel knew that his son was attracted to Pandora, he knew *DJ* understood that his cousin was off limits. Fortunately, Pandora wasn't his cousin. And the fact that she was his wife's relative didn't stop him from driving a couple of times to North Carolina to see her dance again. He hoped that he would be one of the lucky men to get pleasured on stage. It never happened. Primarily because he never had the nerve, more so, he didn't have the courage to even attempt to climb on stage with her. Instead, he called her one day and the two connected. Again, he was fully aware that she was his wife's cousin, but at the time, it didn't matter to him and it certainly didn't matter to Pandora.

This particular evening, as soon as he knew his wife was leaving to take his mother-in-law to the hospital, he convinced Pandora to come over. She obliged him right away. At first, he wanted her to dance for him as he sat like a king in a wingback chair. He was still dressed in his business suit while he watched the young stripper dance him into an aroused frenzy. He enjoyed what he saw and he enjoyed the way she made him feel. She sat on his lap and moved her round *ass* about his crotch; she could feel what he had to offer. It felt good to Pandora, but it felt much better to him. Her moves were pushing him on the verge of an explosion.

He led his houseguest into the family guest bedroom and got naked as she already was. He wanted her to pleasure him, but she wanted him to pleasure her first. He sucked on her breast and kissed her all the way down to her shaven vagina. He spread her legs wide and tasted a mouthful of her inviting womanhood. His tongue moved about her like he was eating an oyster. He licked and he sucked. It drove her wild. She moaned.

He moved his kisses from her vagina to the inside of her leg. He sucked each spot until passion marks appeared. She moved around on the bed while he pulled at his hard manhood. He was ready for action and his dripping manhood was evidence of his excitement for her. It was obvious he wanted her and she wanted him. She opened her legs wide to allow him to insert himself into her slowly. Upon full penetration, she squealed like she was a virgin. It hurt. He was larger than she anticipated, but she didn't push him

away. Instead, she held onto his firm ass as he grinded slowly and gently inside of her. His thrusts forced her to open her legs wider to invite more of him inside her—his manhood was now fitting inside her perfectly.

He wasn't surprised by how good she felt, it was just as he had imagined. Listening to the way she was moaning, it made him feel like he was twenty years old again. On a regular basis, he and his wife made love, but it was nothing like this. It didn't come close to this. This was the best he had ever had. He never wanted this to end.

Then *DJ* walked in. "Dad—what are ya'll doing?!"

CHAPTER THIRTY-EIGHT

Christopher was opening the stack of mail that had been delivered to the church. The first envelope he opened contained a grant approval letter in it. He knew Mychael would be excited to know that the funds for the educational center had been approved. He thought about calling him, but changed his mind. A few minutes passed then he toyed with the thought that if he called Mychael, his pastor and boss may want him to bring the letter to him. In his mind, he knew he didn't have time—he had other plans.

After a month on the job, he was finally settling into his new position as the church secretary. He was really enjoying working in this setting. He couldn't believe that his cousin Beatrice had messed up such a good opportunity like this. Who could have asked for more? He had the freedom to do whatever he wanted and got paid a good salary to do it. True enough, while on the church premises, he had to train himself to refer to his pastor as Reverend Dovely and not as Mychael, but that was easy compared to the ton of responsibilities he had as his secretary and as clerk to the trustee ministry.

Four days had passed and he still had not spoken to Pierce or Jorge. The thought was making him sad...really sad. He missed them both. Then again, he figured that Pierce was probably following Mychael's directive and Jorge was probably following the information he had been given by Pierce.

He knew Pierce very well and he never told a story the way it happened. In every situation, his friend made sure to put his *own* spin on the matter— regardless whether he told it correctly or added a few lies. Even though he knew the type of person his best buddy was, Pierce's actions didn't erase

the fact that he missed talking to them. Especially, on a daily basis, they all spoke to each other by phone.

He put the grant approval letter back into its original envelope then he laid the same envelope to the side. He knew he needed to finish opening the remaining stack of mail, but he kept getting distracted thinking whether he should call Mychael or not. Then again, he knew hearing Mychael's voice would do nothing for his bad mood. Minutes passed and he thought about calling his pastor again and he almost convinced himself to dial Mychael's cell phone, but his intentions were interrupted when the office switchboard began to ring.

"Thank you for calling the Tabernacle of Praise Church, may I help you?" he said through his headphones.

"Yeah, this is Pastor Dovely here." He heard him say. It was too late, just hearing his pastor's voice had made his mood go from bad to worse.

"Yes sir, how can I help you?"

"I was calling because I am looking for a response letter this week from the Department of Education about the Educational building proposal. By chance, has it arrived yet?" Mychael asked.

Christopher was shocked and wondered whether the man was a psychic. He hadn't had the letter in his possession an hour and strangely, Mychael was now calling about it.

"Yes, it came today." He told him.

"Good, could you drop it by the house tonight?" Mychael asked.

"No, I can't Mychael because I have something to do after work." He explained. He couldn't believe that his pastor thought he was going to drive around town delivering mail after his shift had ended at the church. Don't get him wrong, he would do anything for a man of God, especially this one, but he had to draw the line somewhere.

"What kind of plans to do you have, other than hanging around those no good friends of yours? Don't forget what I told you about being around those two?"

"As a matter fact, I *no* longer have any friends—thanks to you."

"Then you won't have a problem bringing me the letter."

"I'm not bringing this letter to you. My shift ends at five o'clock and I have something to do. If you want me to put the letter on your desk, I will be happy

to do that. Maybe you can stop by on your way home," he said. He waited for a response and for a few moments he didn't hear any sound or movement on the other end of the phone.

"Hello, are you there?"

"Yeah, I'm here." Mychael said, mildly then he went on. "Christopher, what have I done to you? You act like you hate me. I give you whatever you ask me for. You wanted that new bedroom group—I went and got that for you. You wanted to upgrade your cell phone—I went and paid for that. You whined about needing new clothes, I gave you my credit card and let buy whatever you wanted. I didn't even ask you how much you spent. You know why—because I didn't care. But now you can't take an extra ten minutes to drop off a letter for me, how unselfish can a person be?" Mychael added.

Hearing Mychael mention all the things he had done for him, Christopher was now feeling bad and it was Mychael's turn to experience silence on his end of the phone. He knew Mychael was right about everything he had said, except he had failed to mention that he written him a check to keep his checking account balance at two-thousand dollars.

"Alright, I'll bring it by there, but I really do have something to do. What time will you get home?"

"That's *my* boy."

He hated when Mychael called him his boy. He wasn't a boy. He was a grown *ass* man.

"You can bring it by around ten o'clock." Mychael said.

"Oh no, Mychael…I mean Reverend Dovely. I thought you meant you wanted me to bring it by after I got off work. I'm not coming to your house at ten o'clock."

"Why not?"

"I'm just not."

"Okay, you've left me no choice. I'll have Mother Eloise keep Hannah tonight and I will come by your place to pick it up," Mychael said, seemingly in a threatening manner.

Christopher knew that was a bad idea. He didn't want to go to Mychael's house at ten o'clock and he certainly didn't want Mychael at his house—no matter what time he planned to come by.

Frustrated, he said, "No, I'll just leave the letter on your desk. Bye."

Mychael disconnected the call without saying a word. He tapped his cell phone gently against his hand. As different thoughts ran through his head, he wrinkled his mouth; he nodded his head up and down. Then he realized he was going to have to show Mr. Christiansen who was the person that controlled their partnership.

Later on, Mychael arrived at Christopher's condo. He got out of his car and walked past Christopher's parked vehicle. Then he stopped and went back and pressed his face against the driver's side widow. He noticed all the papers on the front seat. He noticed all the spare change that was out in the open. He even noticed the pair of athletic shoes in the back seat.

When the neighbors saw him looking inside Christopher's car, Mychael moved quickly away from the vehicle and jogged up to the door then pressed the door bell. He didn't want to run the risk of anyone calling the police on him. Christopher had mentioned to him before that a few people had experienced break-ins to their cars.

After ringing the door bell a second time, Mychael waited and no one answered. He waited a few more minutes, before pressing the door bell a third time. He had no plans of leaving until somebody came to the door—he knew that Christopher was home.

Within moments, an agitated Christopher opened the door. He wasn't smiling and it was evident he wasn't thrilled to see his pastor. He was dressed like he was ready for bed.

"May I come in?" Mychael said.

"I didn't bring the letter home with me. I left it on your desk like I told you," he let him know.

"That's not what I asked you. Now may I come in?"

"Yes…" he said, moving to the side as Mychael walked past him.

"Christopher, why are you treating me like this? Just tell me what I've done and I promise I'll fix it."

"You can't fix it because somebody as controlling as you, won't change over night," he stated, snatching the newspaper from the spot where he wanted him to sit.

"You think I'm controlling because I asked you not to hang around those *faggots* you call friends."

"Mychael don't call them that."

"Oh, pardon my language... What do you call your buddies, men who live an alternative lifestyle or men who have sex with the same gender? Wake up Christopher, it all equals the same, they are still *faggots*."

Christopher shot back, "So what are you, now that you are casting titles on everybody, doesn't that mean that you are a faggot also?" he voiced to his lover and pastor.

By reflex to what he had heard, Mychael back hand slapped him. Quickly, blood began streaming from his nose. It spilled onto his white t-shirt. Mychael's actions shocked his lover as well as himself. Christopher had never been hit anybody before. Not even by his mother. "Don't you ever as long as you live use that word to describe me," Mychael said.

Instead of hitting him back, Christopher held his hand over the bruised side of his face and pulled his shirt up to his bleeding nose before rushing to the door to throw Mychael out.

"Close that *damn* door. I'm not leaving until you understand what I just told you," Mychael said.

"I understand perfectly. Now I want you out." Christopher said.

A couple living next door walked past the open door, both glancing through the door, noticing Christopher's back and the angry expression on Mychael's face.

"Close that mutha— door," Mychael said barely moving his mouth.

Christopher closed the door without thinking twice about it, only because he was afraid of what Mychael might do if he didn't. Obviously, his threats had made Mychael angry because Mychael grabbed him around the collar and slammed his body against the wall—the impact was painful. Christopher grabbed his shoulder and ran to the telephone, but was only able to press the nine key.

"It would be in your best interest not to do that," Mychael told him.

He slowly put the phone down on the table as Mychael started to walk towards him, the closer he got, the more afraid of him he became. He picked up the phone again, but threw it in Mychael's direction. Mychael moved away as the phone smashed into the door. Then he lunged at his lover, this time, he clutched his hands around his throat, chocking him until his eyes bulged, becoming blood shot red immediately.

Mychael looked like he was choking a rag doll. He clutched his hands

around Christopher's neck so tight until he watched him eventually fell unconscious. He looked dead to Mychael and he was frightened that he had killed him.

Breathing heavy himself, Mychael stood over Christopher and to him, he didn't appear to be breathing. Nervous, he dropped to his knees next to his lover's limp body. His first reaction was to grab him into his arms before rolling him onto his side.

Moments later, Christopher began coughing. As his vision came into focus, he looked at the crazed maniac that was kneeling next to him. He felt around his neck, it was burning. To him, it still felt like Mychael's hands were attached to his throat. Like a wounded animal, he jumped from the floor running to the bathroom, locking himself inside. He stood there staring in the mirror as both his eyes were now bloody red. He knew what had happened because he had seen this many times on the discovery health channel. The documentary explained that after a person has been choked, sometimes the act can cause the blood vessels in the eyes to burst. And without a doubt, that's exactly what had happened to him.

Mychael stood outside the bathroom, he was a lot calmer, he begged for Christopher to open the door, but mostly for him to forgive him. Angry, Christopher opened the door, bypassing Mychael saying as he walked toward the front door again, "I hope you take a good look at what you've done. And if people ask me tomorrow, what happened, I'm going to tell them," he threatened, sounding hoarse.

"Come on now, I'm sorry, I just lost my temper. Why don't you take the day off? I promise nothing like this will ever happen again," Mychael said.

"I know it's not going to happen again and no, I am not staying home tomorrow. I want everybody to see me like this," he informed Mychael. He continued to stand at the front door, he hadn't opened it yet. He had something else to say, "I can't believe you think I am some kind of punching bag," he said, now standing with the door open.

Mychael didn't say anything, but held his head down as he passed his assaulted lover. Christopher closed the door quickly and tightly, making the door hit against the heel of Mychael's shoe. Then he turned the lock and pressed his back up against it.

He had to admit that he showed a tremendous amount of bravery, but

honestly, he was scared to death. He had seen Mychael angry before, but he didn't know that he was capable of violence of such a highly and aggravated nature. He grabbed his cell phone as he walked into his bedroom. He began dialing Jorge's number, then Pierce, connecting everyone on three-way.

As Christopher spoke with his friends about the incident, his lover/pastor/boss skipped down the concrete steps to his car. Mychael pulled the key ring bearing the letter *C* from his pocket and he looked at the group of metal pieces. He thought for a couple seconds then he tossed the set of keys down the sewage drain. Acting as if nothing happened, holding his own alarm gadget, he pressed the alarm system to his car. He opened the driver's door before placing his key in the ignition then driving off.

CHAPTER THIRTY-NINE

Christopher woke up early, dressed in a hurry, but spent a considerable amount of time searching for his car keys. He searched everywhere, high and low and he still couldn't find them. In his mind, he could remember the exact place he had put them the night before. Now, strangely this morning, he couldn't put his finger on them. During his search, he walked past the mirror that hung on his living room wall—he looked a horrifying mess. His face was swollen and his eyes were redder, much redder than last night. Damn Mychael for doing that to him! Even still he was determined to go to work.

He sat down in a chair feeling sorry himself. He was unsure whether he was angry because his face was all messed up or because he couldn't find his car keys. Either way, he felt like he wanted to cry. He knew if he did, the tears would only make his eyes burn, the way they had burned the night before. *Maybe I should take the day off?* He thought to himself—giving Mychael's suggestion consideration.

He thought about the suggestion some more and realized he *wanted* people to ask him what had happened. Really, he had no intention of telling those that were brave enough to ask him that Mychael was responsible for the way he looked. Yes, a small part of him wanted people to at least mention it to his lover/pastor and hopefully Mychael would feel convicted each time he heard the story. Then a larger part of him realized that Mychael probably didn't care how many times he heard the story; he would think he had provoked the assault.

If he had listened to his friends last night, his pastor—their pastor would be in jail this morning. Jorge and Pierce tried for an hour to convince him to

press charges. They thought the psycho preacher needed to be brought to justice. Even though Christopher didn't like the idea of walking around like an assaulted victim, he wasn't going as far as to have a man he loved arrested.

Once his friends realized he wasn't going to agree to their suggestion, they resulted to calling him every name in the book, starting with Tina Turner and ending with Robin Givens. He accepted their insults because he didn't expect them to understand. Often times, people who don't fully understand a situation sometimes have the most suggestions, he thought.

Later into their conversation, his friends seemed to think that his altercation with his lover was a laughing matter. Actually, this matter was funny, since it all transpired because he was defending their honor and now they were laughing at him. Who needs enemies when you have friends like Pierce and Jorge, he thought to himself. They had no idea he was defending their reputation and he wasn't going to waste his breath telling them otherwise. They just wouldn't understand. Simply because neither one has ever had anyone to care about them the way Mychael cared for him.

Truthfully, listening to his friend's advice and taking none of it. Christopher understood he had the potential to be many things, but a fool he was not. In no shape, form or fashion was he about to give up the thick pulsating muscle his lover had, not to mention, his large bank account. With all things considered and as far as he was concerned....*Beat me Ike...Beat me.*

Finally, after searching for an hour, he decided to grab his spare set of keys from his bedroom nightstand. Luckily, the week before, he had made copies of all the keys that were on the missing key ring. He couldn't imagine where the keys could be. He thought, maybe they were somewhere looking at him. Then it hit him, maybe last night, Mychael had took the keys while he was in the bathroom. He refused to call and confront him about his suspicion. He didn't need the keys, as he said before he now has a spare set.

When he reached the church, he didn't turn on his computer and he didn't answer the ringing switchboard. He grabbed the yellow telephone book because he needed to make an appointment to see his therapist. He needed to speak with someone and soon. He located the number very quickly, dialed it, the phone rang three times before a lovely voice answered, "Hello, you've reached the office of Dr. Kenneth Marson, may I help you?" the woman said.

"Yes, this is Christopher Christiansen and I need to see if I can get an appointment with Dr. Marson today," he said.

"Yes you can Mr. Christiansen. We just had a cancellation about thirty minutes ago. Is it possible to come in around 11:30 this morning?" the receptionist said.

"Yes, that'll be fine."

"Okay, we'll see you at 11:30."

Christopher made a note and placed it on his pastor/boss' desk to inform him that he had an appointment and he would have to take an extended lunch. His lunch was going to be extended all right, it wasn't even eleven o'clock. Normally, he would have called Mychael's cell phone and left him a message, but after observing his swollen and bruised face again, he didn't even want to speak with the abuser by phone.

He left the church office at eleven wearing sunglasses. As adamant as he was earlier about showing off his appearance to the public, he really didn't want anyone to see his bruises or see him visiting a therapist. When he eased into the parking lot across from the doctor's office, he grabbed a hat from the back seat and pulled it down on his head. He couldn't run the risk of someone recognizing him. He hated that Richard's corporate office was now located on the same block as his therapist's storefront office. This reason alone prompted him to rush through the lunch hour traffic and into the office of Psychiatry.

He walked up to the front desk and wrote his name beneath the three names that were already on the sign-in list. Feeling safe, he removed the cap from his head and the sunglasses from his swollen face. He must have really looked awful because he saw the reaction of the receptionist after he exposed his bruises to her.

"Hi Mr. Christiansen, Dr. Marson is running slightly behind this morning, but he'll be with you shortly," she said, looking at him then she added, "If you don't mind me asking, what happened to you?"

He wasn't trying to be rude, but he wasn't in the mood to be interrogated. "Actually, I do mind," he said.

The friendly woman didn't take offense to his response. She held up her hand as a gentle way of apologizing. She repeated the statement she had said to him earlier then she closed the sliding glass window separating her from the half empty waiting room.

Christopher sat for about twenty minutes before they were calling his name, "Mr. Christopher Christiansen, please come back."

He walked into the spacious area to find Dr. Marson sitting behind his big oak desk. He was jotting down notes in the file of the last patient. As he walked in further, Dr. Marson quickly glanced at him, before returning his attention to the file in front him.

"Mr. Christiansen, you may have a seat and I'll be right with you," Dr. Marson said while writing at the same time.

He sat in his usual spot. Dr. Marson usually sat in a matching chair next to his long leather sofa. He didn't say anything, he knew he would have plenty of time to talk and answer the million questions asked by his mental health professional. He soon heard his therapist close the thick folder he was writing in. Then the Morgan Freeman look-a-like walked over and sat in the spot just like he had imagined. Before he began the session, Dr. Marson pulled his reading glasses away from his eyes. "Young man, it appears that you've been in a fight. And from the look of things, you didn't win." Dr. Marson commented.

Christopher forced himself to laugh. "I wasn't fighting, someone attacked me," he said in response to his therapist's comment.

"Oh, I see. So what's the reason for today's visit?" Dr. Marson said, crossing his long legs.

"Dr. Marson, I'm in a bad situation and I need someone to help me figure it out."

"Does this have something to do with the bruises to your neck and eyes?"

"Yes."

"A new boyfriend I imagine? The last time you were here, you were happily in love," Dr. Marson recalled.

"No, he's not new, but he's changed."

He knew what was coming. His therapist always tried to get him to reveal the name of the person he was seeing. He felt Dr. Marson had an idea that the man was someone prominent, but he wasn't going to confirm his idea. He knew if he were to learn that their pastor was the person he was referring to, the fallout from it all could be bad. Frankly, his therapist's need to know was actually none of his business and his mental health condition should be his primary concern.

"Christopher, I hope you don't mind my speaking with you about this? But what do you actually get out of having sex with men?" Dr. Marson said.

"Are you asking me, do I get satisfaction?" he asked, rearranging Dr. Marson's question.

"I guess I am. When I see two men kissing, holding hands or even being affectionate, it grosses me out. When a guy comes up to me and I suspect he's gay, it literally makes my skin want to crawl," Dr. Marson stated.

"Is that right?" Christopher said, looking at the frown on his therapist's face. He immediately went into education mode.

"Dr. Marson, how do you determine that a person is gay?"

"I usually do by the way a man moves his hands or if he switches when he walks. The pitch of his voice is sometimes a dead giveaway," he said confidently, like he knew about the characteristics of gay people.

"I can assure you that you can't tell if a person is gay by those characteristics. I remember in college, I had a professor who had all those characteristics you just described and was stereotyped just as you have done, but that professor was happily married with three adult children. Another scenario would be a famous professional football player I know, who was the best quarterback in the league, his statistics were unbeatable. He didn't switch when he walked, he didn't hold his hands different and his voice was as deep as Lou Rawls and you know what?" Christopher explained.

He and his therapist answered at the same time, "And he was gay."

"People often think that every gay guy wants to look at their butt or wants to have anal sex with them. Do you know there are different types of homosexual behavior— some guys only want to penetrate guys through anal sex, some guys want to penetrate and be penetrated, and some guys only want to be penetrated. I've heard gay men say, penetrating another man grosses them out and I've heard gay men say, having a man penetrating them, grosses them out. Therefore, Dr. Marson, being gay is not as black and white as some people think."

Dr. Marson continued to sit with his long legs crossed; switching them from one position to the other as he absorbed the information he was receiving from his patient. Instead of him helping Christopher, his patient was helping him to understand the gay culture and gay life style.

"Christopher, you have really taught me a lot here today. Now, not to change the subject, but do you care to tell me about the situation with your bruises?" Dr. Marson said.

271

Christopher on the other hand, was embarrassed and couldn't bring himself to look at Dr. Marson. He said with his head down, "I can't tell you who my lover is because he's a very prominent man. But he and I had a big disagreement last night and what you see is the result of that."

"Did you have to get the police involved? I can't imagine anything being that serious, whereas the two of you would have to get into a physical fight."

"Well, Dr. Marson, since you don't know my friend, it's hard to explain. He's one of the brothers that don't like to be associated with gay people. He wants you to sneak around with him in the dark and plead the fifth every time we have sex. But actually, in regards to last night, he wanted me to choose between a new job and my best friends. His mentality is similar to how you stereotyped certain people as being gay."

"Humm…I see. And what type of work do you do?"

"I'm the church secretary," Christopher said to him before he realized what he had just admitted—by this time he couldn't take his answer back.

"Christopher, I'm sorry our time has gone by so fast, but you really have taught me a valuable lesson about how to treat human beings and to be careful about casting judgment on people. Going forward I remain enlightened that things are not always what they appear to be."

CHAPTER FORTY

At the same time, Mychael was walking into his best friend's office. Alton was certainly surprised to see him. It showed in his expression, mainly because he knew this time of day his friend was supposed to be working.

"Well surprise…surprise…" Alton said, rising from his chair, clasping hands and hugging his best friend. "You must be playing hooky from school today?"

"I had to man. After I dropped my daughter off at daycare, I called in and told my principal I was taking a sick day. Man, I feel like crap," Mychael said, admitting how he felt at the moment.

"No offense, but you look like it to. Still grieving about losing your wife?"

Mychael didn't say anything as he sat comfortably in a chair across from Alton. He rubbed his mouth with his hand like a nervous person. He was really trying to stall for time because he didn't know where or how to begin this conversation.

"Myke, I can't counsel someone who doesn't talk back to me. Now, what's the problem?" Alton stated.

"It's definitely not about losing my wife."

"Oh goodness, here we go, that problem again.…Myke, please tell me I'm wrong."

Mychael shook his head because he wished that he could say his friend was wrong. Then he said, "Come on man—you act like I come to you with these types of problems all the time."

"Let me guess, the light skinned choir director?"

Mychael was shocked that his friend had guessed his problem correctly.

It forced him into his shell again—a place where he felt safe. He looked at his friend, before saying, "Alton man, he's been the only one. I have never slept with any other men."

"I know… so you tell me, but one person or one time is still too many." Alton paused. "My brother I will always have to tell you what the word of God says about homosexuality being a sin. And if you expect me to give it to you any other way then you've come to the wrong person. There's no gray area when it comes to God's word. Now if you really want to know the truth, you are deceiving that congregation. Those people think that you are on the up and up and look at you…you're letting yourself get all messed up over a dude. Man, you don't know how good you have it at Tabernacle of Praise."

Alton hated having to be so stern with his best friend, but he wanted him to understand that as a minister he was obligated to share this type of revelation with him. Sometimes the authoritative and stern method worked and sometimes it didn't.

This particular day, as Mychael spoke, the conversation forced Alton to remember the time he tried to be stern and counsel one of his young male church members, who was so full of energy about the sin of homosexuality. Not only was the young man constantly snapping his fingers after every statement, he was upfront and honest with his pastor. He told him that life for him had been rough and finding a good job was hard to come by. Consequently, the young man used his body to get what he wanted, also shocking Alton when he named the caliber of men that he slept with. He mentioned clients that included doctors, lawyers, bank presidents, etc. and explained that not only did he get paid for his sexual acts; he even acknowledged that he knew the acts were a sin, but he said it was a sin that he liked.

Forgetting that Mychael was sitting across from him, Alton chuckled to himself when he thought about the time the young man's mother passed away and he visited their apartment to see all the expensive furniture that lined the walls. He even recalled the first time he saw the young man pull into the church parking lot driving a top of the line Lexus SUV.

Alton shared his thoughts with Mychael and they both laughed.

"Man…I don't expect you to understand and by all accounts, I know what the word says. But, what about me as a person? I believe

wholeheartedly that God understands that I didn't choose to be this way," Mychael said. He used his fingers to illustrate his point of view to Alton. "I assure you that I wasn't molested as a child nor did I play with girl toys when I was younger. I even had both my parents until I was sixteen years old. I remember the day; I was sitting in the bleachers watching the cheerleaders take the floor. Out of the twelve people I saw, it didn't matter to me that eleven of them were girls—I was attracted to one person and that person wasn't wearing a skirt."

"The choir director?"

"That choir director has a name and his name is Christopher. Why do you think I'm talking about him?"

"Because."

"Because what?"

"I remember at your wife's repast when we were sitting at the pastor's table and he walked into the fellowship hall. I saw your eyes follow him around the room. And when he came up to our table to speak to us, that voice, not to mention, the way he stood over you, massaging your shoulders. I don't think anyone else noticed, but I certainly did."

Mychael laughed; he remembered the date and time that Alton was referring to. "It was that obvious, huh?" he asked.

"I'm afraid so. What is it about the choir dir—? Excuse me, Christopher that attracts you to him?"

"Man, he is everything Monica wasn't. Don't get me wrong, I loved my wife, but she could learn a thing or two from her cousin…"

"Do you care to elaborate?"

"Well, she was quiet and he is outgoing. She was too sensitive and he has thick skin, he wasn't offended easily. She was jealous and it doesn't bother him that I spend more than five minutes with my female members."

"Both you and I know, she had plenty of reason to be jealous of you and the women. But it sounds to me like you are pretty smitten with this guy."

"Yeah, I guess you could say that. We had a big argument last night or maybe I should say a big fight. That's the reason why I'm here today."

"What happened?" Alton asked, forgetting about his twelve o'clock appointment.

"I asked him to cut off his friendship with two known gay guys at the

church and he got upset about it. I called the guys faggots and he called me a one and I slapped and chocked him. Yeah…Yeah…I know already, I shouldn't have done it."

Alton just looked at his friend. He could see the remorse in his eyes.

"It gets worse." Mychael informed.

"I'm almost afraid to ask how much worse?" Alton remarked.

"No, I didn't kill him, but I did steal his keys and threw them down the sewage drain, plus I chocked him so long, I burst the blood vessels in his eyes." Mychael confessed.

Alton let out a hearty laugh. As a matter of fact, he couldn't stop laughing.

"Man, please tell me you didn't…you really are sprung?"

"Come on man, don't say that. I just lost my cool."

Alton tried to remain serious, but it was hard listening to his friend's drama. "How long have you known this guy?" he asked Mychael as he watched him feel for his waist clamp that held his cell phone then checking both front pockets of his pants.

Mychael said after he realized he had left his cell phone at home. "I've known him since he was a sophomore and I was a senior in high school. I didn't see him again until he was a junior in college, by that time I had graduated from college and married his first cousin."

"Man, this is interesting information you are sharing. So, when did ya'll hook up?"

"Alton, I've told you this story before."

"No you haven't. I didn't know who this dude was until Monica's funeral and then I only had an idea."

"Well, he was home one summer and came by to visit his cousin. At the time, we had just built our new house next door to his aunt, Monica's mother. My wife wasn't' there and one thing led to another and we ended up having sex."

"Man, you mean to tell me, that you boned him in your wife's new house?"

"Yep…It's not something I'm proud of. But I have to be honest, after I got a taste of that, I was hooked. Don't get me wrong, I don't sleep around with him all the time. I can go for years and not think about doing anything like that. But when I get that urge, I'm like a dog in heat. No matter how many times *Monnie* and I make love, it just wasn't enough to satisfy me."

"Wow, man this is deep… You really have some serious issues. Have you ever thought about getting counseling?"

"That's why I'm here, jerk," Mychael teased.

"Oh no, this is way beyond my league…"

"Come on man…do you really think I need to see a shrink?"

"Ah…yeah!" Alton laughed, as his friend joined in.

"I'm just joking man, it's almost one o'clock, obviously my appointment is not going to show, let me treat you to lunch and get your mind off of *Christopher*," Alton said to Mychael, bending his wrist when he said the name Christopher.

"Alright, Mr. Comedy man, you got jokes I see," Mychael replied, fighting hard to keep from laughing.

CHAPTER FORTY-ONE

Beatrice sat on her front porch enjoying the fall breeze. The sun was shining, but the occasional breeze was a reminder that the season was still fall. Her son Jeremiah, now a year old was playing in his sand box along with his Cousin Hannah. He loved his cousin and playmate. Thanks to God for getting Mychael to the place where he could trust their family again and allow his daughter time to play with her son. Mychael had called earlier to ask could someone pick up Hannah from school. He didn't say where he was and he didn't call from his cell phone, the number that appeared on the caller display had a North Carolina extension.

Motherhood was something that didn't come easy for Beatrice. It took almost a year for her to get the maternal instinct in perfect order. At first, she was terrified about being a mother. After Jeremiah was born, he had to undergo detoxification from all the crack cocaine found in his system. So much that hospital officials launched an investigation, forcing her to be tested for drugs and as she already knew, the results came back negative—simply because she wasn't the one who had smoked crack cocaine. By far was that the end to all their questions. Social Services were persistent to find out how her son was born with such a large amount of narcotics in his system. At the advice of her late Cousin Monica, she lied to the investigators that she wasn't aware that her boyfriend was a drug addict. She waited for weeks, hoping and praying that the investigators would believe her story. On the third week, by mail, she finally received a letter informing her that the investigation was complete and she had been cleared of all subsequent allegations.

It has been a long time since her son's father had last tapped on her

window and his absence had forced her to convert back to using her sex toys. In the past, she could whip out the gadgets whenever she took a notion, but now she had to use caution—real caution. She could only pleasure herself while her son was sound asleep or away for the weekend. If she had to admit to herself, she would have to say she missed seeing Eddie on a weekly basis. He filled in the gap between the times when she couldn't use the toys.

All the while, she realized that her part-time boyfriend didn't mean her any good and was only using her for sex and money. Money she no longer had. Her income dwindled from $400 a week to $225 a month in the form of a TANF check. She remembered a month after Jeremiah was born; Eddie tapped on her window. She was excited to show him the son they had created, but all her addict boyfriend wanted was sex and money for drugs. Foolishly, she gave him the money, but didn't mention sex to him only because she knew she hadn't returned to the doctor for her six-week check-up. After he left, she thought about how fidgety and nervous her son's father was and she didn't recall him taking a second to look at their sleeping son. If her mind served her correctly, Eddie did walk over to the crib but moved his head so fast she wasn't sure whether he received an image to remember.

Currently, life in the Shaw household was going good and Jeremiah had grown like a wart on his grandmother. Because of this, Agnes was finally cutting her daughter some slack. She enjoyed her grandson calling her *Granny*, rather than Agnes, like her daughter and husband has done for years. It was something about the way he pulled at her dress tail and pointed his small fingers toward the refrigerator whenever he wanted something out of it. She wasn't short patient when it came to him the way she was with her husband and daughter. He made her happy and excited to be his *Granny*.

Joe was another happy story. He had always wanted a son, but was never blessed with one. His wife agreed that Beatrice was enough—more than enough. Therefore, as you can imagine, he treated Jeremiah like the son he never had.

Beatrice didn't have to worry about a babysitter as long as her father was alive. He would take her son to get his curly hair cut and sit outside with the toddler to play sponge football and basketball with him. He would make the comment that he was going to be professional baseball player when Jeremiah would run around the yard like he was running to first, second and third bases.

It was a joy watching the two together as Jeremiah would refer to his Grandfather as *Grandpa*.

Today, Beatrice watched her son as he emptied sand on his head from his red bucket. He was so cute. He was a pale looking toddler with curly black hair, thin lips like his father and green eyes like his Grandmother, his father's mother. A feature she had recognized from a photo Eddie kept in his wallet.

The Simon's had never laid eyes on their grandson. Although Eddie told her that he had mentioned to his parents that he had fathered a child with a black woman, she still didn't believe him; she would never think he would have the nerve to disclose anything like that to his parents. But from what Eddie told her about the conversation, he said after his father heard about what he had done, the Archie Bunker clone cursed him for almost three hours straight and in the midst of his ranting, he used the *n* word to describe him, her and their son.

Personally, she didn't care what they thought about her because she had what she wanted and that was the support from her family. Her relationship with her parents couldn't have been better; her cousin Christopher agreed to be Jeremiah's Godparent and her son was crazy about them all. Jeremiah even looked forward to spending every other weekend at his God Dad's house to receive all the new clothes and toys that Christopher would buy him.

At that moment, Beatrice was sitting in a daze, looking from Jeremiah to Hannah, but not really watching them. She heard Hannah say, but still wasn't quite paying attention. *Who is dat?* She hadn't seen the car pulling into the driveway. She only snapped out of her daze when she heard car doors slamming one behind the other.

She didn't recognize the white man and definitely, not the white woman. Then again, maybe she did. The man looked familiar. The petite woman stopped in the area where the children were playing, the man kept walking. As he passed the children, leading up to the porch, he smiled at her.

"Bet you don't recognize me do ya?" the man said in his southern accent. Once she heard him speak, she knew exactly who he was. It was Eddie. He looked different. His hair wasn't dirty and greasy and his clothes weren't filthy and wrinkled. He didn't look the way she had remembered seeing him last. In fact, he was wearing a pair of beige slacks and a neatly ironed shirt.

"Miss Bea, how's life been treating ya? I bought my *whyfe* by to see my son," Eddie said. "I know, I haven't been the best daddy I should be, but I've changed now Miss Bea. I'm working at the bank downtown," he continued.

"The bank… When did they start hiring drug addicts to work in the bank?" Beatrice said.

"Miss Bea, I told you I've changed, I've been clean for about six months now," Eddie explained. His wife walked up, stopping to stand next to him. She was dressed very conservative, even more conservative than her.

"Hi, I'm Bethany, nice to meet ya'," Eddie's wife said, extending her thin hand toward Beatrice.

"Hello," Beatrice said, choosing not shake the woman's hand.

"Your son and daughter are beautiful."

"The boy is mine, the girl is my cousin," she corrected her.

"Oh, pardon my stupidity."

"I'm sure," she said. Then turning her attention to Eddie, "What can I do for you? If you think for one minute you are going to take my son anywhere near that prejudice father of yours, you need to think again."

"No, Miss Bea, I won't take the boy near my father, but I would like to spend some time with him and I bought my *whyfe* here today, so she won't be jealous of ya'. Honey, do you believe me now about how fat she is," Eddie remarked.

Beatrice was embarrassed. Where were Agnes and Joe when she needed them? Usually, one or the other would come to the door to make sure she was parenting Jeremiah correctly. Right now, she couldn't believe what her former boyfriend had said. She said to herself, *that he didn't care how fat I was when he was on top of me doing his business*—the nerve of him, she thought.

"So, Miss Bea, do you still have a crush on your preacher?" Eddie asked, turning to his wife, "Honey, she use to use these sex toys and all and when she came close to her moment, she would call out her preacher's name," he said, laughing as his wife joined in.

Beatrice heard their laughter, it seemed to last forever. Her head felt dizzy like she had been riding a merry-go-around. She had had enough. She got up from her chair and walked in a fast pace by her unwanted house guest. She grabbed young Jeremiah in her arms and pulled Hannah by the hand, making them both scream for having to leave their sandbox.

"Mr. Eddie and Miss Bethany…I don't think it will do either of you any good to come around here anymore. My son won't be visiting or getting to know ya'll. And Mr. Eddie… you really want to know why I had to use those sex toys…Miss Bethany, I'm sure you know already…because what I was getting from you, just wasn't enough!" She said as she climbed the five steps, entering the house and slamming the door behind her.

Both Hannah and Jeremiah watched from the front window as the man and woman they didn't know returned to their parked car and pulled out of the driveway.

CHAPTER FORTY-TWO

Two hours later, Hannah and Jeremiah were still staring out the window. Both looking and laughing at the cars that drove down the street. Jeremiah could barely talk and understood very little, he only laughed because he saw his Cousin Hannah laughing.

"Ooooooooo, I see her boom...booms...I see her pocketbook," Hannah said, pointing through the window.

"Hannah, what are you talking about?" Beatrice asked the inquisitive toddler.

"Her over there," Hannah answered, continuing to point through the window.

Thinking that Eddie and his anorexic looking wife had returned, Beatrice got up from the chair she was sitting in and walked over to the window. She didn't see Eddie or Bethany, she saw her naked Aunt Grace walking to the mailbox.

Yelling through the window, she said, "Aunt Grace, get in the house and put on some clothes." She went to door as she yelled for her mother, "Agnes, get out here!"

Grace couldn't hear her niece and probably wouldn't have paid her any attention anyway. She continued her stroll to the mailbox, grabbing her mail and taking her time to open a few letters like she was fully dressed.

Agnes soon appeared at the door, not really knowing what her daughter was calling her for. She was surprised to see her sister who hadn't left the house since her daughter's funeral. For months, the only thing Grace did was sit in the dark with all the blinds closed. Between her and Carolina, the two sisters made sure she took her medication, bathed and ate on a daily basis.

"Lawd have mercy! Grace, get in the house!" Agnes yelled, rushing down the stairs and into her sister's yard. The children followed her out to the

porch. They were yelling for her to let them get back into the sandbox. "Bea, take those kids back in the house," Agnes told her.

"Come on kids."

"Look at her boom...booms," Hannah continued to say, mesmerized by the long jugs that extended from Grace's chest.

Carolina came to the door to see about the commotion she had heard from inside her house, immediately she started running like she was in a marathon. By the time she had reached her two sisters, Grace was tussling with Agnes. The two together, were having a hard time getting Grace to move. Cars were passing the road and a few blew their horns while they continued their struggle to get their unstable sister in the house. Grace really didn't understand what her sister's were doing to her. She was incoherent. She wasn't arguing with them, but acting more like a stubborn mule.

Agnes was exhausted and frankly, she didn't have the time to be wrestling with her nutty sister. While Carolina tried to use her body to get her sister to move up the stairs to her house, Agnes went to the nearest tree to break off the thickest limb she could find. She returned to her mentally ill sister and immediately went to swinging the thick branch.

"Get yo' fat ass in that house...Who wants to look at all this cellulite on your fat ass?" Agnes said, extending one lick after the other to her sister's large rear. Obviously, feeling the pain that was being inflicted upon her, Grace squealed and screamed as she ran in the house like a scolded animal. Agnes and Carolina both ran inside behind her. Agnes wasn't finished, she continued to hit her sister lick after lick amongst her head and back. "Agnes, that's enough, she's inside now," Carolina informed her older sister as she walked toward the bedroom.

"Oh," Agnes said, coming back to her senses. She was out of breath as Carolina walked from the bedroom with a house dress in her hand. She too was trying to catch her breath as she helped Agnes pull the garment over their sister's head and onto her naked body.

After that, Agnes moved from the living room into the kitchen. She opened the refrigerator door and noticed the food that they had brought over for the past two days and the cups of medication had not been touched. She grabbed one of the three medicine cups and shoved the pills down Grace's throat.

"Dumb ass, you have to take this medicine if you want to be able to function," Agnes told her sister.

"Agnes, don't call her that," Carolina said, giving Agnes a mean look.

"Well, she is dumb. If you are supposed to take medication to help you function and you don't take it—to me that makes you a dumb ass."

"Will you stop it? She's not dumb, she's sick," Carolina insisted, also looking in the refrigerator. She grabbed the plate she had made the day before. She warmed it in the microwave as she pulled her sister to the table. Grace was starting to yawn, the medication was taking affect.

Carolina hurried and placed the food in front of her sister, who ate like it was her last meal. She didn't use a spoon or fork, but dug at the food with her bare hands and shoved it all in her mouth. Rice fell from her face and meat hung from her lips as she smacked on the remaining portions in her mouth.

"Grace, don't do that," Carolina said, picking up the food her sister was dropping.

Grace sat wide eyed as she laughed out loud. She laughed uncontrollably and nobody had shared a joke. Then she laughed with her mouth wide open, exposing the food she was chewing.

Both Agnes and Carolina recognized the signs they were seeing only meant the medication was entering Grace's system and soon enough she would be fast to sleep. They were correct as they watched their sister's inability to keep her eyes open.

Agnes shook Grace awake when she saw her dozing at the kitchen table. She grabbed her sister by the hand, pulling her in the direction of the bedroom, so she and Carolina could put her to bed. Before they could leave the room, Grace was snoring louder than a hibernating bear.

"Do you think we should stay with her tonight?" Carolina said to Agnes, looking back at their sister now resting so comfortable.

"It doesn't make sense for both of us to stay. One of us should stay tonight and the other tomorrow. We can rotate back and forth," Agnes suggested. She knew Sunday was the Women's day program and Carolina needed to be there. "I guess you're right. You can stay with her tonight and I'll stay with her tomorrow," Carolina said as her sister agreed, turning off the bedroom lights.

Chapter Forty-Three

Today was Sunday morning and Eloise was wearing an off white dress and as usual, both her shoes and hat matched perfectly. She was very concerned about who would be getting the woman of the year award. Each year, the church gave an award for the female that exhibited dedication and outstanding service to God and the Tabernacle of Praise Church.

Eloise sat for awhile then as people began filling up the sanctuary, she got up from her seat and mingled with the members of her sister circle. She roamed the sanctuary to speak with people who were present to attend the annual Women's day problem. A few people she spoke to she hadn't seen in a long while. She walked past her Cousin Clara, the two still weren't speaking. She heard Clara snicker to her granddaughter Pandora as she went past. She didn't care, she knew she looked good.

What Eloise didn't know was the female who would be getting the honor this year—Mychael had decided to handle the recognition differently this year. In years past, the previous recipients included all three of her daughters, her daughter-in-law and herself. In her mind, she couldn't imagine anyone who would be deserving of the current year's award. That was her real and true reason she wanted to speak with her pastor. In her opinion, she wanted to speak to him before he made the mistake of giving the honor to some undeserving individual.

Leaving behind the crowd in the sanctuary, she took a peek into her pastor's office; she wanted to see if he needed her to do anything in particular. Truthfully, she wasn't there to work, but more so to get the information she was seeking.

"Good morning young man," she said.

"Good morning to you too Mother Eloise. How are things going?" Mychael said. Eloise noticed that her pastor didn't look like his usual self. He looked thin, he looked worried, and he looked concerned about something.

She asked him what was wrong. She could tell something wasn't quite right, but Mychael kept telling her that everything was fine.

"Things are going well, where's my gorgeous grandbaby?"

"She's coming later with Sister Beatrice."

Eloise turned her nose up like she smelt something.

"I know Mother Eloise, but Sister Beatrice helps me out a lot with Hannah, and besides she enjoys playing with Jeremiah."

"Hum…I forgot she had that little boy. As bad I hate to admit it, he's pretty handsome. Is his father black or white?" she asked with her arms folded.

"Now, Mother Eloise, how would I know that? I dare not ask them folk about Jeremiah's paternity. You know as well I do, I'm not one of Deacon Shaw's favorite people and we have been getting along fine and I don't want to ruffle his feathers."

"Well, what about your mother-in-law? I heard through the grapevine she ran through the neighborhood naked as a jay bird," she stated.

"Mother Eloise, I haven't heard such a thing. And as much as you dislike Sister Grace, she's still my mother-in-law, therefore conversations about her are off limits," Mychael said, closing the book of information he was reading. He was about to place the same book in his desk drawer when Ernest, Jr. walked in.

"Good morning Mother," he said, planting a kiss to his mother's cheek.

"Hello there son, where's your brother? I didn't see him in Sunday school."

"I just spoke with him, he's on his way. As a matter of fact, I came in here to tell Pastor Dovely that Richard will be picking up the plaque from the trophy shop. Is that okay, I didn't get a chance to go by there yesterday?"

"I guess so. But I didn't know they were open on Sunday," Mychael said, now studying the introduction of his guest minister. He was able to get Minister Paula White to deliver the Women's day sermon. And her introduction bio was impressive, but long to say the least.

"They aren't, but I called Mrs. Price at home, and she's going to open the shop for us and allow Richard to stop by to pick up the plaque."

"Well Pastor, are you going to tell me who's getting the award this year?" Eloise said, interrupting the conversation between him and her son.

"No Mother Eloise, it's going to be a surprise. But I'm sure you will be very pleased. This person is more than worthy."

Eloise didn't question Mychael any further. She and her son turned away, walking out of the office at the same time. He escorted her into the sanctuary and to her seat, before taking his own seat among the row of deacons. Before she could settle in her seat, Eloise snatched her head quickly to the touch of a familiar hand.

"*Sista*, can I sit next to you?" Flossie asked, waiting for Eloise to move over. A broad smile came on Eloise's face. Flossie was out of the hospital and looking better than ever. She was dressed in an off white outfit, appropriate for her age. Miranda stood next to her mother. Eloise and her didn't exchange words, but grabbed and squeezed each other's hand. They both knew what it meant. For Eloise, it meant, she had forgiven her for what she had said and done to her. For Miranda, it meant, she was sorry for the division she had created within the family. In other words, they both silently apologized to one another.

Flossie rocked to the musical rendition being rendered by the choir. She clapped her hands together. She raised them in the air. The old Flossie was back. She was never ashamed to show how much she enjoyed worship services at Tabernacle of Praise. And today wasn't any different.

Moments later, Mychael was standing at the podium about to introduce the speaker of the hour.

"Tabernacle of Praise, we are about to hear from Heaven this morning. I'm pleased to introduce to some and present to others a mighty…mighty…woman of God. Her reputation proceeds her…her preaching can stand on its own. But before I present Minister Paula White, I would like to recognize this year's woman of the year. To some she's a sister, to some she's an aunty, to one she's *simply* mom. But to me, she's a woman who has always respected me as her pastor. After I lost my wife, she took great care of me and my daughter like I was her son-in-law. Breakfast, Lunch and Dinner, I had it. She kept my house in order, she kept

our laundry clean and most importantly she showed me what a true Christian was supposed to be. This year's woman of the year award goes to none other than Sister Carolina Christiansen."

Carolina covered her face as the excitement could be heard throughout the sanctuary. Eleanor left her seat and helped her best friend to her feet. She knew how shy Carolina was so she walked with her from the choir loft to the front of the church, standing next to their pastor. She looked on as Mychael and Carolina exchanged kisses to the cheek. Mychael finally handed Carolina the plaque, then the microphone. "Thank you Pastor Dovely and Tabernacle of Praise," she said, handing the microphone back to him.

Mychael returned to the pulpit to finish his introduction of the world renowned Minister Paula White.

"Tabernacle of Praise, without any further delay, let us welcome our speaker of the hour, Minister Paula White."

Parishioners throughout the sanctuary rose to their feet as Minister White now stood at the podium. She was covered in a long white robe with a gold cross on the chest area of the garment. Like always, her makeup was perfect, her nails were well manicured and her hair was flawless, it even maintained its place as she turned her head from side to side to recognize the Pastor and his officers.

"Tabernacle of Praise, look at your neighbor…Say, neighbor, oh neighbor, today's message is: It's time to be real."

The congregation began laughing. Some members were giving each other the high five, while others nodded their heads in agreement with the topic.

Minister White walked from one end of the pulpit to the other saying, "The word tells us that we must worship the Lord in spirit and in truth. Then the word also tells us that the Lord is the light of our salvation." She paused, looking over her shoulder at Mychael. "Pastor, do you mind, if I go down on the floor and talk to my sisters? I know you didn't invite me all this way to be formal. I want this message to be as informal as possible and I just want to have a one on one conversation with my sisters, is that all right?"

"Now sisters, we've established that we must worship the Lord in spirit and in truth. So tell me…why can't we still get it together? Our hair is in place, our nails are done and our clothes fit us perfect…some fit us a little too perfect… Amen. It appears that we have it together, so why aren't our hearts right and why don't we take our salvation more serious?"

A few members were standing on their feet as commotion could be heard throughout the crowded room.

"We say with our lips that we love the Lord, but as soon as a good looking man approaches us, we forget about our morals and the Lord, finding ourselves lying in bed next to a person we've only known a few months, a few weeks and on some occasions, a few hours."

"Tell me sisters, what's wrong with that picture? Why can't we wait for the man that God has destined for us?" Sisters, tell me… just tell me, why? It's okay… we can talk about it, today is your day. Today is Women's day, right?"

The congregation answered back in reply to her question, "Yes."

"I thought so, it's just me and you sisters, let's talk. Tell me… Why are we supposed to be saved, sanctified and filled with the precious Holy Ghost, but we try our best to sleep with the Pastor…Ooops, did I say that? We lust after our best friend's husband…Ooops, did I say that? And finally when we can't get any of the above, we result to pleasing ourselves…Glory to God, somebody is going to get saved and delivered here this morning."

"Well, my sisters, I'm here to tell you…God is not pleased about you lusting after your pastor nor is He pleased with you lusting after your best friend's husband, I know you're best friend wouldn't be pleased—if she knew. And to give it to you plain and simple, masturbation is just NASTY…amen"

"Come on… let's be real here today, married sisters you're not off the hook, this word is for you to. Some of you don't know the meaning of being submissive to your husband. And men, that scripture doesn't mean that you treat your queen like she's second best. That simply means that you are the head of your household and you are responsible for what goes on in your household."

"All right, preach it Reverend," a male in attendance shouted.

"Tell it like it is preacher," another said.

"Now women…being submissive is simple, we make it harder than it actually is. Submissiveness doesn't mean keeping a clean house, that's something you have to do already. Submissiveness doesn't mean that you have to take physical or verbal abuse from your spouse. Submissiveness means that you want the best for your spouse, it means that you want him to look his best, act his best and your role is to support him in those efforts."

"I counseled a couple once, who said they had been married for over forty years. And the husband said, I would trust my wife with my life, because she always wanted the best out of me and the best for me. And in return, he said, he knew he had to respect her, love her and honor her. So married women, if you show your husbands that you support him and want the best for him and out of him, in return he won't have any choice but to love, respect, and honor you."

"It's time to be real in the way we treat each other."

"It's time to be real in the way we handle our finances. What man of God wants a sister who can't bring anything to the table? Today, I encourage you to open a savings account, pay your tithes first, then pay your savings second, pay your bills third and what's left…you have my permission to spend it as you please. I take authority over the directive I've just given you and if you do these things in that order, I promise you that the every area of finance in your life will be abundantly blessed."

"It's time…It's time…It's time…" Minister White continued to say. "It's time to put restraints on our mind and body. Women, we are more than a one night stand, we are more than a fist to the face or that push to the floor and we are more than that conversation men often have after we've wholeheartedly given ourselves to them. Women we are so much more."

"It's time to be real with ourselves. Real in the sense that we stop looking for our husbands in the nightclubs, at the mall or the grocery stores, I don't care what those magazines are telling you about finding your mate in all these places, I tell you today, right now—this hour your husbands are in the body of Christ. It may not be in this congregation, I said in the body of Christ. It may be the small church down the road; it may be at a Christian concert or at a single's ministry setting. But he is and I say this with every ounce of conviction within me, in the body of Christ," Minister White said, pointing at one sister, then to another. She walked to the back of the church, turning quickly to walk back to the front, stopping in front of Eloise. "My dear sister, I've never seen you before, but God has sent you a message. Are you married?"

Eloise shook her head that she wasn't.

"God says that a man you've been avoiding is your next husband. You've attached him to a conflict in your life, but this man can't be held accountable

for who he's related to. God says open your heart. Love and happiness awaits you."

Minister White walked away from Eloise and returned to the pulpit. "Oh thank you God for that. Where is the sister that received the plaque this morning?" she asked, looking around. Carolina raised her hand. Mychael pointed the guest minister in the direction where Carolina was sitting in the choir loft. Minister White spoke directly to her, "Sister, I don't have to ask you have you ever been married. My spirit says you haven't because you are still in love with a man from your past. I don't know who he is, but be encouraged that the bond that the two of you share hasn't been broken. It's not too late. He's on his way back to you."

Carolina wiped her eyes, as Eleanor fanned her. The minister began speaking in tongues. "Thank you God." She spoke in tongue more. "Ah, thank you God. God I need for you to be make it plain, yes God, I will God, thank you God." She turned to face Carolina again. "My sister, God says be patient. He says trust in His will. I see in the spirit, you holding hands with a little boy, and a tall gentleman, but I can't see the man's face. The spirit says the little boy is the bond between the two of you."

Carolina began screaming while she bucked back and forth in her seat. She shook her head so vigorously that she shook out the curls in her hair. Christopher left his seat in the choir to walk over to his mother to keep her from hurting herself. He fanned, she bucked. Eleanor fanned, her best friend screamed, "I receive it God…I received it God…Oh God I receive it."

CHAPTER FORTY-FOUR

After service, Christopher lost track of his mother and was having no luck finding her to take a picture of her for the front vestibule. He searched everywhere and even had Beatrice to check the women's bathroom, she wasn't in there. He wondered to himself, where could she be? He moved from the bathroom area toward the fellowship hall, he stopped at the table where his aunt was sitting and interrupted her feeding Jeremiah and Hannah.

"Aunt Agnes, have you seen my mother?" he asked her, looking through the crowd of people entering the fellowship hall.

"No baby, not lately, last time I saw her she was walking down the hall with Deacon Lorde," she told him. Hearing his aunt, Christopher jerked his neck back and blinked his eyes twice. After that, he left the fellowship hall in pursuit to find his mother. He just knew his aunt had to be wrong. He continued walking down the long hall and stopped when he heard voices coming from inside the conference room. He didn't enter, instead he listened—oh well, he eavesdropped on the conversation.

"Ernie, she's not talking about you and me," Christopher heard his mother say.

"I believe that she was. Carolina, please tell me if Christopher is my son. Is he the little boy God showed Minister White?" Deacon Lorde questioned.

Before Carolina could answer, Christopher tapped on the door.

"It's open."

He looked behind the door to find his mother standing there.

"Hey, I've looked all over for you. I want to take a picture of you with your plaque for the front vestibule to put in the church newsletter," he said, ignoring Deacon Lorde, his father, according to his mother.

Carolina was glad her son showed up when he did. She was so close to revealing to her high school boyfriend that he was indeed the father of her son.

"Okay son, let me touch up my makeup and I'll be right down."

"Mom, are you okay?" Christopher asked her, not wanting to leave the room.

"Oh yes, I'm fine. You run along and I'll come find you when I fix my makeup," she said, trying to assure him.

Deacon Lorde didn't say a word. He listened to the exchange between Carolina and her son. He saw that Christopher was reluctant because it showed in the wrinkles in his face and the slow manner in which he closed the door.

Christopher angled toward the fellowship hall, but bypassed the door to enter as he made a quick left to enter his office to get the digital camera from the locked file cabinet. He didn't know Mychael was sitting in his office until he heard him talking.

"Christopher, can I speak with you a minute?" Mychael asked softly, covering the phone with his hand.

Christopher took a long sigh before he answered, "I guess so."

"I promise it won't take long," Mychael said now a little more cheerful, returning to his phone call. He informed the person on the line that he needed to end their conversation. He came out of his office and sat on the edge of the desk as his secretary sat in the chair fumbling with the camera.

"Christopher, what can I do to make things better between us? It's been a month and you have not said two words to me. I've told you how sorry I was that things got out of hand. I promise, I won't let anything like that ever happen again, just tell me what I need to do?" Mychael pleaded.

Christopher was silent and didn't move his eyes from his stare of the carpeted floor. "Do I have to stop being friends with Jorge and Pierce?" he asked Mychael as if he needed his permission.

"It's not a problem for you to be friends with them. As a matter of fact, all four of us can go out to dinner and I'll pay. From now on, your friends are my friends," Mychael said.

Christopher chuckled slightly. He had heard that comment before. He raised his eyes from the floor and looked briefly at his lover and pastor. Mychael knew right away what he was trying to say with his eyes—he got his message. Then Christopher returned his stare at the floor again.

"And what do I have to do in exchange for all of this?" he said.

"Nothing, you don't have to do anything. Let's just start over and I promise not to control you or your life. Is that a good enough deal?" Mychael said.

They both stood to their feet at the same time and they hugged momentarily before Mychael moved his lips slowly towards Christopher's. At first, Christopher snatched his face away then he realized what he was doing. It seemed innocent and the few seconds he felt Mychael's lips, they actually felt soft against his.

Once their lips separated, Mychael took the opportunity to take in Christopher's scent, giving him a second kiss similar to a peck on the cheek. He kept his eyes closed as he moved his nose against his lover's neck. He embraced him, much tighter than he intended to, but he didn't know whether he would ever get another chance like this one. His actions shocked Christopher, making him unsure whether he should hug him back—instead he stood coldly.

At the same time, Beatrice stood at the partially open door, observing the end of the exchange between her cousin and their pastor. She wondered what had taken place before she appeared at the door. She stood in silence unable to make out the words the two men were saying to each other. She continued to watch.

"Man, I think I'm falling in love with you." Mychael said, shaking his head like he was embarrassed by his confession.

"Then you should act like it," Christopher said as a response. He was now sitting on the edge of his desk with his arms knotted together.

"I know…I know. I'm going to start though."

When the two men moved from their places, walking toward the door, Beatrice quietly back away from the partially open door and stood in the hallway. She still didn't understand the exchange she had witnessed, but she knew she would have to seize an opportunity to question her cousin further.

Unknowing of Beatrice's observation, Mychael and Christopher walked out of the office to find her standing against the wall with Jeremiah on her hip and Hannah running the halls similar to an energized bunny rabbit.

Mychael lifted his daughter from the floor into his arms, greeting her as he always did, "How is daddy's little girl doing?"

"Pine."

"Pine, huh?" Mychael said, mimicking his daughter.

"Yeah DaDa…I doing pine," Hannah answered.

They all laughed as they each continued their stroll toward the fellowship hall before Mychael excused himself and walked over to the pastor's table to find the guest ministers all eating. He didn't have an appetite to eat; in fact, he hadn't been able to eat much the last month. But now that he had fixed things with Christopher, his appetite would probably come back. While the others ate, he made small talk with his guests and occasionally wiggled his fingers to tickle his daughter.

"Reverend Dovely, have you finalized everything for the weekend retreat next month?" A middle age pastor asked.

"I'm not exactly in the loop on that, I have a committee that's handling everything. Why, are you guys planning one also?" Mychael said referring his response to the pastor of the church located around the corner.

"No, I was hoping that you guys would allow us to go in with you all. We only have fifty members."

"Well, you will need to contact Carolina Christiansen. She's the chairperson of the committee."

As Mychael watched the minister write down the information he had given him, he noticed Minister White watching him. He tried to pretend that he didn't see her. To distract the attention from him, he played with his daughter, tickling her again, this time making her laugh out loud.

"I'll call her tomorrow," the middle age pastor said.

"Reverend, do we have to worry about some of your members bringing guns and knives with them to this retreat? We don't have to deal with that kind of stuff over here."

"Rev., what are you talking about?"

"I'm talking about that metal detector you have posted at the front entrance of your church," Mychael answered. All the ministers laughed, even the middle aged pastor had to laugh. As much as he hated to admit it, his church was located in a bad area. Earlier that year, during worship, there was a drive-by shooting and a man worshipping in the congregation was shot in the arm.

After she finished her meal, Minister White got up from her seat and

walked over to Mychael. She placed her hand on his shoulder, discretely telling him that she needed to speak with him. Slowly, leaving the pastor's table, Mychael followed her out into the hallway. He put his daughter on the floor and let her run up and down the hall.

"My brother, the spirit is showing me that you need to be careful, someone is out to destroy your reputation," she said.

"My reputation, how?" Mychael said.

"God doesn't always reveal everything to us. Sometimes he will give us enough information to make us aware of our surroundings and friends."

Mychael continued to walk along side Minister White as they reached the exit leading to the parking lot. He had to yell at his daughter several times to stop running, but all the while hearing what the minister was telling him. He didn't have any idea who would want to ruin his reputation. In his heart, he received the warning from Minister White. In his mind, he stored in a safe place, the information she had revealed to him. Then he grabbed Hannah by the hand and walked his guest minister to the parking lot as her driver waited patiently for her. Minister White hugged and assured him that she would keep him in her prayers. He felt like she would.

Mychael returned inside the building with his mind turning a mile a minute. He conceded that he wasn't going to worry about what she had told him— he felt protected by God and covered by prayer.

CHAPTER FORTY-FIVE

Eloise was doing some last minute dusting while she waited for her daughters to pick her up for their mother/daughter night. Tonight, they all were going to have dinner and catch a movie. Even though the mother/daughter nights took her away from her Monday cleaning, she still enjoyed the time she spent with her daughters. At one time, they were having them on a continuous basis, but after she offered to take care of Flossie, the time she spent with her daughters became less frequent.

Come to think of it, the last few months had become very lonely for Eloise now that Flossie was living with her daughter. Surely, she desperately wanted to move back with her and Flossie stated this every time she saw her. She made Eloise feel bad with the way she begged and pleaded. She still felt bad because of the disappointment she saw in Flossie's eyes when she had to tell her she couldn't go home with her, but that she had to return home with her daughter Miranda.

Eloise agreed with her conscious that regardless of how she felt about Miranda, she genuinely cared about Flossie and her concern made her call to check on her more often. As a matter of fact, today, she had checked on her once already.

Over time, she began missing Flossie's presence because her house had the tendency to become spooky at times. Despite her concern for her ex-patient, she knew in her heart, that at this stage in Flossie's condition, she needed to be with her children, even though she and Miranda had patched up their differences.

Eloise was about to climb onto her step stool to dust the top of her

bookshelf when she heard her daughter blowing the horn. She had been expecting them, but the sound still startled her. She grabbed her purse and house keys and headed out the door and down the stairs to the car. She smiled when she saw them, but smiled more when she saw her daughter-in-law Overa—it had been a long time since she had gone out with them. Overa had become very active with her sorority and on Mondays, she was usually involved in some type charity work. In fact, she was the incoming Vice-chair and rightfully so, she felt she needed to be more visible and available to her young followers.

Eloise reached the car and opened the rear door. When she got in, she closed the door shut as she spoke to everyone. She massaged with her hand the shoulders of Alma and Eleanor then she squeezed the hand of her daughter-in-law. Usually, she would have kissed them all, but this time she didn't. After showing how glad she was to see them, she took in the scent her daughter-in-law was wearing. It was a strong, but nice fragrance. She had never smelt it before so she couldn't help asking her about it. "Hey there stranger, what made you want to hang out with your boring family?" she said to Overa. "I love that perfume you have on, what kind is it?" she added, before Overa could answer her initial question.

"Thank you and I didn't want to be alone at home tonight."

"Okay. Well I'm sure you can only add to the fun we're going to have. So, everybody is doing okay?"

"Yes ma'am," they all said together.

"Where are we going to eat tonight? I'm starving… I attempted to fast from 6am to 6pm and Chile I was hungry thirty minutes after I started." Eloise informed her daughters.

"So, Mother you didn't finish the fast?" Eleanor asked.

"I stayed on it, but I could've sworn my blood sugar went to zero throughout the day. I got so fatigued around three o'clock, I couldn't help dozing off to sleep. When I woke up, it was after five."

They all laughed at Eloise.

"I thought we'd go to the Apple Hornet tonight, everybody agree?" Alma suggested. She continued to drive through town, turning on Main Street as they all agreed with her suggestion, also enjoying the ride and scenery as she made two right turns and a left before pulling into the partially empty parking

lot. She drove around the parking lot looking for a space close to the front entrance.

"That looks like my husband's car. I thought he said he had a meeting," Overa said, looking at the license tag closely. It was quite obvious that it was him—his tag said *Lorde*.

"Maybe he did and the meeting is here," Eloise assured her daughter-in-law. She saw how anxious she had become. Overa didn't allow the car to completely shut off before she leaped from the back seat, headed toward the restaurant."

"Overa honey, at least let us all walk in together," Eloise suggested. "You make it seem like my son has cheated on you or something. Why are you being so anxious, like you are trying to catch him with a woman?" she continued.

"Okay, I do seem to be a little nervous, don't I?"

"A little," Eloise said.

Once they entered the restaurant, they all stood around talking among themselves before a hostess approached them. The four of them looked very sophisticated, dressed in various styles of different colored pants suits, accessorized with expensive jewelry around their necks and on their wrists. They clutched designer handbags with their fingers and they looked like business executives to onlookers as their host guided them to their seats.

As the four women walked toward the area where they would be sitting, Eloise and her daughter-in-law scanned the restaurant trying to locate Ernest, Jr.

"Eloise London, is that you?" an older woman asked.

Eloise stopped at the calling of her name. Her daughters were ahead of her, but they stopped when she stopped. She looked at the woman and recognized her right away. "Millicent Brickhouse!" she said bending over to hug the sitting woman she recognized. Apparently, the woman was a high school classmate of hers and the woman didn't live in Ramblewood anymore. She was home visiting her family—the same family she was ignoring while she spoke to her.

"That's Brickhouse-Walton. Girl, I haven't seen you in years. How have you been?" Millicent said. "Is your husband still the pastor over there at the Tabernacle of Praise?"

"I'm doing well, but Chile you haven't been home in awhile? My husband,

God bless his soul, passed away nearly two years ago. Reverend Mychael Dovely is the pastor there now."

Pausing, Eloise continued, "I don't think you know my daughters…" she pointed out, introducing her daughters and daughter-in-law. Millicent was sitting with three younger women looking similar to her. After Eloise, she introduced her three children. The sitting women looked at the four standing women in a way that seemed envious. One daughter stared at Eloise from head to toe. She even took the opportunity to sneak a peek at her shoes while Eloise continued her conversation with her high school classmate.

Eloise could tell that Millicent was embarrassed to be seen with her daughters. She seemed to have it together. But her three daughters sat around her with large portions of food in front of them, dressed in polyester pants with the elastic waist and varied colored sweaters. "It was good to see you again, tonight is our mother-daughter night and we are planning to eat dinner and catch a movie. Millicent, if I don't get to see you again, I hope you have a safe trip home," Eloise said, walking away. Before she could leave the area, she heard Millicent say, "Eloise sure does look good for her age." But she knew that already.

While they were talking, the hostess stood patiently next to their table. On the way to the table, Eloise and Overa again tried to scan the restaurant—still nothing.

In response to the commotion behind him, Ernest, Jr. turned his head toward the noise in the booth next to him and immediately recognized his family. They hadn't seen him before now. He did have a meeting. Right away, he stood to his feet as they all took their seats.

"Ah ha…caught ya'll trying to spy on me," he said, arousing laughter from his female relatives. He leaned over to kiss his wife, his mother and sisters. Then he introduced them to the gentleman he was meeting with.

"Reverend Givens, this is my wife Overa, my mother Eloise and my sisters Alma and Eleanor."

The preacher nodded his head behind each introduction. In return, they all said hello.

"Haven't I seen you somewhere before?" Eloise asked, first studying the folder in Reverend Givens' hand, moving her eyes up to his face. "I know where…you did the eulogy for Monica Dovely's funeral. You are Pastor Dovely's friend from college."

"That is correct. You have a very good memory. Well, it was good seeing you all again, but I have to get home. Deacon Lorde, thank you for meeting with me on such short notice."

"No, Rev. I was glad to do it."

The two men shook hands as Reverend Givens walked away.

"Son, doesn't he live in North Carolina?"

"Yes," Ernie, Jr. answered, watching the preacher walk through the front entrance.

"And he drove two hours to have a meeting with you? It had to be pretty important?" Eloise said.

"Not really," Ernie, Jr. answered, no longer looking in the direction of the exit. His mind was somewhere else.

"It wasn't?"

"Mother, order your food…I hope ya'll have a good night out. Honey, I'll see you when you get home."

"Okay, see you later," everyone said, as Ernie, Jr. walked away from their table, through the front door and to his car. They all looked at their menus unsure about what they wanted to order.

"What did I get the last time I was here?" Alma asked.

"Alma, you ask the same question every time we come here," Eloise, reminded her. "Who's sixty-six years old, you or me?" she added.

"I just can't remember. I'm probably going to get just a salad."

"*Ah* salad! Chile you must be sick." Eleanor remarked.

"Yes a salad and what's wrong with a salad every now and then?" Alma said then she paused before she spoke again, "and according to my husband, he says I could stand to lose a few pounds."

"He said what?" the three women asked at the same time. They all put their menus to the side, leaning their heads near the center of the table.

"Chile, you know what *they* say when a man starts complaining about your weight?" Eloise said to her eldest daughter.

"No Mother, what do *they* say?" Alma said, not really in the mood to hear her mother's philosophies.

"Darling, I hate to be the one to tell you this, but I was married to a man for fifty years, and I believe I know a thing or two about them. But anyway…the comment your husband made is a sign he's losing interest and he could be putting his tool in someone else's garden."

"Mother, where do you get all these crazy sayings?"

"Call me crazy, but your mother is not going to tell you anything wrong. You better keep your eye on him. Overa honey, I know he's your brother, but he's a man first," Eloise explained.

"She's right about that ya'll," Overa said, agreeing with her mother in-law. "But I hope you use that same assessment when it comes to your own sons."

* * *

"Hey man…I was calling to see how things are going with you?" Alton said, not wanting to go right into his real reason for calling Mychael.

"Things are going great man, but you caught me at a bad time," Mychael said.

"What, are you with that choir director?"

"No man and I've told you his name is Christopher. I'm actually putting my daughter to bed and I'm reading her a bedtime story. Can I call you back?"

Alton could hear Hannah in the background. He heard pages turning then it sounded like she was trying to read the book herself.

"DaDa read…read DaDa," he heard her say. "Isn't that nice?"

"Okay, I don't want to hear anything from you when you become a father," Mychael said in a good mood. He was very proud to be a father.

"Yeah right…I can't wait. Seriously, I need for you to call me back; I want to run something by you."

"Give me about thirty minutes, are you at home?"

"No, but you can call me on my cell phone."

"Okay, bye."

Chapter Forty-Six

DJ quietly entered his parent's house to find his father sleeping in his recliner. He checked the other rooms and realized his mother wasn't at home. He shook his father until he opened his eyes, they were red. His father didn't say anything. He just looked at his son with blurry vision.

"Dad, where's mom?" *DJ* said, shaking his father harder.

"What the *hell* is wrong with you hitting me like that?" Daniel asked his son.

"I need some money and Mom's not here."

"It's Monday, you know every Monday night your mother goes to dinner with your grandmother. She should be home around ten or so."

"I can't wait until then. I need a hundred bucks."

Daniel's eyes were now stretched wide. Did his drug addicted son think he was actually going to give him a hundred dollars? Maybe he did.

"If you think you are going to get a hundred dollars from yo' Mama, you are sadly mistaking," Daniel said to his son.

"No, I don't. I'm going to get it from you," *DJ* said, looking at his father with a straight face.

His father laughed out loud—but realizing immediately that his son wasn't playing, "Are you for real?"

"Um…hum."

"Boy, are you high? I'm not giving you any *damn* hundred dollars to smoke up—now get your ass out of here."

"Dad, have you forgotten about last week? I still can tell mom about my catching you and don't forget that she believes everything I tell her," *DJ* reminded his father.

"*DJ* lets go," an unknown female yelled while moving around like she had to use the bathroom.

"Who is that?" Daniel asked, looking around.

"Don't worry about her, she's with me."

Daniel had mellowed out very quickly. He really had forgotten about his son catching him and Pandora having sex. Slowly, he grabbed his wallet and looked through his row of bills. He didn't have a hundred dollar bill, but he pulled from his wallet five twenties and handed them over to his son. *DJ* grabbed the money without saying thank you and became scarce with the unknown female.

After his son had left, Daniel became real angry. He hadn't realized until his son was out of his sight that he had been blackmailed. At that moment, he made up in his mind that he was not going to stand for this again. Well, maybe he would. He could only hope that this was a one time situation. Upon realizing that he should probably count his lucky stars that his son had only asked for one hundred dollars and not five hundred, the house phone rang. He thought it was probably his wife, but it wasn't—it was Pandora.

"Hey *daddy*," she said. Her remark made Daniel smile. He liked when she called him her *daddy*.

"You know you shouldn't be calling here," Daniel informed her.

"I tried your cell phone, but you apparently have it turned off." While listening to Pandora talk, Daniel picked up his cell phone and saw that it was off. He remembered when he had mistakenly turned it off. At the time, he thought he was changing the phone from vibrate to loud, but by mistake he had turned it off.

"So, what's up?" Daniel asked his young mistress.

"I want to see you."

"Baby, Charlotte is too far to drive at this time of night."

"I'm not in Charlotte. I'm at my grandmothers."

"Well, I know you don't think I'm coming over there."

"Let's get a room in town. I'll go first and call you with the room number."

Daniel thought about it. He looked at the clock on the wall that read a few minutes before nine. He continued to think about it more while Pandora sat on the other end of the phone. He sighed, trying to make himself decline the offer she had made to him. He couldn't. The memory of the week before wouldn't let him.

"Okay, get the room and I'll meet you there. But I have to be home at least by eleven," he said into the phone. He hung up and thought out loud, "What lie am I going to come up with now?"

* * *

Hannah was now sound asleep. She had made her father read the book, *little red riding hood* three times. Reading the book so often, Mychael now knew the story like the back of his hand. He could probably read it with his eyes closed. As many books as his daughter had resting on her pink bookshelf, she always grabbed the same one. After returning the thin book to an empty space on the bookshelf, Mychael left his daughter's room and returned to the family room. The television was playing. He muted the sound before picking up his cell phone to return the call of his friend as he promised. Alton answered the phone on the first ring.

"Hello."

"Okay, I'm free, what's up?" Mychael said.

"Man I need to borrow some money, I have this investment that I can't pass up," Alton said to Mychael.

"How much?"

"Two hundred and fifty thousand," Alton said, making Mychael start coughing.

"You're kidding right; you really do mean two-hundred and fifty dollars?"

"No, negro, I need two hundred and fifty thousand dollars!" Alton said louder than he intended to.

"Wait a minute now man, slow your roll, don't be yelling at me. You are the one who needs this money;" Mychael declared. "And where do you think I get that kind of money?" he added.

In actuality, he did have that type of money. In fact, he had that amount and more, but he wasn't about to loan that amount of money to Alton. The two of them were friends, but in Mychael's opinion, Alton could use a lesson or two about money management.

"Listen at Mr. high and mighty…don't you forget where you come from. Remember, when I loaned you money a few years back when your pastor's daughter loaned you that church deposit? When you came to me, I didn't think twice about it."

"Yes, I do remember because you won't let me forget it, but remember it was five thousand dollars and not two hundred and fifty thousand dollars?"

"People like you always come out on top," Alton said out of the blue.

"Alton, what are you talking about?" Mychael said.

"You came up here last week and took up all my time, listening to you go on and on about some *punk* whose got your head all screwed up and now I need you to help me and I can't get any."

Mychael couldn't believe what he was hearing. He held the phone away from his ear. It sounded like his friend, but then again the words he was hearing weren't the type of comments that would come from his best friend. He returned the phone to his ear; he could hear Alton continue to rant about everything, including his lack of friendship. Alton hadn't even noticed that he had held the phone away from his face.

"Myke, I need that money. You need to make it happen or else."

"Else what?"

"Or that big congregation you preach to every Sunday may receive an anonymous tip about their pastor being a fudge packer."

His comment really took Mychael by surprise. He was at a loss for words. He started to put Alton in his place, but he thought better of it. He couldn't believe he had disclosed all of his personal business in confidence to someone he thought was his friend and now the same person was threatening to use it against him.

"Myke, are you there?"

"I'm here."

"Do we have a deal? If we do, I need the money by five o'clock tomorrow," Alton instructed.

"Man, I can't get that kind of money tomorrow by five. I need to get with my accountant to have them print you a check."

"Okay, I'll give you forty-eight hours. Man, I really hate to do this, but you left me no choice, you understand, don't you?" Alton explained.

"I understand more than you know," Mychael responded, hanging up the phone.

* * *

It was after midnight and Daniel and Pandora were still making love. This was their third round. Earlier, he had watched her pleasure herself with a penis sex toy. He stood and watched as she moved the vibrating penis around her most sensitive area. He listened as she whimpered like a puppy missing its mother. He reached over to rub her firm breast, but she pushed him away. She didn't want him to touch her. She only wanted him to watch. She continued to whimper and her noises were making Daniel aroused. All of a sudden, he noticed her vagina contracting and a stream of clear fluids drained from her vaginal opening. He thought by this time she was ready for him, but she began to jerk with each contraction as more of the same clear fluids squirted out of her like she was urinating. She had wet the area where she was laying and she couldn't move from that spot. She looked paralyzed. She lay in a disoriented state for a few moments before she allowed Daniel to get on top of her. Their love making began aggressively like he couldn't get enough of her and she couldn't get enough of him.

At the moment, she was straddling Daniel, grinding back and forth, driving him wild. He held her around her waist with one hand and squeezed her breasts with the other. After the third round, he was now exhausted. She wasn't. He wanted to stop. She wanted to ride him more. Soon, he reached his sexual peak for the third time. He begged for her to let him go home. His cell phone had already rung at least five times since eleven o'clock. He knew it was exactly five times because he kept count in his head. Becoming so preoccupied, he still hadn't thought of an excuse to give to his wife. Even with him having a good time, he knew once he made it home, he could possibility be sleeping in the guest room.

Finally, Pandora was letting him free. Lost in his thoughts, he hadn't realized that Pandora had rolled off of him. When he came to his senses, he sprung from the bed. He wobbled a bit. He was weak and dizzy. Was his blood pressure up? He wondered. The room started spinning, making him hold onto the bed, the television then the wall until he was able to reach the bathroom. After that, he sat on the porcelain. As he sat the room kept spinning, but not as fast. He still felt nauseous. He sat on the porcelain a little while longer, until the room began to settle.

After a thirty minute lapse in time, he was able to get in the shower. Once in there, he had to stand his ground to keep Pandora from jumping in with him.

She thought he was joking with her until he raised his voice. She stopped suddenly then slowly backed her way out of the small bathroom. He hated having to yell at his young lover, but he had to get home. He knew letting her get in the shower with him would only delay that effort. The ten minute bath made him feel better, much better and more relaxed. He wasn't dizzy anymore and the room was no longer turning. The only problem he had now was the time—it was now one in the morning.

CHAPTER FORTY-SEVEN

Christopher glanced at the clock on the wall, noticing that it said four thirty. He was thrilled that he didn't have much longer before his shift ended. It was the night of his house warming party and he was happy. He loved receiving gifts. But no one could be happier and more excited than Jorge and Pierce. They both insisted that he have one. In the beginning, he said no then he reluctantly agreed with the understanding that he had to have two separate parties. One, where he would invite his mother, his family and people from the church and a separate gathering that would allow him to invite a select group of people—not his friends, but mostly friends of Jorge and Pierce.

Sitting at his desk, he jotted down all the things he needed to pick up from the grocery store. He had all his belongings packed away and sitting next to his desk on the floor. Usually he would be gone by this time, but since the contractors were surveying the grounds for the educational center, it prevented him from leaving early because the contracting company didn't stop working until exactly five o'clock.

Surprisingly, at four forty-five, he looked up to see Mychael walking into the reception area. He was wearing a pair of black shorts, his Ramblewood High shirt and a pair of new looking athletic shoes. He couldn't help glancing at his legs. They were so muscular and hairy.

"What are you doing here?" Christopher said.

"I am still pastor aren't I?" Mychael responded sarcastically.

"You know what I mean smarty pants."

Mychael didn't make small talk. He grabbed his mail from his box and entered his office. Before Christopher could remind him about the house

warming party, he heard the door behind him close. Ten minutes later, his desk phone rang.

"Thanks for calling Tabernacle of Praise, this is C—," he attempted to say.

Mychael interrupted him. "I'm expecting someone in the next thirty minutes. Could you let me know when he gets here?"

"What are you doing, why do you have the door closed?" he asked Mychael.

"I'm praying…why?"

"I just asked. Are you still coming to the house warming tonight?"

"Oh man, I forgot about that and I don't have a baby sister for Hannah. Do you think you're mother will baby sit for me? Let me call her. I'll let you know."

"Wait a minute superman… You can't mention to my mom about this housewarming," he reminded Mychael.

"I know. And by the way, who all is going to be there?"

"I dunno, I let Pierce and Jorge handle the guest list. It really doesn't matter to me as long as they bring a gift."

"You let Pierce and Jorge handle the guest list to your house warming," Mychael said, repeating what he had heard Christopher say.

"Are you coming or not?"

"Do I have to?"

"Yes you do. Remember, friends of mine are friends of yours?"

Hearing Christopher make that statement, reminded Mychael of the promise he had previously made. He said slowly, "That's right, I did say that? If I do come, I'm not bringing a gift because I'm broke."

"That's okay. You being there will be my gift," Christopher said to him.

Mychael laughed out loud. Christopher could hear him through his closed door.

"Is that right? Some people will say anything to get what they want. Man…see you done got me all sidetracked. I'm supposed to be in here praying," Mychael said.

"Okay, I'll let you go. Oh wait a minute. I think your visitor is here," Christopher said, holding the phone away from his mouth as he spoke to the short gentleman, "May I help you?"

"Yes, I'm Mr. Givens. I have an appointment to see Pastor Dovely."

"One minute." Christopher placed the phone back to his mouth and ear. "Your appointment is here. Can I send him in?"

"Yeah," Christopher heard Mychael say.

Alton walked into his friend's office with his head down. He couldn't face him. Mychael made it a point to watch him as he entered the door to his office. He wanted to make him feel as uncomfortable as possible and he was doing a good job.

"You didn't tell me that the choir director was your personal secretary," Alton said nervously as he stood on the opposite side of Mychael's desk.

"Why would I, you're not a member here." Mychael snapped as he observed Alton attempting to sit down in the empty chair on the opposite of his desk. "There isn't a need to sit down," Mychael said, handing his ex-friend a white envelope with a check enclosed. By the time Alton opened it, Mychael was standing to his feet. He was ready for him to leave.

"Man, I was hoping you would give me a chance to explain."

"There is nothing for you to explain. I've given you the money you blackmailed me for and as far as I am concerned we have nothing more to discuss." Mychael was stern with his words. He was direct, he was angry. He stared at Alton as he stuffed the half opened enveloped between the folders he held in his hand.

Alton stood in one place for a moment then he forced himself to make his way to the door, through the reception area and down the hall to the first exit.

"What was that all about?" Christopher asked, turning to face Mychael standing in the doorway.

"Nothing," Mychael said, closing the door to his office again.

Christopher jumped from his chair to catch him before he got on the phone. By the time he opened the door, he caught his pastor bending down on his knees. Mychael looked at him; Christopher could tell he was annoyed.

"Brother Christopher, I closed the door for privacy," Mychael said.

Christopher didn't get a chance to open his mouth. Instead he hurried out, closing the door behind him. He knew whatever was going on with Mychael had to be serious. He hadn't called him Brother Christopher in over a year, more or less snap at him the way he did. He could definitely take a hint. Not giving the matter a second thought, he grabbed his belongings then turned out all the lights, leaving his pastor to his praying.

He had plenty to keep him busy, starting with his stopping at the grocery store and the party store to get some decorations before getting ready for his housewarming gathering… it was party time.

Hours later, Christopher had arrived home to find his condo partially decorated. Only the decorations that were in his shopping bags needed to be spread throughout the room. Pierce and Jorge had set up tables for the food and drinks and placed extra chairs equal to the guest they had invited. All Christopher had to do now was bring the party trays inside and let his friends finish decorating the remainder of the condo.

Jorge had suggested for him to get a blue table cloth, but the only color he could find was a white one. He probably could have located the color blue, but he chose not to take the time to ride across town to a second party store. He knew Jorge was going to be mad, but the color white was going to have to do.

"Whose idea was it to put that ugly reef on the front door?" Christopher asked out loud.

"Jorge," Pierce said. He really didn't have to tell Christopher who had put the reef there because Christopher was aware that he wasn't the decorator of the group. However, Jorge actually thought he was a decorator and many times, compared himself to Nate Burkus from the *Oprah* show. And no matter how many times his friends told him that he wasn't, Jorge refused to think otherwise.

"Where is he anyway?" Christopher asked.

"In the bathroom," Pierce responded.

"Doing what?"

Pierce said, "Number two," holding up two fingers at his friend along with his words.

"Mind ya'll business," they heard Jorge yell from behind the closed door.

"No, just make sure you clean it when you finish, *messy*." Christopher remarked to his Jorge's comment. "How many people did ya'll invite?" he added.

"I don't know. Jorge handled the guest list. I just invited one person."

"And who might that be?" Christopher asked, looking at the expression on Pierce's face. "On second thought, I already know…Michael."

"Alright *Miss Thang!* Don't get me confused with yo' pastor."

"My pastor? I was referring to Michael Jackson, not Mychael Dovely," Christopher said with a bit of comedy in his statement.

"B-I-T-C-H!" Pierce said, both of them now laughing.

Christopher rushed into the master bedroom then into his master bathroom to take a shower. Twenty minutes later, he was standing in front of his mirror trying to decide what kind of cologne he was going to put on. In that short time, people were starting to arrive. He heard his Cousin Beatrice's voice and he invited her to come into his room. She appeared at the door and he was impressed at how well she was dressed. She really looked nice. If he didn't know any better, she even looked like she had lost a few pounds.

"Hey," Beatrice said, walking into the room and taking a seat on Christopher's bed.

"Hey to you too, you look really nice," he said.

"Thank you," Beatrice responded, seeming embarrassed by the comment, even though it was coming from her cousin.

"You think a lot of people are going to show up?"

"I hope so girl. You know I need my gifts."

"I brought you something, I hope you like it."

"I'm sure I will. You didn't tell Aunt Agnes and Uncle Joe where you were going, did you?"

"No…she didn't ask."

"Not even when you asked her to keep Jeremiah?"

"She's not keeping Jeremiah. Aunt Carolina called to say she was keeping Hannah for Pastor Dovely and she asked could he spend the night with her and Hannah?"

"Oh, okay."

Christopher pulled off his bath robe. He walked around his room in his t-shirt and briefs. He wasn't bashful to walk around half dressed in front of his cousin. She had seen him half dressed before and he her. It wasn't like they hadn't been around each other all their lives.

He slipped into his new jeans and a matching new shirt. His jeans were a little tight, but he wanted them to fit that way. He stopped dressing momentarily to allow his cousin to grab a pair of scissors from the nightstand to cut the tag hanging from his shirt collar. He looked at himself in the mirror

again, turning in a circle so he could see himself from the front, side and back angles.

"How do I look?" he asked Beatrice.

"I like that outfit. Those jeans fit you nice."

"Do they look too tight?"

"Kinda," Beatrice said, shocking him with her response.

"BEA!"

"Well they do. But who is going to be paying attention?" she said shyly.

"I will be paying attention."

"Can I ask you something?" Beatrice said with a hint of caution in her voice.

"Yeah, what's up?" Christopher responded, still checking himself out in the mirror.

"Are you and Reverend Dovely like this?" she asked, moving her hand like a see saw.

"What do you mean?"

"If ya'll are, It doesn't matter to me. I was just wondering…I just noticed how the two of you get that *look* when ya'll are around each other."

"What look?"

"Those looks… like ya'll are in love or something?"

Christopher waited a few seconds. He was about to confirm her suspicions for her, but decided not to. He didn't want to devastate his cousin, since she had once been in love with their pastor. Plus, he didn't want to run the risk of her repeating his confession to her mother and father, not to mention his own mother.

Instead he said, mimicking her white ex-boyfriend, "*Miss Bea…* I think you asking a bit too many questions. "

After hearing Christopher's southern dialogue, Beatrice fell backwards onto his bed, laughing as if her tickle box had been turned over. Christopher knew then he had caught her by surprise. He knew she didn't see that twinge of comedy coming.

Still partially laughing, Beatrice said, "Okay, you don't have to answer anymore of my questions just don't ever call me *Miss Bea* again. I literally hated when Eddie called me that," she added still laughing.

Next, they heard the door bell ring as they conversed with each other.

Beatrice raised herself from the bed and followed her cousin to the living room, turning the light off as she exited the bedroom.

"Hey everybody," Christopher said, hugging Richard and Larenz as they walked into the open living room. He noticed that Richard looked very thin as he took his seat then removing his jacket. Of course, Larenz couldn't resist looking around. He couldn't help it. People like him would be considered as *nosey*.

Christopher offered them a drink and gestured his hand in the direction of the table of food. Richard declined, but Larenz made a mad dash for the wide variety. He piled his saucer sized plate high with chicken wings, potato salad, pasta salad, little smoke sausages, and deviled eggs. He had so much food on his plate, as he took his seat, a chicken wing fell to the floor. Richard looked at his roommate first then he looked at the plate, before shaking his head in shame.

In the kitchen, Jorge was putting ice in a cooler as Christopher opened a new pack of plastic cups when Pierce entered. He approached his friends from behind whispering, "Is that *fat* bitch gon' leave any food for the other guests?" His comment aroused laughter from his friends. "If we knew *she* was coming, I would have had the event catered rather than try to do it ourselves," he added.

"Be nice Pierce. That is Richard's friend and we have to be nice to him. I don't want him to think I'm being jealous or anything," Christopher said.

The door bell rang again. Christopher left the kitchen angling toward the front door, as he passed the table he placed a sleeve of cups on the table near the drinks. He opened the front door.

"Hi, we are the James family and we live next door—welcome to the neighborhood. We *thought* you were having a housewarming. Here's our gift," the woman said, later telling Christopher her first name was Jameka. She shoved a tiny gift into his hands as her husband stood behind her. Then the two entered the house like they had been invited.

Jameka was a bubbly woman who reminded you of a shorter version of Angela Bassett. Her husband, Dewey reminded you of the Neil Winters character on *the Young and the Restless*. He seemed the complete opposite of his wife. He was quiet. She was talkative, very talkative. They were a true odd couple. Jameka came in and immediately became the center of attention.

Right away, she recognized Richard and hugged him. Her hug was followed with a handshake between Richard and her husband. Then the pair moved on to take a seat at the dining room table.

"Shane, you have a lovely place. I hope you enjoy living here," Jameka said, becoming comfortable in an empty chair.

"Thank you and thank you for the gift," Christopher said, shaking the box to his ear.

The condo was getting crowded rather fast. Christopher kept looking at his watch. It was almost eight o'clock and no Mychael. Arriving after Jameka and Dewey were Pierce's young date, Ashton. He and Pierce too looked like the perfect odd couple—much odder than Jameka and Dewey.

Ashton was a short petite mocha colored brother. He looked terribly thin, almost borderline anorexic. His jaws sank into his long face, not accenting his large eyes at all. His hair was in dreads and hung long past his shoulder. If you were to blink your eyes, he could easily remind you of a female. He followed Pierce around like he was afraid to be in the room with everyone else. Honestly, Christopher didn't even see him exchange pleasantries with his Uncle Larenz, who happened to be among those in the room.

Of course Pierce loved the attention he was getting, since he never got this amount of attention from his many, many, many other partners. If the young teenager only knew…but Christopher figured he couldn't stay eighteen forever; at some point he would have to learn about life.

Finally, Mychael arrived, still dressed in his shorts, school shirt and sneakers. At first, Christopher just looked at him. Then through clinched teeth he said, "Why are you still wearing those shorts and shirt?"

Mychael didn't react to his comment as he walked past his lover into the living room; he also passed Richard and Larenz without speaking to them. He was about to sit at the table next to Jameka and Dewey. By this time, the husband and wife were pretty tipsy.

Mychael and Dewey clasped their hands together like they were buddies. Mychael had never seen the man he was clasping hands with before and Dewey hadn't seen Mychael until tonight—but alcohol will make you do that. Yes, Mychael's breath was reaping of alcohol. As he was about to take his seat, Dewey said in a slight whisper, "Man you better be careful, this house is full of sissies."

"Dewey shut you mouth, before you get us thrown out of here," Jameka said to her husband as she scanned the room to take notice of her husband's observation.

Mychael laughed. Then he walked away from the couple now arguing about the comment her husband had made. He stood at the food table and began arranging himself a plate. Christopher followed behind him. Richard watched the couple from where he sat while his roommate danced from his seat, not paying attention to nothing going on around him.

Christopher nudged Mychael with his arm. He did it just to make him laugh. It worked. Mychael laughed slightly as his tongue traced the corner of his mouth. Then he whispered something in Christopher's ear, making him laugh. Christopher looked over his shoulder, before he stood on his toes and whispered a sexual remark to Mychael. Now they both were laughing.

Watching the interaction between Mychael and Christopher made Richard feel uneasy. He didn't know his pastor was going to be there. But he should have figured that he would. At first, he had thought about not attending and he probably should have followed his mind. Then he would've had to come up with an excuse and he really didn't have a reason that he couldn't attend. True, he was feeling a little jealous of the closeness between Mychael and his best friend, but he and Christopher both had agreed that they could be friends only. In his mind, Richard wished that he was seeing someone else besides Mychael Dovely interacting with the person he has known all his life. But he agreed with his thoughts that all of this was his own fault. He was the one who decided that he wanted to get married, not knowing the woman he had fallen in love with was a killer. And yes, he was well aware that she had been acquitted. He didn't care whether she had been or not—to him and his family, she was still a murderer.

Interrupting Christopher's conversation with Mychael, Jameka walked up to the two men standing near the food table. She put her arm around Christopher's waist. "Shane, we had a good time, but I need to go and put my husband to bed, if you know what I mean," she said, winking her eye at Christopher.

"Okay. I thank ya'll for coming and it's Christopher," he said, walking the couple to the door. He stood on the concrete stoop while Jameka tried to help her staggering husband down the stairs. She wasn't much help—she

was staggering herself. As the husband and wife angled toward their own condo, Dewey turned to face his new neighbor, he said, "Christopher man, I don't have a problem with yo' kind—to each is own. My buddy, you are still welcome at our house at any time—day or night."

Dewey was certainly drunk. Christopher on the other hand was offended. Not only did they come to a housewarming that they weren't invited to, but Dewey had the nerve to insult the host in the process. Christopher started to leave the two outside and let them find their way home the best way they could. Rather than be mean, he braved the cold and watched them walk to their door. Then he returned to his party—which was still going strong. He entered the condo as some guests danced while others carried on their individual conversations.

Christopher walked over to the dining room table to sit in an empty chair next to Mychael, who was nodding his head to the *Kenny G* jazz CD. He also watched the guests dance and enjoy themselves. "Looks like you racked up," he said, dipping his chicken into his side of ranch dressing.

"I guess you can say that," Christopher said.

Moments of silence fell between them. After that, Christopher hit Mychael on the arm to get his attention. The lick made Mychael leaned his head over to see what Christopher wanted.

"Are you going to tell me why you were in such a bad mood earlier?"

"Oh it was nothing," Mychael answered, turning his attention back to the amusing crowd. "How old is that boy that's talking to Pierce? Isn't he on the choir?"

"Yes, he's on the choir and he's eighteen."

"Does his Grandfather know he's like that? Before you answer, please tell me nothing is going on between him and Pierce?"

"Not yet... I jokingly called him Michael Jackson."

Mychael was eating a piece of fruit when Christopher told him about the name he had called Pierce. He started laughing and couldn't stop. "Man, for real, you called him Michael Jackson," Mychael said, repeating what Christopher had said to him. After he stopped laughing, he raised his cup to his mouth and drank the last bit of soda.

"Have you been drinking?"

"Yeap."

"Yeap?!?!?! So you're not going to lie about it?"

"Nope," Mychael admitted again, now pouring ice into his mouth. "Does the choir have rehearsal tomorrow before the choir anniversary Sunday?" he asked, changing the subject.

"Yes, at five. Why are you coming to sit in?"

"No. I'm going to spend the day with Hannah. I've been putting my baby off on everybody this last month," Mychael explained. He turned his head from Christopher to face Richard and Larenz as they walked up.

"Well man, it's getting late. We really enjoyed ourselves, everything was really nice," Richard admitted, as Larenz looked on. Unknowingly to Richard, Larenz gave Christopher a smirk look.

"I'll see you tomorrow at rehearsal," Richard said. Then he turned his attention to Mychael. "Pastor, I guess I will see you Sunday morning," he added.

"You fellas have a good night," Mychael said, surprisingly extending his hand to both Richard and Larenz.

After the two men walked through the front door and disappeared out of sight, Mychael couldn't hold his comment any longer. He turned to face Christopher again, "A son and a grandson that's gay is a huge pill to swallow. I hope Deacon Mayweather never has to learn about that."

"Learn about what? His son is living with a man and his grandson wears his hair in dreads and in case you haven't notice—it's longer than his mothers. Let's not mention, he has more female features than those of a male," Christopher explained to Mychael.

"I see you're point. He probably knows then," Mychael agreed.

Their conversation was interrupted when Beatrice walked up to say goodnight. Christopher walked her to the door and waited until she got into her car. It appeared that everyone was leaving at the same time. Beatrice was followed by Pierce and Ashton, leaving behind Mychael, Jorge and him.

"Why hasn't Jorge left yet?" Mychael asked.

"He's staying the night. His parents don't allow him to come home after midnight." Christopher said.

"You're kidding me right."

"Mychael don't start. Remember, you said you don't have a problem with my friends?"

"How can I forget, you keep reminding me?"

"I don't mean to, but you keep acting like my friends are a problem."

"Well can you at least get rid of *him* long enough for us to spend some time together?"

"Get rid of him how?"

"I don't know…but don't tell him why you're doing it."

Mychael didn't know that asking Jorge to give them time alone was easier than he thought. Little did he know Jorge already knew about his and Christopher's relationship? Out of formality, Christopher walked up to his friend and asked that he take his car, ride around town for a couple of hours and he would call him when Mychael had left. Mychael didn't know this, but the two friends found great humor in his paranoia. Smiling slightly at Mychael, Jorge grabbed Christopher's car keys from the dining table and left out the front door.

Christopher walked into his bedroom first, leading the way as he pulled Mychael behind him. A second later, Mychael was pressing him against the wall, kissing him passionately. At the same time, they dropped their clothes to the floor and dived under the new comforter that was covering Christopher's king size bed.

Mychael lay on his back and watched as Christopher crawled on top him. He caressed him about the neck while licking his lover's lips with his tongue. Christopher loved when Mychael did that. The physical attraction between the two was so strong it was indescribable. Christopher could tell Mychael had missed him. He could tell Mychael wanted him. He could even tell that Mychael had to have him.

The lovers kissed more. Mychael reminded Christopher of a snake every time he licked his tongue quickly against Christopher's lips, finding Christopher's tongue then the sensitive part of his neck. Unconsciously, the two men maneuvered around on the king size bed that Christopher now laid against as Mychael gazed down at him. "Oh baby, I've missed you so much," Mychael said to his lover. "It's been so long…why have you been keeping this from me?" he purred while they bumped and grinded under the covers. "Tell me that it feels good. How good does it feel to ya'?"

"Yes baby it feels good," Christopher eventually said because he couldn't deny any longer that it actually felt that way.

In the same moment, Christopher's legs were now propped evenly over Mychael's shoulder. The two kissed seductively on the lips then sucked on each other's tongues. Moments later, Mychael moved from his lover's tasty tongue and began sucking again on his neck and his chest, leaving behind one passion mark after the other. This time, Christopher didn't mind being branded. In fact, he enjoyed it. He enjoyed everything about this moment of love making. The foreplay, the middle play and what he could imagine as the after play. He was enjoying it all.

Grinding faster and moving in perfect rhythm. Mychael was reaching the height of his sexual peak.

"Oh baby, I'm about to cum. Can I cum inside of you…I want you to feel all of my hot juices. Oh I'm about to cum…I'm about to cum…here it comes…"

CHAPTER FORTY-EIGHT

It was the day before the choir's 30th choir anniversary; Alma stood at the floor podium to make a few announcements and statements as President. Her nephew Emanuel sat at the keyboard waiting to begin rehearsal as choir members entered the sanctuary one by one.

Alma had begun her remarks when Pandora walked into the meeting. She was surprised to see her since her cousin hadn't sung with the choir in over three months. Today, Pandora was wearing a t-shirt that read *God's finest* and a pair of daisy dukes shorts and a pair of flip flops. Totally disrespecting the fact that Alma was before the choir speaking, Pandora moved past Alma while she in the middle of her address to the choir to take a seat on the front row.

"I just want everyone to know that we are wearing black this year and Pastor Dovely and I are asking all the ladies to wear dresses that are appropriate. Nothing snug, tight, or low cut, that may show too much cleavage. And ladies please wear hosiery and small stud earrings, no loop earrings," Alma said.

Pandora raised her hand. There were several people with their hands up in the air, but Alma called on everyone else before she addressed her cousin.

"What do you mean about not wearing dresses that are snug and tight? All of my dresses are tight and snug, I have a shape and I'm not wearing anything that is falling off me," Pandora said, explaining her reason for wanting to wear a form fitting dress.

"Pandora, that's the rule. Pastor Dovely and I have discussed this at length and he agrees that we should dress appropriate."

"You would make a rule like that because you'd look a mess in anything form fitting," she said under her breath. The choir members sitting next to her laughed at her comment, but Alma could only glare at her cousin, then choosing to continue with her comments.

Alma knew exactly why her cousin was coming to this rehearsal. It was not a secret anymore that she had been sleeping with her husband. The affair was now public knowledge and Pandora no longer respected the marriage that she and Daniel shared.

As a matter of fact, Daniel had admitted his indiscretion to her after their son revealed to his mother that he had caught the two in bed. As you have probably imagined, since then, Daniel has been staying with his sister Overa and brother-in-law, which happens to be Alma's brother.

This particular day, Pandora was driving Daniel's Cadillac Escalade, making it obvious to those that didn't know that the two were an item. Alma was clueless to this fact while she stood in front of her choir members. She was shaken with nerves when Christopher whispered it to her as he handed her the copies outlining the anniversary program. Even though the revelation hurt like hell, Alma had to admit, Christopher was a lot more respectful than her cousin. Instead of walking across the front of the church, he parked himself on the front pew while Alma spoke.

Personally, Alma was trying her best to hold it together. She tried not to look like she was bothered by Pandora's presence, but she *really* was. Especially since she now knew she was driving her husband's SUV and it worried her, that after rehearsal, everybody was going to know that she was. Nonetheless, she continued to smile through all of her younger cousin's negative comments.

As she braved her present dilemma, Alma caught her sister looking at their grown twelve year old cousin each time she made a childish comment towards her. She and Eleanor were as different as night and day. She was the prissy daughter and her sister Eleanor was the fighter—the tomboy kind and proud of it. She would fight you at the drop of a hat. And Alma knew today wouldn't be any different—she could tell her sister was ready to take up her slack.

Fortunately for Pandora, Richard sat next to Eleanor, and being next to her, it allowed him to keep her calm. They both figured their cousin was young

and naïve. In fact, so naïve to the degree that she didn't realize that she was being used.

Alma didn't doubt for a minute that she and Daniel would move beyond their marital problems. They had so much invested in their marriage and her cousin was not going to come between that. She was a firm believer that everybody is entitled to make a mistake and her getting down and dirty with Pandora wasn't about to happen—not today, not ever.

"Does anyone have anymore questions? If not, please take the choir loft," Alma said.

"I have a question…yes ma'am I sure do." Pandora said, smacking her lips, arousing laughter from the choir members that knew about the animosity between them. "Are we going to have a section for special guests? My boyfriend is the assistant chairman of the deacon board and he will be here so I need to let him know where to sit," she added, trying to keep from laughing herself.

Alma didn't address the question. Instead, she directed the choir to take their places in the loft. Everybody rose from their seats as the sopranos lined up to enter the choir loft from the right and the altos lined up to enter from the left. The majority of the members were in their places when Pandora's cell phone rang.

"Hello," she said loudly. "I'm at choir rehearsal. Our anniversary is tomorrow."

"What? You haven't been on that choir in months, what are you talking about an anniversary?" Pandora heard her Grandmother say.

"Grandmother, I gotta go," she said, closing her flip phone. She walked up to the choir loft and stopped on the second row. She turned her body to slide past those already seated.

"Pandora, you don't sing on this row anymore. You need to get…," Alma attempted to say.

"Who are you supposed to be? You don't run this choir. The last time I was here I was on this row and this is where I am going to sing today," Pandora said, moving past Alma, then past Eleanor.

"Pandora, there isn't a space on this row. You need to go to the back," Eleanor said, repeating the directive her sister had given earlier.

"I'm not!" Pandora said, attempting to kick Eleanor's legs out of her path.

Eleanor jumped to her feet and immediately got in her cousin's face. Although Pandora was much taller, Eleanor didn't appear to be afraid of her. Knowing that she had a height advantage, Pandora used her index finger to push her cousin by the head. The force caused Eleanor to fall backwards onto the person sitting next to her. Losing her balance, Eleanor managed to grab Pandora by the hair and the two women starting fighting. Pandora's height allowed her to get the best of Eleanor, who by this time had fallen between the seats.

Alma screamed and yelled, "Somebody stop 'um." Before anyone could move toward the two cousins, Christina came out of no where, jumping over seats onto Pandora's back. She scratched Pandora's face, before grabbing her by the neck, giving her mother enough time to get on her feet. Regaining her balance, Eleanor got up swinging, punching and clawing.

Holding Pandora around the neck, Christina pulled Pandora out of the choir loft and down a couple of stairs as she kicked wildly, trying to keep Eleanor away from her. Christina kept her grip hold around her cousin's neck as she flipped her over into the pulpit. The maneuver made Pandora land on top of one of the wooden chairs, causing it to break in half. Appearing dizzy, Pandora didn't see Eleanor and Christina coming, but she felt their blows as they both pounded their fists about her face also kicking her with their feet.

It took the man power of Richard and Emanuel to break up the three women. To teach his cousin a southern lesson, Richard took the liberty of adding two or three licks to the altercation. He was full aware that he could have been charged with assault, but to him, family was family. Still angry, Christina was ready for round two as she wrestled with her brother to turn her loose. When she finally broke free, she tried to get around him to attack Pandora again.

"Girl, take a chill pill," Emanuel said aggressively to his tom boyish sister.

After the mother and daughter finished with their cousin, she now looked like she had been in a car accident. Her hair was standing straight on her head and she couldn't find her purse. At this point, she was wearing only one flip flop. Once she found the second one, she decided not to stay for rehearsal, leaving the sanctuary limping, wearing one flip flop on her feet and carrying the other in her hand.

Eleanor and Christina returned to the choir loft with only minor scratches and bruises as they rehearsed with the choir for two hours straight, perfecting all of their songs for the next day's anniversary.

* * *

The next day, there wasn't a choir in attendance that could out sing the honorees.

Christina lead the verses to *Spirit fall down* and turned church out. She crooned the song like it was her last time singing.

"Spirit, I can't make it without you," she sang.

"So I can walk right, so I can talk right," she crooned.

"Yeah...fall down," she continued to say.

After the choir finished their verses, only the music could be heard playing in the background. In the spirit, Christina jumped up and down until it left her and fell on her mother. Then it fell on Alma, who screamed and hollered and shook her head from side to side. She shuffled her feet back and forth. From a distance, it seemed like she was tap dancing.

"Thank you God!" Alma said, raising her hands. She continued to shuffle until she fainted, having to be carried out by two male tenors.

"Jesus! You're awesome! Jesus!" another choir member declared.

The congregation was standing to their feet singing along with the choir. Some were rocking from side to side as others clapped their hands to the lyrics. Mychael came to the podium to give the benediction as Emanuel played the cords while crooning the words to the hymnal, *He's sweet I know*.

He began singing, "He's sweet I know...He's sweet I know...Dark clouds may rise... Stormy winds may blow...I'll tell the world" Then the choir followed his lead, "I'll tell the world wherever I go...That I've found a savior...and He's sweet I know..."

The choir continued to sing until every parishioner in the packed sanctuary had left the building.

"Pastor Dovely, I need to give you something before you leave," Christopher said, stepping off the last step of the choir loft.

"Give me what?" Mychael asked as he watched his secretary open his appointment book.

Christopher grabbed a brown envelope and handed it to his pastor. Mychael opened it and saw that it was the same check that he had written

327

the previous week to Reverend Givens. He looked at Christopher, puzzled. "Where did you get this?"

"A woman gave it to me when I got out of my car and she told me to make sure that you get it," Christopher recalled. "Why?"

"No particular reason. That was a *really* good program today, wasn't it? I really enjoyed it," Mychael said.

"Yeah, I must agree. Despite what all took place yesterday, it was really a strong way to close things out."

Mychael and Christopher left the sanctuary and walked into the reception area of their offices. They jumped when they met an older gentleman dressed in a suit and tie.

"Excuse me sir, may I help you?" Mychael said, extending his hand. The man didn't exchange small talk with him. He looked quickly at Christopher then turned his attention to him again.

"I'm looking for Eloise Lorde. I was told she was a member of this church."

"Yes she is, but Mother Lorde has left for the evening."

"Did I understand you to say Mother Lorde, is she your mother?"

"I'm sorry sir, but her late husband was the pastor of this church and since his passing, she's now known as Mother Lorde or Mother Eloise," Mychael explained.

"Oh, I see…thank you gentleman for your time, but I will catch up with Eloise, excuse my rudeness…Mother Lorde at another time. You all have a good evening," the stranger said.

As he left, the man placed the black hat he held in his hand on top of his head and exited the office reception area headed toward the church exit.

"Wasn't he strange?" Mychael noticed.

"Very…when I first saw him, I thought my Great-Grandfather Amos had come back from the dead," Christopher said still a little shaken.